HEATHER WEBB is a contributor to the popular writing blogs *Writer Unboxed* and *Romance University*, and she manages her own blog, *Between the Sheets*. When not writing, she flexes her foodie skills, or looks for excuses to head to the other side of the world. She is a member of the Historical Novel Society and the Women's Fiction Writers Association and lives in Connecticut with her family. Connect online at www .HeatherWebb.net, Twitter/@msheatherwebb, or Facebook/Heather Webb, Author.

Praise for Heather Webb and Her Novels

"Dazzling! . . . In *Rodin's Lover*, author Heather Webb brings to life, with vivid detail, the story of brilliant and tormented sculptress Camille Claudel and the epic love affair with the legendary sculptor who worshipped her. Deeply moving and meticulously researched, this book will capture your heart, then hold it tightly long after the final page."
—Anne Girard, author of *Madame Picasso*

"*Rodin's Lover* is a textured historical novel that captures the indomitable spirit of artist Camille Claudel, a woman whose mighty talent was nearly eclipsed by her potent love for fellow artist Auguste Rodin. Can two passionate, creative talents thrive together or will one flame inevitably consume the other? Webb gracefully explores this ignitable relationship while illuminating Claudel's untold heartbreak and evocative artwork. A story of human emotion, once raw and malleable, now preserved to lasting stone."

—Sarah McCoy, *New York Times* bestselling
author of *The Baker's Daughter*

"Webb holds up a light into the inner recesses of a fascinating and contradictory woman. . . . *Becoming Josephine* is an accomplished debut."

—*New York Journal of Books*

"Webb's portrayal of the range of Josephine's experience—narrow escapes from bloodshed and disease, dinner-table diplomacy, and her helpless love for Napoleon, her children, and a small dog—is exceptionally concise and colorful. A worthy fictional primer on Empress Josephine."

—*Kirkus Reviews*

"A debut as bewitching as its protagonist."

—Erika Robuck, author of *Call Me Zelda*

Rodin's Lover

A NOVEL

Heather Webb

P

A PLUME BOOK

PLUME
Published by the Penguin Group
Penguin Group (USA) LLC
375 Hudson Street
New York, New York 10014

USA | Canada | UK | Ireland | Australia | New Zealand | India | South Africa | China
penguin.com
A Penguin Random House Company

First published by Plume, a member of Penguin Group (USA) LLC, 2015

P REGISTERED TRADEMARK—MARCA REGISTRADA

LIBRARY OF CONGRESS CATALOGING-IN-PUBLICATION DATA
Webb, Heather, 1976 December 30–
   Rodin's lover : a novel / Heather Webb.
      pages cm
   ISBN 978-0-14-218175-1 (paperback)
      1. Claudel, Camille, 1864–1943—Fiction. 2. Rodin, Auguste, 1840–1917—Fiction.
3. Sculptors—France—Fiction. I. Title.
   PS3623.E3917R63 2015
   813'.6—dc   2014028322

Printed in the United States of America
10 9 8 7 6 5 4 3 2 1

Set in Baskerville MT Std.
Designed by Eve L. Kirch

For my parents, Jeff and Linda Webb, my biggest fans

Go, bloom near the somber captive,
And tell her truly that we love her.
Tell that through fleeting time
Everything belongs to the future

—Louise Michel, L'Œillet Rouge

Part One

1881–1885

L'Aurore
The Dawn

Chapter 1

꧁꧂

Camille dropped to her knees in the mud. Her skirts absorbed last night's rain and the scent of sodden earth. She plunged a trowel, stolen from her neighbor's garden, into the red clay and dug furiously, stopping only to slop hunks of earth into a wooden trough. She needed one more load to mold the portrait of Eugénie. The maid *would* sit for her again, regardless of her protestations.

The sun climbed the sky, though it did little to warm the damp chill. Thankfully, the heat of summer had not unleashed its force to scorch the grass and dry the earth. It made for easier digging.

Camille breathed in a lungful of air laced with the mineral scent of clay. Perfection.

"Read to me, little brother," she said. "If you're not going to help, that is."

Paul dangled his legs over the edge of the boulder on which he sat. "I'll help you lug it home, but I'm not listening to Mother's howling over my soiled trousers again."

"Coward."

Paul cared for appearances, with his proud chin and shining blond hair, his perfectly polished boots, even at the young age of thirteen. Camille grinned. It was a fatal mistake in a household with a sister obsessed with clay.

Her brother ignored her and flipped to a page in Verlaine's *Poèmes Saturniens*. He read aloud.

How far away now is all that lightness
And all that innocence! Ah, backwards yet,
From black winter fled, to the Springtime of regret,
From my disgust, my boredom, my distress.

"Can't you read anything more lively?" Camille stood and stretched her aching back. It would not do to feel so fatigued already. She had too much to accomplish today. "You're always so melancholy."

"As you're always spiteful."

She gouged her fingers into the slick clay and lobbed a fistful at Paul. It splattered his vest and the cuff of his once-pristine shirt. She laughed and gathered another handful.

"Cretin!" He jumped down from his perch and chased her through the wood toward the edge of the riverbank.

She squealed as she fled. "You'll never catch me in your fine shoes." Her dark hair came loose from its haphazard knot and streamed down her back. She laughed as she laced through maple and chestnut trees and leapt over underbrush. How easy her brother was to goad.

Paul threw himself forward and caught her arm, spun her around, and smashed a wet mound of earth on her cheek. Camille shrieked, then grasped his free hand and tugged him toward the water's edge.

"Oh no you don't. Let go!" He leaned away from her with all his weight.

"You're covered in mud," she said. "You need to bathe."

With a final yank, they tumbled together into the river, a heap of flailing limbs and fabric. Paul sputtered in the cold russet water before he gained his footing on the silt bottom. "You'll pay for this. While you sleep."

"Try it. I dare you." Camille splashed him before she waded to shore, flopping onto the embankment in her soaked gray gown, a fish out of water. Paul trudged over soft riverbank and plopped onto the carpet of grass beside her, tucking his hands beneath his head. He stared up at the clouded sky.

"Rats!" In a sudden movement he scrambled to his feet. "Our lessons! Monsieur Colin will be angry if we're late." He offered his sister his hand. When she reached for it, he yanked it away, and she tumbled back to the ground. He laughed at her startled expression. "You deserved that."

Camille giggled. "So I did." She stood and pulled at the wet fabric sticking to her skin. "I'm sure he started with Louise. You know how long she takes at the pianoforte. We needn't hurry."

Monsieur Colin had traveled to Villeneuve-sur-Fère to tutor the children during the summer months. Gracious of him, considering he had many commitments. Papa paid him well for his services.

They returned to the rocky hillside and hefted the heavy trough back through the windswept fields to their house in the center of Villeneuve. As they passed the town's *église*, the sonorous clamor of church bells tolled the hour from their Gothic tower.

"It's later than I thought," Camille said, lowering the clay to the ground. A sinking dread settled in the pit of her stomach. Mother would be angry.

"Hurry!" Paul urged her.

They dragged their load through a rusted iron gate and around to the barn behind the house. Camille covered the clay with a moistened cloth and left it beside Grand-père's old kiln before following Paul to the house.

Monsieur Colin bounded down the front walk. "There you are." He studied their ruined clothing with shrewd eyes. "It seems you have gone for a swim instead of tending to your studies. I prefer not to waste my time."

"I beg your pardon, monsieur." Camille cast her gaze to the ground. "We didn't realize the hour. I was looking forward to another drawing lesson."

"*Moi, aussi,*" Paul said.

Monsieur Colin gave them a stern look. "I left a list of assignments for next Thursday. I will be in Paris the remainder of this week. And Camille"—his stern tone softened—"your mother isn't happy with you."

The dread reemerged and slithered in her stomach. What sort of punishment would she receive today? She met her tutor's eyes. "She never is."

"Try not to take it to heart. Your studies are progressing well, when you attend to them." Monsieur Colin winked and a smile lifted the corners of his bushy mustache. He continued down the walk and raised his cane in the air. "Paul, keep your sister out of trouble."

"*Oui,* monsieur," he said. "I will do my best."

Camille pinched his arm. He shoved her in response. "Now we must face Mother, thanks to you."

"What's another admonishing? We're always at war." Camille's words were braver than she felt. The last time she had broken a rule, she had been restricted from the barn for a week. She had been reduced to making shapes with her pureed potatoes.

When monsieur's coach disappeared down the street, they entered the familiar stucco house. Mother swept into the hall in her usual gray day dress unadorned by lace, corsage, or frills, embellished only by a modest bustle and a cameo. She wore her hair slicked and shiny, parted down the middle, and rolled into a tight chignon at the nape of her neck. Her sharp expression and rigid shoulders—held stout like a soldier's—did little to soften her austere appearance.

Camille braced herself.

"Where in the devil—" Mother's hand flew to her mouth. "Camille, look at you! You're a disgrace." She stared at the red clay caked on her daughter's gown and boots, the naked forearms and elbows covered in grime. "Those filthy sculptures. I have told you not to wear your good dresses outdoors, yet you insist on keeping up with this nonsense. If you continue to run amok like a heathen, you will ruin the family's reputation."

Camille flinched. She didn't wish to destroy the family's reputation, but she did not see how sculpting could be shameful. It filled her with purpose and joy. Sculpting was all beauty and inspiration—and passion, something Mother had not experienced a single day in her life.

"I'm an artist, Mother," Camille said drily. "Not a whore or a gambler."

Paul snickered.

Mother's nostrils flared. "Yet you appear as one, just now."

Camille's mouth fell open.

"Don't talk to her that way." Paul jumped to her aid.

"Know your place, young man," Mother snapped. "You aren't the head of this household."

"Why do you dislike me so much?" Camille asked. "Because I am not him? Your infant who died?"

Mother's eyes bulged in their sockets—the desired effect. Camille had struck a nerve.

"I had not yet been born, and you deride me as if I made him die," Camille continued. Sorrow and anger clawed at her throat.

"Do not speak of him!" Mother said, her voice strangled. Tears shone in her eyes.

Camille had gone too far, and yet, she knew her words rang true. She had always paid for Mother's pain, for her loss. "I am sorry." She reached out a trembling hand to comfort her mother, despite her instinct to recoil.

Mother pulled away and crossed her arms. "You'll spend the rest of the day in your bedroom. And Paul, you will work off the cost of your ruined shoes."

His face fell.

"I will work for his shoes." Camille tucked her hand through his arm in solidarity. "It's my fault." She bumped him softly with her shoulder. Grateful, her brother squeezed her hand.

"Fine." The rigid lines on Mother's forehead deepened. "And no more talk of being an artist. It's absurd. You will finish your studies and find a husband, Camille, as it is supposed to be."

Camille's insides turned to stone. A husband? She could think of nothing worse. She turned on her heel and stormed up the creaky oak stairs. Mother couldn't force her.

"Wait." Paul raced after his sister, reaching her bedroom just as she closed the door.

"Not now, Paul." Camille paced in the tiny space, littering clumps of mud behind her on the wooden floor. Mother wanted her to behave like every other lady, or better yet, to behave like Mother herself—a submissive, miserable woman. A victim of her own life.

"I can't believe you said that to her," Louise said. Her sister braided her hair before the mirror for the second time that day. She admired her new set of ribbons entirely too much—and her own reflection.

Camille stopped. "Of course you wouldn't understand, because she never reprimands you."

"It's not difficult to follow the rules."

Camille struggled with the laces of her damp gown, freed herself, and tossed the offending garment into the corner with a savage thrust. She could not be a demure, overly sweet creature who shrank beneath the weight of duty. *Marriage*—even the word—turned her stomach. She would not spend her days pleasing everyone but herself.

Paul knocked at the door. "Camille, let me in."

She pulled on a dry chemise and opened the door.

"Don't listen to her." Her brother embraced her. "You'll be a famous sculptor one day. You'll be one of the first women to do it. I know you will."

Thank God for Paul. He would always be there, defending her to the last.

⚜

Camille lit another candle. Evening descended, and soon she would need to sneak the lantern from her bedroom into the barn. She scooped a mass of clay onto an old farm table to roll and knead it, to wick away unnecessary moisture. With forceful thrusts, she pushed against the clay again and again. The sticky lump formed beneath her hands, bent to her will. She could control clay and depend on its soothing smell. She marveled at the way it held a secret identity until she coaxed it to life.

The barn door screeched on its hinge. Camille looked up to meet the intruder. "Papa!"

Louis-Prosper Claudel had returned home after a week's stay in Paris. Camille kissed his cheeks. The familiar scent of his mustache wax hovered about him.

"*Bonsoir, mon amour.*" He removed his morning coat and loosened his cravat. "It's good to be home. Paris is abysmal in the summer."

Camille wondered what abysmal looked like—she had never seen the capital city. Mother deemed it unsafe since the fall of the Paris Commune and the Prussian invasion a decade ago. Still, Camille had pleaded for a visit more times than she could count. She longed to tour the Louvre and see the works of the greats.

"Mother said you haven't eaten since this morning." He rubbed her back. "Come and have tea with your papa."

But she had so much to do—the bust of Poseidon needed some attention and she had to prepare more clay. Perhaps she would work more after a visit with Papa.

"Very well. I'll join you." She dunked her hands in a bucket of water and scrubbed.

They strolled to the house and into the salon, where the rest of the family lounged. Paul snapped his book closed, and Louise ceased her piano practice to greet their father.

"I asked Eugénie to save you a plate from this afternoon." Mother tilted her cheek so Papa could kiss her, but did not look up from her sewing.

Camille noted Mother did not do the same for her.

As Papa turned the cylinder on the gas lamp, a flame blazed to life. Satisfied, he settled on the settee. "And how are your studies, children?"

"*Bien,*" Paul said. "I am ahead again."

Camille sat beside her father. "I spent the entire day in the barn. Paul's bust is finished."

"If you continue with such intensity," Mother said in a curt tone, "your *art* will consume you."

Camille shrugged. Was that a bad thing? To be consumed by what you most adored?

"I look forward to seeing it," Papa cut in. He removed his spectacles and polished them with a handkerchief.

Mother dropped her sewing in her lap. "She missed another session with Monsieur Colin yesterday afternoon. Your daughter traipses through the woods, destroying clothing, ignoring her duties. And of course she has to get her brother into trouble as well." She threw Paul a pointed look.

A rush of blood crept up Camille's neck to her hairline. Mother could never resist the chance to chastise her in front of everyone. She bit her tongue to keep from saying something she would regret.

"Camille." Papa trained his kind blue eyes on her face. "You mustn't miss your lessons or I won't pay for them any longer."

"I'm sorry, Papa." She covered his hand with hers. "I lost track of the time. I had to gather more clay—"

"See to it you don't miss another." He nodded as if to close the discussion.

"*Oui,* Papa." Camille shifted her gaze to the floor.

Mother recommenced her sewing, her lips twitching into a satisfied smile.

"Monsieur Colin wrote to me of your progress." Papa withdrew a

Heather Webb

letter from his pocket. "He is impressed, Camille, and with you as well, Paul. I fear you both may soon outgrow him."

Louise noted his lack of compliment toward her and crossed her arms.

"Would you send me to school, then?" Paul leaned forward in his chair.

"Perhaps, one day."

"And me? Would you send me away?" Louise asked with a nervous tug on a stray curl. She twined it around her forefinger.

"Don't worry," Camille said. "You'll not be sent away, Louise. You'll fall madly in love with a prince who will whisk you away to a castle that would make even Cendrillon jealous."

Louise gave her sister a saccharine smile.

"Don't mock your sister," Mother said. "At least Louise has a real goal. You should set one of your own. One that is actually achievable. In fact, I think it's time to find yourself some suitors."

"I have a goal, though you refuse to accept it!" Camille stood and glared down at Mother. "Tell her, Papa."

He tugged on her hand. "For now, you must finish your studies. Then we will discuss other options."

"Other options?" Mother's voice switched from condescending to shrill. "We spend entirely too much money on her as it is. And for what? So she can pretend she is a man?" She picked up her sewing and jabbed her needle through the cloth.

"I don't *pretend* anything." Camille stalked to the door.

"Where do you think you're going?"

"*Je sors!*"

"You are not going out," Mother declared. "Come back here this instant!"

She ripped open the door and flew into the yard in a fury.

"Let her go." Papa's firm voice drifted through the open window.

Camille raced down the gravel lane and across the square. She ducked under a row of lime trees, passed the silent *boucherie* and the darkened windows of the handful of boutiques that sold figurines, pottery, and other goods made from the red Villeneuve earth, the town's one and only treasure. Her only treasure.

Suitors! The thought of it made her ill. She cared nothing for men

and their lustful eyes and pawing hands. To be married would suffocate her. No man would ever understand her need to create with her
hands day after day.

A mother pulled her children closer to her side and hurried toward
home, something Camille's own mother would never do. Mother would
never embrace her, or take her by the hand. She had never kissed her or
stroked her hair, not even as a child. Camille swallowed hard against the
unfathomable sorrow that rushed up her throat each time she allowed
Mother to make her long for the love that would never come.

She dashed into a wheat field, blond stalks swishing around her
legs. As the rows thickened, she pushed ahead, tendrils brushing
against her face. She ran her fingertips over the stalks, grasping at
heads and plucking off the individual kernels. To touch, to feel anything comforted her. At the edge of the field, she plucked a final stalk
and twirled it between her thumb and forefinger.

She must devise a plan. She could not be married off—that was out
of the question.

The crickets' night song grew louder as she neared the forest, and
the scent of pine needles filled her nose. She followed the sandy path
through the trees that led to her favorite hiding place, now swallowed
in shadows. In her secret garden, worn boulders jutted from the earth,
their grotesque shapes carved by weathering wind and rain. The Devil's minions, they were called. As a child, Camille had created stories
for each of the distorted shapes. When she reached La Hottée du Diable, the dull gleam of limestone shone in the moonlight. She climbed
into the rock's hollow and ran her hands over its rough surface, feeling
every weathered bump.

Night enfolded her in its balmy air, and with darkness came a decision. She would persuade Papa to hire an art tutor, someone more
knowledgeable than Monsieur Colin. Then, she would bargain with
him. If she did not progress in a year's time, she would not waste Papa's money any longer and she would . . . confront those repercussions
when the time came.

Camille leaned into the cradle of stone and peered up at the silver
moon. She *would* become a sculptor; someday she would even show
her portraits. The thought warmed her blood and filled her heart until
she felt as if it would burst.

A fat raven alighted on the edge of the rock nearest her. The bird preened its midnight feathers and then watched her with an inquisitive eye.

"Yes, Mr. Raven, it will be," she said. "You may carry my words to the Devil himself."

Chapter 2

꘠

Camille strode across the lawn to the barn and propped open the doors, flooding the space with light. A fine powder covered every surface. Against the rear wall, a table displayed a bust of Napoléon I and a portrait of David and Goliath, along with several studies of Paul and Louise, and a dozen miniature animal figurines. How long, exactly, had she been sculpting? She thought back to the first figurine she had formed while making mud pies with Paul when he was a toddler. Was she six? Seven? Each day after that first, she had returned to the clay, intent on making some new toy for him or Louise.

She tied an old apron around her waist. Papa had been amenable to her idea of an art tutor, and today the new teacher would view her works and decide if she was a worthy student. Her nerves rattled at the thought. He wouldn't turn her away, would he?

She threw off the damp cloth that protected Poseidon's bust, and the sea god stared back at her with murderous eyes.

"Well, hello to you, too." Camille laughed to herself.

She sliced small incisions into Poseidon's clay forehead, dabbed them lightly with a wet brush, and pressed a loose slab of clay onto the scored surface. Now to shape it just so. She worked the pasty surface with her fingers until a rounded bonelike structure appeared. As she had hoped, the mound threw a shadow across the sea god's prominent cheekbones. Her Poseidon was angry, poised to fight the sailor who had kidnapped his water nymph lover.

All of Camille's portraits reflected ardent emotion. Even her bust of a young girl possessed a vivid exuberance, and not the quiet happiness the model herself had learned to demonstrate through etiquette. She did not see the point in living a life sans passion. She turned the armature supporting the sculpture, examining the bust from different angles. The head tilted too far forward. How to correct the problem? She walked around it once more. She would have to adjust the neck and shoulders, possibly build a new armature. She groaned. This would take some time.

Camille pored over Poseidon, losing track of the hour, until the sound of wheels crunching gravel and a horse's whinny broke her reverie. She peeked through the window to see Papa's trim form alongside a portly gentleman with thick waving hair and a wiry beard.

The tutor had arrived!

As they made their way to the barn, she ducked from sight and returned to her sculpture.

"And here is her work space." Papa led the gray-suited gentleman into the barn, not bothering to introduce him to Camille.

The man immediately absorbed himself in her work. He walked from one end of the room to the other, studying each of the pieces. He grunted and scratched his beard.

Camille pretended to mold Poseidon's head, but watched the stranger examine her portraits.

After several silent minutes, Papa said, "Camille, this is Monsieur Alfred Boucher. A professional artist. A sculptor, *chérie*."

"*Bonjour*, monsieur," Camille said. The gentleman wasn't just a tutor, but a real sculptor! She could hardly hold her tongue. She had so many questions, so many ideas.

Alfred Boucher met her gaze and raised his eyebrows in surprise. "Mademoiselle, these are all yours?"

Clearly he had not expected to see such promise from a young lady. Her smile dimmed. Or maybe he found them lacking.

"Who has taught you, other than Monsieur Colin?" Boucher asked.

"She has had no proper training," Papa said. "Only a little drawing and painting at the girls' school in Épernay."

"I am ready for more instruction." Camille pushed her hair out of her eyes with her arm, careful not to drag her sticky fingers through it. "It is no easy feat to find an art tutor for a girl, especially for sculpture." She tried to remove the edge from her voice but failed. "We are so unworthy of schooling. An artist's life might taint my pure mind and heart."

"Camille—" her father began.

Boucher chuckled. "Young woman, you are more than worthy of schooling. Your use of light, these ridges . . . they are violent in contrast." He leaned closer to the bust of Paul. "And this expression! For a novice it's exquisite."

A surge of pride rolled through Camille. She believed her work good, but it was quite another thing to hear someone else—a professional—say it. So different from the compliments offered by Papa or Paul, or occasionally Louise.

"Monsieur Boucher isn't just any sculptor, Camille," Papa said. "He is renowned in Paris."

Boucher smiled. "Yes, I suppose that is somewhat true. Louis-Prosper, if we could have a word." He nodded at Camille. "It has been a pleasure. Thank you for sharing your work with me."

"The pleasure was mine, monsieur." She smiled again. This man might be the key to expanding her skills, or—better yet—to convincing Papa to send her to school in Paris. Irrepressible excitement coursed through her. She wanted to dance!

Papa followed the gentleman to the door. Once they had gone, Camille tiptoed to the edge of the doorway and peeked outside.

"She has exceptional talent," Boucher said. "You say she is seventeen?"

Papa clapped him on the back. "Yes, she is only seventeen."

"I would be willing to take her on as a pupil," Boucher said. "I could travel to your home a few times per month, as time permits, but I must warn you, I spend a great deal of my time in Paris. I cannot commit to a regular schedule." He clasped his hands behind his back, thinking. "If there is any way . . . Pardon my candor . . ."

"Go on, man," Papa said. "I invited you here for your honesty."

"You really should send her to Paris. She could learn from me as well as from other students. There is an art school where young women are now permitted—the Académie Colarossi. She would certainly

benefit from their teachings. The school even uses nude models. Unusual for a school with female students, but necessary for learning
sculpture. And, as luck would have it, I know the director. I could talk
with him if you wish."

Art school? Camille bit her knuckle to hold back a squeal.

Surprise registered on Papa's face. "We will discuss it," he said
slowly. "This is a sudden move, and possibly more than we can afford.
And it would divide the family." He ran a hand over his hair. "I can't
very well send her to Paris alone."

She fought the disappointment that crushed her unchecked hope.
She had to go! She would never flourish at home, in this *ville nulle*, with
no training and no opportunity. Mother would force her to give up
sculpting and marry some boorish man.

"Did you say *nude* models?" Papa asked.

Alfred Boucher smiled. "Yes. To properly learn the human form,
the musculature and bone structures, you need to study them nude. It's
shocking for those outside of the art world, but I assure you, the greatest sculptors study nude models—even if their pieces eventually wear
clothing." He removed his hat. "You don't have to decide now. Take
time; consider it well. A move to Paris is a grand decision. An invest-
ment for her future, and would be for your son as well. I hear he's a
gifted student in letters and philosophy? You have a talented family."

Their voices trailed off as Papa led Camille's only hope away to the
house.

⚜

Two weeks had passed since Monsieur Boucher's visit and Camille had
yet to see him again. She peered over the edge of her book from her
position on the settee, chewing one nail after another. When would
they receive word? Had Monsieur Boucher rejected her after all?

Papa reclined in his usual spot, nestled in his favorite chair with a
stack of newspapers on the floor beside him. Paul sat at the dining
room table, writing furiously by lamplight, pausing only briefly to flip
through one of the many books beside his inkwell. Mother and Louise
had retired to bed.

Camille's anxiety swelled and she stood. "Papa, would you like to
stroll with me in the garden? It's a perfect night."

"A splendid idea," he said, oblivious to her distress. "I'll just get my walking cane."

They filed through the door and around the side of the house. Moonlight spilled over the scraggly hedges and the red roof of the neighboring house. Though they walked without speaking, Camille's stomach churned.

"Papa—"

"Camille—"

They spoke at the same time, then laughed.

Papa slid his arm about her shoulders and kissed her head. "I have something to tell you."

Her stomach plummeted to her toes. This was it. Monsieur Boucher had decided not to tutor her—she wasn't good enough. Suddenly the moon turned into a glowing eye, mocking her from its exalted pedestal in the sky.

Papa lifted his cane to point at a movement near the roses. "Look, a family of rabbits. They had better hide before that old fox comes around."

"Go on," she said, her impatience plain.

He chuckled and turned to face her. "I have a proposition for you."

She nodded.

"The family will move to Paris."

"You mean it?" Her heart leapt into her throat and she squeezed his arm.

He held up his hand. "As I said, it's a proposition. We will move to Paris—I will do my work in Wassy during the week and travel to Paris on the weekends. You will no longer have to move about with me every time I am sent to a new town." He sat on the stone bench in the garden. "Your brother will go to school. I've already spoken with him about this."

The little rat. Paul hadn't told her.

"Louise will continue with a tutor at home and you, my dear," he continued, his eyes twinkling, "are enrolled at l'Académie Colarossi. Now, I know it isn't l'École des Beaux-Arts, but—"

Camille threw her arms around his neck and kissed his cheek. Sheer joy bubbled inside her. "You won't regret it. I'll show those stodgy old men at l'École a thing or two about art. They'll wish they admitted women."

"There's more," he said in a firm voice. "In exchange, I've promised your mother you will meet with a few suitors."

She froze. That would mean . . . She shook her head.

"Camille"—he rubbed his thumb across her cheek—"I'm not asking. I'm telling you—you must."

Her mind raced. They could not force her to marry. She could meet a few gentlemen. What did she care? She would be a sculptor—that was all that mattered. She smiled triumphantly. "I'll do it."

Chapter 3

❧

Camille and family rode the ninety kilometers to Paris in silence until the number of houses and buildings increased, and she knew they had reached the city.

"Here we are!" Papa said.

They entered the northern edge of the city and traveled south through Montmartre. The carriage made a sudden turn down a narrow side street dotted with makeshift workshops. Half a dozen carts filled with *tableaux* lined both sides of the cobblestone street. Views of the Seine and its bridges, assortments of flowers, and seascapes were all for sale to passersby. Artists perched on stools, their easels propped open, prepared to sketch a willing customer.

Warmth surged through Camille's limbs. Others would understand her passion. A fierce happiness seized her and she laughed aloud.

"Look." Paul nudged her with his elbow.

A man in a faded bowler hat made swift strokes on paper with a chunk of charcoal. The bald head and beady eyes of Jules Grévy, elected president of the Third Republic, emerged. The caricature displayed an overly large head and a narrow body. The latest bloody revolution had converted France from an imperial state to a republic once more. Papa debated Grévy's election with the neighbors incessantly. "A moderate man who enforces change at a pace the people might digest, rather than those damned radicals," he argued.

The sudden screech of police whistles split the air.

Traffic stopped. Their caravan of belongings halted. Artists slammed their cases closed and sprinted into alleyways or ducked into open taverns. People scattered in every direction. Two hackneys stacked with artwork pulled into traffic, dodging coaches, pedestrians, and street vendors, and sped away to their next destination. An officer on horseback thundered after them.

"What's happening?" Camille asked, eyes wide.

A mustached policeman in black uniform stalked from vendor to vendor, flashing the pistol at his hip.

"You need a permit to sell art on the street, or to rent a gallery space," Papa explained. "Otherwise, you will be fined, or arrested if you have been warned before. Boucher explained this when he escorted me through Paris last month."

A third policeman blew his whistle and urged the traffic forward. Their caravan began to move once more.

As they continued through the city, Camille studied the sprawl of houses and apartment buildings. Sculpted fountains, monuments of statesmen, and Grecian figures decorated the city's gardens. Windows framed with ornate structures and carved cornices adorned the public building fronts and the more expensive homes. She longed to stroke the bumpy stone vermiculation on their facades, or the smooth marble animals guarding their entries.

They turned down Rue du Parc Royal and Camille pressed her face to the glass.

"The Hôtel de Ville," Papa said.

She gawked at the dozens of statues and intricate friezes that seemed to spring to life from the stone. Her fingertips tingled in anticipation. There must be so many working sculptors in Paris, her new home. She smiled.

Their coach wound through narrowed streets and across grand boulevards.

"Look at all the boutiques." Louise squealed and kissed Mother on the cheek. "Imagine the gowns."

Mother patted her favorite daughter's knee. "You would be lovely in yellow silk. Too bad we won't have much to spend on frivolities."

Camille looked past the shops at the astounding number of gentle-men, boys, and even the odd woman on *bicyclettes*. She had seen a few before in town—the newsboy had one, the occasional neighbor—but never had she seen so many at once. Gentlemen wheeled around pedes-trians and splashed through puddles, muddying the bottoms of their trousers. Some managed to ride without so much as tipping their hats. Camille cringed as one young man in a checked sac suit narrowly missed a flying hansom cab. He did not flinch and looked ahead as if nothing had happened.

The odor of garbage rotting in the summer heat permeated the air. Mother pinched her nose. "This city is foul. How will we stand it?"

Papa's smile tightened, but he did not let her spoil his good humor. The rest of the family was thrilled to be in the city.

"*Regardez.*" Paul perked up. "La Bibliothèque Nationale. Can we visit it, Papa?" Paul studied the towering library, now under construc-tion for expansion.

"Of course, my boy." Papa squeezed his shoulder.

At last they neared Montparnasse, in the fourteenth arrondisse-ment, their new home.

"This district is considered part of the Left Bank," Papa said, "the home of many art schools and studios, though not Bohemian like Montmartre." He pointed to a pack of students streaming from a nar-row doorway between two brasseries.

Every student was male.

Camille eyed a man not much older than she. He carried a blanket-draped canvas and a satchel stuffed with paintbrushes; flaxen bristles poked from the top of his bag. A blob of violet paint smeared his cheek. "I'll need a work space," she mused aloud.

Mother snorted. "And how do you propose to pay for it?"

"All that occupies your mind is money, Mother," Camille said, her voice laden with sarcasm. "Perhaps you should get a hobby, or a goal of sorts."

Mother huffed, "You ungrateful—"

"Enough!" Papa said. "We are almost there."

The traffic moved and they continued on their way. When they reached their apartment, Camille sprang from the coach. She could hardly wait to explore.

꿍

Within two weeks, Camille had settled into their apartment on the fifth floor at 135 bis Boulevard du Montparnasse, and Papa headed to his newest post in Wassy. When the first day of school arrived, she nearly skipped through the carved front doors of l'Académie Colarossi. Young women and men filed inside and scattered to their respective classrooms—drawing, painting perspectives, classical studies, sculpture. Camille inhaled a whiff of heaven: pine turpentine and paint, the chalky odor of plaster powder, and the acidic tang of shellac. Her nose sought out her favorite smell of all, the earthy scent of clay.

She wound through the rooms and at last found the proper studio. Large windows spanned the entire length of one wall, leaving the room awash in sunlight. On the opposite wall, a system of shelves displayed finished busts of all shapes and sizes, animal caricatures, and a smattering of tools and supplies. She chose the only free stool. A petite blonde sat next to her, and beyond her, a plump yet pleasant-faced brunette. Camille glanced at the cloths covering two large lumps in front of the girls. Their current works, no doubt.

"*Bonjour*," the first girl said with a thick English accent. "*Je suis* Amy. And this is my friend, Emily. You're new here."

Camille smiled. "Yes," she replied in English. Papa had harped on her learning it, though she had never mastered the difficult language.

"Good morning, students." Their professor, a nondescript middle-aged gentleman, removed his hat and slipped into a gray smock. The remaining students shuffled to their places.

Camille studied her classmates while the professor began the lesson. Her heart beat faster with excitement. She would work side by side with men! She'd have the same education as they.

Students removed sheets from their models, revealing half-finished torsos and heads.

"Before we begin, please welcome Mademoiselle Claudel. She will be joining our class this semester."

A dozen pairs of eyes turned to stare. Camille fixed her gaze on a spot on the wall and avoided eye contact. She wished the professor would get on with the lesson.

"You may prepare the plaster for your table today, mademoiselle," the professor said.

A dark young man dressed in a white *chemisier* and a colorful foulard strolled into the room. His angular jaw, aquiline nose, and high cheek-bones were striking, though he could not be called handsome.

Our model, Camille thought. A *real*, hired model.

"*Parfait.* Giuseppe is here. Let's get to work. The plaster, mademoiselle." Professor Jacques motioned toward several covered buckets at the rear of the classroom.

Camille chose a bucket of plaster, dragged the heavy container to her work space, and began to stir. She turned her body to get a better grip on the stirring rod and found herself facing Giuseppe.

The model smiled as he loosened and removed his scarf and laid it on a nearby stool. Camille's heart thumped a bit faster. Next, he re-moved his shoes, and then unbuttoned his shirt, showing patches of richly colored flesh and black chest hair.

When he reached for his trouser buttons, a flush burned Camille's cheeks. She averted her gaze. Why didn't he undress behind the parti-tion? She dipped the thick rod into the viscous mixture with too much force. Plaster splattered her arms. She looked up to see who had wit-nessed her first blunder.

Giuseppe winked. Camille bowed her head, swirling the stick in her bucket one last time.

Amy leaned toward her. "You will grow used to seeing him naked. His . . . well, *it* is not as frightening as it seems." She chuckled as she cleaned her wire end tool.

"I'm not frightened of . . . *it*," Camille said, straightening.

Amy and Emily giggled softly.

Camille flipped open her sketchbook. She would need several pre-liminary sketches before she would be ready for plaster. She stole a glance at the model again—just in time for him to strip away his un-dergarments. An inaudible gasp escaped her lips.

His "it" dangled between his legs, encircled by a forest of dark hair. She could not tear her eyes away. So different, a man's physique, when seen in reality rather than stone. She wondered at his member's tex-ture. Was it truly as soft and squishy as it seemed?

Her cheeks grew hot once more. It was perfectly normal to wonder about his . . . texture, she told herself. She was a sculptor, for God's sake. If she were to reproduce him well, she must know the sense and movement of every part of the human anatomy.

Giuseppe sauntered to the front of the room and mounted his stand. He settled into the stance he had held, no doubt, for many days. He stood as if poised for battle, one arm suspended with a faux shield, the other raised to grip his sword. His features assumed a noble expression, though he stared at the wall and not a battlefield.

Camille plopped down on her stool and wiped her hands on a towel. She sketched the model's body, careful to accentuate the patches of shadowed skin, the highlighted angles of his face, his muscular stomach and well-formed chest. At last she drew his thighs, feet, and his . . . flaccid member.

She wondered how he felt on the platform. Could she stand naked for all to scrutinize? She shuddered at the thought of prying eyes measuring and assessing her every curve.

The class continued their work in silence for hours. The professor floated around the room, making suggestions and demonstrating techniques. When he stopped at Camille's table, he did not say a word, but stood and watched her.

Monsieur Jacques handled the miniature portrait she had made of Giuseppe, turning it this way and that. "There should be more harmony here between the chin and jaw. And again here." He pointed to the shoulder blades. "These grooves are too deep and create too much shadow. The lines should flow from one to the other."

"*Merci*, monsieur," Camille said.

He fished in his pocket and produced a watch. "Now we break for luncheon. Everyone, meet back here at three this afternoon. Please do not be late. You will have only a couple of hours of proper daylight left to work."

Camille's face fell. She had just started to make progress. While she packed her things, the other students milled about before leaving for home.

Giuseppe jumped down from his perch and moved to the back of the room. As he passed her table, he smiled.

"You have all the luck," Amy said, winking. "One day in class and already you have the model wishing you were his girl."

Camille laughed. "I doubt that." She wrapped her clay models in a towel.

Amy touched her hand. "Emily and I like to dine at a café across the street. You are welcome to join us."

Camille regarded Amy's clear brown eyes and plain features. She had not had many friends and couldn't help but be a little suspicious of her intentions. In the past her classmates had turned on her when her work outshone theirs, or when she had received attention from boys, and now men. She did not have time for such nonsense. She was here with one goal in mind: to break the rules restricting her sex so she might become one of the greats.

"Come! We won't bite, I promise." Amy smiled, melting Camille's defenses. She seemed genuine and friendly.

"That would be grand," Camille said.

"*On y va!*" Emily replied. "I'm famished." She removed her smock, which covered a gaudy yellow dress with red floral print.

Camille smiled. Things were already better than she could have hoped.

❧

Camille settled into her routine at the Académie Colarossi. Her classmates, the weekly schedule, even the model's nakedness became familiar. Yet frustration came again and again when she tried to work at night in the dimly lit makeshift studio in their apartment. She would never advance in such a cramped space.

After a long night of cleaning the hardwood over and over, she posed the idea of an atelier to Mother at breakfast.

"Out of the question," Mother said. "It isn't acceptable for a woman to have her work space outside the home."

"We're in Paris. Everything is acceptable." Camille dropped her slice of bread slathered with strawberry jam onto her plate.

"That is not true." Mother sipped from her dainty espresso cup. "I've spoken with several new lady friends in the city. They're appalled I have a daughter in art school at all. Can you imagine what they would say about an atelier? Absolutely not, Camille. The idea is preposterous, and you know it."

Camille clasped her hands together beneath the table. Frustration choked her. "How will I become a well-known sculptor if I don't have a proper place to work? I want to be one of the greats. I despise being a woman."

"One of the greats? Really, child. You are delusional. And look at you. Your flushed cheeks and bright eyes, chestnut hair and dainty form. Even a mind too intelligent for your own good. You're everything a woman could hope to be," Mother said, her tone brittle. "Yet you want to be something you are not. It makes me ill."

Camille shifted in her chair. Mother's list betrayed her own envy. She had never been quick-witted or beautiful; neither did she possess any skills outside of sewing. Though Camille had been chastised many times before, it never ceased to make her uncomfortable and worse, guilty for being herself.

"I suppose I will continue to dirty your floors and furniture," she said, ignoring Mother's comment. She gulped the remainder of her coffee and pulled on a linen jacket the length of her dress, trimmed with a stout black collar and buttons.

She needed an atelier and soon. She would think of something.

⚜

Once at the academy, Camille took out her frustrations on the clay. She dug at her piece with fury, gnashing at the surface to create uneven planes. Garlands of light and dark wreathed the maquette's neck and torso. Her emotions seeped from her hands into the clay.

Why did Mother compare herself to her? It did not seem natural for a mother to be jealous of her own daughter.

"Striking, mademoiselle," Monsieur Jacques said. "Smooth this portion here, if you want it to be more realistic." He ran his fingertip along the bust's nose. "It is too pointed, especially from this angle." Camille stared at him for a moment, her expression fierce. The professor cleared his throat, his unease apparent. "Do you have a private tutor?"

"*Oui*. Monsieur Alfred Boucher. But it has been difficult to meet with him in my small work space, and my mother won't pay for an atelier. She would have me quit altogether." She tucked a piece of hair behind her ear, smearing her cheek with clay.

He rubbed his chin. "There are others in your predicament. Perhaps you should consider sharing a space and expenses." He motioned toward Amy and Emily.

Camille had eaten lunch with them several times, but would not call them friends. Still, to have an atelier away from the house . . . Perhaps she would speak with them.

The professor touched her shoulder. "To advance, you must take risks." His brown eyes were kind.

Her shoulders relaxed. She hadn't realized how tense she felt. She did not have to defend her desires to her teacher, or to her classmates. They were on her side. At the very least, they understood her. She watched Amy carve curls onto the head of her bust with absolute concentration.

A plan formed in Camille's mind. She had not used the supply money Papa had given her the past two months. The sum would be a fine down payment for rent. And the girls—she must convince them to join her.

"Let's break," monsieur said to the class.

Camille dampened her cloth with a sponge and placed it over her piece. "May I join you at the café?"

"Of course," Amy said. "I'll just wash up."

They made their way to the door and bolted across the cobblestone road, narrowly missing a gilded carriage. "Watch where you're going!" Amy called after it.

"Idiot!" Camille shouted. Emily laughed.

They entered the brasserie and chose a table near the window. The girls removed their coats and gloves and chose their seats. Camille looked around the cozy, well-lit brasserie, perfect for a chilly afternoon. As she sat, she noticed Amy talking to a gentleman a few tables away.

"Does she know him?" Camille asked.

Emily sat beside her. "Amy talks to any man who will listen. She has kissed a few as well."

"Desperate to marry, is she?" Camille thought her new friend would not last long as a student at this rate.

Amy swept over to their table, her cheeks glowing from the attention, and sat down. "He called me lovely."

"Don't they all?" Emily said. Camille laughed.

A man in dusty trousers and a coat with frayed cuffs set a carafe of wine and glasses on the table. He filled each of them. "We have *côtelettes de lapin*, spinach, and pureed potatoes today."

"Fine," Camille said, waving him away.

"Did we just order rabbit?" Emily wrinkled her nose. "I don't eat rodents."

Camille laughed. What an odd thing to say. She had never met an English person before. They clearly had different views of food *and* art, else the serious female artists wouldn't flee to Paris.

"Don't the English eat rabbit?" Camille said. "Or are you too civilized there?"

"Some eat rabbit," Amy said, "though I would call it a dish for the lower classes. It isn't common in our circles, but then, neither are naked men on pedestals." The ladies laughed.

After a moment of silence, Camille said, "I have a proposition for you both." She could not wait to plunge into the topic weighing on her mind. "Would you be interested in sharing a studio?"

Emily bobbed her head forward. "I would love to, but I'm not sure I could afford it."

Camille swigged from her wineglass. "If we pool our resources, we could split all costs three ways. Tools, materials, models. Rent and firewood. Just imagine—we could work on whatever we like without distractions."

Amy rotated her glass on the table over and over again. "What about a teacher?"

"I have one already. You may have heard of him—Alfred Boucher?"

"I have heard his name." Emily blotted her mouth.

"Here we are, ladies." The waiter placed three steaming plates before them. "I'll bring more wine."

"Would your tutor work with all three of us?" Amy asked.

"I'm certain he will. He's generous and kind. I've had to put off my lessons with him many times because of school, but we could schedule regular sessions with him. What do you say?"

Emily forked a large bite of chicken into her mouth.

Camille leaned across the table toward them. "Monsieur Jacques said we must take risks to advance. Women have few chances. This is ours."

Amy drummed her fingertips on the tabletop. Finally, she said, "I could teach piano lessons for extra money."

"I'll ask my father for an increase in my monthly stipend," Emily said. "I caught him with his mistress so now he gives me whatever I ask for."

"Emily!" Amy nearly choked.

"So you're in?" Camille said.

"We're in!" the ladies said in unison.

Camille whooped. "A toast!" She held up her glass. "To taking risks!"

⚜

At the conclusion of class, Camille packed her things and walked home. Her fingers throbbed and her stomach rumbled. A hot bath and a little food would go a long way. Yet she still had a series of sketches to do before bed for a new piece. *Madame B*, she would call it.

She entered the front door of the building and climbed the stairs to her family's apartment. She dreaded speaking to anyone. If she could, she would disappear before the family retired to the salon. They had all grown accustomed to seeing her less and less often these days. As she removed her hat and unwound the burgundy scarf at her neck, she felt a trickle of water dampening her shoe. She had knocked over a bucket at school, by accident, and trudged through the puddle. Now, her hem dripped water on the floor. She sighed as she ran a hand, thick with clay, over her hair.

Mother's voice drifted through the small apartment. "She's quite beautiful and very intelligent. Your mind for science would be a match for hers. She adores the outdoors and dabbles in artistic pursuits."

Camille's hand flew to her mouth. Who in the world could that be?

An unknown male voice replied, "I look forward to meeting her. When did you say she would return?"

"I thought I heard the door now. Camille, is that you?"

Camille froze. Mother had already arranged for a meeting with a suitor? She leaned against the wall for support. The payment had finally come due.

Chapter 4

꧁꧂

Auguste pointed to his empty snifter. A barkeep with muttonchop whiskers raised an equally furry eyebrow. Rodin pointed again and fixed the barkeep with his ice blue eyes. The man nodded and pulled a bottle of brandy from the shelf.

Rodin didn't often drink liquor, but this day required it. He had molded a dozen or more maquettes for his current piece, but none seemed right. His problem wasn't that he lacked inspiration—quite the opposite. So many ideas bombarded him that the true message of his work eluded him. Usually the miniature clay models helped. Not this time. The fine arts ministers had commissioned a set of bronze doors to pose as the entryway to the Musée des Arts Décoratifs—a building not yet built, but planned for more than thirty years.

He took a long draft before peering at his reflection in the glass. The burnt orange of the brandy matched his amber hair, and his eyes looked, well, distraught. The doors had proved to be hellish so far, but he was happy, was he not? The project meant he would have a fighting chance at the prestigious Légion d'Honneur. With it, he would secure true recognition and acknowledgment from the bastards who had shut him out. Breaking through their *ancien* sculpture styles, their gilded gates, had been a struggle for twenty years.

Rodin's own furry eyebrows shot up. *Gates!* The gates of hell! He looked at the man to his left and back at the barkeep. Had they witnessed this miraculous revelation? Did they know what this meant? A rush of jubilation tingled over his skin. He had to restrain himself from grabbing the barkeep by the collar and shaking him in a fit of joy. Instead, Auguste swirled the ochre brandy in its pear-bottomed glass and gulped it down.

The Gates of Hell, or the gates guarding the museum, would be infested with souls—fools—clamoring outside them, consumed with ambition and lust, begging to be allowed entry.

Auguste's mind raced with a flurry of ideas. He would read Dante's *Inferno* again. He could see the sculpture burdened with man's suffering, the quivering needs of the flesh. He would create it all! He slammed his fist down on the mahogany bar.

The barkeep, shining a set of glasses, paused to direct a weary glance in his direction.

Auguste smiled and glanced around the room. A smoky haze hovered above the heads of the patrons. The far corners were cast in shadow, though Auguste could make out a pair of drunken young men with pomade-slicked hair and expensive suits. In another corner a woman with an ample bosom laughed at something her companion had said, jiggling the black feather that sprang from the top of her hat. She leaned forward and cupped her lover's face in her hands. He kissed her greedily.

Auguste grunted and faced the bar. Fools. Their sentiments would fade and veiled dislike would be all that remained. Rose's haggard face came to mind. Though she was loyal, her desperate need to please him, to control him, grated on his nerves. He avoided spending too much time in her presence. At this point, he considered his live-in lover more of a *camarade de chambre*. He'd never known love, not as poets spoke of it. As far as he was concerned, there was nothing as romantic, as awe-inspiring as the day he had first touched clay.

A gentleman with a thick salt-and-pepper beard slid onto the barstool beside him. "The same." Claude Monet pointed to Rodin's glass. He removed his coat and beret.

"Glad you could make it." Rodin grunted. "I thought you weren't coming."

"It took me a while to hail a damned cab," Monet said. "I despise this infernal city. I'm leaving as soon as I find a place in the country."

"Where are you going?"

"I am not sure yet." He took a swig from his glass. "But I'm done with my father's place in Le Havre. The pain of it wears on my soul. It washes me out to sea with the tide."

Auguste snorted. "You're a poet."

"I'm a *con*."

Auguste laughed, a hearty sound.

"What are you laughing at?" Monet asked. "You're an ass yourself."

Auguste laughed again. "I suppose I am." He scratched his bearded chin. "What are you working on these days?"

"A tableau of sunflowers. Nearly finished, in spite of the dismal light in this town."

"And how are . . . things?" His good friend had lost his beloved wife two years before and couldn't shake his melancholy.

A fleeting look of pain filled Monet's eyes, but he quickly composed himself. "Well enough. I'm still here, still working." He drained his glass. The barkeep filled it again without asking. "Congratulations on your commission. It's quite an honor, my friend."

"My first large commission," Auguste said in disbelief. "I'm not sure if it's an honor or a curse. They have sent over visitors to check my progress. One even questioned my assistants to see if they cast from wax." His face heated as anger surged once more. Ever since the blasted scandal with *The Age of Bronze*, his skills had been in question.

"Let them watch you work. Prove to them you aren't a cheat."

Rodin rubbed his eyes. "At least I finally know what I want to do with the doors. I found the cohesive element I was missing."

The young men in the rear of the room rose from their table and stumbled to the entrance, laughing and shoving each other. Two chairs crashed to the barroom floor. The barkeep made his way across the room and followed them out.

Monet scowled at the men before asking, "Aren't all projects a curse? They haunt you until you put the image on canvas and out of your head. Even then I hardly sleep at night."

"This one's different. I must prove myself to them, or I'll never see another commission from the *institut*. My career won't flourish without it."

"You will have many others. This one isn't different. You need to create for yourself, not them." Monet poked Rodin in the chest. "Find your focus here. If you don't, your work will be lacking in spirit. You always were too cerebral."

Auguste raised an eyebrow. "And what should I do? Take up your habits? Brood and carry on with each new project, agonize over details? You don't need to agonize; you need to work. Pencil on paper. Brush on canvas. Stop lamenting and busy yourself."

Monet's expression darkened.

He had said too much. His friend had only meant to help. "We have different processes, that is all." Auguste stroked his copper-colored whiskers. "I do just fine capturing others' sentiments."

"And you strive to please those who prevent us from attaining success! The fine arts ministers who only look to the past. They spurn you and still, you try to please them."

"I look to make a name for myself," Auguste said. "I don't give a damn if they like my work or not."

"You're a talented man. I admire your work, but you need to channel what burns inside you. Sort it out, and your genius will be unparalleled."

Auguste thought his friend would understand his need to be accomplished, to turn the art world inside out. Apparently they had different ideas of how to do that. He grunted. "The next round is on me."

❧

Auguste slammed the door to his atelier on the Rue de l'Université. A bevy of sculptors, stonecutters, models, and other assistants looked up from their stations. A chorus of *bonjours* filled the air.

"*Bonjour*, all!" Rodin bellowed.

He strode through his spacious atelier, one of his two public studios. He had earned it after years of stonecutting and working under others. The time to propel his career forward had arrived.

Three assistants heaved an enormous block of marble into a work space. Another wrapped a finished bust to prepare it for the founder for bronzing. Two men mixing plaster squabbled and pushed one another. One stumbled into the bucket, slopping the liquid on the floor.

"*Attention!*" Rodin threw his coat and hat over the back of a chair and rolled up his sleeves. "You'll waste the plaster." The men glared at each other and returned to their task. Rodin motioned to a female model who idled on a chaise with her handsome male counterpart. "Come."

Adèle, already undressed, climbed onto her platform.

Rodin walked around her four times, five. She sat with one leg straight, the other propped over it, knee jutting toward the ceiling. Her torso muscles twisted as she looked over her shoulder.

Auguste hadn't gotten the line of her neck quite right. He ran a well-muscled hand down her bare neck and shoulder. Goose bumps rose on her skin and her rosy nipples hardened. She pushed out her rounded breasts in invitation.

"Don't move, Adèle."

"After last night, I cannot resist your touch." Her pretty mouth formed into a pout.

He had taken her in the back room, after the others had gone. He knew she had bedded several of his assistants. Adèle had little self-control—few of his models did. Once they undressed, they removed their propriety and their sense of womanly decency. Rodin didn't care. He craved the liveliness of youth, esprit de corps. If she gave, he would take.

He reworked his maquette for more than an hour with a wire end tool, skimming away the excess clay until the dip between her collarbone and her neck emerged.

"I could use a break," she said at last.

Auguste ignored her. The girl complained every quarter of an hour. If he listened to her constant gripes, he'd never get anywhere. And he paid her well, far more than most sculptors. He did not settle for inferior tools or materials, and certainly not for inferior models—and, despite her complaints, Adèle was one of the best.

Auguste continued to shave bits from the molded thighs of his maquette for another hour. At last, he glanced out the window. Buildings blocked what he imagined as a colorful blaze of sunset. All he could see was an orangey glow fading to evening blue.

"You may go," he said. "The light is waning and I need a break."

"Finally." Adèle stood and stretched, bending over before him. She righted herself and threw her slender arms around his neck. "I'm available . . . if you are." She pressed her body to his.

"François asked after you this morning. Perhaps you should meet with him." Auguste pulled her arms from around his neck and cleaned his hands. "I have more work to do at home."

She frowned. "You are no fun."

He admired her lithesome limbs and the curve of her hips as she sorted through her pile of clothing and pulled on her underclothes. "And you, my dear, are too much fun. Go play with someone your age." He kissed her on the forehead like a father.

She laughed. "How old are you? Forty?"

He didn't see why his age amused her. "Thereabouts." He removed his apron and tossed it over a chair. "Marcel?" His voiced echoed in the vast expanse of ceiling.

A young man in a filthy smock scurried across the warehouse to meet Master Rodin.

"Tidy my station," Rodin said. "I'm going for the day."

"*Oui*, monsieur," Marcel said.

Auguste pulled on his wool coat and cap, snatched his sketchbook from his desk, and strode to the door. Adèle's twisted torso, her seductive look, had given him an idea for *The Gates of Hell*.

He walked several blocks down the Rue de l'Université, lost in thought. He didn't notice the lacy drizzle coating his jacket and beard and dampening his face.

Adèle's eyes had brimmed with lust. Longing burned inside a woman as it did a man, perhaps even more. The weaker sex had to present a refined and docile nature, despite their yearnings. Yet many of those he had bedded longed to break free of those restraints. Somehow it seemed unfair.

Rodin dodged an omnibus packed with passengers as he crossed the street, perched in the doorway of an inn to avoid the rain, and flipped open his sketchbook. In hurried charcoal strokes he outlined a woman on her knees before a man, sitting outside the gates of hell. He smudged the woman's shock of hair with his thumb, then closed his book and smiled. That image, or some variation, would be a brilliant addition to his work. He would start on the studies in clay right after dinner.

He leapt into a hackney cab and rode the remaining stretch to his apartment. Once indoors, he tossed his hat and overcoat on a white chaise.

Rose rushed from the kitchen to greet him. "Really, Auguste, can't you hang your coat?" She plucked it from the chair and hung it on a rack. "It's wet. I do get tired of cleaning up after you."

Auguste glanced at her shriveled lips and mousy brown hair, her dirty apron. He tried to remember how he had come to love this little dressmaker. But still, he could not leave her. She cared for his maquettes when he was busy with others, kept his home in working order, tended to their bills. And she was the mother of his seventeen-year-old son. The thought of young Auguste left a bitter taste in Rodin's mouth. The drunken lout had no skills, no interest in holding a job or attending school. He slunk out of sight for stretches of time, reappearing only when he needed money.

"Can you put on a pot of tea?" he asked. "I'm going to be up late tonight."

"You won't have dinner?" Her face fell. "Who is your muse this time?"

"Would you prefer we pay back the advance?" Auguste asked, tone sharp. He avoided the topic he knew Rose wished to discuss. He would not be baited to talk about the women he had bedded. She had not warmed his bed in years as per her choice, so in his eyes she had lost the right to care.

"We can live on the street. Would that suit you?" He clutched his sketchbook to his chest and headed toward the kitchen. "I'll prepare my own tea and retire in my room. Suddenly I am not hungry."

"Don't you love me?" Tears filled her eyes.

He spun around. "Love? How can you ask me that? Do I not put a roof over your head? Haven't we toiled together in our poverty? I dine with you in the evenings and we share Sunday afternoons."

Must she harass him every moment? Rose's constant need for reassurance wore on him almost as much as her constant admonitions. He never seemed to be enough for her. Yet once, they had shared a passion of sorts. He wondered how it had withered so easily.

"Yes." Rose dipped her head. She understood the limits of his love, though it was not the love she wished for. But he knew she would not leave him. She had nowhere to go. He was everything to her, and yet, she could not keep from grasping at his coattails as if he might slip away.

Auguste met her watery gaze. "I am finished discussing my emotions for one evening." He mounted the stairs leading to his bedroom. The only emotions she evoked in him now vacillated between irritation and gratitude. Love? He didn't know the meaning of the word, nor did he care to. Love was for fools and for mothers and children. And he had work to do.

He closed his door and turned the key in the lock.

Chapter 5

❧

Camille removed her cape and hung it over a chair. Mother could have warned her about the suitor's visit ahead of time, though if she had, Camille might have done her best to avoid him.

"Join us, please," Mother called from the salon. "There is someone I would like you to meet."

She glanced down at her soiled dress, shrugged, and tromped into the salon.

"Goodness, dear, you're quite disheveled." Mother strained to keep her tone light.

"It was a usual day of mixing glue and playing with mud. A true lady's pursuit." Camille smiled sweetly.

The stranger in their salon chuckled.

Camille raised an eyebrow. The gentleman had a sense of humor—one victory for him. She stared, unabashedly, at the man in a black sac suit and cravat. His wavy hair gleamed in the waning daylight, and his perfectly trimmed beard and stout posture exuded arrogance. He thought he was someone special.

The gentleman set down the teacup he cradled in his hands and stood. "Mademoiselle Claudel, I presume." He crossed the room toward her to make a proper greeting.

"The same." She stiffened as he neared.

"I present to you Monsieur Alphonse Bertillion." Mother bared her teeth in a self-satisfied smile. "Sergeant at the Paris Prefecture of Police."

Sergeant Bertillion leaned toward her and the scent of ink and bergamot wafted from his person. He doled out a peck on her cheek as if it pained him to part with it.

"Has someone been arrested?" Camille's mouth fell open in mock surprise. "Paul, perhaps? No! It's Louise, isn't it? She has been stealing again. That devilish sister of mine."

"Camille!" Mother fumed.

"Or perhaps you are here on account of my pilfering from the local church?" She batted her eyelashes at Sergeant Bertillion.

He chuckled again.

Camille could not stop the smile that sneaked to her lips. As a policeman he did not scare easily. An unfortunate circumstance, for she had no interest in him, or any other gentleman caller, and she would do what was necessary to unnerve him.

His rigid posture thawed ever so slightly. "A woman with a sense of humor is a rare thing, mademoiselle. Would you care to sit down?" he asked.

"Why not?" She perched on the edge of a chaise, ignoring the weight of Mother's glare.

He sat opposite her and chose a sugar-glazed biscuit from the serving platter. "Your mother tells me you attend art school. You've heard there is a new Ministry of Art?"

"Headed by Antonin Proust. Yes, I read it months ago."

He glanced at her sodden skirts. "Do you paint, mademoiselle? It is quite an acceptable pursuit for young women."

"I am a sculptor," she said, her tone disinterested.

"What precisely does a sculptor study?" he asked. "I am intrigued."

She picked at the crud dried beneath her fingernails. "I study anatomy. Each day I look upon naked men and women and compose their likeness."

He choked on his mouthful of biscuit until his face flamed red. Horror registered on Mother's face. The tick of the mantel clock reverberated in the room like a gong.

Camille selected a biscuit of her own and nibbled at its edges. While Monsieur Bertillion drained his teacup, she glanced at his hands. They appeared soft and thin, without calluses or the mark of one who labored, though his right hand was ink stained. She looked at her own, scarred from a slip of a rasp and caked in filth. She smiled. As any sculptor's hands should be.

Mother glared at Camille. *Say something*, her eyes said.

"I am also a student of emotion." Camille broke the silence. "I am fascinated by how it shapes our choices, and do my best to reflect those sentiments in my works."

Sergeant Bertillion replied, "I see we aren't so different, Mademoiselle Claudel. I, too, study men's motives and how their unchecked emotion leads them to crime."

"Oh? It is my understanding policemen merely detain their victims and haul them to prison."

"That is true, but I spend more time in prison observing criminals, writing extensive notes of their behaviors, and doing clerical work. I examine the shape of their skulls and eye sockets, the structure of their bodies. I am in search of patterns, you see. If one could determine a pattern in criminal behaviors, in their anatomical structures, perhaps we might prevent crime. Or, at the very least, discern whether or not they are truly guilty."

That was why he had smelled of ink, Camille thought. All of his feverish note taking, no doubt.

"As far as I can see, there is no science to one's emotions, monsieur. They sweep over you and consume you, often with an intensity one does not expect. Nothing more than a familiar scent or texture to spark a memory, and voilà! A flood of disgust chokes you, or the sweetest memory fills your heart."

Mother said nothing, but listened to their banter.

"Still, I believe there is a science to it all. I have not found the missing link yet, but I shall," he said.

"I am certain if anyone can discover that link, it is you, monsieur. You seem the inquisitive sort."

"Thank you." Pride pushed his shoulders back a fraction. "I like to think so."

"I imagine you spend many hours poring over your documentation," Camille said. "What a life you lead, spending hours in prison and chasing criminals! Your work is admirable."

"Why thank you, mademoiselle." He sat a bit taller.

"You are so passionate! You must be consumed by the nobility of your career," she said with false admiration.

"I hope to serve justice in whatever way I can. I would like to change history."

She smiled. "And changing history is not such a lofty goal for someone of your . . . intelligence. But I suppose your dedication requires endless focus—near obsession, even."

"Very often, yes." He nodded. "I do not sleep well at night for my churning mind."

"One might say you have no time for a wife and certainly not a family at all."

A grim smile crossed his face. At last he understood her game of words.

"More tea?" Mother interjected, oblivious to Camille's victory.

"I would love some, Mother." Camille smiled in spite of herself. Any man as proud as Sergeant Bertillion would not let himself be outwitted by a woman. He would not return.

⌘

Camille had argued and pleaded, somehow persuading her parents to rent an atelier. The thought of all that "mud and grime" coating the furniture and floors disturbed Mother greatly, and once Camille had proposed shared expenses with other women, she had tipped the argument in her favor. She swept up the final pile of dust and debris on the studio floor. She would not have bothered, but Monsieur Boucher would be by for a lesson at any moment.

Emily prepared her workstation while Amy reshaped an ear on her bust of an angel for the third time. The ear sagged and flopped to the floor with a thud.

Camille smothered a laugh. Amy was trying to force what was not natural. She didn't feel the contours of the clay, or mold with light fingers when necessary. Camille had already shown her the technique twice and she could not seem to catch on.

"Clay has a memory," she had told Amy. The ear had once been a nose and did not wish to be an ear.

"That's absurd," Amy had retorted. "You can shape the clay to be whatever you like. And I don't want to waste it."

But now the misshapen lump lay on the floor. One could not force something to be, simply because one wanted it to be so. And pushing made no difference at all.

Emily ignored them and continued to sketch at her worktable.

"Why don't you help me instead of laughing?" Amy wiped her hands on a towel and stretched out in a chair.

"Perhaps your angel doesn't want to listen," Camille said. When she noticed Amy's exasperated expression, she stopped. "Come now, that's funny." She leaned her broom against the wall.

"It is all so easy for you, isn't it?" Amy retrieved the flaccid disk of clay from the floor. "I grow tired of your smug tone."

Camille's smile faded. She had never been smug with Amy—only helpful. But the girl she had liked immediately at l'Académie Colarossi had proven to be envious and insecure in her abilities. Now Camille understood why. Amy lacked true talent—though sad to admit, it appeared to be true. Her comrade worked hard, but it did not make up for her lack of inspiration. Emily possessed more raw aptitude, but did not work as hard as Amy did. In all, neither would advance if they continued on these paths. Being a female artist was far too difficult.

"Having confidence in my abilities does not make me smug." Camille drew a tin of tobacco out of her handbag and sat at the table. "Besides, I have helped you many times, have I not?"

Amy did not reply.

"Don't lose heart," Camille said, her tone softening. "Why don't we take a break? Have a cigarette, and I will show you a trick to fix the ear." She licked the edges of a small square of rolling paper and placed a clump of sticky brown tobacco in its center.

Amy's furrowed brow relaxed. "Thank you. I could use your help."

"Glad to," Camille said while keeping her eye trained on her task. She lit the rolled tobacco with a match; the cigarette paper caught and the end glowed with a tiny orange ring of fire. By the third puff on her cigarette, her tongue tingled and her head began to vibrate.

A knock sounded at the door. Camille stood and moved to the door to welcome their tutor inside. "Monsieur Boucher, please, come in," she said, inhaling once more.

Boucher's eyes widened as he took in her cigarette. Such an impolite habit for a young woman.

"Good day, monsieur," Amy and Emily said in unison.

Amy straightened her smock. "I would offer you tea, but we need to refill our bin. I apologize for our lack of hospitality." She blinked rapidly, fluttering her lashes at the sculptor.

Oblivious to Amy's flirtations, he said, "No need, but thank you." Monsieur Boucher glanced around their work space, noting the Oriental rug covering one wall, the stove, and even a makeshift vase with dried flowers. "A charming nest. Quite the perfect place for women to work."

"I should bring my sewing and some lace curtains," Camille said, smashing her cigarette in a dish. "Perhaps some china with a pretty flower pattern?"

Monsieur Boucher held up a gloved hand. "Mademoiselle Claudel, you know I—"

"No need, monsieur, for I am only teasing you." She grinned. She couldn't help but be sarcastic. He meant well, but he did not know how offensive his comments could be. She truly detested being assigned a "woman's" duties and interests. She found them dull and demeaning.

He smiled. "*Très bien.* This morning, we will begin by choosing a model. They're gathering soon." He fished inside his coat for a pocket watch. "We don't have much time. The schools will select their models first and we may do so after."

"This is so exciting," Emily said. A dimple made a groove in her round face.

Camille leapt to her feet and squeezed Emily first, then Amy, with all her might. "We shall have our own model!" she exclaimed. The ladies laughed at her exuberance.

After a short and bumpy ride to Place Pigalle, they alighted from the coach to join a crowd gathered in the square. Carriages and bicycles skirted around the mass of people milling by the fountain.

Camille gaped at the throng. She hadn't realized there were so many models, or working sculptors, for that matter.

A sculptor in a beret with an auburn beard appeared to be important; many models crowded around him. She watched in fascination as the gentleman scrutinized each face and figure, dismissing those he did not want. At last he settled on three models. Three! She couldn't fathom having the ability to pay for more than one at a time. She eyed the gentleman once more with interest.

"The best models apply directly to the renowned sculptors." Boucher leaned close to Camille's ear to be heard above the din of the city. "Then the schools choose, and we pick last. You won't have the luxury of knowing which models are the most reputable or which make the best study, but you must start somewhere."

"I trust your opinion, monsieur."

"Oh, you shall choose, mademoiselle." His smile reached his eyes.

Camille returned his smile, pleased to be selecting her first professional model.

"It isn't uncommon for entire families to model. They make it the family business of sorts. There." Boucher pointed at a family of husband, wife, and two children clustered together. Their fair hair and squared jaws resembled one another's.

A man shoved Camille aside, nearly knocking her and Boucher off their feet.

The man raised his hand. "DeRossis!" he shouted. He pointed to a family of raven-haired beauties with long, straight noses and high cheekbones. A child of no more than four leapt into his mother's arms. The father nodded and the family followed.

"Most certainly an Italian family," Boucher said. "Many travel to France for opportunities."

Amy and Emily stood to the side, arms crossed, watching as Boucher led Camille through the crush of bodies. She did not miss the jealousy etched on Amy's face. Amy wanted Boucher to take her under his wing, rather than Camille; that was clear. Perhaps if Amy spent less time flirting with the male students in class and took her work more seriously he would.

A gentleman approached Camille. "Are you employed with someone yet, mademoiselle?" The man's shrewd gaze appraised her appearance as if sizing up a thoroughbred.

Her mouth fell open but emitted no sound; she was stunned.

The man looked to Boucher. "What have you agreed to pay her? I will double it."

Camille wanted to slug him. "I am a sculptor, monsieur, not a model."

"You owe Mademoiselle Claudel an apology. She is an artist," Monsieur Boucher said.

The man winked at Camille and disappeared among the crowd.

Boucher regarded the anger on Camille's face and placed a hand on her shoulder. "Never mind. Come."

Minute to minute, the throng thinned as models followed their employers.

"How about her?" Camille pointed at a woman of medium height in a showy gown nearest the fountain. A large bustle jutted out behind her in layers of forest green brocade, cinched with bows. The woman appeared wealthy, though Camille knew better. Most models were as poverty-stricken as the artists who sketched them. "She isn't precisely pretty, but her brow is interesting and her form is healthy."

With a perfect mix of interesting features and a touch of classic beauty, the woman would make a fine model. The arc of her lily white neck was as graceful as a swan's.

"A good choice, mademoiselle." Boucher said.

Camille wanted to sing. Their own model!

The group made their way through the crowd. When they had reached the model, Monsieur Boucher began introductions. "Pardon me, mademoiselle, but I am Alfred Boucher—"

"Boucher!" the model interrupted. "I am honored to work with you, monsieur." She smiled brightly. "I've heard many great things about your work."

"*Merci*, but you will not work with me, but my protégé and her classmates—Mesdemoiselles Claudel, Fawcett, and Singer." He indicated each of them.

Camille smiled. "*Bonjour.*"

The model scrutinized Camille from the tip of her navy hat to the hem of her unadorned dress. "But you are a woman," the model said. "You are all women."

"The power of your observation is impressive," Camille retorted.

The woman pursed her lips. "My name is Maria Botticelli. And I do not work with amateurs."

"Mademoiselle Botticelli, these women are serious sculptors," Boucher said. "They will pay the wages you request. Your association with them will not diminish your reputation. On the contrary, you may find yourself with more work. They are a talented group." He looked pointedly at Camille—a warning for her to be polite.

Camille wasn't certain she wanted to work with this woman. Her sour attitude might interfere with her ability to do as she was told. "We will find another model," she said. "I will not be looked upon with derision and I certainly will not tolerate a poor attitude in my atelier."

Amy and Emily snickered at her blunt assertion.

"I apologize, mesdemoiselles, monsieur," Maria said quickly, glancing at the diminishing crowd. "I have never worked with women, but I am happy to accept the job and follow your instructions. When shall we begin?"

Camille scrutinized Mademoiselle Botticelli for an instant, making the model squirm under her intense gaze. She absorbed Maria's proud demeanor, her lovely features, and the insecurity that rolled off her person. She would make an interesting study.

"You start today."

Chapter 6

❧

The heat in the foundry always surprised Auguste, perhaps because his ateliers were bone cold in winter. Today he came to ensure his *fondeur* made a negative cast of *Dante*, exactly as he had sculpted it. He trusted Henri Lebossé—he had cast most of Auguste's pieces in bronze perfectly—but one never knew when a detail might be missed or Lebossé had a bad day on the job. Auguste would not hesitate to ask him to recast a piece if that day ever arrived. Imperfections were unacceptable.

"No bubbles in the mold?" Rodin asked.

"None." Lebossé presented the bust for inspection.

"You've chased the seam lines nicely." He ran his thumb over the filmy edges of the piece's legs. The mold had left crease marks in the wax that an expert hand had blended until no longer visible. "You've done a brilliant job along the muscle lines."

"Thank you, monsieur." Henri smiled, displaying a set of teeth that jutted too far from the line of his jaw. The poor fellow looked like a damned rabbit with his teeth, bushy beard, and corpulent belly, but he knew how to bronze better than anyone.

Lebossé carved a hole in the wax head to prepare it for shelling; the piece would be dipped in solution and sanded in layer after layer over weeks to form a strong outer mold. Once the outer mold had hardened, the bust would be heated and the wax drained.

Auguste walked into the next room to survey the other copy of

Dante. It had already been layered and heated, and now sat filled with molten bronze. Even after years and several pieces, he still enjoyed watching the founder's assistants chip away the outer sandy crust to reveal a bronze replica of his original. He browsed a hall of finished works. The metallic patina gave the myriad of shapes a lustrous finish in the light.

Rodin frowned at his pocket watch. He expected Jules Dalou, one of his closest sculptor friends, more than half an hour ago. They had agreed to meet at the foundry and walk together to the Café Américain. Jules said he had news.

As if conjured by his thoughts, a familiar voice resonated behind him. "I am sorry I'm late."

Rodin turned to find his wiry friend red faced and blowing hot breath on his hands to ward off the cold. "I was just wondering where you were," he said.

"Monsieur Rodin." Lebossé joined them. "Your busts will be ready for shipping tomorrow."

"Thank you." Auguste nodded and followed Jules to the door. A blast of icy air greeted them and he lifted his collar against the cold.

"Boucher said he would join us later," Dalou said. "He's working with a student of his. Someone named Claudel. Said he couldn't let her down by canceling. Whatever that means."

"He couldn't reschedule with a *female* student?" She must be important to him, Auguste thought. He smiled to himself. The dog. Alfred was probably sleeping with her.

"There's talk of reestablishing the Société Nationale des Beaux-Arts." Dalou broke into his thoughts. "It's not organized yet, but the Artistes Français selected another round of inexperienced louts to sort through Salon submissions. Our fate lies in the hands of the least qualified men in the country."

"Who will lead the group?" Auguste asked through frozen lips.

"I would like to be the president, if the others will have me." Jules tucked his hands under his arms for warmth. "But first, we will have to choose a location for an annual salon."

"The move will enrage the Artistes Français. Are you certain you want to anger the people who support you?"

Dalou had received the Medal of Honor for his reliefs of the *Estates*

General, Meeting of June 23, 1789 and another titled *Fraternity*—both dedicated to the memory of the French Revolution. Auguste had been so proud of his friend he had sculpted a bust of him in celebration, though Jules had yet to congratulate him on his own success of several smaller bronze commissions.

"I don't give a damn about the ministers and their awards," Jules said, avoiding a slippery patch on the sidewalk. "And I'd like you to join us."

Auguste would join his friends, but he wouldn't turn away the Artistes Français. It would be career suicide. They still held the majority of influence, not to mention most of the funding for public commissions.

Another gust of cold air sliced through the waning warmth of his coat and hat. The men increased their pace. The café lay just around the corner.

"You said you have news," Auguste said. "Are you going to tell me or do I have to beg?"

His friend laughed. "You will never believe it."

When they reached their destination, Auguste whipped open the café door and heat enveloped them. The men removed their coats and hats and chose a table.

"Well?" He blew hot breath on his frigid fingers.

Jules frowned. "They have awarded me the Légion d'Honneur."

"Why on earth are you frowning? Congratulations!" Rodin held out his hand for a hearty shake.

Jules pursed his lips in displeasure, giving his already thin cheeks a sunken look.

Auguste lowered his hand, surprised by his friend's rebuff. "You're an anointed one now. This is fantastic."

"It's a medal devised by that imperial tyrant. Awarded to pieces deemed as art in the eyes of the Bonapartes, who, might I add, knew nothing about art, but merely stole it from other countries."

Rodin would kill for the recognition, regardless of who had originally put the award in place. "Now it's an award granted by the republic. It's prestigious. A golden seal."

"I am not going to accept it. It's an assault on my integrity." Jules sipped from his wineglass.

Auguste knew other artists who had refused the honor. He hated the *institut* and the standards of the old guard as well, but he couldn't conceive of refusing the award. The public revered the winning artists. The greasy unease of envy swam in his stomach. No, he would not be jealous of his friend. He wished him the utmost happiness and success; he truly did.

"It means freedom in your work, *mon ami*," Auguste said.

"I will have more work, yes. But it is your busts of Legros and Laurens that have garnered all of the support in the papers. 'Rodin is the artist to watch' and so forth." Dalou's eyes darkened.

Auguste flinched at Jules's implied jealousy. His friend had received two of the highest honors an artist could win, yet he worried over a few write-ups about him in the newspaper. They had been friends for years—Jules had even appeared at his father's funeral, a comfort Rodin had appreciated in the midst of his devastation—yet he had not seen this side of him.

Dalou went on, "What good is an award when I am not respected? Certainly you are."

Though Auguste's cheeks had thawed, he struggled to fight the ice water in his veins. A confidence between him and his oldest friend had come to an end.

⋖⋗

"Maria Botticelli is a real trial." Camille rolled over on Paul's bed. "She thinks she is above my instruction, and it is I who pay her."

"What do the others say?" Paul asked.

"Amy and Emily don't reproach her. They allow her to prattle on, complaining about every pose, sniveling about the cold, the crick in her neck, after only minutes in her position. If she doesn't like the work, she shouldn't do it. I am fed up with her and it has only been a month."

"Perhaps you should give her more breaks." Paul peered at her over the edge of his book. "I have posed often enough for you. You're a demanding little wench."

She tossed a pillow at her brother. He blocked it with his fist before it reached his face.

"Maria is paid to be still." She crossed her ankles and eyed the polished leather of her boots. "I allot plenty of time to stretch or take meals. Monsieur Boucher says it is difficult to find good models. He believes paying her more will encourage her to shut her mouth."

"Why don't you take his advice?"

"We do not have more money, and I don't believe she will behave better." She snapped one of Paul's suspender straps.

"Ouch! What did you do that for?" He rolled upright into a sitting position, giving her his back.

Camille laughed. "You lie there so innocently." She rubbed his back. "I'm sorry, brother." Something about their relationship brought out the child in her, despite her nineteen years.

He looked over his shoulder. "I have just found out I have the highest marks in the class in letters and literature."

Camille propped herself up on one elbow. "Of course you do! Shall we celebrate? I will buy you *une demi*. Whatever beer you wish."

"Don't you have a gentleman caller this evening?"

She flopped against the pillow and groaned. "Monsieur Bertillion. He isn't all bad, but I am not interested. I had hoped to frighten him the last time we met."

Paul laughed. "Better luck next time."

There wouldn't be a next time. Camille jumped to her feet. "Come on!" She pulled on her pelisse and fastened a burgundy hat to her hair with pins.

"You don't think Mother will notice us walking out the front door?" he asked, skeptical.

"We'll make a quick getaway." She tugged on his hand. "Let's go to the Étoile area. I've been dying to see the electric streetlamps."

Paul ran a nervous hand through his blond hair. "My hat is in the front hall."

She smiled, her eyes alight with mischief. "Fetch it, quietly."

Camille inched the bedroom door open. Paul tiptoed down the stairs behind her, nearly knocking over a vase perched on a decorative table in the corridor. She pushed a finger to her lips. When they reached the front hall, Paul snatched his hat from the rack and followed Camille through the door. It stuck as he tried to pull it closed.

"Come on!" Camille raced down the apartment stairs.

"It won't close." He jerked on the latch, slamming the door. He thundered after her without regard to the clattering he made in the hall. Camille threw open the building's main door and paused to venture a look over her shoulder. The maid poked her head out.

"Run, Paul!" she squealed.

He held his hat to his head and dashed after her. They had run ten meters when the building door opened and Mother peered out into the dark.

"*Arrêtez!*" she shouted. "Right this instant!" She waved her arms about as if the house were on fire. The crinoline under her cream skirts swayed like a bell. "Camille, Paul! How dare you leave our guest unattended! Come back here!"

Camille laughed in glee, nearly slamming into a figure clad in a striped suit.

"Pardon me," the man said.

At once Camille recognized the astute face of Alphonse Bertillion. "I apologize, but I must go!" she shouted without slowing. Paul ran fast at her heels.

They ducked around the corner and huddled in the doorway of a church, Ursulines de Jésus. Paul leaned over, panting. "We'll be in for it when we return."

Camille laughed, her stomach aflutter from the thrill of stealing away. "Mother will yell, but I am a grown woman. I make my own decisions."

"Which are usually *merde*," he said, shoving her playfully.

She guffawed and then gulped in another breath. "My decisions aren't shit."

The echo of heels on stone drew closer. "Do you think Bertillion is following us?" Paul's clear blue eyes widened.

"He'll never follow us in here." Camille pushed her brother inside the church, through the vestibule, and into the nave.

A hush enveloped them. Not a soul graced the rows of polished pews, though a priest must have lurked about. A circle of candles flickered on the altar. Their light dissipated in the vast darkness.

Camille stared at the towering ceiling. Their slightest movement would be amplified in such a cavernous space.

"This place is creepy," Paul said, craning his neck to take in its wide expanse. When he looked down again, he met Camille's watchful gaze. Her stillness unsettled him. "What?"

She saw the fear shining in his eyes. "They built those ceilings with purpose. To make us feel insignificant and small. To steal our sense of self. If God is all-loving, why would he wish for such a thing? If he exists, he does not reside here."

"You miss the point, sister."

Camille rubbed her hands together, the leather of her gloves slipping as they shimmied back and forth. "Have you become religious, then? Papa would laugh to hear such a thing. Perhaps that school is not so good for you after all."

Paul looked down at his boots, a sheepish expression marking his features. "Your skepticism doesn't erase someone else's faith, or God's existence—if there is a God," he added quickly.

"Our family has been skeptical about religion our entire lives, and you as well as any." Her brow furrowed.

"Can we change the subject?" Paul glanced around the dim room and shuddered. "Let's go. I feel as if—"

"You feel his eyes upon you, do you?" she goaded him.

He ignored her quip and hurried to the door.

When had he turned into such a coward? Camille looked over her shoulder a last time. A shadow stretched from the altar's crucifix across the floor. A shiver tingled along her spine.

She felt the sudden need to escape as well, and hurried after Paul into the night.

⌘

Camille wiped her hands and peered out the studio window. Something wasn't quite right with her piece, but she couldn't discern the issue. The sun beamed over the rooftop tiles, peeped in windowpanes, and flooded the alleyways between buildings. The sunshine did not fool her; her morning walk to classes and the atelier had been brisk, but she needed fresh air to clear her head. She untied her stained apron and tossed it over a chair.

"I'm going for a walk," she said to Amy and Emily, who looked up briefly and then retrained their eyes on their sculptures.

Maria straightened from her awkward pose. "Finally." She rotated her head back and forth to stretch her muscles. "I'll break for luncheon and return in three hours."

"Three hours?" Camille looked at her with an incredulous expression. "I'll lose too much light by then. An hour and a half at most."

Maria screwed her perfect mouth into a pout. "How am I to eat in such a short time? I'm meeting someone across town. Besides, I have been working for two hours already."

Anger overwhelmed Camille's contemplative mood. She wouldn't finish the piece before she ran out of money at this rate. Not to mention she would miss the submission deadline for the May Salon.

"You've worked for two hours and expect three to repose?" She clenched her fists. "It seems you have forgotten I paid you for the entire day."

Maria pretended not to hear her, slipped into her undergarments, and reached for her vermillion day dress.

"Let her go," Amy said. "We kept her an extra hour last night."

"She stayed an extra hour because she had to stop five times yesterday!" Camille said. "And the day before she did not show at all."

"You don't need to work her so hard." Amy crossed her arms over her chest.

"I only demand what I paid for!" Camille said. "If she is unable to fulfill the hours, she should not accept payment for them."

Emily exchanged looks with Amy as if a secret conversation had passed between them.

"This arrangement is not working." Camille threw her arms in the air. "It seems I am the only professional here."

Maria snorted. "As if a woman will get anywhere in the art world anyway."

"At this rate you won't find me giving recommendations for your service!"

Maria opened her mouth to speak, but Camille's look froze her tongue in place.

"I'm going out for a couple of hours." Camille pulled on her wool cloak and gloves, and tucked her sketchbook under her arm. "I expect you to be here when I return." She slammed the door behind her and lunged into the street.

Maria had some nerve, demanding time off, more money, day in and day out. As soon as Camille finished this piece, she would seek a new model. Perhaps she would begin looking sooner. Something needed to be done about Amy and Emily as well. They seemed not to care whether or not they advanced with their pieces, and what's more, they whispered about her at every turn. It did not make her work any easier.

She ambled along the street in search of a comfortable place to sit. She missed Villeneuve, its wild landscape and even the torrential rain that pelted her skin—the kind of weather that ripped away artifice and deepened the soul. Though Paris had its own sensibility, a heartbeat even, it did not offer her the same comfort as her summer home.

Camille sat on a bench near the entrance of a popular brasserie facing a nook of greenery, a place artists and students frequented. She flipped open her sketchbook and retrieved a pencil from her pocket. A hungry bird hopped about a patch of grass. Pencil to paper and she drew its outline. She lost herself in her drawing, the sun warm on her face despite the chill. As two women passed, she glanced at their heads inclined toward one another, their eyes condemning. She did not care that she sat unescorted, boldly in the middle of the day. Her reputation could be damaged, but it mattered little to her. She did not hold society's mores on a pedestal. She pitied those women. Their lives must be insipid, each moment of their days planned by another, their friends chosen by another, their very dreams dictated by another.

Camille sketched the robin's feathers, the lump of its rusty throat, its curious gleaming eye. She looked up again as a gentleman neared her bench. His agile form moved with grace, his curling dark hair bouncing beneath his cap. He stopped for a moment to retrieve his watch from his jacket pocket. She noted his long thin fingers, his angular jaw—yes, he seemed familiar. He sat beside her on the edge of the bench and nodded, a polite greeting from a stranger. She remembered now. He had been at the fountain, waiting for a sculptor to choose him.

"Good day, monsieur." Camille closed her sketchbook, suddenly excited.

The gentleman smiled. "Good day."

His thick Italian accent confirmed her suspicions. "You are a model?" she said as more of a statement than a question. "I saw you at the Rue Bonaparte."

"*Oui*." He tipped his hat and bowed his head. A smile tugged the corners of his lips. "How do you do?"

"Are you currently employed?" She flashed her most congenial smile.

"Not at the moment." He returned her smile. "But I have worked with Mercié, Bourdelle, and Rodin. Do you know a sculptor who might be interested in working with me?"

"I know none of those sculptors, so I will have to take your word for it. But I am interested in your services, monsieur."

He raised one dark eyebrow. "What did you have in mind?"

"May I?" She held out her hands.

"Of course." He removed his hat and leaned toward her.

Camille tilted his head and probed the bones of his face. "You'd make a fine study."

The gentleman smiled, a twinkle in his eye. "So I've been told."

"I'd hire you for multiple projects, if you are available," she said. And terminate Maria the instant she returned. "Would you care to see my studio?"

Another look of surprise crossed his features. "Your studio?"

"It's not far from here." She gathered her utensils.

⌘

They returned to 117 Notre Dame des Champs. Camille entered the studio in her characteristic rush and tossed her shawl and coat over a chair.

"*Mes amies*, this is Monsieur—" She stopped and looked at him with a quizzical expression.

"Giganti." He removed his hat. "*Bonjour.*"

"Welcome," Amy said, smiling brightly at their guest. Her hand flew to her hair in an instinctive gesture.

Emily dropped the hunk of bread she nibbled on her plate.

"Giganti has agreed to—"

The door opened and Maria entered, out of breath. "I've made it!" She stopped when she saw the handsome Italian. "And who do we have the pleasure of meeting?"

Camille checked the clock on her desk. "It has been two and one half hours. Consider yourself dismissed."

"Camille!" Amy stood in outrage. "You don't make all of the decisions. Not without consulting us. I say she stays."

"Dismissed?" Maria's eyes widened. "But you are in the middle of a portrait. You won't find someone as competent as me for the pittance you paid me." She crossed her arms and stamped her foot. "I won't go."

Emily stuffed in another bite of bread to avoid replying.

"You would continue to let the model take advantage of us?" Camille turned to Maria. "You may go. Immediately."

"I am only half-finished with my angel," Amy said, her brown eyes flashing. "I need her."

"Make your angel a male. Besides, it looks as if you need to start over at any rate," Camille said cruelly. She wrapped a hand around Maria's arm and pulled her toward the door. "You have wasted our money and time long enough."

"Unhand me at once!" Maria looked back at Giganti for help. He shrugged and smiled. He seemed to enjoy the drama playing out before him.

"Good day to you." Camille thrust the woman through the door, turned the key in the lock, and returned to Giganti's side. "Now, as I was saying, this is Giganti and he'll be our new model."

"I'm delighted to work with you all." His smile was packed with square white teeth and dressed with dimples.

Amy crossed her arms over her chest. "Take it back. Take back what you said about my work."

"Amy." Camille huffed out an impatient breath. "I apologize if your feelings are hurt, but I only speak the truth. Your professors and tutors have not told you because they want your money. But I will tell you because I am your friend. Your last few pieces have been not only amateur, but downright dreadful. You spend little time practicing or studying. You need to put in the time to learn technique, or move back to England and marry. All you talk about is men anyway."

At once, Amy's eyes filled with tears. "This is how you repay me for befriending you."

"I am your friend by telling you the truth. And by the way, friends don't whisper about you while you're within earshot—or at all."

Amy tossed her smock on the floor, stomped across the room, and threw on her coat. "I'm leaving." Emily glared at Camille and scrambled after Amy.

Regret hit her instantly. The truth always pushed its way from her gut and up her throat to spill out in the open. To her chagrin, few appreciated it. Now she had lost one of the only girls who had ever been nice to her—even if Amy had been jealous and whispered about her.

Camille sighed.

"Shall we begin, mademoiselle?" Giganti asked.

She smiled weakly. "You just said the perfect thing."

Chapter 7

꧁

Camille reworked a mass of clay with her fingers, softening it, shaping the mound into a human nose. Paul's nose, to be precise. His face had changed into that of a young man and she wanted to preserve him in time. Her mind emptied of every thought save the shape of Paul's proud forehead and chin, his stout posture and probing eyes. The truth in his face, the wisdom and forbearance had always struck her and remained one of the things she loved most about her brother. To chisel beneath the surface of her subjects' skin, to tunnel into their secrets and reflect them on the faces of their busts, or in the movement of their limbs, was her favorite part of sculpting. Paul made for an easy study.

With a fine wire tool, Camille trimmed the clay well of Paul's eye sockets. Last night she had read the early pages of a play he was composing. One day he would be revered for his stories. She could feel it.

An hour passed, two. . . .

The splat of a plaster spatula against its portrait interrupted Camille's reverie. Emily worked intently on her soldier, made in Giganti's likeness. The model had proven to be an excellent choice. He never complained and Camille liked his contagious, optimistic nature. It balanced her own thick sarcasm.

She looked up from her bust. Though Emily had returned, Amy had not, even after the letter of apology Camille had sent. She sighed. Now they would need another student to help pay rent.

A knock came at the door.

Camille rubbed her hands together to loosen the clay crust coating them, dipped them in a basin of cool water, and scrubbed.

Someone knocked again.

"*J'arrive!*" Emily called, before rushing to open the door.

Monsieur Boucher and an unknown gentleman entered. "Bonjour, mesdemoiselles," their tutor said. "I have brought a fellow sculptor and friend to see your work. I present to you Monsieur Dubois."

Camille studied the gentleman. His middle protruded, stretching the buttons of his morning coat, and his shoulders sagged in fatigue. Pouches of purple-black skin puffed under his eyes. Had some sort of tragedy befallen him? She tried to decipher the emotions of everyone she met and filed the information away for later. She never knew when she might need ideas to layer a piece with meaning.

Monsieur Dubois nodded curtly, his eyes locked on the naked Giganti. "I see you are . . . hard at work."

"Always." Camille bit her lip to keep from giggling at the gentleman's shocked expression. She wondered how long her using a male model would garner such surprise. Really, Monsieur Dubois was a sculptor himself. He must have worked with *real* female artists before.

"Can I offer you a cup of tea?" Emily asked.

"Thank you, but no. I have only stopped by to see a Mademoiselle Claudel's work."

Emily's face fell.

"I am Mademoiselle Claudel and this is my friend and fellow sculptor Mademoiselle Fawcett. If you are inclined to view her work as well?"

Emily shot her a grateful smile.

Boucher laid a fatherly hand on Camille's shoulder. "Monsieur Dubois is the director of l'École des Beaux-Arts. He would like to see your last few pieces."

A mix of indignation and awe swirled inside Camille's belly. Women were prohibited from studying at Dubois's *académie*, yet he came to see her.

"Of course. Right this way." She whisked around the room, unveiling several of her studies: a bust of young Paul, *David and Goliath*, and a maid bent over her washing. When she removed a sheet covering a plaster bust of *La Vieille Hélène*, a cloud of dust filled the air.

Monsieur Dubois sneezed, then hacked and wheezed as dust particles filled his lungs.

"Here, man." Boucher pounded him on the back.

Camille reached for a carafe on the table and poured him a glass of water. "Monsieur?" She placed it in his hands.

Dubois sipped from the glass. "Goodness." He removed a handkerchief from his breast pocket and wiped his eyes. "Thank you." He set the glass down and perused her remaining pieces. Camille watched as he ran his fingers over the varied surfaces of the offending sculpture, detecting the grooves and dips, the smooth planes and violent peaks.

"Simply incredible," the sculptor said.

A flicker of glee sparked in Camille's chest and spread until a full smile blossomed on her face.

"You mimic Monsieur Rodin beautifully," Dubois said. "He has taught you well."

Her stomach clenched. He thought she copied the styling of another? Her work mimicked no one's. She hadn't met a single person who used light, or its absence, exactly as she did. Few artists wrenched the soul from the depths of their subjects and portrayed it with such vigor and detail. Only the masters had managed this feat. Humble or not, she ranked her work among the more skilled artists.

Monsieur Boucher looked taken aback by the minister's statement. "There may be some similarities, but Rodin prefers harmony in his silhouettes and musculature. Look here." He ran his pinky finger over a furrowed section of the sculpture of Hélène's head. "Camille's works show violent contrast, light and its absence, and an intimacy all her own. The very antithesis of Rodin's style."

Monsieur Dubois scratched the yellowed beard on his chin. "Perhaps." He shot Camille a questioning look, as if he did not understand her.

The glee Camille had felt vanished, and she restrained herself from saying something vulgar. Her temper had sprung up more and more often these days, though she did not understand why. Yet, even if she detested the idea of his assumption, she must mind her manners.

She stuck out her chin. "Pardon my impertinence, Monsieur Dubois, but how might I mimic Monsieur Rodin? I have heard his name mentioned only once before in passing, and I've never laid eyes on the man or his work."

"No?" Monsieur Dubois's eyebrows shot skyward. "Perhaps you should."

Chapter 8

❦

Auguste pushed an array of clay maquettes to the corner of his desk and opened his sketchbook. He thumbed through its pages, careful not to smudge the charcoal drawings, until he came upon a series of cathedrals. He squinted and pulled the book closer to his face. His blasted eyesight grew worse by the day, but he refused to wear spectacles. They warped his perception of surfaces, which did him no good. He rescued a drawing pencil teetering on the edge of his desk and flipped to a fresh page. The outline of his *Gates of Hell*, its facade adorned with tormented figures, emerged on the page in several strokes.

He paused and tapped the paper with his pencil. Hell meant longing without respite, never attaining satisfaction. He drew a woman, desire on her features, and a man reaching for her, his agony plain. Auguste's longing took shape in the form of lust for his legacy, that magical inspired moment—the scent of a woman's skin.

The sound of shuffling feet alerted him to a visitor, and he looked up from his drawings. Alfred Boucher, his friend and colleague, stood in the doorway.

"Come in, Alfred. Sit." He motioned to a chair on the other side of his desk.

Boucher eyed the brown stain and the fine dust covering everything. "I prefer to stand, thank you. I've just had my trousers cleaned."

Rodin took in the joy that lit Boucher's eyes. "You look cheery. What's happened?"

"I have just heard," Alfred said, his voice bubbling with exuberance. "I have won the Prix de Rome."

The winning artist received a stipend to study for eighteen months in the Renaissance capital, a very competitive prize and quite difficult to obtain. Nearly every artist Auguste knew had applied and failed.

He jumped to his feet and extended his hand. "Congratulations! Marvelous news." He shook Boucher's hand vigorously. "You are on your way."

"Thank you, my friend."

Despite Auguste's show of enthusiasm, the familiar tide of yearning rushed over him each time a friend advanced and he ran in place.

"When do you leave for Italy?" he asked.

"I don't begin my studies for another two months, but I depart within a fortnight." He cleared his throat. "Which brings me to the reason for my visit. I have a favor to ask of you." Rodin raised his tawny eyebrows. "I'll be leaving behind a protégé."

Auguste returned to his chair. "I am far too busy to take on a student."

"She's not just any student."

"She?" He stroked his mustache with his thumb and forefinger. "Is this the woman you are sleeping with?"

"Good God, no!" Alfred said, astounded at such an accusation. "She is my pupil and nothing more."

"I'm sorry, Alfred, but the women I have tutored do not commit themselves to their studies as heartily as they should and rarely advance. I couldn't possibly devote more time to someone who isn't serious."

Alfred cracked a smile. "You'll never meet a student more serious than Mademoiselle Claudel. Her love of sculpting rivals yours and mine. And it is more than that." He leaned on the edge of Auguste's desk to meet his eye. "She is . . . special. She learns quickly and I would call her skill near advanced."

Auguste grunted in disbelief. "She has talent?"

"She needs direction and practice, but her will is fierce, her devotion unquestionable. I daresay she is a woman possessed. And yes, she's the most talented student I have ever worked with to date."

"I don't know. . . ."

"Meet her. Take a look at her work. If you aren't satisfied with what you see, decline." He straightened once more. "I will find someone else in your stead if you aren't interested. But I am loath to send her an inferior tutor whom she will quickly surpass in skill."

Auguste heaved a sigh. "I'll give her a chance, but please warn her. I have no time for tomfoolery and if she cannot keep pace with my instruction—"

"Mademoiselle Claudel will show her work one day. Soon, I'd say, especially under your direction."

Rodin held up his hand to halt Alfred's assumption. "Now, don't get ahead of yourself."

Alfred smiled and put on his derby hat once more. "You'll see soon enough."

❧

Camille's shoulders and neck ached with fatigue. She had been working on Paul's bust for hours without rest. She rubbed her sore hands. "Is there any bread left?"

"It's gone." Emily bent over a bucket of plaster and stirred the thick mixture.

She groaned. "I bought an entire loaf yesterday. You ate it all again?"

"There's no need to be cross," Emily said. "We will get another."

"*We*, or do you mean *me*? You haven't paid your share of the expenses this month and now you eat all the bread."

"If you had not insisted we purchase the most expensive tools, I would have paid you already." Emily flicked her wet hands over the bucket of plaster, showering the floor in snow white droplets.

"You wish to work with inferior supplies?" Camille knitted her brow. "I would prefer not to cast our lot with artists who lack proper instruction and materials. No one takes their work seriously. If you'd like to join their ranks, then go."

Was she so abnormal that no one understood the depth of her passion, of what she would sacrifice for her vision? One day there would be someone who grasped her driving need to create.

"You don't need to be so testy. Of course I do not want inferior supplies." Emily tossed a rag at her. "And I have already sent for more money from Papa."

Camille dropped into a chair and rubbed her face. "I'm sorry. I am hungry, is all."

Emily saw a figure approach the door through the window and scurried to greet the unknown visitor. "*Oui*, monsieur?" she said.

"Rodin. Auguste Rodin." The man removed his black beret. "Monsieur Boucher sent me to evaluate your work."

"Please, come in. I am Mademoiselle Fawcett. And this is Mademoiselle Claudel."

Camille's eyes fixed upon the stout man with fiery hair and flowing beard. It was the sculptor at the fountain who had been surrounded by models, the one who had looked so important. "You are the tutor Monsieur Boucher has sent?" She smoothed an errant lock of hair out of her eyes.

After a lengthy apology, Monsieur Boucher had explained why he must take his leave. Though the news had saddened Camille, she could not help but wish the best for her kindly tutor. Ever generous, he had assured her of Auguste Rodin's accomplishments and talents, though she doubted his assertion that Rodin's talents rivaled his own.

Monsieur Rodin nodded, and moved through the atelier without invitation, pausing to peer at each piece. Intensity exuded from his person.

Was the sculptor timid or self-important? Camille could not tell, for he did not say a word. Confidence emanated from his square shoulders and direct gaze, yet he did not have an exalted air about him. Intrigued, she watched him tour the atelier. The skin between his eyes wrinkled over a sloping nose. What could he be thinking?

Despite her interest in the sculptor, Camille pretended to busy herself with cleaning and rearranging her tools. Emily folded her hands like a well-mannered Englishwoman and leaned against the wall.

Monsieur Rodin paused to assess several of Amy's unfinished pieces.

"Those belong to a student who no longer works with us, monsieur," Emily explained.

The gentleman nodded, then continued to Emily's Roman soldier, and finally to Paul's bust. He leaned closer, eyes scrunched. Camille held her breath. Rodin circled the piece twice, pausing to view it from several angles.

"Whose piece is this?" he asked.

"It is Mademoiselle Claudel's," Emily said in a rush.

His gaze flickered over Camille's frame and returned to *Paul at Thirteen*. "These others are yours, I presume?" He motioned to several other studies Camille had begun but not yet finished.

"*Oui*. They are mine." Tension vibrated in her shoulders and neck. The man distinguished her style easily from the others, but did he like them or not?

"This is your best." He placed his hand atop Paul's head. "But the contrast is too great between the fabric and his skin. Also between his skull and hairline."

Her stomach tightened. "Thank you, monsieur, for pointing out my faults."

Rodin did not react, but examined her array of tools. He picked up a molding knife, examined it, and returned it to the pile on the table.

Camille clenched her fists at her sides, poised to receive more criticism. She did not know why, but suddenly she cared very much what the mysterious gentleman had to say. His presence unsettled her.

"I will send word tomorrow to inform you of my decision," he said at last. "If I am unable to tutor you, I will send recommendations for others." He replaced his beret on his head. "For now, I must go."

Rodin strode to the door and paused. He locked eyes with Camille. She raised her chin, determined to appear calm under his unwavering gaze, though she quivered inside.

"Thank you for sharing your work with me, mesdemoiselles," he said. "Good day."

"Good day, monsieur. And thank you!" Emily tripped over herself to see him out and close the door behind him.

Camille stood stunned in the middle of the room, struggling to pinpoint her feelings. This Rodin had swept through her atelier in a flurry, criticized her quickly, and disappeared. Had he found her lacking in ability? She thought of his gaze once more and his intensity—vigor, barely contained by limbs and flesh, rolled off him and filled the room. Such a quiet man, he was, with a large presence.

"I guess we will hear his verdict tomorrow," Emily said, picking up her chisel.

After another long moment, Camille returned to the bust of Paul and worked with renewed alacrity. She would show Monsieur Rodin smooth lines—if he deemed them worthy of his attention.

She worked long beyond sunset, until her fingers throbbed with cold.

⤜⤏

Auguste soaked a hunk of bread in his cabbage soup and gulped down a salty bite. The young woman had too much pride. He could see it in the arrogant tilt of her chin. Mademoiselle Claudel had not been broken by rejection as he had, yet he sensed she had steeled herself for criticism just the same. She was a woman in a man's world, after all. He could not help but be impressed by her passion. It was immediately apparent in her pieces.

He slurped down his soup until the spoon clinked against the bottom of his tin bowl. Camille Claudel would be a difficult pupil, but she held a great deal of promise—if she would listen. He mused at the way she had rankled at his criticism. The other student showed no more talent than his mother, who had dabbled in painting on rainy afternoons, but he would work with both women if he chose to visit the atelier again.

"Auguste, would you read to me this evening?" Rose's whiny voice never failed to grate on his nerves. "I have missed you this long day." She kissed him on his crown of dark amber hair.

"Not tonight. I have work to do."

Her face fell. "You avoid me."

"Don't be absurd." His voice remained calm, though he prickled at her words. He tired of the same arguments.

Sensing his irritation, Rose wrung her hands and said, "I will send up a pot of tea and biscuits."

"Thank you." He kissed her cheek and rubbed her shoulder for an instant, then disappeared up the stairs.

Auguste closed his office door behind him and turned the knob of his gas lamp. The dark room came alive with clay studies, their shadows dancing across the ceiling in the light. He opened his sketchbook. He'd had an idea for his *Gates of Hell* this afternoon: a man climbing on top of a woman, desperate to exit the hell of his tortured desire. The woman accepted him greedily.

Auguste's charcoal swept over the paper as if it moved on its own. His vision blurred and a soft mound, then two emerged, a hollowed navel and curving hips. An oval head and sweep of dark hair, piercing eyes—the kind that could discern one's soul—jumped from the page. Vivacity undulated from the flesh, beauty and its seduction. He dropped his utensil and stared at his drawing in amusement and surprise. His heart sped up its pace.

Mademoiselle Claudel peered back at him in all her naked splendor.

Chapter 9

꩜

Camille tiptoed past the maid pulling a ham from the oven. Her stomach rumbled at its rich scent, but she would eat later. For now, she had somewhere to be.

Mother caught sight of her from the salon and followed her to the door. "Where are you going at this hour? We will dine soon."

"I am meeting a friend for tea," she lied.

Martin Larousse, a fellow student, had told her of a spot to find clay on the outskirts of an estate's property, though he did not have the nerve to take any for himself. Giganti had agreed to help her dig it up and carry it back to the atelier. If Mother knew, she would lock her in or, worse, send for the police. It could not be legal to dig up someone's property, but Camille didn't care one whit about legalities.

"Absolutely not," Mother said, eyeing the clock on the mantel. "It's half past eight. Only prostitutes or society women with proper escorts are out at such an hour."

Camille fastened the last of the buttons on her overcoat, jammed a hat on her head, and snatched two buckets and a pickax she'd stashed near the door. "I'll be home in a few hours."

"I don't know why I bother at all!"

Camille slammed the door behind her. She did not understand why Mother still took the pains to yell at her. She would always do as she pleased.

She raced up the street and hailed a coach. Once inside, she glanced at the moon, bright and nearly full. She wondered what Monsieur Rodin was doing tonight. Working, or perhaps enjoying an aperitif by the fire? Was he alone? She shifted in her seat, at once surprised and alarmed by the course her thoughts had taken. It did not matter what the artist was doing. Surely, Rodin was not thinking of her.

The coach stopped at the edge of a park abutted by several large houses.

"Please return in two hours," Camille said to the coachman.

"By then I'm in Montmartre to pick up the gents and prostitutes." The coachman leered. Even in the dark, she could see he had no front teeth and stubble covered his chin.

"I'll pay you double the fare," she said firmly.

"We'll see 'bout that, ma'meselle." He cracked his whip and his horse lurched forward.

She hoped he would return. Toting buckets of clay for a kilometer before she met another cab would be a brutal undertaking.

A dark figure in a bolero hat stepped from the cover of trees at the rear of the closest house. The rhythmic thumping of her heart increased. "Giganti?" she whispered. "Is that you?" The figure slid along the side of the enormous house and onto the spit of cobbled street.

"*Si, signorina.*" A smile split Giganti's face and his teeth gleamed in the moonlight. "A perfect night to steal clay, no?" He waved his hand at the swath of black sky dotted with sequin stars. He chuckled, positioning his shovel on his left shoulder.

Camille swatted his cheek in a playful gesture. "Let's go before someone sees us."

They stole through the yard, damp grass clinging to their boots, their breath streaming around them in a cloud. The crisp air chapped Camille's cheeks and stung her lips. She hoped the ground would not still be frozen. It had warmed the past few weeks with the coming of an early spring.

When they reached the edge of the wood, she ducked under a bough. "Martin said we should walk no more than five minutes and we will see the pond."

"For why does he know such things?" Giganti asked, his Italian accent thick as ever. "Does he make a habit of sneaking through people's gardens?"

Camille giggled. "He knows the people who live here."

After several minutes traipsing through dense forest, the trees thinned and a pocket of water glistened silver in the moonlight. Its clean scent permeated the chilly air.

"We'll take turns digging." Camille kicked a stone aside with the tip of her laced boot. "Yesterday's rain softened the ground. It should be easy enough."

Giganti plunged the shovel into the soil, using his full weight against the head of the tool. He grunted as it hit rock. "It's solid rock."

"The clay is below it." She pulled on her kid gloves and grasped the pickax in her hands.

"You say that as if it is easy to find."

She swung the ax at the ground with force. A cracking and thud met the point of her tool. She launched it again and again, until her hands grew clammy with sweat and slipped inside her gloves.

Giganti watched her with a mixture of amusement and bewilderment.

The exertion warmed Camille's blood and she no longer felt the raw air. Sweat dripped from her nose. She paused to catch a breath. "Now give it a try."

He forced his shovel into the earth. It gave way easily.

"Ah, see there?" She dropped the ax and took the other shovel.

They dug in silence. The lonely hoot of an owl drifted through the forest branches in an eerie echo. The pond's glassy surface reflected the light of the moon, casting the oblong well of water in an ethereal glow. If Camille were more superstitious, she would swear they were being watched by woodland elves.

When at last they hit clay, they heaved load after load into the empty buckets.

Giganti lifted a bucket to test its weight. "They're heavy. We should stop now or we'll never be able to lug them through the forest."

Camille dropped her tool and flexed her sore fingers. "What time is it? I told the coachman to return in two hours."

He flipped open the luminous brass lid of his pocket watch. "It's nearly eleven. We need to leave now or we'll never make it."

They looked across the clearing to the woods. It would be a long, difficult haul. Camille's jaw set in determination. "No time to waste."

They dragged their loads, pausing every few meters to rest. Her shoulders ached, but she ignored the burn. She trudged through the woods in almost total darkness; only a smattering of silver light sprinkled down through the thicket of trees. After a few meters more, she slammed the edge of her bucket on a bared tree root and stumbled.

"Are you all right?" Giganti huffed behind her.

A series of lit windows winked in the distance. "We're nearly there," Camille said, fastening her gaze on the edge of the field, where the line of grass met the street. Only a little farther now.

When twenty meters remained, the rumble of wheels on cobblestone echoed in the stillness. Camille attempted to run, dragging her bucket with one hand and her tool with the other. "Hurry!"

"I'm going as fast as I can!" Giganti caught up to her, his breath coming faster now.

The carriage pulled to a stop and the coachman stood on his perch, horsewhip in hand. "Make it quick. I don't have all night," he growled. He adjusted his manhood in his trousers.

"Everything settled now?" Camille asked.

"Not quite." He grabbed himself once more.

A burst of laughter erupted from Giganti beside her.

"You are too much man for me to handle," Camille said.

Giganti roared until a tear slid down his cheek.

"Shut it and get your hind end on board!" The coachman reseated himself.

Camille climbed into the hackney, ignoring the one other passenger, and took the supplies as Giganti handed them to her.

The steady gallop of horse's hooves beat against the cobbles, shattering the night's stillness. Camille peered out the coach door and down the street, half-afraid to see who approached.

"You there! Stop!" A policeman emerged from the darkness, the shiny buttons of his black uniform and the telltale shape of his hat giving him away.

"Police!" Giganti heaved the last of the tools inside and leapt into the carriage.

Camille shoved the lady passenger over—if one could call her a lady. She had come straight from Montmartre, no doubt. Her body had been wrangled into a gown several sizes too small and her rouge appeared layers thick. She didn't even wear gloves, not that Camille cared. She looked down at her own muddy hem, her filthy gloves and dirty boots.

"*Excuse-moi!*" Anger contorted the painted woman's face. "You didn't need to push me."

The policeman thundered closer.

"Cover the buckets," Giganti hissed.

"And how am I to do that?" Camille asked as a swell of panic washed over her.

"Your coat. And your pelisse, mademoiselle." Giganti gestured to the woman.

"Why should I help the likes of you?" She pushed her already heaving bosom out a bit farther.

"Because you don't want me to report you as a thieving prostitute. Our night together was not up to my satisfaction and I would like the money you stole from me. I'm sure the policeman will side with me."

The woman glared at him and removed her pelisse with haste. She folded it over her arm, draping its train over the bucket under her legs.

Camille fumbled with the buttons of her overcoat.

The policeman sidled up next to the coach, dismounted his horse, and opened the door to peer inside. Camille said a silent prayer of thanks for the darkened street.

"What brings you to this end of Paris on this fine evening?" the policeman asked.

Suddenly the situation seemed hilarious. Camille began to laugh.

"Do you mind telling me what's so funny?" the lawman asked.

"I—we"—she motioned to Giganti—"are playing a game, you see. A friend, a fellow sculptor, thought it would be a great trick to steal my tools and lead me on a scavenger hunt," she added quickly. "That Monsieur Rodin!"

Oddly, her stomach clenched at the mention of her potential tutor's name. She pushed the image of the intriguing man from her mind.

The officer raised his eyebrows. Before his skepticism could grow, Camille rushed to complete the lie. "I've found them in this field. And now, it is my turn to repay the favor. What would be a fitting punishment for such a wicked deed, monsieur? Perhaps I hide the plaster bust he is slaving over? Or maybe his favorite chisel and mallet should disappear? Silly man. As if Rodin could get the best of me!" She pursed her lips in a pout.

"Well, mademoiselle, I . . ."

She winked at him as if he were her accomplice. "Don't worry. I will come up with something."

Shock stamped the policeman's features.

Camille laughed again. The man did not know what to make of her. "I am certain you have many more important things to do this evening. Please, don't let us keep you." She brushed Giganti's lips with hers in hopes of making the policeman uncomfortable.

"I-I apologize, mademoiselle, monsieur," he stammered. "I'll be on my way. *Bonsoir.*" He tipped his hat at Camille and the prostitute.

"Good evening," Giganti replied. He covered his mouth with his fist.

When the carriage pulled away, the duo burst into laughter. The policeman remained frozen in the street, staring after them.

"You, my friend, are brilliant! A bit crazy, but brilliant." Giganti flicked a chunk of dried mud from Camille's chin. "It's a good thing he didn't know Rodin. The man would never play such a prank. He is far too solemn." He gave her a conspiratorial wink.

"Thank you for your help tonight," she said.

His features sobered. "Your kiss . . . You know I have a taste only for men?"

"It was a friendly kiss." She squeezed his chin in her hand. "And now the policeman will assume we're lovers looking for a bit of mischief, rather than thieves stealing through the night."

"Well played, my dear Camille."

Chapter 10

After six weeks, Camille had used nearly all of the clay she had stolen, but her bust of *Madame B* was coming along nicely. She munched on a bite of bread smeared with layers of goat cheese and confiture, and returned to her work. She and Emily had decided to skip a proper meal to work through the afternoon.

"The tea is ready. I bought some cakes as well." Emily cut the string on the bakery box and raised the lid. Two fruited tarts glistened with glazed sugar.

"You really are English," Camille said. "Tea and cakes in late afternoon."

"And you are truly French."

Camille stuck out her tongue and the women laughed.

"Sugar?" Emily filled two cups with scalding black liquid and fished two cubes from a bowl.

"Of course." Camille examined Paul's bust a last time before joining Emily at the table by the stove.

They sat in amiable silence; the only sound drifted in from the city's street noise and the marching hands of the clock.

"I wonder if we'll have a visit from Monsieur Rodin." Camille broke the silence. She shocked herself at the sudden mention of his name. "He said he would send word the next day, if he was to accept the position. It has been nearly two months." She grimaced. "I suppose we are beneath him."

Camille remembered his expression as he raked his eyes over her work, how he had pointed out her shortcomings. Emily had gloated all afternoon about his not mentioning any of her flaws. She chewed her bottom lip at the thought.

"I've just heard some gossip about Monsieur Rodin," Emily said. "A friend in London wrote to me when I mentioned he might be our new tutor."

Camille clenched the teacup with force at the sound of his name on another's lips. "What did she say about him?" She affected a bored tone.

"It's quite scandalous. Judy said a French sculptor by the name of Auguste Rodin was accused of working directly from life castings for a piece called *The Age of Bronze*. The sculpture's likeness to reality was claimed too real to be made by hand."

Her pulse began to skip. "Is he a fraud as they say?"

Emily shrugged and popped a chunk of buttery crust laden with custard in her mouth. "Mmm. I am never disappointed. French food really is superior."

"Of course it is," she snapped, her irritation plain. She wanted to hear more, not talk about their national differences. "What happened to Monsieur Rodin? Was he banned from showing the piece?"

"It was shipped from Brussels to Paris for the Salon, but the same talk followed him here. His assistants and models were called in to attest to his honesty, but the Belgian authorities wouldn't allow the models to cross the borders into France. Can you imagine?" Emily wiped her mouth with a cloth. "Several artists came to his aid. Dubois, Boucher, and Chapu. They all verified Rodin's work. Apparently, his greatest problem is his refusal to conform to the classical approach. We should demand to see proof of his work if he returns here." Emily's eyes danced with excitement.

"I don't care to see him again, or his work." Camille stared at her reflection in her cup. "He stalked through here like a panther, criticized me, and left as quickly as he came." She did not say how much she had hoped he would return, or that she waited for the post each day. But the letter did not come. A gray malaise gnawed the edges of her good humor. Monsieur Rodin had not found anything redeeming in her work.

Emily perked up at the knock at the door. "I will answer it."

"It is likely to be my sister, Louise," Camille said, standing as well to rinse her cup. "She said she might stop by today to see the studio."

"Is Mademoiselle Claudel here?" A male voice drifted from the door—a voice Camille knew after only one meeting, a voice that had come to her in more than one dream since. The tempo of her heart increased.

Emily showed him inside. "Camille, Monsieur Rodin is here to see you."

The sculptor walked into the room. "Good day, ladies." He held his worn beret in his hands.

Camille cursed herself for the nervous energy pulsing through her veins. "Monsieur Rodin." She did not hide her irritation. "I thought we would not have the pleasure of seeing you again."

Emily gaped for an instant, then snapped her mouth shut.

"Forgive me for the delay. I have been very busy and did not have the time to respond as I had hoped. Until today, that is."

"A letter would have been sufficient." Camille couldn't help herself. His indifference had made her feel foolish and undeserving, a little girl in a grown man's world. It made her want to spit.

He frowned. "I won't apologize again, Mademoiselle Claudel. I am a busy man."

"So you said." She crossed her arms to prevent the current of anger that roiled inside her from boiling over. She did not understand her reaction to him. Somehow he had managed to get under her skin, after she had met him only once.

"Would you care for a cup of tea?" Emily attempted to dispel the tension.

"No, thank you," he replied.

"If I may be so bold to say, I am a great fan of your work," Emily said.

Camille snorted. Emily had never seen his work.

Monsieur Rodin glanced at her, a question in his eyes. She got the distinct impression he had no idea what to make of her. But that was just as well. If she said what she really thought, she would need *another* tutor. She glanced at him and looked away. How *did* she feel about him? She flushed with embarrassment, though she hadn't the slightest idea why.

"Thank you, Mademoiselle Fawcett," he said. "May I see what you have been working on lately?"

"I would be honored." Emily held her hands together as if her prayer had been answered.

A pang hit Camille—of envy, or was it disappointment? Monsieur Rodin had not asked to see her pieces. She shook off the absurd feeling and focused once more on *Madame B.* The first rendering of the bust had been a mess. Today she would come close to completing its improved design.

Monsieur Rodin followed Emily to her statue of a little girl.

"Nice work here," he said. "The folds of her dress appear fluid. A swirl of silk and cotton around her knees."

"Thank you, monsieur." Emily wrung her hands again.

At last Rodin turned his azure gaze on Camille. "And yours, mademoiselle?"

She tossed her head to flick the fringe of dark hair out of her eyes. Why in God's name did this man make her feel less than confident? Without a word, she removed the cover over Paul's bust.

"You have repaired it, I see." He peered at the piece. "This line of his jaw." He stepped back and squinted.

She tried to appear disinterested, yet clung to his every word.

"A job well done, Mademoiselle Claudel."

Her rigid shoulders melted like a mound of clay in a rainstorm.

Monsieur Rodin ran a thumb gently over the bridge of Paul's nose. "If you are still in need of a tutor—"

"We are!" Emily cut in. "Pardon me, monsieur. We would be honored to accept your aid."

He nodded and looked to Camille for verification.

Something stirred in her breast—relief, delight, and something more she could not name. She relished his uncertainty. But she knew the moment she had first laid eyes upon the man she would not reject his help. Something about him . . .

"When will we begin?" she asked at last.

Monsieur Rodin smiled somewhere beneath his beard.

⤜⊷

Auguste found himself on the doorstep at the atelier on the Rue Notre Dame des Champs the following day. He had planned to work all afternoon, but his feet had a mind of their own. His hand hovered near the brass knocker. Would Mademoiselle Claudel accept his assistance? Last night he could not shake the woman's face from his mind. Her demeanor intrigued him—sharp, yet eager for praise. He saw it in the way the muscles in her face relaxed at his compliments, the way her indigo eyes shifted from challenging to warm.

Auguste looked down at his newly polished shoes and adjusted his scarf.

The door flew open without warning. He stumbled backward, knocking into a man on the street. "I beg your pardon!" he said, flustered. The man grimaced and kept walking.

"What a pleasant surprise, Monsieur Rodin," Mademoiselle Fawcett said. "I was on my way to fetch a few things. Would you care to come in?"

"I've come to begin lessons. I had some extra time today," he lied. He didn't have a single spare moment and yet, suddenly this was the only place he wanted to be.

An eager smile lit her face. "Very good. I will go later."

Inside, a model lounged on a chair as if waiting for instruction. Auguste stopped to stare. He knew well the dark ringlets that framed the model's high cheekbones and angular chin. Giganti, who hailed from Naples; he had worked with him several times in the past. Curious he should find Giganti here, in a novice's studio. As a professional, he could work with anyone he chose. Auguste felt a strange twinge at his presence there. Perhaps he would hire the model again.

Mademoiselle Claudel, engrossed in her task, did not notice his arrival. She pounded a pile of mushy clay with a wooden rod. A few minutes more and she could roll it into loaves.

"*Bonjour*, mademoiselle." Rodin stopped beside her prepping table.

The thwack of her tool ceased and her vivid blue gaze met his. "You've returned, Monsieur Rodin?" she asked, her surprise evident.

A nervous twinge niggled in his stomach. "I have extra time today. Unexpected, but pleasant, so I thought we would begin your lessons. We will start at the Louvre."

"We'll not work in the studio?" She dropped the wooden instrument into a bucket with the others and began massaging the clay into thick ropes. Her dainty hands moved swiftly over the length of them, doubling them in width.

The twinge returned and he looked at the floor.

Giganti rushed to greet the famous sculptor. "Monsieur Rodin! Am I to have the privilege of working with you this afternoon?"

"I'm afraid not," he said, "but I'm certain we will sometime soon." He glanced at Mademoiselle Claudel, as if seeking her agreement. She continued her work without looking up.

Auguste cleared his throat. "Mademoiselle Claudel, will you join us?" Somehow he knew he should request she join them and not require it. This woman would not be told what to do.

"Indeed, monsieur, I will." She washed her hands in a basin and dried them on a dingy cloth.

"Allow me, *mon amie*." Giganti helped her slide on her coat.

Auguste raised an eyebrow at the familiar tone with which the model addressed her. Was there something between them?

Mademoiselle Claudel smiled and kissed Giganti on each cheek. "We'll pick up again tomorrow morning? The clay is prepared so we can get started immediately."

Giganti beamed at her. "Of course. Whatever you need. I'll see you in the morning."

A foreign sentiment gnawed at Auguste's stomach.

Mademoiselle Claudel met his eye once more, but this time mischief lurked there. "May I?" She tucked her hand in the crook of his arm. Surprised, he said nothing, though his blood warmed.

Mademoiselle Fawcett stared for an instant, appearing surprised by the gesture as well.

Auguste didn't know what to make of the young woman's bold behavior, but it appealed to him. She was different from any woman he had ever met.

⚜

Monsieur Rodin had begged off this week's lessons. Camille wanted to ask him why, but did not want to intrude. Neither did she want him to think she tracked his movements. She only wanted to be sure he would not desert them. Yes, that was all. She chewed her thumbnail. She had struggled with her drawings all evening, despite the fact that she had the apartment to herself. The rest of the family had accepted an invitation to dine with one of Mother's friends and she had faked being ill.

Camille tapped her pencil against the desktop. Why hadn't Monsieur Rodin shown them his studio? She had yet to see any of his work outside of the occasional maquette he carried with him. She imagined the Dépôt des Marbres to be a grand place, packed with many materials, tools, and statues and busts galore. She glanced at the time. Nine o'clock already? She hadn't made any progress at all. Perhaps she needed a break.

In a split second, Camille made a decision. She jumped from her chair, pulled on her winter things, and hired a coach. She would go to Rodin's atelier to peek in the windows. There would be no harm in that. No one would be there and she could get a sense of who this man really was.

As the coach rumbled through the city streets, she wrestled with herself. What if he *was* there? She must stay out of sight.

When she descended from the coach, a flutter of nervous energy swarmed her stomach. Light blazed in the windows. She crossed the street quickly and put her back against the stone facade to shield herself from view. She smothered a laugh. She was a spy, embarking on a clandestine mission. She leaned toward the window and gazed inside. Dozens of pieces, armatures, and platforms filled the space. Her eyes darted from one corner of the room to another, and settled on the solitary figure inside.

Monsieur Rodin. He bent over a bust of what appeared to be a young woman, and he was so absorbed, he did not see her. He likely noticed nothing outside of his piece. Camille knew that sensation well. She stepped into full view and pressed her face against the glass to watch him. At last she had met someone as consumed with sculpture as she was. She smiled in the dark.

❧

The Hôtel Continental was lavished in gilded molding, chandeliers, and velvety crimson fabric. Dozens of windows reflected the candlelight and the flicker of lamps, casting the ballroom in a haze of gold. Befitting for the birthday celebration of a national hero, Auguste thought. He still could not believe he had been invited to Victor Hugo's birthday celebration—Edmond Bazire, journalist at the radical *Intransigeant*, critic, and new friend, had secured his invitation and Auguste, in turn, had managed to bring Jules along to the soiree as well. He would work at their friendship until there was no hope—they had known each other so long. Perhaps they had hit a rough patch, was all.

Attendants in black-and-white livery swarmed the crowd like an army of worker bees, silently refilling empty glasses, wiping soiled surfaces, and whisking trays of delicacies beneath the noses of their distinguished guests. Auguste enjoyed watching them, their smooth expressions a thin veil that did not disguise their disgust for the wealthy, or perhaps a desperate longing to be like them. He studied the wrinkled hands of an attendant, saturated with fatigue, and the hump in his back. He found no pride in his work, but burden.

It was a sentiment Auguste could capture, and he understood it well at times. He felt his breast pocket in search of cigarette papers, a habitual gesture. His desk drawers overflowed with small scraps covered in sketches made on the go.

"You haven't brought them, have you?" Jules Dalou asked.

"I should know better." Auguste sipped from his glass of Mouton Rothschild 1870, one of the more expensive wines he'd ever tasted. "Inspiration always comes when it is inconvenient."

"Artists see something noteworthy in life the rest of us lower beings never notice," Edmond said, a wistfulness in his voice.

Jules chuckled and picked up his fork. "Perhaps writers rival our talents, or musicians, though I doubt it."

Edmond cocked a fair eyebrow and glanced at Auguste.

Rodin drank deeply from his glass to prevent himself from saying something rude. Jules should show more humility. His awards had made him feel invincible and above the rest. Auguste knew an artist was only as respected as his next piece in the eyes of the critics. Consistency mattered more in the long run, rather than one dazzling piece.

Edmond swallowed a bite of roasted chicken. "My cousin is to voyage on the Orient Express."

"The luxury train?" Jules's eyebrows knitted together.

"Lucky man, isn't he? It stops in Vienna and Constantinople. I heard the food and exotic vistas are well worth the trip. Intricate paneling, silk sheets, leather armchairs. I must admit, I'm envious."

"Won't they have to stop at every border?" Auguste asked, unconvinced. "Sorting through all of the travel papers must be cumbersome for the crew. But Constantinople I would like to see."

"Think of the intrigue." Edmond's brown eyes danced. "At each frontier, spies could jump aboard and hide from their enemies."

Auguste laughed. "You have a rich imagination."

Jules waved his fork. "I don't know who would consider traveling to be a luxury. I detest it. And riding among all of the wealthy would put me off for certain."

Edmond grunted his disagreement, putting an end to the conversation. This evening, Jules was not winning any hearts.

The men ate in silence.

Auguste looked past his tablemates to the place of honor where Victor Hugo sat. He had watched the great man from afar all evening, his stately stature and noble expression. Hugo never stroked his beard and comblike mustache, nor did he fidget. The man possessed composure and grace, even at his advanced age of eighty-one. Hugo was his childhood hero, a Goliath among his contemporaries. Republicanism, the common man, his legendary love for Juliette Drouet—all of the writer's accomplishments, the allure of his personage, echoed in Rodin's mind.

"I must thank you again, Edmond," Auguste said, breaking the silence. "I am honored to be here, and for the chance to bring a guest." He nodded at Jules. He had hoped bringing his friend to such a coveted event would smooth over their last, uncomfortable meeting.

"They are honored you're here." Edmond bent his blond head over his almost empty plate.

Auguste smiled. "You flatter me."

"I have a surprise for you." Edmond's eyes twinkled over the rim of his wineglass. "I may have convinced Monsieur Hugo to allow you to sketch his likeness."

Jules's fork clattered against the porcelain.

Auguste didn't know what to say, how to express his gratitude. It would be a dream to work with the great Hugo.

"I have left you speechless." Edmond flashed a crooked smile. "Don't be intimidated. Monsieur Hugo appreciates art in all its forms, though he doesn't care for posing. Write to him with your request. Whatever his rules are, you must agree to them."

"Well, aren't you the fortunate one," Jules said, his voice full of spite. He dabbed at his mouth with a serviette. Auguste flinched at his friend's tone.

Edmond's easy manner grew tense, and he looked sideways at Jules. "Are you feeling out of sorts this evening?"

Jules's ears reddened. "Do I seem cross? I'm just in awe of Monsieur Hugo and such a wonderful opportunity."

"Perhaps you will have your own," Edmond said, pressing his lips into a hard line.

Auguste noted with satisfaction Edmond did not extend the invitation.

"I sketch models in their natural state, lying on the sofa, walking around, crouched on the floor," Auguste said, redirecting the conversation. "It will not be so difficult to do the same for Hugo, though I won't have near as much time." He grew more animated as his excitement mounted. Dalou's envy would not get the better of him. He could already envision Hugo's bust in plaster. "But I am grateful for any at all." Smiling, he leaned forward in his seat and held out his hand. "How can I ever thank you?"

Edmond shook his hand and smiled. "Create a great piece, my friend. That's how you may thank me."

"Well, then," Jules said, "let us hope Hugo will be amenable to hosting you in his home. If not, perhaps I will give it a go."

Doubt clouded Auguste's good humor. He would do his absolute best to accommodate Hugo's requests. Jules would not take this opportunity from him.

Chapter 11

❦

Afternoon sunlight filtered through the streaked salon window and pooled on the cold tile, hardly warming the winter chill in the air. Auguste could see the vapor of his breath. Perhaps he would spend a bit less on marble this month and more on wood. He rubbed his hands together for warmth and picked up his novel once more—*Les Misérables*, Hugo's most notable work, despite the widely negative reviews it had received. He grunted. The critics always had much to say, but neither the skill nor the will to create themselves.

He read to pass the time until seven o'clock, when he would venture to the writer's house for his first visit. The only sound came from the rustling of pages between his fingertips, the faint tick of his timepiece.

"Auguste?" Rose's voice drifted up the stairs. "Would you care for a bowl of soup?" She appeared in her usual navy house dress, her skirts brushing the tops of her sensible boots.

"No, I'm expected at Monsieur Hugo's at seven for an aperitif."

"I could wear my white and yellow gown, put a hot iron to my hair." She fingered a frizzy lock sticking out from beneath her cotton cap.

"This isn't a social call, Rose. It's work. I'll not be dining, but sketching Monsieur Hugo while the others eat. It's unlikely he will even speak to me."

"Of course he'll speak to you. And you'll talk about literature and politics and woo them all."

Rodin examined her squared fingernails, the chapped skin of her working hands. "And you detest reading. If we discussed literature all evening, what would you do?"

An image of Mademoiselle Claudel came to mind, her lounging in a chair in her atelier, book in hand. How very intent she'd been. When he had placed his hand lightly on her shoulder she had startled. He smiled at the memory of their passionate discourse afterward.

"Do not mock me." Rose noticed the smile and crossed her arms.

"I'm not teasing you, woman." He stood and made his way to the door. "I simply speak the truth. You would grow tired of the talk about Jules Ferry's laws of education and Prime Minister Duclerc, of political pamphlets, and poetry. I doubt they will gossip about bourgeois socialites and other feminine interests in front of us. We aren't their friends, after all."

"You're meeting a woman there, aren't you?" Her face flushed in anger. "I embarrass you, yet you parade your mistresses around town."

"I said I'm working." Auguste detested conflict and avoided it at all costs. He simply didn't have time for the angst it inspired. He sighed and stood. Yet he owed Rose his attention. Despite her nagging and insecurities, she had been his first love, and a friend.

Her face softened as he approached. He cupped her cheek in his palm. "Why don't we go to dinner somewhere tomorrow evening? Wear your best dress."

She smiled and kissed his hand. "I would like that very much."

❧

Two hours later, Auguste found himself on the Avenue d'Eylau. He paused to assess the row of redbrick homes, their windows facing a park in the center of *la place* and the traffic of carriages and omnibuses zipping around the square. He ducked into the covered passageway beneath the building. A woman in a bombazine gown tugged her son closer to shield him from the brittle wind.

Rodin pulled up his collar and continued past several doorways. At number six he paused on the doorstep. Anxiety streaked through his limbs. Though he must remain "unseen" by Hugo, he needed to befriend the others, if possible. The Société des Gens de Lettres, a group of renowned writers, would sponsor an upcoming commission of

Hugo and he wanted to be considered. For now, this private bust would make the perfect stepping stone in his studies.

Auguste inhaled a breath of razor-sharp air and knocked. A servant admitted him and led him through the house. Burnished mahogany, cherry, and walnut furniture filled each room. He had heard Hugo had a penchant for antiques and even carved furniture himself, and by the looks of it, the rumors were true. Auguste paused to admire the dovetailed corners of an exquisite table in the study and an ornately carved lattice mounted on the library wall. Chandeliers of Murano glass, burgundy wallpaper and silk drapes, decorative dishes and handiwork covered every centimeter of wall and ceiling, and rich Oriental carpets blanketed the floors. The man had expensive taste—quite the opposite of Auguste's own humble abode. He spent his every penny on his ateliers.

"Follow me, monsieur," the servant said, motioning him forward.

The tinkle of glassware and the hum of voices drifted from the salon. Auguste slipped into the room unnoticed, amid famed writers and socialites.

Monsieur Hugo cradled a glass of what looked to be sherry in his hand. From the side, Auguste might be able to sketch his profile. He spied a chair in the corner of the room and headed toward it.

"Not so fast, *mon ami*," Edmond Bazire said, eyes merry with the excitement of his company, and perhaps the sherry. "I'd like to introduce you."

"Of course." Auguste followed Bazire around the room, greeting various guests. When they made their way to Hugo's side, his heart bumped a rapid pace in his chest.

"May I present Auguste Rodin, brilliant sculptor, at your service," Bazire said.

"*Bonsoir.*" Monsieur Hugo's pale eyes had the watery film that came with age, his wrinkles deepened when he spoke, and a heavy frown perched atop his brow, leaving Rodin little doubt as to his feelings toward him. "I have not had a pleasant experience with artists and I refuse to remain in one position." The hand that clutched his glass shook slightly. "I hope that is clear."

"Quite, monsieur," Auguste said. "I will be as invisible as breath. You'll not hear me, nor see me if I can help it." Yearning to immortalize the great man burned in his veins.

"Excuse me." Hugo moved toward Juliette Drouet, his lover of fifty years.

Rodin had heard Juliette appeared less and less often at her salon and not in public at all. Her illness prevented it, and given the pallor of her skin and the protruding bones in her cheeks, he did not doubt it.

Swiftly, he moved to a chair opposite Hugo, pulled cigarette papers from his pocket, and put pencil to paper.

꩜

Camille deepened a groove in the collarbone of her *Madame B* bust. Soon it would be complete, just in time for the May Salon. Monsieur Rodin had already told her he would enter it under his tutelage in a very coveted spot. She hummed a tune Louise had played every evening these past weeks. Though melancholy, the notes of the beautiful melody crept into her sketches. She admired her sister's musical abilities, despite their avoidance of each other, and had even bought her a new book of sheet music to encourage her playing.

Rodin sat at her studio table, drawing. He had come a day earlier than his typical Friday this week, though she tried not to read into his behavior. In the months since they had met, he had missed three sessions, all days Camille could recall with anxiety. Why did his presence mean so much to her?

Because she thought of him at night.

Rodin looked up as if he had heard her thoughts. She diverted her eyes to her piece.

"I have been to Victor Hugo's home," he said, his voice raspy from working many hours in silence.

Camille tossed her tool on the tabletop and dropped into a chair. "Oh? And you've come to brag, have you?" She smiled to soften the blow of her biting words.

"Is that how you view me, mademoiselle?" Monsieur Rodin's voice was soft, disappointed.

She grinned. "I view you as you are. A gentle man, contemplating something most serious. Perhaps a little divertissement is in order."

"Camille, really," Emily said, her tone incredulous. "Have you lost your manners?"

"Monsieur Rodin has visited us for months now," Camille said. "He knows my temperament."

"I am learning." A smile touched his lips. "You are a spirited and engaging woman."

"What is life without spirit? Passion drives an artist, wouldn't you agree?"

A fierceness filled his eyes, and he captured her in his gaze. She warmed to his sudden intensity. What she wouldn't give to read his thoughts! To stroke his beard and gauge his reaction.

He looked down, breaking the tension, and pushed his sketch away. "I'll begin with clay next week, but I'm frustrated by my lack of time with Hugo. He is not a fan of artists, or sculptors at the very least."

"I'm certain you will do a fine job." Camille walked to the desk and covered his hand with hers—an apology for her tart comments, a reassurance of her faith in his ability.

Monsieur Rodin studied her face with such concentration, she shifted away from him. The man absorbed her thoughts, her spirit.

Emily cleared her throat. "Should we go to the park? I would like to do a bit of sketching outdoors."

"The Luxembourg?" Camille asked.

"Let's," Rodin said.

❧

Camille dried an array of wire end tools, knives, and chisels, wrapped them in cloth, and tied the bundle with string. She tossed it into her bag and glanced at the visiting student once more. Professor Moreau had sung the young woman's praises that morning in front of the class; Jessie Lipscomb had won two prizes from the Royal College of Art, a prestigious school in London: the National Silver Medal and the Queen's Prize. Now she sought real art instruction in Paris, a land that opened more doors to women. Camille couldn't help but wonder how impressive Jessie's work really was. She swallowed a lump of jealousy. It was silly to worry about another artist's work. Jessie's fine sculptures did not diminish the quality of her own. But the professor had never breathed a word of admiration about *her* work.

Camille watched the Englishwoman as the remaining students cleaned their stations and filed into the corridor. Jessie wore her tightly curled hair in a chignon, and stood tall in a pearl gray costume with a blouse corsage, typical of English styling. Camille did not have a particular eye for fashion, but Louise had spoken of nothing else since they had moved to Paris.

As Professor Moreau spoke with Jessie, Camille slid her sketchbook into her satchel and pretended not to stare. If only she were closer to make out their conversation.

"Mademoiselle Claudel?" Professor Moreau motioned for her to join them near the door. "I would like you to meet Mademoiselle Lipscomb. As you heard, she is a medal winner."

Camille's grip on her satchel tightened. He need not remind her of the medal. She forced a smile. "Pleased to meet you."

"How do you do?" Jessie smiled, transforming her plain features. She looked the sort who rarely smiled. Life was a serious matter—a sentiment evident in her drawn features and folded hands, the gray and brown hues of her day dress.

"You two may learn from one another," the professor said. "Your styles and subjects are different, but you both possess strengths unlike any students I have ever taught."

Camille tingled at the praise.

Monsieur Moreau flipped a hat onto his head. "Now, if you will excuse me, ladies. I am off."

"Congratulations on your award," Camille said.

"Thank you. I am thrilled to be in Paris." Jessie's pale cheeks glowed. "I am surrounded by such talent and excitement! I could walk the museums and parks all day." She dropped her eyes to the floor, suddenly realizing she had shown too much zeal.

Without doubt, Mademoiselle Lipscomb was an Englishwoman.

"Professor Moreau tells me you have an atelier," Jessie continued. "Would you care to share your work? I would be honored to see it."

Camille smiled. She decided that instant she liked Jessie's humble yet direct nature. With a swift motion, she threaded her arm through the Englishwoman's. "I would be happy to show you my work, but I am starved. Would you care to dine with me at home first?"

Jessie blinked, surprised at Camille's overt gesture. She shifted uncomfortably. "My aunt is waiting for me in the hall."

"You are both welcome. Mother will be thrilled to meet a new friend. Particularly a lady artist with proper manners." A wry smile crossed her face.

"We would be most grateful to dine with you," Jessie said.

Camille's smile widened at Jessie's formality. "Off we go."

⚜

After only a month in Paris, Jessie departed for England with a promise to return. Camille was dismayed at her friend's leaving. They had gotten on well; their love of art was the strongest bond between them, as well as their temperaments.

When Jessie's first letter arrived by post, Camille opened it with haste, slitting the skin on her index finger. "Ouch!" A drop of blood rose to the surface. She suckled the small wound while reading the letter.

Jessie spoke of returning! Camille strode into the salon.

"Mother, she wants to move in with us!"

"By *she*, I presume you mean Mademoiselle Lipscomb?" Mother stuck her needle into the frilly skirt of her pincushion doll and finished the last of her tea. "Her mother doesn't mind sending her daughter across the channel to stay in a stranger's home?"

"Everyone who wants to become an artist moves to Paris, even women." Camille refilled Mother's teacup.

"I cannot be responsible for her welfare." Mother added a sugar cube and stirred. "I am sorry, Camille, but she'll have to find another place to stay."

Must Mother fight her at every turn? She had enjoyed Jessie and her aunt's company immensely. The only thing that might change Mother's mind . . .

"She will pay rent," Camille said. "Her sums will help with the expenses of the atelier, and our apartment."

Mother's dull expression perked up. Camille knew she could not resist additional income.

"Papa will be delighted to have some of the pressure relieved." Camille could not hide her smile. She knew she had her.

"Louis-Prosper would be pleased," Mother mused aloud. "Especially to give you a regular lady escort and artist friend." She let out a long sigh. "Very well. I will write to her mother and arrange it immediately."

Camille jumped up from her place on the settee and embraced her mother's stiff form. For once they could agree.

❦

A servant placed the final course of fruit and cheese on the table before Auguste and company, while another poured champagne. He never ate Monsieur Hugo's food; he did not wish to disrupt the gentleman's elegant meals, and he certainly did not expect to be fed. Yet despite his delicacy, he received increasing weary looks each time he returned to the Rue d'Elyau. Tonight, Auguste nearly lost his calm when Jules Dalou not only entered the room, but conversed easily with Victor Hugo and his guests. How had Jules managed to count the clan among his friends so quickly?

"How are you this fine evening?" Jules asked, sidling up next to him at the table. "I have been invited to dinner again next week, and drinks with a few men from the Gens de Lettres. It seems the old man has taken a liking to me."

Auguste willed himself to control his emotion. "How nice for you."

"Hugo complimented my work. Perhaps they will consider me for their commissions." He swigged from his wineglass. "How are your sketches coming along?"

"Fine. Now, if you will excuse me, I have work to do." Auguste wanted to knock the haughty expression off his face, but instead, he bent over his cigarette paper to sketch the top of Hugo's head. A sketchbook at the table would be far too intrusive, though he wished he could use one now. His studies had advanced enough that he needed more detailing. He observed the writer intently to imprint his measurements and mannerisms on the folds of his mind. Without a proper sitting, this was the only way.

Monsieur Hugo drank from his goblet. His eyes drooped at the corners, his cheeks sagged, and grief etched lines around his drawn mouth. Juliette Drouet would pass soon, and all joy had drained from the household.

With a stroke of his thumb, Auguste smudged the circles under Hugo's eyes on his sketch, and darkened the eye sockets. He sympathized with the man's struggle to retain his composure.

In a swift and violent gesture, Hugo pounded his fist on the table, rattling the dishes atop it.

Auguste dropped his pencil. Jules looked startled, as did everyone else *à table*. All conversation lulled and Hugo's guests turned to face him.

"Stop staring at me," Monsieur Hugo said, his voice gruff. Despite his eighty-one years, his menacing tone made everyone squirm in their seats.

"Monsieur—" a gentleman at the table began.

"You." Hugo pointed at Rodin. "Stop staring at me! I am not a circus animal or some science experiment. You capture my pain on paper as if it pleases you."

Auguste stiffened. "Monsieur? I assure you it does not please me. I apologize—"

"What the devil takes so long?" The creases in Hugo's forehead deepened. "I look the same today as yesterday!" He stood, bumping the table. His plate chinked against his goblet and it tipped.

Edmond's hand shot out and righted the crystal glass just in time. "An artist's work takes time and diligence, something you are well versed in yourself, Monsieur Hugo," he said. He looked quickly at Auguste, an apology in his eyes, and back to Hugo. "But perhaps you would like time alone? We are more than happy to oblige."

Jules refused to make eye contact, though the telltale lift of his chin meant he had abandoned the bonds of friendship to side with his idol.

To be seen as a pest made Auguste ill, as did Dalou's betrayal. He wanted to immortalize the great man, but he possessed integrity. He captured a subject's pain in his art so another might find beauty in man's struggle and not feel alone—not to delight in it. If Hugo did not understand his intentions, he must go.

"Get out. All of you! And you"—Hugo directed his ire at Auguste—"your work is finished." Monsieur Hugo threw down his serviette and strutted from the room.

Rodin flushed in embarrassment and anger.

Dalou paled. "How dreadful. I'm sorry, Auguste."

"He isn't himself," Edmond attempted to reassure him.

Auguste stood, his face still aflame. He wanted to tear into the ass who had ruined his chances with Hugo. The previous artist must have been dreadfully unprofessional.

A footman appeared with Rodin's coat and hat. "Your things, monsieur."

"Good evening, everyone." Auguste nodded at Edmond and the stunned diners, and quickly departed from the room and the apartment.

A wall of rain greeted him, soaking the passage walk and streaming down the arched roof. Auguste popped open his umbrella and joined the sea of black-and-navy-clad pedestrians shuffling to their destinations. Hugo had no right to be so rude to him—he had kept his promise. Still, he could never fault a man in such pain. The old man watched life's breath trickle from his lover's lips and the night close in around her.

To lose one's great love must be the most acute, exquisite pain.

Auguste sloshed through a puddle, drenching his shoes and trousers. The tunnel of death loomed for Hugo, too. The inevitable slip of time weighed on a man's soul.

A vision of Auguste's father with gaunt face and gray skin vibrated in his memory. Those final days before Papa's death had leeched his spirit, and were a horror to behold. Even a strong man would wither in this life and meet his maker. He moved his umbrella to the side and let the cold rain wash over his face. He must seize his passions while he had the time, and allow emotion to flood his soul, feel the rain on his face. Taste the sweet fruit of elusive love. Such precious, short time there was.

Chapter 12

꧁ ❦ ꧂

Jessie returned to Paris and joined the atelier at Notre Dame des Champs. The months slipped by in an easy rhythm. Camille admired the way her friend adapted to her new home and fell into the same arduous work routine as hers. For the first time in her life, she felt as if she had a true friend who understood her, other than her brother. Emily, by contrast, had appeared less and less often at the atelier—and classes—and rarely helped with bills.

One spring afternoon, the ladies strolled through a park with Rodin along patches of manicured lawn and rows of hedges. Camille bent to stroke the satin petals of a pink tulip, her strong hands turning gentle, then snapped the flower's head from its stem to twirl it between her fingers.

"I beg your pardon," Jessie said, pushing aside a tree branch heavy with buds. "You aren't to pick them."

"They won't miss one." Camille took a seat on a nearby bench to soak in the spring sunshine.

Jessie sat beside her. "I prefer peonies. My mother's garden is full of them. And roses."

Rodin joined them, but he focused on the passersby instead of the flowers. After several moments, he squinted and adjusted his position. "There," he said. "Do you see the gentleman in the Homburg hat speaking with the lady in the flowered dress?" He opened his sketchbook. "The movement of his jaw, and his neck muscles, straining as he leans closer to her." His hand moved over the paper in swift strokes, though his eyes never left his subject. A charcoal outline of a body appeared, then a head with cords of muscle pulsing along the neck and shoulders.

Camille gazed at his hands, his face. She marveled at his concentration.

"You must capture it—not just the musculature, but the life that feeds it," Rodin continued. He sketched another figure similar in scale, still without looking down, as if the image had burned into his mind. After he'd finished, he rooted through his satchel and retrieved a lump of clay. In a few short minutes, he shaped a maquette between his thumb and forefinger and the man's form emerged.

Camille flipped open her sketchbook, but rather than drawing the man, she outlined the woman—the fervor in her expression, the laughing mouth, the joyful twirl of her white silk parasol dotted with black spots.

"Oh, she's lovely," Jessie said, peering over Camille's shoulder. "Brava. Her expression is perfect."

"I'm sure her companion hasn't noticed her expression," Camille said. "He can think of nothing but her ample bosom."

Jessie covered her mouth with a gloved hand and laughed. "You do love to shock us, don't you?"

"I speak the truth." Camille smudged the folds of the stenciled gown with her thumb.

Rodin watched her sketch. When she looked up, she searched his face for an answer—did he approve? He stroked his coppery beard in silence.

"Well? What is wrong with it?"

"Not a single thing. In fact, it's excellent. A perfect sketch, slavish devotion to your work . . . I think, mesdemoiselles, it is time."

❧

Camille set her shopping basket on the dining table next to Papa.

"I've bought some things," she said, unloading her items one by one. "Flowers to brighten the room for Mother. And for you, a new tin of your favorite tobacco and some chocolate biscuits."

"Generous of you, dear girl, but why the gifts?" Papa looked up from his newspaper.

"A thank-you." She kissed him on the cheek. "For the atelier, and for believing in me."

"I am pleased to see you happy." He slurped tea from a petite porcelain cup etched with bluebells and silver vines.

Camille plopped down in a chair and wrung her hands in her lap. She had something else to tell Papa. "I need to speak with you." She poured her own *tasse* of tea to busy her hands.

He removed his spectacles. "What is it, *chérie*?"

Mother breezed into the room humming a Chopin tune.

Camille stilled. Mother wore an evening gown in chartreuse silk with lace appliqué on the sleeves and neck. Her skin looked sickly next to the yellow-green fabric, and she reeked of lavender perfume. Camille stared, awestruck, as she touched her hair, fastened with a *cache-peigne*. The looped ribbons dangled from the decorative comb onto her shoulder.

Not only did Mother very rarely dress for an occasion, but she never wore rouge. This morning she had painted her cheeks heavily enough for two.

"You're dressed for the theater." Camille glanced at her father's equally incredulous expression. "Are you going somewhere?" She seemed . . . odd today.

"Must you always criticize me?" Mother's bright mood turned stormy in an instant, like a blustery autumn sky. "Such a negative child."

"It was a simple observation," Camille said.

"You were saying, my dear?" Papa asked, diverting the conversation, though his brow creased with concern at his wife's strange behavior.

Camille chewed her bottom lip. She didn't want to share the news in front of Mother, but she may as well be out with it. "You have heard of the sculptor Monsieur Auguste Rodin?" she said. "The tutor Boucher appointed."

"I have read reviews of his work from time to time." Papa leaned forward in anticipation. "Does he like your work?"

"Very much. He invited Jessie and me to join his atelier on the Rue de l'Université. We are the only female students to work with him."

Papa sprang from his seat and cradled her face in his hands. "*Mon amour!*" He pulled her into a tight embrace. "I knew it! I knew they'd see your talent one day."

Excitement fluttered in her stomach. If she had Papa's blessing, she could accept, and it was a good thing, because she already had. "Thank you, Papa."

"It is an all-male atelier?" Mother said, her voice an octave too high.

"You know how few women have had the opportunity to develop their talents."

"Except you, of course." Mother cleared dishes from the table. The china rattled in her shaking hands. "Camille, the genius child." She said her name as if it were a disease, then let the dishes crash to the floor.

Corinne, the maid, scurried into the kitchen at the alarming sound of breaking china. Her jaw dropped when she saw Mother's attire.

"What is the matter with you?" Papa clenched his hands into fists. "Your daughter may promote the reputation of this family. She may very well influence the art world. Why are you so ungrateful, woman? She has been given a gift. *We* have been given a gift!"

"She humiliates us, cavorting with those self-important fools. They put filthy ideas in her head and now you allow her to work with them. In the company of whores who remove their clothes for money! That does *not* promote our reputation." She clasped Camille by the shoulders and shook her. "You'll be a whore, too!" Her lips pulled back to reveal gritted teeth, like those of a growling canine.

"Let go of me!" She tried to pry Mother's viselike grip from her arms.

Papa wrenched his wife away. "Get hold of yourself, woman!"

With a huff Mother yanked on her gown to straighten it. "I've received a letter from Monsieur Bertillion."

Now Camille understood why she was so livid.

"He is no longer interested in courting our 'lovely daughter,' but wishes her the best of luck with her art. I assume he was put off by her skipping his calls to the house."

"I didn't want to marry him, Mother." Camille sniffed.

"You ungrateful wench!" Mother lunged toward her once more. Camille ducked and Mother stumbled over the leg of a dining chair.

Papa caught her around the middle. "Stop this at once!"

"You love her more!" Mother screeched. "You've always loved her more than any of us—your other children, even me." She dissolved to the floor in a weeping pile of expensive silk.

Camille rubbed her arms, eyes wide. How had she been born from such a woman? Had she gone mad? She would never be like her, Camille swore to herself.

⁓❦⁓

The following week, Jessie and Camille stood on the Rue de l'Université across from Rodin's famed atelier, the Dépôt des Marbres. Iron balconies jutted from windows in the building's stone facade, and an array of workers streamed in and out through the double doors, their shoes and trousers covered in dust. Sunlight burst through the cloud cover and Camille smiled.

"Here we are." She clasped Jessie's hand. Beyond the opportunity, she could hardly wait to work alongside Rodin, though she would never say so aloud.

"I am anxious to begin," Jessie said.

Two men hauled a block of white marble indoors.

"We'll have less time for our own pieces. That's my largest concern."

Jessie squeezed her hand. "But just think! We might have a chance to show at Salon with Monsieur Rodin at our side. And we will be paid."

Camille nodded absently. A kernel of fear lodged in the pit of her stomach. Their association with Rodin might also mean their identities as artists would blur. Still, the opportunity could not be missed. She had learned so much in the year since she had met him.

They followed a pair of assistants inside. The odor of clay and resin permeated the air, and the enormous space echoed with the sounds of artists hard at work. At least two dozen apprentices scurried about in their splattered trousers and smocks; several bent over a bucket of plaster, while others sawed pieces for a wooden base, or twisted metal frames to support a protruding limb. Two nude models perched on a platform, their posed forms as graceful as ballerinas. A select few workers chipped away at a hunk of marble, a skill reserved for the best of artists.

Camille longed to work with marble, but the material was too expensive to practice upon. She glanced at Jessie and saw a reflection of her own bewilderment on her features. How had Rodin created such an operation? He must have more private commissions than he could complete. Hardly an artist alive owned such a large work space with so many apprentices. She clasped and unclasped her hands. Why was she so anxious? She cursed herself for her weakness.

A man with overgrown facial hair and a blocky body shouted, "Are you coming in or not?"

"He looks like a woolly mammoth," Camille whispered to Jessie.

Jessie laughed. "What on earth is that?"

"You haven't heard of the elephant creatures covered in hair?" She had read not only mythology and literature as a child, but anything about science as well. In fact, she read almost anything when not sculpting.

A man whistled in appreciation as they passed. Camille glared at him and he laughed.

"No need to be prudish, sweetheart," he said. "You'll be naked on the stand soon enough."

"*Je suis sculpteur*, and you are an ass."

He laughed again, revealing brown teeth. "Did you hear that?" He snorted and a glob of mucus flew from his nostril. "We've a lady sculptor on our hands."

A chorus of male voices murmured; a few whistled. "She's a pretty one. I'll have her, Alain. You can have the other." The rail of a man named Alain guffawed.

Another man rearranged his manhood in a lewd gesture. "She'll join the likes of the rest."

Jessie's jaw fell open in shock. "I beg your pardon!"

"It seems, Mademoiselle Lipscomb," Camille said, projecting her voice loud enough to be heard, "that we've joined the house of apes, though they have fewer brains among them."

A titter of laughter rippled through the room.

Mother's face, screwed into a disdainful sneer, came to mind. She would have much to say about such a scene. Thankfully, she'd never know.

"*Ça suffit!*" a familiar voice roared—an uncharacteristic outburst for the rumble of hammering, chiseling, and male banter ceased. "These women are my pupils and fine *artistes*. You'll treat them with respect or find another place of employment." Monsieur Rodin loomed in a doorway leading to an adjoining room. His ginger beard blazed in the room awash in pale light.

Camille noted the immediate attention his quiet yet commanding presence demanded. His frame exuded strength, a power derived from years of experience, from passion and talent. He seemed solid as granite—unmovable, even unbreakable.

Suddenly she longed to see his softer side.

"*Oui*, monsieur," a few of his assistants called out.

Camille smirked at Alain and the woolly mammoth. She had the master on her side. Still, she must prove her worth or she'd look a fool. But that would happen soon enough.

"Follow me, ladies. I will show you the rest of the studio." Rodin abruptly returned to the room from whence he came.

Camille did not miss the female models watching them as they disappeared through the doorway. They would get over their shock as well, and show her respect. She would not be viewed as another of Rodin's conquests.

"This is my office." He motioned to a room with a simple oak desk and shelves packed with volumes on cathedrals and history, and artist manuals. Each corner of the room was piled with a mountain of abandoned maquettes on the verge of avalanche.

Camille plucked a severed goblin's head from his desk and poked her thumb inside the gaping mouth. Even his small pieces appeared alive. She turned it over in her hand, leaving a trail of chalky grit on her palm. "May I?"

Rodin nodded and she slipped it into her satchel.

"Come. I'll show you the marble room." He led them down a short corridor and into another large room.

Camille gazed at the array of unfinished statues, broken limbs, and uneven blocks of marble: Parian and Pentelic, the fine-grained limestone from Carrière, and blue-gray Carrara, all sorted by type. The men they had seen carrying the block outdoors now placed their load in the designated lot.

"I've always wanted to work with marble." Camille caressed the bumpy surface of a small stone.

Jessie leaned against another milky slab.

Camille's eyes lost their focus as she retreated into the dreamy haze of her mind. She knew exactly what she would do with this piece if it were hers.

"All in good time." Rodin's features displayed his amusement. "You have much to learn first. Let me show you the studies for the piece you'll be working on. *The Gates of Hell.* This way."

Camille sighed. Today marked the beginning of her labor being devoted to another's cause. She would have to sketch her new idea that evening.

⌘

After several weeks, Auguste couldn't help but notice Mademoiselle Claudel's sullen behavior. She possessed such a playful energy and yet he saw none of it in his atelier, only her scarcely controlled irritation. He scooped a coil of clay from beneath a damp cloth and squashed it between his hands. She had arrived every day as they had agreed, except Fridays, when he visited the Rue de Notre Dame des Champs. He read the frustration in the way she heaved load after load of plaster up a ladder, in the way she snapped at the other workers, and in the scowl on her pretty face that deepened as the day went on. She seemed to detest everyone, and above all, him.

A shot of pain coursed through him, a pain he did not understand. Why should he care what Mademoiselle Claudel thought of him?

Auguste molded one torso, then a second. Despite her talent, the young woman must learn humility and flexibility—it was the only way to survive the rejections awaiting her. He knew their sting well.

A tap at his office door pulled him from his thoughts. "*Entrez,*" he said, tossing the intertwined bodies on his desk.

Mademoiselle Claudel entered, her wavy mane slipping from its pins. Several clumps of hair stuck to her sweaty forehead. He took in her slumped shoulders, her downturned mouth.

"It has been twelve hours," she said. "I'm exhausted."

He nodded. "These are the hours any professional atelier keeps. You may go now."

For the second time that day her fleshy lower lip protruded slightly. "I'll never have time to work on my own pieces. I have class tomorrow."

"You will find a way. I've walked the same path. It's imperative to our growth and our humility."

A mixture of yearning and frustration filled her eyes. She looked down, and rubbed her hands together to loosen the grime caked in the grooves of her skin.

Auguste sensed she might cry and he felt his insides soften. The thought of crushing her passionate spirit, even for an instant, sent another wave of pain through him. His road had been more difficult initially—so what? Did that mean she must suffer as he had? It was difficult enough to make a name for herself as a woman.

"Follow me, mademoiselle."

She crossed her arms over her chest. "I won't do another thing today, Monsieur Rodin."

He waved her forward. "I have something to show you."

After a moment of hesitation, she followed him to the marble room.

The sun had begun to set; streaks of gold and pink filtered through the windows and glittered over the facets of irregular stone, casting the entire room in a shimmering, rosy light. Auguste stopped in the center of the room and spread his arms wide. "Select any piece you like."

Mademoiselle Claudel's lovely eyes widened and the first smile he had seen in weeks played on her lips. He did love to please a woman, but somehow, she was different, more important. Her happiness set his blood humming in his veins.

"Any piece?" she asked.

Auguste nodded.

Mademoiselle Claudel surveyed the uneven slabs of marble, some with rivers of gray, others with speckled sand or beige, even a rare hunk of jade. She stroked their surfaces lovingly and inspected their shapes from many angles. At last she lifted a small alabaster stone.

"You've chosen a fragile stone," he said. "It cracks easily unless you have had quite a bit of practice with it. Perhaps a more solid stone for your first try?"

Her eyes settled on his face. "No, I've found the one I want."

Chapter 13

꩜

Camille rolled her head from side to side, chisel in one hand, hammer in the other. She had worked with the gifted alabaster all week. She did not mind exerting such effort for her own sculptures, but the endless days of ladder climbing, lugging buckets of water or plaster—the menial chores—bored her senseless and suffocated her inspiration. The pay Rodin awarded her was hardly worth it, though she had to admit she liked to be near him.

She looked out her atelier window at the cheery morning light. She would skip classes, though it had already been weeks since she had attended. She did not have the energy for it. She bent over her piece once more and brushed the crumbs of rock away. Should she go to the atelier today to appease Rodin, or work more? Stupid girl, she berated herself. He did not care whether she was there or not. That settled it. She put chisel to stone and hammered against it with her mallet. She had too much to do here, at any rate.

꩜

Mademoiselle Claudel did not return to Rodin's atelier for a week and then two. Auguste sighed for the fifth time in the span of an hour. Both her absence and a letter from a minister to check on his progress of the *Gates* grated on him.

"It'll be finished when it's finished," he muttered under his breath. They didn't seem to grasp how much time it took to create something worthwhile. With a fine wire tool, he scratched at his figure's nose and threads of clay fell away.

Why hadn't Mademoiselle Claudel returned? His apprentice did not seem interested in rejoining his crew. She was so talented; in time her pieces would rival those of any man. Hell, they already outshone those of most of his male apprentices.

"What did you say, monsieur?" Adèle asked without shifting a single muscle.

"Be still," he replied.

Mademoiselle Lipscomb had returned, day after day, and claimed she had no idea whether or not her friend would return. Maybe she had been sworn to secrecy? Women loved their secrets.

Adèle yawned.

"Get dressed." Auguste pitched his tool in the pile with the others with more force than necessary. "I'll return in a couple of hours."

Adèle stared at him in surprise—he rarely left in the middle of a session, especially with such good light. Sunshine radiated through the glass panes.

He would see for himself what had kept Mademoiselle Claudel away.

❧

After some time dallying in the street, Auguste knocked at Mademoiselle Claudel's atelier door. She must be there. He knew she would not waste such a grand day for sculpting. He met no answer.

Two ladies passed behind him on the street, one leading a poodle on a leash, the other talking at a clip, relating the details of some family drama.

He knocked again. Still no reply. He peered up at a clear sky to see a bird dip after its insect prey. Another moment and he would go.

The screech of a hinge in need of oil put a smile on his face. As he suspected, she was working.

"What brings you here, Monsieur Rodin?" Camille stood in the doorway, a cigarette perched precariously on the edge of her plump lips.

His heart leapt in his chest. "You have missed work," he said.

She shrugged. "I have been occupied. Would you care to come in?"

"What have you been working on?" His shoulders tensed as he followed her inside. Had she joined another atelier?

"These." Mademoiselle Claudel uncovered a pair of hands extended from the hunk of alabaster he had gifted her. Slender fingers laced together as if uncertain whether or not they would poise for prayer.

Rodin stared intently at the piece, rotating it slowly, the better to examine the lissome fingers, squared knuckles, and fingernail grooves. The surface felt as smooth as any he had done himself.

"When did you learn to do this?" He tore his gaze away from the hands.

"I've watched the *praticiens* in your studio a hundred times. I memorized their techniques. Now I emulate them."

"It is your first piece of stone?"

She nodded.

"Camille . . ." He stopped, aware he had breached a formality. He had no right to call her by her christened name. "I apologize—"

"Don't." She tapped her cigarette to free the end from its burden of ashes. "I am not offended."

"This piece," Auguste began again. "You are very skilled." She should be one of his *praticiens*. He wanted her there, working beside him. He wanted her.

The realization struck him at once and he leaned on his heels to steady himself. Her frank demeanor and the direct ardor of her gaze got under his skin and soaked into his very core. He would happily drown in the indigo depths of her eyes, in her fierce passion. And yet, she would laugh at him if he dared say something so inane aloud, he was certain. He walked to the window to regain control of his emotions.

"Do you like my hands?" She exhaled a stream of smoke.

He turned to face her. "You are as skilled as any of my *praticiens*. These hands pulse with life."

"I am not sure if I'll return, monsieur. As you can see, I am quite busy here and I do not like to sacrifice so much of my time." She dragged on her cigarette once more.

She did not want his instruction and she certainly did not want him. His head drooped forward at his own stupidity. Of course she did not want him; he was twice her age.

"Have you seen my bust of Giganti?" she drawled in her provincial speech. "I think you'll find it agreeable, as you would say."

Auguste followed her to her worktable.

"It's nearly finished," she said. "I would like to show it in May at the Salon."

He ran his hands over the plaster, eyes closed, feeling each lump and groove. "Shave this cheekbone, and lift his chin a bit and this will be ready."

A spark lit her eyes and pure happiness dawned on her face. He tingled at her smile, an unwitting gift to him.

Mademoiselle Claudel averted her gaze and crushed the butt of her cigarette in a plaster ashtray.

Auguste would write a letter to a minister friend on her behalf. She deserved to show there—this piece would do well.

"Do you often work alone?" He shifted his weight from one foot to the other.

She moved across the room to wash her hands. "Yes, I often work alone. Jessie is dedicated, but I suppose I am—"

"Possessed?"

"Obsessed." She laughed. "*Exactement.*"

"I understand the sentiment well," he said quietly. He stared at her unwillingly, as if he could not help but be captured by her.

The laughter died on her lips. "I'm certain you are the only one who does."

The intensity that radiated from her person pressed against him. God, but he wanted to take her in his arms.

He cleared his throat. "Can you pause for a break? I am going to dine. Would you care to join me?"

She removed her smock, a brilliant smile on her lovely face. "I'm starved."

Camille entered the Café Ormond, Rodin at her heels. He had come to check on her—he valued her work! Excitement fluttered in her chest.

Monsieur Rodin pulled a chair out for her and she sat, pretending not to notice his eyes following her. To have his approval filled her with pride, yet she did not wish to be a slave in his workshop, despite how much she had learned in the months since she had joined him. But perhaps she could stomach it a bit longer . . . if he asked her to. She had not realized how much she missed his face during the weeks she had not returned to work.

They ordered a meal of filet of pork with potatoes and greens, and red wine.

"How is the *Gates* coming?" she asked. "I assume you're still in hell?"

A hearty laugh rumbled in his throat. How she liked to make him laugh. He didn't seem put off by her provincial speech and brash nature—a good thing, as she had no intention of changing herself for anyone. She knew who she was.

"Yes, I'm in hell," he said, "though I've created studies for new figures."

"And your Monsieur Hugo?"

"I have several maquettes, dozens of drawings. I'll commence the bust next week." He forked a thick slice of pork into his mouth.

They ate in companionable silence.

After Camille's final bite of potato, she asked, "Have you seen the new vehicles powered by steam? I'd die to ride in one. Who can resist the adventure?"

That expression crossed his face again—the arched brow followed by a twinkling in his eye and a smile. He seemed amused by everything she said.

"A friend of mine owns one," he said. "They're an abomination, all of these inventions. Industrialization chokes our countryside and clogs our minds. 'Progress' diminishes beauty. It separates man from nature."

Monsieur Rodin's ice blue irises dilated and a cloud perched upon his peppered brow. His coppery hair reflected the passion lurking beneath his cool exterior, though from what little she knew of him, he did not often show it, but channeled it into his work. His aloof manner covered a deep sense of humility and timidity, and the sharpest mind she had ever encountered.

"The noise and the smoke," she agreed. "I miss Villeneuve some days. The wind, moonlight on wheat fields. The feeling of stark wilderness and being completely alone."

"One day our art form will disappear completely. Our handwork will no longer be admired. Machines will carve marble, and they'll sell replicas of our busts like candy."

She sat back in her chair. "I disagree. What man can do will always be admired, despite machinery and progress. There is no substitute for human understanding of emotion."

Monsieur Rodin leaned forward. "Except for one issue. What is determined beautiful will shift, just as it has through the ages. And I fear that ideal may not include man at all." He folded his napkin and laid it across his plate. "Industrialization is nothing but a ruse to make man feel as if he is above his work, not tied to the fields he plows, the house he keeps day after day, his relationships. But he is not above any of it. In fact, he needs those things to feel whole."

Camille met his gaze a moment too long without speaking, and her face warmed.

"Perhaps I am struggling too much with the *Gates*," he said.

She set down her glass. "You struggle because you focus on the form and movement. Vitality emanates from your work—that is true—but you don't capture what tortures your subjects."

The look she had come to recognize appeared on his features once more. "You critique my work, mademoiselle?"

She flipped her knife over and over again on the table next to her plate. "Can't we all learn from criticism?"

He did not answer, but fixed his blue eyes upon her. She squirmed under his gaze—he had a way of making her feel exposed.

"So we can," he said at last.

"You are under a lot of pressure to produce. You mustn't let the ministers come between you and your passion, though they may try."

"They certainly try. But we artists must band together to beat them down."

"Us against them!"

He held up his glass. "Us against them. To always learning, to moving forward!"

She clanged her glass against his and smiled. To moving forward, indeed.

❧

The day's light sputtered and waned and with it, artists vacated their posts to head home. Marcel, the last of them, waved his hat at Rodin and closed the door behind him. Camille should have left as well, but did not look up from her task. She chipped another fragment of marble away. The set of feet would soon need to be sanded and polished. After her fifth pair, she could create them almost without thinking.

Monsieur Rodin flitted about the studio, lighting the lamps. Soon, the shadows retreated to the corners of the room and crept toward the gulf of ceiling and the darkened loft. He planned to continue working. Camille glanced at a woman's bust across from her station. Her eyes appeared suspicious of Camille's intentions.

"I am here to work, nothing more," she whispered to the bust. How had the object read her thoughts? She puffed out a sharp breath and blew away the crumbled bits of stone covering the feet.

Rodin bent over a study of a seated man leaning forward on his hand to contemplate theories of the universe.

"I would place his hand slightly over his mouth. As he is now, he appears as if he is posing." Camille put down her carving chisel and selected a rasp to buff the rounded hump of each heel.

Rodin gave her a sidelong glance.

She smiled. She supposed he did not expect her input, but she was no longer a lowly assistant; he respected her opinions . . . or so she assumed. If he did not, she would offer them anyway.

"The muscles in his legs and arms appear flexed," she continued. "He looks as if he might spring from his seat, rather than lose himself in his thoughts. I suppose it depends on the point you are trying to convey."

He rotated the maquette on its base. "I think you may be right."

Camille smiled. They had spent a lot of time working together lately. Though the growing familiarity between them unnerved her, she couldn't seem to leave when the others did, especially when she might have time with him alone.

The soft *thwap* of Rodin's tools floated above their heads and was lost in the chasm of the ceiling. Camille moved to his side to view his piece. "Lovely." His eyes softened. She could sense the rhythm of his breathing and the warmth that emanated from him. She felt a burn spread from her core through her limbs and crawl across her cheeks.

Slowly, his hand stretched toward her. Her heart stopped. He paused for an instant, then brushed the hair off her forehead, his fingertips feather light over her skin. The burn deepened until she felt ablaze. She dared not move, or even breathe.

Her voice came out in a whisper. "I am your student." She knew his reputation with women, though she had yet to see any truth behind the rumors. Still, he had everything and everyone he wanted—but he would not have her. Yet her fingers trembled.

"You are a brilliant woman." His voice came low, guttural. He reached for her again and cupped her face.

Without thinking, Camille closed her eyes and leaned into the cradle of his palm. Her heart pounded against her rib cage. How right it felt, his hand upon her cheek. But she couldn't risk her reputation, regardless of her own desire. No one would take her seriously. She would be nothing more than a mime, his student, not an artist in her own right. Her eyes flicked open to find him inches from her face.

She pulled away, her knees suddenly weak. "I need to go. Mother will wonder where I am."

If he knew Camille better, he would realize Mother no longer assumed she would be home to dine with the family, or even cared as to her whereabouts. She grabbed her hat from the rack near the door and tied its black ribbons hastily under her chin. At the door, she glanced over her shoulder a final time. "*Bonsoir.*"

Rodin raised his hand in a silent wave.

Camille stepped into the night to flee the tenderness of his caress, and the tide of emotion sweeping through her.

Part Two

1885–1887

La Valse
The Waltz

Chapter 14

❧

Camille swirled the last bite of pigeon and tender onion in the wine sauce and chewed it thoughtfully. She needed to scrub her stone this afternoon and prep it for chiseling. The last block of marble Jessie had chosen had a vein running through it and the blasted thing had split in two. Her friend should know better to avoid weak stones by now, but then, that was probably Rodin's reason for not appointing her a *praticien*. She glanced at the empty chair at the dining table. Jessie worked through lunch. Camille often did as well, but today she needed sustenance. The hammering, chiseling, and filing she had ahead of her would take a great deal of strength.

As would her avoidance of Rodin.

Mother scraped her fork against her plate in an uncharacteristic show of poor manners. Camille flinched at the noise. "What was that for?"

"I am speaking to you and you pretend as if you don't hear me," she said. "What is going through that head of yours? You're blushing."

Corinne bustled into the room, carrying an assortment of letters. She handed one to Camille. "Can I get something for you, mademoiselle?" She asked as she placed the remainder of the stack in front of Mother.

"Thank you—no."

Camille opened the single letter and quickly scanned the text. "The Société des Artistes Français has accepted *Giganti*!" She squealed. "It will be displayed in their May Salon!" She jumped to her feet and pecked Mother's cheek. "Perhaps I will receive a commission from a patron."

This was it! The beginning of selling her work and being admired.

The beginning of being loved.

Madame Claudel's blue eyes tightened. She patted the place where Camille had kissed her with a stiff hand. "I suppose all of the money we have spent on you is not a complete waste."

That was the only compliment Camille would receive from her, and so be it. She did not care—her work would be on display for all of Paris to see!

"I must tell Monsieur Rodin." The mention of his name ignited the burning once more, and it spread from her middle to her chest and face. She laughed aloud. The man made her feel as if she were on fire. Suddenly everything made her happy.

Mother smoothed the lace tablecloth with her hands. "We haven't finished our meal. Sit down."

"I am quite finished, Mother." Camille kissed her hastily on the cheek, snatched up a hat, and dashed through the door.

❦

Auguste squinted at Giganti, then refocused on his portrait. He nudged the shoulder of the clay study with his thumb and a wreath of shadow draped the figure's abdomen. *Parfait.*

His stomach gurgled loud enough for the model to hear. Giganti held back a laugh. The model had learned to be restrained, particularly under Auguste's watchful eye. If he so much as drew in a breath, he would be chastised.

Auguste stepped back from the armature. "Let us break. Apparently I need to eat." He had been unable to think of food the past week, since the night he had touched Camille. Did she find him repulsive, a man—her teacher, no less—much too old for her? But she was a woman, not a girl, he reminded himself. He scrubbed at the clay crust on his hands. She had leaned into his palm, eyes closed and lips parted. Heat shot through him at the memory. But since that evening, she had managed to avoid being alone with him. He glanced about his atelier. He wondered when she would arrive—

That instant, Camille barged through the atelier door, a letter in hand. Her lovely features glowed with happiness.

Warmth flooded his chest. She had received her admission letter. He watched her dash across the room toward Mademoiselle Lipscomb. She found her friend huddled in a corner, crouched beside an armature, her eyes level with the plaster hem of a woman's dress.

"It's been accepted!" she shouted.

Mademoiselle Lipscomb embraced her friend and the two hopped up and down, then pulled each other round and round in a circle like schoolgirls.

Auguste smiled. So full of life and excitement, they were.

"Congratulations!" Mademoiselle Lipscomb embraced her again.

Giganti, now dressed, joined them and Camille launched herself into his arms. The model laughed and twirled her around before placing her on her feet. She leaned in to kiss him. Auguste felt his joy contract. Giganti slung his arm around her shoulders possessively.

Perhaps they were lovers. The thought hit him like a blow to the gut. No wonder Camille had fled from him that night. He turned his back on the happy trio and curled his hands into fists.

"Monsieur!" The musical voice that haunted his dreams, *her* voice, called to him. He looked over his shoulder to find a beaming Camille. "Did you have something to do with this?" She waved the letter at him.

"I thought *Giganti* deserved recognition," he said. He had spoken at length about her talent to his critic friends and written a letter to the director of the *société* on her behalf. "It's a remarkable piece."

Camille crossed the room, stood on the tips of her toes, and placed a kiss upon his cheek. A triumphant smile lit her face. Auguste's jealousy dissolved. *Dieu*, he loved to make her happy—and that frightened the hell out of him. He nodded and continued to his office and closed the door.

❧

Paul perched on the faded velvet pillow in the window seat of Camille's room while she applied rouge to her lips. For the Salon, she must look a proper lady.

"*Écoute.*" Her brother thumbed through one of his books and read aloud.

I summoned plagues, to stifle myself with sand and blood.
Misfortune was my god. I stretched out in the mud.
I dried myself in the breezes of crime. And I played some fine
tricks on madness.

"Are you reading Rimbaud again?" Camille asked.

Paul closed his book. "How did you know?"

"Because the passages are either about hell or they make no sense."

"He makes perfect sense to me." Paul licked his thumb and rubbed at a spot on his shoe until it shone.

A soft knock came at the door. "Camille?"

"Come in, Mother." A tide of sadness swelled in her breast. Mother refused to attend the Salon, lest she be seen amid the "infidels of Paris." Camille had hoped she might go anyway, perhaps show support for her daughter's success for a change. At least Papa would be home tomorrow in time to see *Giganti* on display, even if he could not escort her on opening night. Paul and Louise would join him.

Mother stood beside Camille at the mirror. "I . . ." She looked down at her folded hands. "I wanted to wish you luck at the Salon. Even if sculpting is a foolish waste of time . . . you have done well." A certain vulnerability and a touch of pride shone in her eyes.

"Mother?" Camille's own eyes widened in shock. She squeezed her mother's hand and kissed her on the cheek. "I will make you proud of me yet."

Mother attempted a smile. "Don't let me keep you. You mustn't be late." She left the room in a rush, clearly uncomfortable by the display of emotion.

Camille glanced at Paul in disbelief. He shrugged. That was the first time Mother had complimented her artwork. Sure, she had praised her for high marks in letters and history, or an occasional witty comment when the family bantered, but never for her sculpture. Unexpected tears threatened. She blinked several times to keep them at bay.

"You've been in front of that mirror for an hour," he said. "Aren't you ready yet?"

She launched one of her hats at his face. "You will spend twice the time on your toilette tomorrow."

"Very funny," he said, having caught the hat easily.

Camille smoothed the front of her black-and-gold-striped skirt and peered over her shoulder to check her bustle. All appeared in order. Filigree eardrops of shiny black stones dangled from her lobes and an ebony velvet ribbon encircled her neck, the perfect complement to her low neckline. She pulled on one black silk glove, then another. Perhaps Monsieur Rodin would be pleased. Camille frowned in the mirror. She had far more important things to think about tonight.

A tramping of hooves clamored in the street. Paul pushed aside the lace curtain and peered into the street. His face screwed up into a scowl. "Monsieur Rodin awaits."

Camille glared at him. "He is my tutor and employer, Paul."

"He steals all of your time. I miss you."

She smiled. "I miss you, too, but I've learned a lot from him. His connections are a big part of why my bust was accepted."

"Your talent is why your bust was accepted." He stood. "I fear for your reputation. He is known to be a lady's man, Camille. You do know that?"

"Of course." She snapped her powder box closed. "And yet, I haven't seen him with a woman as long as I have known him." She noticed his crossed arms. "Do not worry about me." She leaned over him and mashed her lips against his cheek to blot her rouge. She laughed at the scarlet ring left on his skin. He swatted her hand and fished for his handkerchief in his pocket.

Jessie stepped into the room, still fiddling with her gray pelisse. The jacket blended with her unassuming gown. When she saw Camille's attire, her hand flew to her hair. "You're wearing feathers . . . Shall I?"

Camille eyed Jessie's simple hairpins, bulging with a mass of dark curls. Jessie would not feel comfortable in a more ostentatious hair ornament or a flashy dress. No sense in making her worry all evening about her appearance. Her friend's intelligent discourse would make up for her wanting beauty.

"Here, wear my brooch." Camille fastened a sterling oval etched with a blooming rose to the high lace collar of Jessie's costume. "You look lovely."

Paul followed them downstairs.

"Good evening." Rodin exited the carriage so the ladies might sit first.

"Meet my brother, Paul," Camille said.

Paul extended a hand in greeting, though his features were pinched. "Monsieur Rodin, take care of my sister."

Camille laughed at Paul's possessive reaction. "There's no need to worry, brother. Jessie and I are in good hands."

Paul nodded tightly and watched them mount the carriage.

Once settled, Camille noted Monsieur Rodin's elegant suit and top hat, and a red carnation at his lapel. She wondered who had fastened the flower there. The thought made her squirm.

"I see you own clothing that isn't spattered in plaster," she said. "Strangely enough, we do as well." She laughed, her good humor plain. "The flower is a nice touch. Your wife has excellent taste."

He glanced at her painted lips. "I do not have a wife. And you, *mes filles*, are stunning." Though he addressed them both, his gaze never left Camille's.

Her smile widened. He wasn't married, then.

Jessie cleared her throat. "You must tell me how to behave, monsieur."

"Admire the art, be gracious, and above all, do not take offense at the criticism. Some opinions you may like, but often you will dislike what is said about your work. Remember those who render judgment do not understand the inspiration behind them or the care with which we shape them." He clutched the polished head of his cane. "It's not them we please. It is ourselves."

Rodin could make such a declaration because he had so many commissions, Camille thought. His list of admirers grew by the day.

The carriage stopped in front of the Salon de Champs-Élysées. Gentlemen milled about in elegant suits decked with silk ascots, beaver-felt top hats, and dress coats with swallowtails. The ladies hurried indoors to escape the light rain, resplendent in silk, their sleeves adorned with ruche detailing or frilly ribbons.

"Look at all their lovely hats," Jessie said, touching her rather plain one.

Women sported miniature derbies, porkpie hats, or the newly fashionable tall felts trimmed with flowers, feathers, or lace.

"What a crowd." Camille swallowed hard. She had not expected so many people to attend. Suddenly she wished she could hide in the private confines of her studio. She did not enjoy being in a room full of people. Her fingers itched to sketch or mold, or even hammer at a block of granite—anything to calm her nerves. What if the critics despised *Giganti*? She must begin her career on the right foot. She looked frantically to Rodin.

"Are you ready?" he asked, his eyes sympathetic.

Camille smiled bravely. He must have learned to enjoy these events, though she knew he preferred the solitude of his studio as well.

"My work will be at the next Salon," Jessie said emphatically. "I will do everything in my power to be here."

"Of course you will," Camille said, squeezing Jessie's hand.

Monsieur Rodin took a lady on each arm.

The evening flew by in a blur of clinking glasses and light chatter that grew louder as the night wore on. Camille and Jessie floated from one piece to another, scrutinizing each.

"I like this one," Jessie said, stopping before a sculpture of a woman in full gown and hat.

"You prefer the realist tradition, I see. They are similar to your own pieces."

Jessie nodded.

Camille recognized the beauty in the same pieces, but found them rather dull. She preferred the more radical approach in her own work: to adapt proportions of the human form to reflect the emotion she wanted to convey—just as the Impressionists, as the painters called themselves, demonstrated an altered view of reality. She admired that quality about the painters' vision.

"I am going for another turn through the main room," Jessie said. "Care to come?"

"I think I'll head over to *Giganti* again, to observe the viewers." She cracked a smile. "I will meet you later."

Camille watched the wealthy patrons flit about, critiquing her bust as well as several studies for *The Gates of Hell* by her own Rodin. She put her fingertips to her lips. *Her* Rodin? She glanced around the room quickly. Had anyone heard her thoughts? No one had the slightest idea who she was, she reminded herself. Right? She scanned the room again.

Rodin stood across from a sculpture of a warrior dressed in helmet and sandals, grasping a sword, the muscles in his forearm flexed from the weight of the steel he carried. The statue had been fashioned in the classical Roman style and was technically perfect, but lacking in spirit like the dozens of others she had seen. It was a wonder Camille had been asked to be in the Salon at all, with such repetitive samples in the showing. She sipped from her wineglass. At least the wine was good. She looked from one unknown face to the next and wondered where Jessie had stolen off to—probably with the English couple she had met earlier in the evening.

A beautiful woman in a sparkling gown with a low neckline approached Rodin. She laughed and touched her earlobe in a coquettish fashion, then brushed away a gold curl from her forehead. Rodin appeared enthralled by their conversation. He leaned closer to the woman, his lips so very near her ear.

Camille's mouth went dry. She had put off his subtle advances, and yet, she could not stand the sight of him in another woman's presence. She drained the last drops from her glass and set it on the base of a nearby Madonna.

An elegant woman in rose brocade sneered at her obvious lack of respect.

Camille glared back. She had seen one hundred Madonnas. This one was not so distinguished and neither was it well crafted, but it had been made by a man and that is why it had been accepted. Camille selected another *vin rouge* from an attendant's tray. It must be so easy to be a man. But she would show them all. This Salon was only the beginning for her.

She returned to *Giganti* and retreated to a nook just within eyesight of it. Two gentlemen stood before the bust, measuring its worth.

"I wonder what he is thinking." The man with the square head and thick black hair leaned in for a closer view. "Don't you agree? It's magnificent."

"It looks as if it was made by an amateur," the other said, pushing his spectacles higher on the bridge of his crooked nose. "The detailing is all wrong."

Camille felt as if she had been struck in the gut. An amateur would not show at the most prestigious Salon in Paris.

"I disagree," the dark-haired man replied. He leaned closer to the bust. "Look at his eyes. It's as if he is being consumed by some inner sorrow, yet he juts out his chin proudly, to ward off the next offense that might come his way."

A rush of gratitude filled her heart. Camille wanted to embrace the gentleman.

The tall man shrugged. "It looks like one of Rodin's castoffs." He sauntered away.

Camille bit back an unexpected wave of tears. She was accustomed to Mother's rebukes, but not those from strangers and certainly not from those who might attack her work. The man's words stung more than she had anticipated.

The dark gentleman looked over his shoulder at her. "What do you think this *Giganti* is thinking?"

Camille buried her wound and put on a brave smile. "I cannot share his secrets, monsieur."

He raised his eyebrows in surprise. "You are the artist?" His eyes dropped from her face to her bare shoulders and neck. "Mademoiselle Claudel?"

"*C'est moi.*"

"I am Joseph Archambault." He tipped his head forward in a polite gesture.

"Are you an artist as well?"

"Of sorts. I am a composer."

Though he was not attractive, the gentleman's intelligent gaze appealed to her. Besides, he possessed a refined taste in sculpture. She smiled, suddenly thankful for the distraction from both the harsh criticism and the blonde in the sparkling gown, who still held Rodin's attention.

"I should like to hear one of your melodies, monsieur," she said, feigning a chipper mood.

Rodin turned his head that moment and found her face across the room. A sense of recklessness enveloped her. She tilted her head toward Monsieur Archambault.

"Do you need to join your tutor?" The composer had not missed Rodin's glance. "Monsieur Rodin?"

The burn returned, and an unfamiliar ache. The sparkling woman had glued herself to his side. "No." She choked on the emotion welling inside her. "Not at all."

"I would be honored to escort you on a turn through the Salon, Mademoiselle Claudel, artiste extraordinaire." He smiled.

She took his arm. "That would be lovely."

As they paraded through the hall, Camille tried to listen to the gentleman but could not focus on his words. In the doorway to one of the adjoining rooms, she paused to dare one last glance in Rodin's direction. He had gone.

He would abandon her on her first showing for that woman? She frowned as jealousy swarmed her unsettled stomach.

Chapter 15

꠸꠸꠸

Adèle and Giganti sat entwined on their base per Camille's instruction. She had been working feverishly on an idea that had awakened her in the middle of the night three months before. The night it came to her, she had lit a candle in her bedroom, enraging her sister at the ungodly hour, and padded down the stairs to the salon. Under the halo of a solitary lamp, she had sketched the Indian princess Shakuntala, once abandoned by her husband and lover, the King. Unbeknownst to the princess, her husband was bewitched. When the spell broke many years later, he returned to her on his knees, his heart full of longing and remorse. The pain of the past melted away at their reunion and their spirits rejoined as if never parted. Camille would show Shakuntala's forgiveness, the couple's sacred bond.

She peered at her nearly life-size maquette. This piece would be nothing like the others shown at Salons. A nude couple, slave to their love and desire, would rock the foundations of the Société des Artistes Français. She might very well be thrown out for it . . . or she may be revered. No other woman had designed such a risqué piece. Excitement pinged around her stomach each time she thought of the work's potential success.

Camille pinched a coil that would become Shakuntala's hair.

Jessie looked up from her own piece, a young girl in a fanciful hat. "Do you think Emily will rejoin us? She has not been by in weeks." She cleaned the excess clay off the end of her tool.

"I doubt it. She has skipped out on her share of the rent. Besides, she talked of being homesick." Camille sniffed. A friend run off without a proper good-bye—this was why she rarely expended the effort to cultivate her friendships. They always failed her. But she was so thankful for Jessie. With a sudden burst of gratitude, she crossed the room and kissed her friend on the cheek.

Jessie laughed. "What was that for?"

"For being a lovely friend."

Jessie smiled. "You mean unlike Emily?" She selected another tool on her worktable. "I think she's gone back to England."

"Perhaps, or maybe she joined another atelier."

Both Camille and Jessie had abandoned their lessons at l'Académie Colarossi when they became employees for Monsieur Rodin, so they did not know if Emily had attended class. But what could be better instruction than working with a master?

"I am surprised she did not tell us her plans," Jessie said, frowning.

Camille shrugged.

Adèle scratched her nose, then rested her arm at an incorrect angle, too close to Giganti's head.

Camille sighed heavily and adjusted the model's arm to its intended place. Adèle did not like her but had agreed to pose with Giganti for the right price—and at Rodin's request. It had taken additional persuasion to get the model to pose in her atelier. Camille could not tell if Adèle detested taking orders from a woman or if she felt uncomfortable being examined by one. In a man's eyes, Adèle was an object of desire; in a woman's, she was only an object.

"I need to be finished by one o'clock," Adèle said. "Auguste will be expecting me." She squirmed on her perch.

Exasperated, Camille stamped her foot. "You will miss your appointment if you move again." She didn't care a whit for the model's plans. Rodin had been locked in his office for days, poring over sketches to submit to a competition. He wouldn't need Adèle's services today. The model had lied to her. Not to mention, the hag had the audacity to use his first name. She dared not guess if they had been intimate, or she might throw the model into the street.

Camille rolled a pellet of clay between her hands and massaged it into place on the haunches of her male clay figure. Yet with such familiarity, Adèle had no doubt slept with him. She mashed the clay a bit harder than intended, flattening the rump too much on one side. She huffed and threw her hands in the air. "Take a break," she said. She could use an espresso, at any rate.

The pair of models stretched and slipped on their clothing, while Camille flexed her fingers.

"I'm headed home." Jessie removed her gray smock. "Are you coming?"

Camille shook her head. She had no intention of suffering through lunch with Mother. She had been in the worst humor lately. Besides, Mother seemed to prefer Jessie to her, and she could not withstand her disdain again today.

A pounding came at the atelier door. Giganti moved wordlessly to answer.

Rodin appeared, his eyes red, his beret knocked askew. He all but sprinted toward Camille, sketchbook under his arm.

⤜❧⤛

"Is there something wrong?" Camille asked.

"I need to speak to you privately," Auguste said, slightly out of breath. He needed to talk to her immediately; it couldn't wait.

Giganti ran a hand through his hair and pulled on a hat. "To the brasserie I go. When you are finished here, would you like to join me, Camille?"

She nodded.

"*Perfetto.*" Giganti smiled.

"Are we meeting today at one o'clock, Auguste?" Adèle twirled a lock of blond hair around her finger. "I canceled a rendezvous to meet with you."

Auguste looked at Adèle as if she were a stain on a newly pressed shirt. "You may go," he said. "I am occupied this afternoon."

The model sniffed, her discouragement plain. "Very well. But I am busy all week." Without a second glance, she left, slamming the door behind her.

Auguste grunted. Models could be so self-indulgent. Camille stifled a laugh.

"I will return in a couple of hours." Mademoiselle Lipscomb threw her smock over a chair. "Good day, Monsieur Rodin."

Silently, he nodded. Once Jessie had gone, he gave Giganti a pointed look. "Please excuse us." Giganti winked at Camille and disappeared through the door.

Auguste dropped his sketchbook on the table and picked up a hunk of clay. He rolled it between his palms into coils, then made a figure in the matter of minutes.

"What is it?" Camille said.

In silence, he continued until he finished a fifth man, slightly leaner than the others, and placed them in a triangular arrangement. After some time he said, "I am to present my idea for a new commission."

"I have noticed your absence this week."

A thread of hope began to throb inside him. She had noticed? He forced himself to focus on his figures. "The town of Calais is going to demolish its medieval fortress walls to join the *vieux quartier* with the new development," he said. "They want to install a monument as a marker. One that honors the martyr Eustace Saint-Pierre."

"Yes, I know the story," she said. "He and five others forfeited their lives to King Edward of England so their city would not be destroyed."

Camille knew the history of Calais? He shouldn't be surprised; he noticed she read very often. When he flipped open his sketchbook, Camille stood beside him, close enough for the scent of amber and clay to envelop him. She moved closer still, to get a better look. The throbbing increased.

He cleared his throat. "What do you think of their arrangement?"

"I've never seen anything like it. No man atop a horse, or in religious robes." She peered at the maquettes and again at the pad.

"The men are marching to their doom."

"Very clever," she said. "I'm surprised the ministers have agreed to it. This pushes the boundaries of anything I've seen."

The taut muscles in Auguste's shoulders relaxed. Her approval washed away the pressure, the self-doubt with which he had wrestled the better part of the past two weeks.

"They haven't agreed to it," he said. "Not yet."

Camille crouched so she was eye level with the figures' arrangement. After several minutes, she eyed the sketch once more. "Something seems . . . off." She moved the maquettes a hair farther apart and bent their bodies.

Auguste stroked his beard, his mind buzzing. The figures were united by their cause, their sacrifice.

"He is Eustace?" She pointed to the man nearest the center.

He nodded.

She moved him right of center, then shifted another figure slightly. "They are individuals, even if their destinies have collided."

That was the missing piece! They were individuals, yet joined. Their forms needed to display as such.

Auguste picked up one of the clay men and bent his torso forward, as if he might collapse in grief. He pulled another's shoulders back, making him proud of his own courage and willingness. He rotated them and widened the base; it would be square, rather than a pyramid.

"*C'est ça!*" she said, her excitement plain.

He lunged at her, wrapped his arms around her middle, and twirled her around. "That's it!" She laughed and threw her arms about his neck. After another spin, he placed her on her feet. His hands lingered on her hips. The laughter died in her throat. He gazed at her with the intensity that pulsed in his veins. Her lips parted and a blush burned her ivory skin. The space between them seemed to vibrate.

"Well then, you have work to do," she said. "As do I."

"You are an inspiration," he said in a throaty voice.

She gazed at him with her bewitching eyes. "It would be criminal for them to reject such a design. I can think of nothing more compelling."

He squeezed her slightly. When she did not pull away, he leaned toward her and slid his hands slowly over her back. He felt the rapid thud of her heart on his palm.

She inched closer. "You could also—"

He silenced her with his lips. She pulled him closer and pushed hungrily against his mouth. A groan rumbled in his throat. Liquid heat surged through his limbs. The wall built long ago inside him melted with the softness of her lips.

In a swift movement, she tore away from him, gasping for air. "Did you say something?" She looked past him to the corners of the room and the windows, then rubbed her temples.

"No," he whispered. The searing need to have her pounded against his will.

"A voice." She whirled around to assure herself they were alone. "I heard a voice."

He frowned. "There is no one here but us."

"But I heard someone. I thought . . ." Her puzzled expression faded, but she maintained the distance between them.

"It must have been someone in the street. My dear, Camille," he whispered. "Every inch of me is alive when you are near." He closed the space between them once more and traced her cheekbone with his thumb.

She bristled at his touch. "Please. Just go."

He regarded the wildness in her eyes, the fear quivering in her limbs. God, he ached for her—a gnawing, consuming ache that kept him from sleep. He ignored her plea and swept her into his arms once more.

"Leave me!" She pushed against him. "You care nothing for me. Only for my *jeunesse*."

"My darling girl, if you only knew."

"Let me go or I'll scream!" Her voice grew savage.

Auguste released her as if she had bitten him. Embarrassment, then hurt crashed over him. She did not want him—and of course she did not! What was he thinking?

He gathered his pride and quit her studio at once.

Chapter 16

꒚

Camille shifted closer to her brother on the settee and leaned against his shoulder. "I'm telling you, I heard it. A voice told me to run from Monsieur Rodin or he might hurt me."

Paul puffed out an exasperated breath. "We have been over this all afternoon. Must we talk about it again?"

"How would you feel if a demon voice spoke to you?" she insisted.

"Monsieur Rodin won't hurt you, Camille." He wrapped an arm about her shoulders. "He may steal all your time, perhaps an idea of yours, but he would not harm you."

Her mind whirred. Was she hearing things, or had some part of her subconscious warned her about him? She wasn't sure. She squeezed her eyes closed and forced the thought away.

It had to be nothing.

꒚

The heat of midafternoon pressed upon Camille and Jessie while they worked. Camille wiped her forehead with the sleeve of her smock. She had perspired all morning and now the afternoon had become unbearable. Though it was early autumn, the sun had not yet ceased its punishing heat. She jumped down from her perch above her maquette, submerged a cloth in the water basin, wrung much of the moisture from it, and remounted the ladder. It had been difficult to keep her sculptures moist in the oppressive heat, despite the humid air.

"I've had enough," Camille said, covering *Shakuntala*. Not only was she boiling from the sun's heat, but she burned at the thought of Auguste. She could not expel him from her mind and she resented it, never mind the strange voice. It had spoken to her that night he held her, and warned her about him. Still, they had kissed twice more; the last time Camille had pulled him against her and threaded her fingers through his beard. He had moaned and rested his forehead on hers. Her knees had nearly buckled in response to the delicious sound.

"Stop it," she mumbled to herself. She had more important things to ponder—finishing her next piece for the Salon and landing a commission, for example. Her wages from Auguste and the money from her parents scarcely covered her expenses for supplies.

"I am ready for a pause as well," Jessie said, placing a cloth on her own piece.

"Shall we go to the Musée des Antiquités?" Camille asked. "Do some drawing?"

"It's a bit far for today, isn't it?" Jessie washed her hands and face in cool water.

She shrugged. "Less than twenty kilometers, and a quick ride by train. It would be a nice reprieve from the city heat."

And from her thoughts.

Jessie patted her face dry with a cloth. "An escape from the city *would* be lovely."

A short ride later, the girls descended from the train at Saint-Germain-en-Laye. The afternoon sun slid from its pedestal in the sky, yet heat radiated from the paved walkway, and muggy air stuck in their throats and clung to their clothing.

"It is days like these I detest being a woman," Camille said, swishing her skirts to create a breeze on her sweaty legs. She regarded the array of fountains, the gardens and gravel pathways laid out in a geometric pattern. Their mathematical design seemed in opposition to the riotous beauty of the flowers bursting from their pots. She peered up at the stone castle, once a king's playground, a hospital, and now the museum's showroom—one of her favorite places to derive inspiration. She glanced back toward the fountain. "Come!" She grabbed Jessie by the hand and led her toward it. "First, we cool off."

"No." Jessie pulled her hand from Camille's grasp.

"Don't be such a prude. If you come with me, I will tell you a secret."

Jessie stopped in her tracks. "Is it a commission? Has someone bought a piece of yours?"

Camille barked a laugh. "I wish that were true." She skipped the remaining distance to the fountain.

"Really, Camille." She caught up to her. "One might think you were a little girl."

"Aren't I?" Her laughter burst with glee as she unlaced her boots.

"You aren't going in?" Jessie asked, horrified.

"Why not?" She gathered her skirts and climbed over the edge of the fountain, sighing contentedly as a current of cool water curled around her sweltering toes and ankles. "The water is divine. Come in." She held out her hand to assist Jessie.

Her friend crinkled her nose. "Absolutely not. You are embarrassing yourself."

Several couples gawked at Camille as they strode toward the museum. She splashed around and laughed, spraying Jessie in the process.

"Do not get me wet!" Jessie moved away from the fountain's edge. "Come out of there at once. We will be asked to leave!"

Camille skipped her foot over the water's surface once more, spraying a bevy of cooing pigeons, who skittered out of the way. Lower skirts drenched, she sloshed to the edge and hoisted herself over the rim of the fountain once more. Rivulets of water streamed down her legs and pooled around her feet.

"You've ruined a perfectly good pair of stockings," Jessie said. "And perhaps your dress."

Camille looked down at her clothing. Why did she behave so brashly? Her will was stronger than her sense of reason at times. Was that the price for being so passionate? "They will dry soon enough in this heat," she said.

"You had better dry or I won't sit by you on the train," Jessie said, crossing her arms over her chest. "Now, out with it."

"Out with what?" Camille laughed wickedly.

"Do not play coy with me, young lady. Your secret!"

While wringing out her skirts Camille said, "He kissed me."

"What? Who kissed you?"

"Monsieur Rodin."

Jessie stared. "No! Camille, that won't do. He is our teacher. He's—"

"I know." She tilted her face to the expanse of summer sky and sighed. "And yet, my senses betray me. I step into the circle of his energy and I am consumed."

"I cannot condone this," Jessie said. "You must control yourself, no matter how hard that may be."

Camille flinched at her disapproval. She did not wish to be entangled with Rodin—she had promised herself she would steer clear of him. Yet she found herself thinking of little else. Each night when she closed her eyes, his scent of sandalwood filled her senses. Her fingers tingled, anxious to probe the shape of his face, the curve of his lips.

"Oh, Camille." Jessie rested her hand on her chest as if surprised. "You have a fire in your eyes. Your cheeks are blooming. You are in love with him."

The words hit Camille like a blow. She couldn't be in love with him. Her art meant too much to her. If things disintegrated between them, it would be a disaster extricating herself from his influence.

"You know he lives with a woman and has a son with her. Rose Beuret." Jessie's face was a mask of concern.

Rodin lived with the woman still? Her damp skirts became irritating against her skin, the beauty of the museum and its gardens insulting. The euphoria buoying her for days drained from her body, leaving her hollow. She knew he had a son, but she hadn't realized he lived with a woman still. Had Camille been in the privacy of her bedroom, she would have smashed something and dissolved into tears. But she would not appear a fool in front of Jessie.

"What has that to do with me?" Her words came out strangled.

Jessie's mouth fell open. "That doesn't concern you?"

Camille picked the leaves from a low-lying branch one by one, shredded them, and watched them flutter to the ground. She couldn't imagine why the woman stayed with Rodin. Everyone knew he'd had lovers, or at least the rumors claimed he did. Mademoiselle Beuret must know. She clamped down hard on her tongue. How could she have feelings for a man who treated his lover with such disregard? She must keep her distance.

"I suppose it does. A little," Camille admitted at last. She swallowed hard. "Are you ready to go inside?"

Jessie embraced her. "Keep your distance and all will be well, my friend."

The girls ambled toward the museum.

⚜

Auguste pulled his lantern closer and hunched over his desk. He put charcoal to paper, and the hunk cracked and split, leaving a trail of black crumbs on his sketch. The martyrs of Calais stared vacantly in the distance and were now crowned by a dusting of black stars, vacuous and absent of light. The stars absorbed life from the weary men. Auguste pressed his finger on the specks and smudged them across the page. A wind tunnel appeared beneath his thumb, poised to suck Eustace, leader of the martyrs, into oblivion. He thought of the swirled tangle of Camille's hair after a long day's work.

Perhaps it was he who would be swept away.

A smile played on his lips at the thought of her wildness, her bold expression. Her advice on the placement of the statues had been brilliant. He labored over his visions, while she drew on her inspiration and never questioned its validity—a both admirable and foolish trait. Fledgling sculptors should question their techniques and the structure of their works to grow their talents. He snorted. He liked to pretend he was a master and she, a mere pupil, but she could hardly be called a fledgling sculptor. She learned in a few lessons what had taken him years to master. And she taught him as well.

Auguste plucked the maquette of the Calais monument from the corner of his desk. Omer Dewavrin had been pleased with his design, though many others opposed Auguste's vision and crucified him in their reviews. But he would not produce the same tripe as every other sculptor before him. He turned his model over in his hand. His men appeared resolute, yet anguished to leave behind all they loved, to sacrifice their lives. Nevertheless, pride and nobility emanated from their stance. He would not succumb to his opponents' lackluster vision. They did not recognize fine art.

Auguste pitched a loose hunk of clay across the room. It thudded against the window, then plopped onto the amber-colored hardwood floor. If only his most ardent supporter had been reelected mayor. Omer had advocated for him, but now with him out of office, the commission was threatened. Auguste fished his friend's letter from his drawer. Several other ministers wanted him out of the running, but he wouldn't let that happen. He would leave for Calais tomorrow.

꒰ᵕ꒱

Auguste descended from the train in a pristine suit and hat. Rarely did he wear clothing not splattered or stained, but he knew when to put on airs, and he knew the right people to impress. He clutched his valise and crossed the platform at the Gare Calais-Ville, hired a cab, and rode the distance to Dewavrin's home. The gentleman had offered him room for a few nights and to coordinate a meeting with another of the ministers of the *conseil municipal.*

On Dewavrin's doorstep, Rodin inhaled a steadying breath. His lungs filled with salty air tinged with the musty odor of seaweed. He could smell the ocean from here, though he had never laid eyes on its glistening waves. He knew its beauty only from Monet's paintings, but one day he would venture to the shore.

The handle rattled and a lock turned. A maid ushered him inside while another carried his valise to his room.

"Monsieur Rodin," Dewavrin greeted him. "A pleasure to finally meet you in person. And this is Andre Calin, one of the ministers on the council."

"Very good of you to come, monsieur," Rodin said to Calin. "I am pleased to meet you both."

Monsieur Calin's expensive clothing did not hide his lumpy frame and scabrous skin. The poor bastard had probably never bedded a woman in his life.

"The feeling is mutual," the councilman said.

"Shall we take our meal in the garden?" Dewavrin led them through a set of glass doors. "The breeze and shade will be more refreshing than this stifling room."

The trio sat near a sweep of willow trees, which from a distance looked like a furry mop of hair. If Auguste were a painter, he would capture their unusual beauty.

The maid poured glasses of Chablis for each of them. "We are serving moules frites, messieurs. We purchased fresh mussels early this morning."

"Very good. Thank you, Céline." Dewavrin shooed her away.

Rodin took a sip of the refreshing Chablis, at once cool and crisp in his dry throat. "Tell me more about Calais. I am fascinated by medieval histories."

An hour of polite conversation and Rodin felt himself grow restless. He scooped the last of the broth with a mussel shell and poured it into his mouth. The savory liquid spread over his tongue. He needed to talk about the monument, but did not want to rush the ministers.

After the gentlemen nibbled on a platter of cheeses, the maid poured an aperitif of Calvados, the region's famed apple brandy.

Auguste cradled his aperitif in his hand, liquid courage to bolster his bravery. "I am happy to be here in Calais, the land and peoples that inspire the monument, on such a brilliant day."

Monsieur Calin folded his hands and rested them on the tabletop with an official air. The mood of the conversation shifted with the gesture. "Tell me, what is your vision for the monument?" he asked. "I have seen the initial maquettes, and I must admit, I find the display rather curious. It is not at all what I envisioned."

Auguste sat straighter in his chair. "I chose to display the figures in bondage so we might see their pain and sacrifice. The nobility in their acceptance of death."

Calin ran his fingertip around the rim of his glass several times without speaking. "I think the choice is a mistake. They do not appear noble in prisoner's clothing, but degraded and lacking in humanity."

"Their clothing illustrates how death strips each one of us of our stations and titles, our accomplishments and failings. One who looks upon my burghers will not see the figures as bourgeois, farmers, or the poor, but as men, united in a cause to save their town."

"Bourgeois clothing your onlookers can relate to, monsieur."

"And they cannot relate to the men's humility?" Rodin gripped his brandy glass. "I see we have different views."

"Very. I'm afraid many of my council members are in agreement with me. The design you propose is revolutionary, monsieur."

Auguste embraced the idea of revolution in sculpture. It was long overdue. He did not withhold the defensive note that crept into his voice. "The maquette you have seen is a rough sketch and far from finished."

"Yet I imagine the issues we have just discussed will remain the same?"

"I don't see them as issues, but strengths," Rodin said. He had lost other commissions and he had been mocked with *The Age of Bronze*. Now his skin had thickened, his place among artists more certain. He would not be bullied into a concept that lacked teeth.

Monsieur Calin laced his fingers together. "As I thought. And the square base you prefer will remain over the classic pyramid?"

"For this piece, yes."

"You have chosen a design that breaks tradition in every way. You may see how difficult you are making things for yourself and the council?"

Anger crept along Auguste's spine, but he knew he must restrain himself. Diplomacy won hearts. "I am an outlaw in the eyes of the art ministry," he began, "and, it would seem, in yours as well. But I attempt to create my own masterpieces, not those as designated by the standards of the *école*. For that I will neither apologize nor alter my vision. I am the artist, monsieur, and a fine one at that. You must trust my instinct."

Monsieur Calin wiped his weak chin with a napkin and pushed back from the table. "Well, gentlemen, I see we are at an impasse, and I must be on my way. Thank you for a delightful meal, Monsieur Dewavrin. And good luck to you, sir," he said, nodding to Auguste.

"Good day," Auguste replied. Monsieur Calin did not like his work, nor him, it seemed, but he would not beg for his acceptance. He must gain the commission another way.

"I will see you out." Dewavrin followed his guest through the house.

Rodin looked out at the row of birch trees that marked the end of the property line. Their regal white bark and flittering leaves stood out in the sea of green. He would continue forward with his plan: see the town of Calais and find a location for the monument.

Dewavrin returned, a newspaper tucked under his arm. "I must apologize for him. You know I disagree. Your piece is magnificent, in my view. Even the painter Jean Cazin came to your defense. I know fellow artists speak out for one another at times, but he seemed very impassioned by your design."

"I'm grateful for his aid," Rodin said. He would owe Cazin a favor after this pledge of support.

Dewavrin went silent and watched a lark flutter about in a nearby tree.

"You have something to say." Rodin perched on the edge of his chair. He knew by the man's hesitance to speak, it was news he'd rather not hear. Dread pooled in the pit of his stomach. "What is it, Omer?"

"In the newspaper yesterday, the *Patriote* . . ." He stroked his mustache. "Well, you know how Calin feels about your design. There are others. And now that I'm no longer mayor, they feel the need to make their opinions known."

Auguste stuck out his chin. "This isn't the first time my designs have been rejected—or ridiculed, for that matter."

"Apparently one of the ministers has bent the ear of a local journalist. They've written a review of your design." His eyes were contrite, but his paunchy cheeks puffed in indignation.

"May I?" Auguste held out his hand.

"Are you certain that's best?"

"I read all of my reviews. Since the piece is not yet finished, I find it curious the council should feel so strongly already."

He scanned the text. They had missed the point of his design completely, just as Calin had. In fact, it could have been Calin himself who had submitted the article.

"*Alors?*" Dewavrin asked.

"Their faces show 'sorrow, despair, and endless depression.'" Rodin smacked the offensive newspaper with his hand. The noise spooked a robin searching for crumbs near their feet. It fled to the cover of the trees.

"My figures display a pain *si intense, si claire,* the councilors squirm in their seats. They feel their own cowardice when they view the disquiet of a man marching to his death."

Dewavrin nodded. "It was a backhanded approach to knocking you out of the running for the commission."

Auguste continued reading. "'This doesn't represent what the citizens wish to see.' And how would they know? No one has had the chance to see it! 'The cube shape is "graceless"!'" He tore the article from the paper and stood. "No man is exalted when the spidery fingers of death grasp our souls and pull us to the underworld. These cowards cannot bear to face their own fate!"

"I apologize for their ignorance," Omer said quietly.

Auguste met his gaze. "You need not apologize for them. I need a walk."

He forged a path quickly through the grass. The bastards had used the media to oust him as a top contender.

Two could play at that game.

Chapter 17

Camille rolled the beaded fringe on her handbag between her thumb and forefinger. The baubles glittered each time the carriage passed beneath a streetlamp. She had borrowed Louise's favorite handbag for the occasion—a writer's salon across town. She couldn't wait to introduce Paul to real writers. He had begun writing a play; no doubt he could use advice from experts.

She bumped her brother with her shoulder. "You're quiet this evening. Aren't you excited?"

"Do you know these people?" Paul's voice cracked.

"You're nervous." She squeezed his hand in hers. "Stick close and I will introduce you to a few people. I don't know many, but Giganti will meet us there."

"Isn't it uncouth to invite the hired help?" Paul asked.

"He isn't just the 'hired help'; he's my friend. Besides, no one will know who he is. He's likely to be in a back room with some other man."

Paul cringed beside her. "You mean he is . . . he—"

"Is intimate with men? Yes." A smile curved her lips. Her little Paul was growing up.

"I don't know, Camille. Maybe I should sit in a bar and wait until you're finished."

She shot him a weary look. "Don't you want to meet others who share your passion for writing?"

His brow furrowed. "I won't have a thing to say to them."

"You're seventeen. You will figure it out." She pinched his cheek. "It's time to be a man."

He swatted her hand away. "Then treat me like one."

A balmy night breeze swirled around them in the hackney cab and Camille held her hat to her head. She felt a little guilty luring her brother to such a place. The last salon she had attended, Émile Zola had shown, followed by a pack of friends and fans. Everyone had gotten blistered on spirits and opium, herself included. She had even kissed a gentleman she didn't know, though when she had closed her eyes, there was only one image, one sloping nose and pair of soft lips, one beard grazing her cheek that she'd imagined. She wrinkled her nose at the memory—the stranger had tasted of tobacco and Pernod, nothing at all like Rodin.

A nervous twitch worked its way into her hands. She rubbed her thumb and forefinger together. What if Rodin was there tonight? Her resolve not to be near him felt on shaky ground beneath dark skies and winking streetlamps, and plenty of booze that would be imbibed. She squeezed Paul's knee with all her might.

"Ouch! What did you do that for?" He rubbed the sore spot where her thumb had dug into his flesh.

Why had she? She didn't know, really. Emotion raged through her like a fire at times and she could not contain it. The thought of seeing Auguste tonight . . .

The hackney stopped in front of a nondescript yet elegant home on the outskirts of the Latin Quarter.

At the door, a maid escorted them inside.

Paul gasped.

The hall gleamed in Arabian tiles; cerulean, ochre, and goldenrod flowed into the form of a large peacock on the wall. Orbs of brass and stained glass swung overhead, casting a rainbow glow about the room. Silk curtains swathed the front windows and laughter erupted in the room beyond.

"Brilliant!" Paul squeezed Camille's hand. "I'm already glad you made me come."

She laughed. "Let's get a drink."

They wound through the crowd to a table laden with glasses and a punch bowl filled with red liquid. Camille bent to sniff the concoction. Her nose burned from the sharp alcohol fumes. "The hair on my face is singed just from smelling that," she said.

Paul laughed. "It looks frightful."

Camille moved to the end of the table to take inventory of their choices. An array of glasses and bottles had been carefully laid out and a footman poised, prepared to pour.

"There is guignolet, a cherry liqueur which I adore, and some sort of brandy." Camille pointed from one bottle to the other. "It's probably Armagnac. And this"—she selected two pontarlier glasses from the final row—"is absinthe."

"We will have absinthe," she said to the footman.

"*Très bien*, mademoiselle."

The footman poured a portion of absinthe into the bottom of the glasses. Next he placed a perforated spoon over the rim and set a sugar cube atop it. Paul watched intently as he poured cold water over the cube. The sugar dissolved slowly, turning the liquor in the glass to a murky green liquid. After a quick stir, the footman handed Camille her glass, then prepared Paul's.

"You know I prefer brandy or beer," Paul said.

Camille sipped from her pontarlier glass. "Just try it."

"I don't trust you. Your eyes are full of mischief."

"Don't be such a girl," she said.

He glared at her and took a drink. He sputtered on the burning liquid.

"Push through the burn and your limbs will tingle. It's a delicious feeling."

He swigged from the glass again. "It tastes like a meadow."

She smiled. "It's floral, yes. Shall we?" She linked her arm through his and led him around the room.

Camille did not recognize a single person, but the alcohol emboldened her and she interrupted more than one conversation. She paused at the refreshment table to have her glass refilled.

"Excuse me, but did you say your name is Mademoiselle Claudel?" a Monsieur Jules Dalou asked. "You are Rodin's student?"

"Yes," she said, taking in his sunken cheeks and the challenge in his eyes.

The man studied her with interest and leaned closer, his hot breath on her cheek. "I am a sculptor as well. An old friend of Auguste's. If you should find yourself in want of more reliable instruction . . ." His eyes fell upon her chest.

Camille shuddered inwardly at his lecherous look, yet met his gaze directly. "Monsieur Rodin is a fine tutor and, in truth, a friend. Please respect him in my presence."

Monsieur Dalou gave her a sickly smile that did not touch his eyes. "He is my friend as well. I've known him for years."

"It shows," she said, her tone curt.

"If you will excuse us," Paul said, leading her away.

"The nerve of that man!" she said. He had no interest in helping her unless she bedded him. If she did not know better, she would think him out for revenge against Auguste.

The remainder of the evening Camille wove through the crowd, watching for the face that was most dear. As the hours clicked by, she felt a mingled sense of relief and frustration—Rodin had not come. She plucked a tin of sugared lemon drops from the refreshment table. She would soothe her disappointment with sweets. It was best he had not come, at any rate. She had come to enjoy herself, not to spend her time trying to ignore him.

The voices grew louder and more animated with the passing of each hour. After finishing her absinthe, Camille coaxed Paul through a black silk drape used as a makeshift door to a room off the salon. A single lantern burned, rendering most of the room in shadow. A haze of smoke and the sweet flowery scent of opium permeated the small space. A man with whiskers and a loosened cravat puffed from a bamboo pipe coated with silver. Two couples petted each other openly in the far corners of the room, and a gentleman read a poem aloud from a pocket notebook. Everyone lounged on an array of silk pillows on the floor.

Camille watched Paul's face with delight. He stared through hooded lids and his mouth lay open, his fourth glass of absinthe cradled in his right hand. She giggled. It was good for him, the relaxation. He spent far too much time fussing over his marks in school and his obsessive propriety. Yet judging by his stagger, she would need to get him home soon.

"I've never seen so many hedonists in my life!" Paul said loud enough for the entire room to hear. "Wait until I tell Marc."

Camille smothered a laugh. Lovers on display, an opium den and its blackened souls therein—his new devout friend would lap up the lurid details. She guessed Marc was in love with Paul, but far too pious to act upon it. And a good thing; Paul fawned over their neighbor Cécile, though he tried to hide it.

Paul cupped a hand over his mouth and attempted a whisper. "Does that man have his hand down her dress?"

The poet paused in his reading to scowl at the offending party.

Paul stumbled forward and slammed his head on a beam jutting down from the low ceiling. "Damn!" Laughter floated through the room.

A gentleman sprawled across a vermillion pillow untangled himself from his position on the floor, jumped to his feet, and approached. A familiar face framed with dark curling hair emerged through the smoky haze.

"Camille! I thought you hadn't come." Giganti kissed her cheeks. "And you must be Paul?"

"Who are you?" Paul slurred his words.

Camille took the empty pontarlier glass from Paul's hand. "We were just leaving."

"No, no. Let's stay." Paul pitched forward. A lock of hair fell across his forehead. "I want another drink."

Camille crossed her arms over her chest. "Like hell. I don't need you vomiting on me on the ride home."

"I'll escort you." Giganti tilted his head in Paul's direction. "You may need some assistance."

"You're sure? I hate to take you away from a good party."

"I prefer your company any day." Giganti kissed her cheek.

Paul pushed aside the fabric and stumbled into the main room. They buffered him on either side and half-dragged him through the crowd.

"Let go of me!" He struggled against Camille's grip. "I can walk!"

A chorus of laughter followed them. At last they reached the door and thrust him into the street. Giganti jogged to the end of the block and whistled at a line of hackney cabs parked outside a bustling dance hall. One pulled from the line and he jumped inside. When it stopped, Giganti helped Paul into a seat.

Camille threw her arm around her brother. A sheen of sweat broke out on his brow and all color drained from his face.

"*Allons-y* and hurry!" Giganti called to the driver.

"It's my fault," she said. "I shouldn't have let him drink so much in the first place. And the cigar didn't help. But I couldn't resist. He needed to enjoy himself."

Paul groaned. "My head is spinning."

"Deep breaths, man," Giganti said. "Don't lose it here."

"If you *cons* vomit in my cab, you'll pay triple!" the driver called over his shoulder. He snapped the reins, urging the horses to go faster.

The cart jerked forward and Paul fell into Camille, then slumped against her arm. She patted his hair. A little nap would take the edge off.

Giganti chuckled.

Twenty minutes later, they thundered down the Boulevard de Port-Royal. As the house drew nearer, Camille noted the darkened windows. No one had waited up for them and she was glad for it.

She shook Paul, but he didn't stir. "Paul! We're home!" She shook him once more.

"He's out," Giganti said.

"Whoa." The driver slowed the horses and the carriage came to a halt. "Now, get out!" He leered at them, grease glistening on his face and hair, even in the dull lamplight. He probably hadn't bathed in weeks.

"With pleasure!" Camille sneered. The man didn't have to be such an ingrate.

They hauled Paul's leaden body out of the cab. Just as they reached the front door, something moved in the dark to their left. Camille's gaze darted to a nearby doorway. She gripped Paul's arm tighter. Thieves did not usually loiter on this end of the street, but she knew they could be anywhere.

"Who's there?" Giganti said.

A gentleman stepped out of the shadows. A familiar set of shoulders, a beret atop a serious face with flowing beard appeared.

Camille's stomach dropped and her heart thudded in her ears.

Rodin waited for her in the dark.

Chapter 18

꧁꧂

Auguste berated himself for pursuing Camille. He should have waited until Monday at the atelier to speak with her about the *Burghers*, but he wasn't certain she would be there. He hadn't seen her in the three weeks since he had returned from Calais. Such an idiot he was—she had been out all evening with Giganti. A twinge of pain twisted in his stomach. The two of them grew closer as she distanced herself from him. He might wish for her comforting words about the degrading article, but she did not need his comfort for anything—or him. Damn fool.

Swallowing his pride, Auguste walked toward them. "I beg your pardon. I didn't mean to frighten you. I wanted to discuss a few things with Mademoiselle Claudel, but I should have waited until next week. . . . I've been so consumed with this project. You understand that more than most, mademoiselle. But I can see you are occupied. I will go." He clapped his mouth closed, silently scolding himself once more for rambling.

Paul moaned and leaned his head atop Camille's.

Auguste raised an eyebrow. "Is he hurt? Do you need assistance?"

"I think we can manage, but can you wait for a moment?" Mademoiselle Claudel said. "Let me just bring Paul inside." She and Giganti dragged her brother into the apartment building and up the stairs.

Auguste clasped his hands behind his back and stared up at the moon. Stars speckled the sky like flecks of quartz in a slab of black granite. He wanted to know her thoughts on his recent version of the *Burghers*, and about the article in the *Patriote*, the Calais newspaper. He had written a rebuttal, point by point, to the offending review. As he had hoped, his supporters rallied to his aid quickly and the commission of the *Burghers* was his. Soon, he would receive the first advance payment. Yet, he still wished for her opinion on his piece. If that many had opposed his design, perhaps she could see improvements that he could not.

Auguste kicked a pebble in the street. He could not lie to himself. He needed to see her, beyond the piece, to persuade her not to run from him. He could behave himself—he wanted her near, even if he could not have her.

An ache throbbed inside him. God, how he wanted her.

The door swept open and Camille walked toward him. Tendrils of hair blew softly across her face and neck, and her gown's low neckline hugged the gentle slope of her breasts. The bare skin of her shoulders glowed pearly in the moonlight.

Giganti was on her heel. Rodin swallowed his desire.

"Monsieur Rodin, *bonsoir*," Giganti said.

"Giganti." Auguste tipped his hat.

The model turned to Camille and winked. "And goodnight to you, *mon amie*."

Rodin did not miss the exchange. They had their own secret, perhaps even at his expense. *Putain*, he swore under his breath. He wanted to flee and bury himself in his sketches. He looked down at his thick hands, swollen from the exertion of his day's work. Camille clearly wanted nothing to do with him. If only he could banish her from his mind.

For a moment, Camille watched Giganti walk briskly away, before turning to him with questioning eyes.

"Thank you," he said, "for agreeing to see me. I wanted to show you my new design of the *Burghers*, and—"

"Shall we go to your studio?" she asked. Something smoldered in her curved mouth and dark gaze.

He dared not hope. She had made it clear he should not cross the boundary between them. Yet his pulse accelerated.

"It's rather late," he said. "Are you certain?"

"Quite." Her smile widened.

They rode the distance by hackney cab in silence. Auguste clenched his fists as tension sparked between them in the dark. He must control himself, or he would drive her away.

When they reached the atelier, he unlocked the door and then lit several lanterns. "I have changed the structure," he began, "to emphasize the burghers' pain and their pride." He removed the sculpture's cloth covering.

Camille examined the maquette, now a midsize version of what the final piece would be. Auguste watched her expression for a sign.

A lock of hair sprang from a pin and floated down her back. His fingers ached to remove the remaining pins, fill his hands with her hair, and run his lips over the sensitive skin on her neck.

"It's perfect," she said. "Each face and form tells a story. Their anguish is exquisite."

As was his own. Auguste crossed his arms over his chest to keep his hands from reaching for her. "This is precisely what I told Monsieur Dewavrin in Calais, but the ministers disagree. They find the anguish despicable."

She ran her finger along the base of the figure. "It's about as far from despicable as can be." She locked him in her gaze. "It pulses with life and tormented beauty."

Auguste nodded, his pulse quickening once more.

"They do not understand you. Not as I do." Camille moved closer, never removing her eyes from the maquette, until her scent of amber enveloped him.

"That is true." His voice came deep, unsettled.

The brass clock on the desktop dinged on the other side of his office door. One o'clock, the dead of night.

Camille looked up once more and her blue eyes darkened. She stepped closer.

In a swift instant, he gathered her in his arms. She surrendered her restraint and crushed herself against him. He held her tighter as if she might slip away. He must possess her. She was *his*, this wild, impassioned creature. He would make her his.

Camille wrenched from him suddenly.

"Oh, *mon amour.*" A plea, and a confession.

Her eyes softened and she wrapped her arms about his middle, laying her face against his heart. It skipped in his chest. Could she hear it call for her?

"Mademoiselle—" he began.

"Camille," she said, her voice feather soft.

"Camille," he sighed. "I—"

"Shh." She put her finger to his lips and began to unfasten the buttons of his jacket, one by one. Next, his vest.

Auguste traced a shaking finger over the supple skin of her breasts, the roundness of her shoulders. This time, it was she who moaned, the only invitation he needed. He released her from the clothing that bound her. He would savor this delicacy of a woman, her stark contrasts of cold and heat, of light and dark, her sudden rage and melodious laugh. He would worship at her altar as Mother Nature intended, as she deserved. He would fill her.

In moments, she stood naked. Her porcelain skin glowed like marble in moonlight.

"My darling, beautiful Camille."

She took his hand and kissed it softly, then guided it to her breast.

With his hands he memorized the curves of her body, her silky skin, the bulge of muscle or bone, the sweep of hair.

She writhed under his touch. "Auguste, please," Camille sighed. "I can't bear it."

The sound of his name on her lips set his blood to boiling. She belonged to him. At last he pushed himself inside her. She gasped. "Did I hurt you?" he whispered, then brushed his lips over her cheekbone and temple. He knew he must be gentle.

"Do it again," she said, voice thick with longing, and clasped her arms around his neck.

They made love and lay entwined together, the hours dissolving too quickly.

After a spell of hazy contentment, Auguste said, "How long I have dreamed of you. We have found each other, at last."

"And what are we to do now?" she whispered.

"Create, *mon amour*, together. Stun the world with our art."

"Together." Her lips stretched into a smile, her laughing eyes pools of agate.

He kissed her deeply, until emotion welled from the pit of his being and filled every part of him—intoxication of the most dangerous kind. She curled next to him and he wrapped around her, relishing her warmth.

When first light peeked eagerly through the windows, Camille stood and dressed. He watched her, took in the planes of her body, her sinuous movement.

Auguste sat up with a start. A lover, a kiss. His mind whirred despite his fatigue and his hands itched to draw her portrait.

Camille turned to him, a faint smile hidden in the apples of her cheeks, then slipped from the room without a word.

ॐ

Camille hunched over a pile of sketches while Jessie swept loose chips of plaster, clay, and sawdust into a pile. The sky had gone black and a night breeze stirred from the street and streamed through the open window. She could not stop thinking of Auguste—his lips, his skin on hers. She sighed and pushed aside another drawing of *Shakuntala*. She had the figure's stance wrong. The woman should rest her head on her lover in quiet surrender and forgiveness.

A flash of Auguste's face hovering above hers, his ecstasy, filled her with longing. She had made love to him twice more, each time leaving him behind, reaching for her. She offered her body to him for her own needs, not to be his mistress or his pawn. He kept a woman at home for that, or so she told herself.

The first inkling of guilt swirled in her stomach. But they were not married and Auguste had yet to mention Rose Beuret. She could not be so important.

The soft scratching of straw against wood floor and the sway of Jessie's skirt entranced her. Soon Camille's focus blurred and she heard his voice in her ear. *Mon amour*, the beautiful phrases he whispered to her, the secrets that were all theirs.

"What are you thinking about?" Jessie asked. She bent to scoop debris into a rusty dustpan.

Camille's reverie rippled and faded. "*Rien de tout.*"

"It isn't 'nothing.' You have had that look of enchantment about you for two weeks at least. It is him, isn't it?"

One of two lanterns guttered and went out. Smoke curled through the top of the glass bulb toward the ceiling.

"Rats." Camille carried one of the remaining lanterns to her desk. "I've got at least another hour to do and we need more gas."

"You cannot be serious." Jessie planted one hand on her hip. "You've been working for fifteen hours."

Camille studied Jessie's face. Her thick curls sagged, her mouth turned down at the corners. Jessie needed sleep, possibly a vacation. Her last three pieces had been rejected by the Salon and now her disenchantment colored her usual bright humor a dull shade of gray.

"I need to get this sketch right and I'm not going to bed until I do."

Jessie recommenced her sweeping. "What were you thinking just now? Do not tell me it is *Shakuntala*."

"Care for a glass?" Camille changed the subject. "I could use a stiff beverage before finishing here."

They dressed and, huddling together, walked swiftly to their destination.

"I have something to tell you," Camille said. "You won't like it."

Jessie peered at her in the dark. "It *is* Monsieur Rodin."

Camille crossed her arms over her chest. "We've—"

"Do not tell me," Jessie said quickly. "I don't want to know."

Camille frowned. A rush of anger swept through her. She cared deeply for Jessie, but she needn't be judged by her. Her friend still possessed such prudish values at heart, despite her wish to be viewed as daring. It irked her at times.

"He takes advantage of you." Jessie's tone belied her concern. "He has everything. What will you do when he finishes with you and tosses you aside? You will not be able to benefit from his connections or his instruction. He will leave you with nothing."

Camille's head began to buzz. "*I* take advantage of *him*. Have you ever thought of that?"

Jessie pulled back, face incredulous. "Really, Camille. That's absurd."

She stopped in the middle of the cobbled boulevard, hands on her hips. "And why is that?" Rage clogged her throat.

"I've witnessed your moony expression these last weeks. Either you are oblivious to your own feelings or you lie to yourself. This whole thing is a terrible idea and it's just wrong. Your parents would be furious."

"My parents?" Camille barked an angry laugh. "I live by my own rules and no one else's. I always have. You are jealous of my success."

"Come, Camille. You cannot really think I am jealous of you. You, who make others feel awkward with your antics, who pores over her work to the point of obsession. You must pace yourself, yet you do not seem to know how. And now Monsieur Rodin? Can you imagine how the poor woman he lives with must feel? You will be deemed—"

"I am finished with this conversation." She turned on her heel and stalked back to the studio, her head ready to explode.

Jessie had some nerve. Camille did feel guilty, she must admit, but it was Auguste's responsibility to discuss his affairs with his live-in lover, not hers. Besides, she could succeed with or without him if she chose to, on her own terms. She walked an extra block under the streetlamps and past darkened storefronts to calm her nerves. She clenched her hands into fists. Her time would come, and there would be plenty of commissions. She felt that truth course through her veins. People would know her name. She turned the final corner and headed toward her atelier.

But what if . . . what if Jessie were right? What if Auguste used her and cast her aside? She must leave him first.

The hollow thud of footsteps on stone echoed behind her. A chill ran over her skin and she glanced over her shoulder. Nothing but shadowed buildings.

She dismissed her alarm. It was merely a gentleman returning home after a drunken evening, or perhaps a woman like Camille, eager to reach her destination.

A veil of mist clung to her skirts, her arms and face. Yet something felt odd. The buzzing grew louder and her head ached.

She increased her pace. The footsteps gained momentum in time with hers. Alarm raced down her spine. She could see her atelier door. Faster, she must move faster. The sound of thundering feet drummed in her head. A metallic tang lingered on her tongue and her heart skipped in her chest.

Camille lunged for the door handle and slipped her key into the lock, hands shaking. She leapt inside and slammed the door, locking it quickly behind her. Her breath came in shallow gasps in the dark. Who was following her?

She crept to the window and peeked through drapes made of bedsheets to wait for the mystery person to pass. A minute ticked by and still no one came. Had they changed their mind once she had escaped? She shuddered at the thought of being caught in the street.

Light. She needed light to banish the dark.

Camille fumbled in the shadows. Her fingers brushed the pointed end of a rasp, the glazed surface of a pottery bowl, and a metal tube of paint. Finally, her hand closed around the waxy cylinder of a candle and a small rectangular box. She slid the cover open, retrieved a match, and struck the end against the box's gritty strip. A flame flickered to life, burned the phosphorus-tipped head, and engulfed the wooden stick. She lit the candle just as the heat licked her fingertips.

How ghostly the room appeared by candlelight—a graveyard of broken pieces, half-finished human forms covered in rags, and heads with hollow eyes searching for their missing bodies. She shivered and lit the gas lamp. And there, atop her desk, sat a blob of clay, the wood handle of a plaster knife protruding from it.

Bumps ran over Camille's arms. She hadn't done that—had she? She had been angry earlier, but . . . She wrenched the knife from the mound of clay. A deep groove remained where the utensil had penetrated its pliable body. She didn't always remember her actions during a tirade. Rage welled from her toes and swept over her, strangling her sense of reason. She detested how it took hold of her, but she couldn't seem to control it. Yet she did not recall being angry today.

Not this time. She knew she had not stabbed the clay. And Jessie had not returned. She would have passed her in the street.

Camille's pulse sped up once more. A metallic taste flooded her mouth. Stumbling, she flew around the room, examining every surface, each sculpture, the teakettle, the ashtray overflowing with squished cigarettes. All appeared normal but the plaster bust, which now sat askance.

A tremor of fear shook her to the core.

Her heart thundered against her ribs. She raced back to the window and peered out: doorways empty and cloaked in shadow; an abandoned bicycle missing a wheel and garbage littering the street; a sky swaddled in night's blanket. Nothing appeared out of the ordinary.

Until someone, posed just around the corner of the adjacent street, stirred in the dark.

Chapter 19

꧁

"I am being followed." Camille chose a fig from the picnic basket and sank her teeth into its gritty flesh.

Giganti stretched out on the blanket, tucked his hands under his head, and stared up at the spring sky. "Who would follow you?"

"Monsieur Rodin," she said without hesitation. She shuddered at the memory of the dark figure in the street, the knife in the clay.

A roar of laughter split the air. "Monsieur Rodin?" He sat up. "Following you? Why would he do that?"

Camille chucked a fig at him. "Is he so above me?"

"I just cannot see him stalking you from the shadows. He doesn't seem the sort." Giganti ran a hand through his dark curls and adjusted his posture on the lawn. He looked like a model even when he wasn't trying, with his squared jaw, pursed lips, and tawny eyes. "Honestly, what would he gain by following you?"

Offended, Camille gathered her things and stuffed them into the basket. "What do you mean? He wants my ideas to claim for himself."

"Camille." Giganti took the basket from her hands. "You are a brilliant artist. No one can take that from you. But Rodin is as brilliant as you, so why would he attempt to steal your ideas?"

"I don't know."

Camille frowned. She wasn't sure why she thought Auguste had followed her. She hadn't seen him, exactly. And his words—he had said many beautiful things to her. Would he lie? Her heart tangled with her reasoning.

"Rodin has feelings for you. I've seen the way he looks at you." He squeezed her knee. "But for some reason you believe he would steal from you. It simply isn't his way."

She brushed a few errant blades of grass from her skirts. "You don't know for certain how he feels about me, do you?"

"No."

"Nor do I."

Giganti laughed.

"But Jessie has plenty of opinions about what I should do." Camille looked out at the families walking together, enjoying the sunshine and unseasonal warmth.

He clucked his tongue. "And you measure yourself by the young Englishwoman who will be married before she has made a name for herself? Come, darling Camille, that isn't like you. She's talented, but you are a poet. A poet with stone, that is."

She leaned down and kissed him on the forehead.

"That has earned me a kiss? What would your Monsieur Rodin have to say about that?"

She grinned. "He wouldn't need your services anymore."

Giganti laughed again.

Camille cocked her head sideways and the sunlight warmed her exposed cheek. "We've had an argument, Jessie and me. I don't know what to say to her. She finds my relations with Auguste appalling. I told her she was jealous of my success." She looked to him for guidance.

"She likely is, but she will come around. Jessie cares about you. And if she doesn't, you don't need her." He squeezed her gloved hand. "Besides, you have me. I will always be your friend."

"What would I do without you?"

❧

Sunlight bathed the gravel walk and the expanse of emerald lawn, and splashed over Camille and Paul, who rested on a park bench after a leisurely stroll. Paul crossed his ankles and leaned back in a young man's easy pose. He watched the older gentlemen play *boules* beneath the trees in their rectangular court of crushed stone. A stout man in a derby hat launched his first *boule*. The wooden ball, made of boxwood root studded with nails, rolled toward its target. It spun and stopped just shy of bumping the smaller ball out of place.

The ball's owner threw his hands in the air and whooped with glee. Another player whistled.

"He's won again," Paul said. He chewed listlessly on a long stalk of grass.

Another of the men scowled but ribbed the winner. They began to bicker good-naturedly among themselves.

Camille hated that she had argued with Jessie. She regretted her words and wished she had never told her about Auguste. No matter what Giganti said, she feared she had run off a dear friend. Besides, perhaps Jessie was right. Why would Rodin treat her differently from every other muse?

But the thought of dismissing him tore at her insides. *Merde.* She cared for him already.

"Read to me, Paul." She laid her head on his shoulder and closed her eyes, willing herself to forget poetic whisperings and strong hands, gentle on her skin.

He picked up a book from the bench. An article he'd stuffed in the center fluttered to his lap. "Oh, I saved this for you." He unfolded the crinkled paper.

"What's this?" She snatched the scrap from his fingers.

"You haven't seen it?" He sat up straighter, his face clouded with regret. "Mother assumed you had. She was about to throw it into the wastebasket. Yesterday's paper."

"Mother meant to hide it from me, I'm sure."

"She quarrels with you, but she wouldn't hide this from you, Camille."

She screwed her face into a scowl. "I wouldn't doubt it for a second. I'm surprised you do. When is the last time she congratulated you on your marks at school?"

"I don't expect her to applaud my achievements. She has never even embraced me."

The smallest stab of regret pierced her heart. Warmth and affection were not among Mother's traits.

"Did she tell you the Royal Academy in London accepted my piece?" she said. "*Giganti* will be shown."

"Congratulations!" He squeezed her arm. "You're making your way."

"Jessie's *Day Dreams* was accepted as well. I had hoped to travel with her to England this month."

"And you aren't going now?"

She shrugged. "We've had an argument."

"Women love the dramatics." He cocked a lopsided grin at her. "But it will pass."

She smoothed the paper once more. "I hope you're right."

"Well? Are you going to read the article or must I?"

Camille scanned the text until she saw her name. It was another review of *Giganti*. Her breath hitched and her mouth curved into a smile. "'*Giganti*, by Camille Claudel, is lively and the bust's soulful eyes challenge the viewer to engage with it.'" She continued to read and her smile faded. "'Her style strikes a remarkable resemblance to her teacher, Auguste Rodin, one of the most daring sculptors of our time. Expect to see more from the promising Mademoiselle Claudel.'"

Her mood darkened.

"He compares you to Monsieur Rodin, sister!" He threw his arm about her shoulders. "Did you see that—'one of the most daring sculptors of our time'? His popularity is growing. That could mean only good things for you. I pray for you every night."

She bristled with anger. "I am nothing but a toady. One of Rodin's innumerable admirers."

The pack of gentlemen shouted. A man with a rotund middle and jowls waved his hand about, his voice passionate. Someone had knocked the target out of its position, throwing the whole game of *boules*.

"I agree you must be cautious," Paul said. "You need to forge your own identity." He placed his hands on her shoulders and forced her to meet his eyes. "But he is an excellent teacher. You've said so yourself. And you need him, for now. He will help you win commissions."

"His *Idyll of Ixelles* was rejected by the Royal Academy and my sculpture was accepted. I can win my own commissions," she said, her tone defiant.

But her words felt hollow, even to her. She *needed* him, and she didn't need anyone.

"We'll storm the literary and art world. Throw them all in a tizzy with our brilliance." Paul stood and held out his hand. She accepted it, and rumpled his perfect hair. He laughed and swatted at her. "Let's go home."

⌘

That afternoon, Camille strolled through the *quartier* near her atelier. She grew tired of avoiding Jessie. She paused before a chocolatier and put her face to the glass. A woman leaned over a vat, stirring a pool of melted chocolate with a paddle. The rich mixture whirled in a funnel shape and glided over the wooden blade with each stroke. Jessie loved sweets. Perhaps a gift would ease the tension.

Something bumped Camille's ankle. She looked down to find a kitten with black fur and white paws rubbing against her. The animal ducked under the hem of her skirt and the scratchy edge of a kitten tongue lapped against her stocking-clad leg. She laughed and bent to retrieve it.

"Where do you belong, *minou*?" She held it at eye level, the kitten's back legs dangling. Two large yellow moons peered back her. It kicked and swayed, attempting to leap to flat ground, and finally sank its tiny teeth into her hand.

"Ouch! You're a feisty little girl, aren't you?" She held the animal against her and stroked its matted fur. Soft vibrations of kitten happiness rumbled in its throat. Given its meager frame and filthiness, the kitten must be a stray.

"Perhaps you should go home with me," Camille said. She had always loved cats, but had never been allowed to own one.

The *minou* mewed in agreement.

She tucked the animal firmly against her, its fur tickling her chin, and walked to her atelier. Jessie adored animals as well; she had spoken of her cats at home many times.

When she entered, Jessie looked up from her piece briefly, and then trained her gaze on her bust once more.

"I've brought you a gift," Camille said, breaking their week of silence. "This is Minou."

"Oh?" Jessie picked up a plaster chisel and continued to shape a lace collar.

Camille's hope plummeted. She wanted to put the argument behind them and forget it had ever happened. But it seemed a gift was not enough. She must apologize and plead for forgiveness—not her favorite thing to do.

"I—" the girls said in unison.

Jessie laughed softly. "Let's just forget it, shall we? I should not have been as forthright as I was. It is not my business, nor is it my right to tell you how you should behave. If you are happy, that is all that matters to me. I apologize."

"And my tantrum. The things I said . . ."

"Forgiven!" Jessie crossed the room, tool in hand, and kissed her cheek. "Of course you may see whom you wish, Monsieur Rodin included. Who am I to predict how things will go? Besides, given his humor these last few months, I would say he's quite taken with you."

Camille gave her a rueful smile. "I'm not sure that's a positive thing. Did you see the review of *Giganti*?"

"Yes, congratulations! It was a wonderful review. My friend the 'promising sculptor.'" She looked down. "I must admit, I have struggled with my rejections."

Camille squeezed her arm. "Don't give up hope. You are an excellent sculptor." She smiled. "Plus, your piece was accepted in London! Paris must be soon to follow."

"You really think so?" Hope lit her eyes.

"Absolutely. I believe in you. And I'm proud to work alongside you." Camille meant it. Jessie's style might be different from hers, but her works were beautiful, inspired.

Jessie wiped her hands and reached for the kitten. "May I?"

Minou startled at her touch and leapt to the floor, landing on all four paws.

"Little Minou," Jessie sang in a soft voice. She bent to pet the kitten, which spooked and shot across the room. She laughed and stood. "It seems the kitten belongs to you, not me." Her smile faded at Camille's change of expression.

"The critic compared me to him. To Rodin. That is the third time I've heard it." Her jaw clenched. "I'm not sure what to do. I think I need to get away. Gain some room to think."

Jessie put down her tool. "I'm visiting my parents soon."

"Yes, I know."

"You are still invited to come, if you wish. We'll spend time in Peterborough and London. We cannot miss the Salon, now, can we?"

Camille hugged her. "I would be so grateful."

Jessie wrapped her arms about her. "We'll whisk you tidily away, then. I can't imagine attending Salon without you, at any rate. My parents will be thrilled to meet this talented Camille I always speak of." Jessie glanced at their new addition to the atelier. Minou batted the bottom edge of the bedsheet, which served as a window covering. "May we leave the kitten in your brother's care while we are on holiday?"

"Certainly."

"I'm afraid we will leave as early as next week. Does that suit you?"

"I hoped you would say that."

Chapter 20

※

The ferry moved out to sea and the Calais port disappeared behind a curtain of fog as if erased from existence. The town, even France herself, became a mere memory.

As would *he*, or so Camille told herself.

She sucked in a lungful of briny air and closed her eyes. To be adrift at sea, cool fog coating her skin and no solid sense of earth beneath her feet, reflected her mood.

She floated in a space between.

The foghorn blared its melancholy cry. Her eyes fluttered open to a scene of a packed deck, passengers in an array of hats and overcoats to shield them against the wind. Jessie sat beside her, thumbing through a novel. Camille picked up her own book, a guide of Roman antiquities. She studied the classical sculptors even if she did not wish to emulate their style. There was always more to learn.

A half hour passed and she moved to the bow. The sun burned away the mist and in the distance, the chalky cliffs of Dover stood like a ghostly fortress, a great dividing wall between sea and civilization. Black water and bleached rock imprinted their image on her mind. Perhaps she would paint a watercolor when they arrived; she had been assured they would have all the supplies they needed to sketch and paint. What luck the Lipscombs had, to be so well off.

Jessie had spoken fondly of her parents, particularly her mother. Camille couldn't imagine a mother who caressed her hair, left cheerful notes on her pillow, a loving woman who celebrated each of her accomplishments with kisses, special cakes, and tea. Jessie had it all.

Camille gripped the railing. Wind whipped through her skirts and over her skin. But she did not need any of it—she only needed her work. Her needs and emotions could be channeled into clay and rock, a beautiful container for her sorrows and triumphs, her reflections.

A hand touched her shoulder and she turned.

"We'll be docking soon." Jessie held her hat to her head.

"What if your parents don't like me?" she asked, suddenly timid.

Jessie looked taken aback, then touched Camille's cheek with her free hand. "Impossible."

Camille smiled for the first time that day.

The Royal Academy at Burlington House stood exactly as Auguste remembered it: a proud building with two arms that hugged its central courtyard. Clouds draped the building's spires, poised to sweep over the facade and cover it completely. London possessed every variation of cloud cover, from soft mist to soupy fog laden with soot. He had thought Paris had unending cloudy days before he visited the dreary isle. At least he enjoyed English tea and crumpets slathered in clotted cream. His stomach rumbled at the thought; he hadn't eaten much in days. *Sa féroce amie* had departed to Peterborough without so much as a word.

Auguste still couldn't believe he had followed Camille to England. She ran from him, yet he could not let her go. When her defenses had melted in his arms, he had known what he must do—make her feel secure in his love, somehow. She feared depending on him. Christ, he had done everything he could for her and would always. Couldn't she see that yet?

Monsieur Gauchez at *l'Art* magazine had tried to put Auguste's requests off, but he had insisted the editor include a drawing of Camille's bust of Paul and an article about her in the next edition. Gauchez agreed, only with a bribe of drink and an advanced preview of a sketch Auguste planned to submit for the contest to win Victor Hugo's monument. Whatever it took to help her. She could not seem to help herself.

Rodin stuffed his right hand inside his trouser pocket. His fingers brushed aside a few shillings. He checked the other and found the crinkled missive from Mademoiselle Lipscomb. After some persuasion, she had agreed he could visit Wooton House, her family's estate. He had leapt at the invitation to dine with the Lipscombs, when it finally came. He shuffled his feet over the cobbles and the bottom of his shoes scuffed against the slick stone. Would Camille be angry with him for coming? Had he taken it too far, following her all the way to England? But she had left without explanation, and now her absence tortured him. He needed to be near her or he might . . . He might what? He cursed at himself. He must control this passion somehow. He acted like a madman, gripped by an illness he could not shake.

"Auguste Rodin," Gustave Natorp called through a crowd gathered around a juggler.

He turned to meet his former student, now friend. They would view the exhibit at the academy together. Gustave had no inkling Auguste had traveled to London to be near Camille, and it would remain that way.

"Have you got a shilling for the entrance fee?" Gustave asked, slightly out of breath. His hair had thinned considerably, exposing an almost pointed dome of a head.

"Yes. Shall we go?" Rodin stuffed the letter in his pocket once more, and with it, his anxiety.

⤐⦕⤏

The Lipscombs' house towered at the end of the lane. Camille would call it more of a museum than a home. Monsieur Lipscomb had made a fortune in the London Coal Exchange a few years back and had capitalized on the opportunity. Camille felt strangely alone in the rambling rooms and halls, a solitude she found at once comforting and disorienting. A cozy country home suited her far more.

She had been working on a new concept for a piece, but the viscous images flitted through her mind and whirled through her dreams just out of reach. She tapped her pencil against the tabletop. Though Jessie was reading on the sofa, her eyes darted from the page to Camille's profile every few minutes. She pretended not to see her friend's furtive glances. She knew whatever it was, Jessie would share it soon enough, though it made her ill at ease.

After an hour, Jessie snapped her book closed. "There's something I need to tell you."

"I know. I have caught you staring at me all afternoon." Camille looked up to find Jessie's face carved with worry and her eyes contrite. "You look like a naughty schoolgirl. What have you done?"

Jessie sighed. "I've been meaning to tell you all week, but couldn't bring myself to do it."

Madame Lipscomb stepped into the room, her pale flowered gown swishing around her feet. A straw hat with pink ribbons perched on her head. "I'm going into town before our guest arrives. Care to join me, ladies?"

"No, thank you. I'd like the chance to speak with Camille in confidence." Jessie gave her mother a knowing look. "And then we'll need to tidy up."

"Of course, dear. I won't be long." Madame Lipscomb disappeared through the doorway, her mules clicking on the honey-colored floors.

"Shall we walk?" Jessie asked, standing.

Camille chewed her lip. She had seen the glance between mother and daughter. Jessie was not dramatic and never teased. She wondered what could warrant such behavior.

After donning her hat, Camille followed her friend along the stone path through the Lipscombs' garden. They crossed beneath a trellis threaded with vines, through a thicket of white tea roses and scarlet carnations, fuchsia foxgloves with their bell-shaped heads and spotted centers, and a dozen varieties of flowers she could not name, all arranged to perfection. Camille moved ahead, beyond the formal garden to a field of tall grass bursting with cornflowers, their indigo blooms vivid as the summer sky overhead. She freed her skirt from a prickly bramble and plucked a stray English daisy.

Jessie stopped beside her. "Beautiful, isn't it? It's still hard to believe our change in fortune sometimes. Wooton House has become a real home, ever so quickly."

"Out with it, Jessie." Camille pushed through the tall grass. A flurry of tiny white-winged moths ascended from their resting place, fluttered around her head, and scattered.

"I have received a letter from Monsieur Rodin. It arrived in the post a week ago." She watched her face for telltale signs of emotion.

Camille shielded her eyes from the sunlight and looked out over the garden. "Oh?" She forced a light tone. "And what did he have to say?"

"He suffers. The man is quite in love with you."

"He doesn't love me. He lusts for me, and the moment I call myself his mistress, he will discard me." She pitched the bloom to the ground.

"I know you care for him."

Camille crossed her arms over her chest. "My art is what matters. Above all else, it comes first. This . . . thing between us is inconsequential. I refuse to behave capriciously and throw away my opportunities. He must remain my teacher and nothing more," she said firmly. "I came here in part to escape him. It's best I don't see him."

Jessie cringed. "Then you won't be happy with me—or Mother. She invited him to join us for dinner, and to stay with us, tomorrow evening."

"Why would you agree to it?" Anger throbbed in Camille's temples.

"I know how you feel, but you must also consider how I feel. And my parents," she added. "He is my teacher, too, and my parents admire what he has done for me as an artist. They wish to thank him personally."

A zephyr rolled over the field, and the flowers swayed and bent their heads to the force greater than they.

Camille threw her hands in the air and stormed past Jessie.

"Wait!" Jessie hurried after her, skirts rustling in the grass.

Blood pounded in Camille's ears. Auguste pursued her! Yet despite her anger, unbidden pleasure streaked through her limbs. A foolish pleasure, she chided herself. She had nothing to gain by giving in to her . . . heart. Oh, God. Her heart.

An image flashed in her mind. One of flowing fabric, movement like the sway of golden grass. She raced toward the house for her pencil and paper. Another flash came, of his face, his hands.

The spark of inspiration slipped through her fingers.

❧

By the time Auguste's carriage arrived, Camille had disappeared into the garden with her sketchbook. The remainder of the afternoon she spent in her bedroom with the day's post from France. She refolded a letter from Paul. He would join her and the Lipscombs on their jaunt to the Isle of Wight next month. She couldn't wait to see him. Her brother had ached to travel his entire life and would now have the chance.

The clock dinged the hour. Ready or not, it was time to dine—time to face Auguste. She touched the jeweled comb in her hair. She couldn't put off joining the family a moment longer without offending her gracious hosts.

The salon was lavished in floral wallpaper in yellows and pinks, several lace adornments, and a scattering of mahogany and cherry furniture. Monsieur and Madame Lipscomb sat across from one another on a pair of silk-covered settees, and Auguste, dressed in a black suit, posed on the edge of a burnished leather chaise, the only piece of furniture that looked out of place in its surroundings.

He stood at once and fixed his piercing eyes on Camille. The intensity of his demeanor radiated through the room.

She shivered under his unwavering attention. At once she felt torn—should she throw herself in his arms, or flee? How would she lock away her desire?

"You look lovely this evening," Madame Lipscomb said, surveying Camille's scarlet gown with low neckline trimmed in black lace. "It's so very French."

Camille gave a half smile of thanks. Not exactly the modest Victorian styles Madame Lipscomb wore daily, and she had planned it. A part of her wanted to torture Auguste—make him desire her, long for her, yet she would stay just out of reach.

"Mademoiselle Claudel, how nice to see you." Auguste's voice cracked from strained emotion.

Camille's anxiety turned to anger. He would not behave like a love-sick fool and embarrass her in front of the Lipscombs. She would look like a desperate young woman without sense, falling for her teacher—a common tale and always a dangerous venture for a woman.

"*Bonsoir*, Monsieur Rodin. I trust you've been able to rest after your journey?" Camille remained near the doorway.

"I did, *merci*. I was thrilled by the invitation to visit two of my best students. The studio feels empty without you and Mademoiselle Lipscomb." He crossed the room and, taking her by surprise, kissed her gently on each cheek. He smelled of sandalwood and longing.

Camille flushed and stepped out of his reach. "You flatter me, monsieur."

"Would you care for an aperitif?" Monsieur Lipscomb asked. "John was just going to pour sherry for us on the terrace."

A footman with slicked hair and white gloves moved through the room, tray in hand.

"The fresh air would be welcome." Rodin accepted a glass. He eyed Camille, the intensity welling in his eyes once more.

The footman passed Jessie and madame without offering them a glass. Too masculine a pastime, it seemed, to have a drink before dinner.

Like hell. Camille was not English. "Excuse me." She motioned to the tray. "I'll have one."

The footman paused and looked to Madame Lipscomb, who took a sudden interest in the overflowing pots of petunias lining the terrace.

"Very good, mademoiselle." He offered the tray to Camille.

She took a glass in one hand and placed her other on his forearm. "Wait." She chugged the dry liqueur, then choked as it burned her throat. The footman's eyes bulged in surprise. She took another crystal goblet. "*Merci.*"

Madame Lipscomb regarded her with concern.

Camille felt her impatience rise once more and moved to the open door leading to the terrace. The sun plunged toward the horizon, leaving a trail of blazing gold in its wake. She felt someone join her at her side, but didn't turn.

"Please be polite, for heaven's sake," Jessie whispered.

"Did you see the looks he gave me?" she whispered, her tone fierce. "Your parents must have noticed. I'm humiliated."

"You only confirm their suspicions with your behavior." Jessie slipped her arm around her middle for a quick squeeze of reassurance. "He will be gone soon."

"Monsieur Rodin, would you care to see the stables on the property?" Jessie's father said.

The men started through the garden.

"What in the world are you two whispering about?" madame asked. "Are you quarreling with Monsieur Rodin, Camille?"

"A quarrel of sorts, yes." She swigged from her sherry glass.

Jessie cast her mother a warning look. Madame Lipscomb forced a tight smile. "Well, let's try to enjoy the evening, shall we?"

Camille swallowed the lump of tears in her throat. Where had they come from? She wanted to run through the fields, far from her confusion. "I'll do my best," she said.

⚜

They dined amiably, though Camille could taste the tension in the air. She rubbed her thumb and forefinger together over and over in her lap. She wished Auguste would leave. She had enjoyed her stay with the Lipscombs and their adventures through neighboring towns a great deal. Why did he have to ruin it?

She sank her teeth into a bite of jam roly-poly. The soft yellow cake squished on her tongue and the sweetness of wild strawberry preserves filled her mouth. She forgot her unease for a moment. "Strawberry this time." She cut another bite. "*Délicieux.*"

"I had the cook make it for you, dear," Madame Lipscomb said. "I've noticed it is your favorite pudding."

"I could eat it every day," Camille said, scooping the last bit of preserves on her plate with a spoon.

"Perhaps we should take the recipe with us home to France," Auguste said, his voice light.

For the first time all evening, Camille looked at him directly. "Your wife can make it," she said. "And where is she? She didn't wish to travel with you? A holiday in England may have been just what she needed."

Auguste read the challenge in her eyes. "I traveled for business. I met Monsieur Natorp in London, but I also came to support my favorite students."

She snorted. He had sidestepped the mention of Rose Beuret completely, the scoundrel. And yet, a part of her wanted to take him by the hand and lie in the cornflower field. She hated herself for even thinking it. She took another drink of wine. Why must she feel so torn?

Jessie bit her lip. "Shall we move to the drawing room? I can play for you."

"Sounds lovely," Madame Lipscomb said.

Camille followed the party into the drawing room and sat at the far end of the room. Auguste sat across from her. The Lipscombs took their seats near the piano.

Jessie cast a worried glance her way and then began to play. A Scottish ballad filled the room.

"Melancholy, isn't it?" Camille said in a low voice so only Auguste could hear. "Like a lover scorned." She regarded him. His expression matched the tenor of the music. Her muddled emotions boiled to the surface and spilled over. "Why must you look at me like that? You're making a fool of me!"

Jessie's singing grew louder.

"I accepted a hospitable offer from the Lipscombs, happy to be near you, yet you are angry with me. Why did you leave without telling me?"

"You live with Rose Beuret—a woman I knew nothing about until recently—which I discovered, no thanks to you." Frustration strangled her. "I need to clear my head and yet you intrude upon my vacation, my space, and my thoughts. How am I to work when I can't escape you? I run from you and you chase me."

Hope dawned on his features. "You think of me?" He put out a hand instinctively to touch her.

She jumped to her feet. "Don't touch me."

Jessie stopped playing abruptly.

He reached for her once more. "Camille—"

"Please, go," she said. Her reason warred with her heart and she needed to escape, to untangle her confusion. She could not think in his presence. "If you won't leave, I'll stay locked in my room."

Pain filled Auguste's eyes, and Camille felt as if she had been stabbed. To hurt him made her throb with regret.

Jessie glared at Camille and rushed to Auguste's side. "Monsieur Rodin, my most ardent apologies."

He bowed his head slightly. "Thank you for the delicious meal. I'm going to retire for the evening. And if you would call a carriage for me at first light, I would be very grateful."

"Of course." Monsieur Lipscomb extended his hand and shook Rodin's vigorously. "If there is anything else I can get for you, please ask."

Auguste nodded and left the room, shoulders sagging.

Camille had gotten what she wanted, yet her insides collapsed.

⚬❦⚬

The train to Paris gained momentum as it pulled away from the Calais station, engines hissing and black smoke billowing over the platform in clouds of soot. A thin layer of grit blew in the open window and coated the floor, seats, and passengers. Rodin dusted off his trousers and leaned his head against the seat. He'd made an ass of himself chasing Camille to England. She had seen through his facade of visiting Gustave in London. She always saw through him.

"*Merde!*" he mumbled aloud. He bit his knuckle to keep from cursing more.

A woman seated in his car startled and gave him a look of disdain. She looked out the smudged windowpane. Her cerulean hat and expensive dress hinted at extreme wealth, femininity, and well-bred manners—the exact opposite of the precious woman he adored. How could he make Camille believe she could trust him? Yet there was Rose. . . . And he could not turn his back on her. It would not be honorable.

As the train increased its speed, Rodin concentrated on its rocking sensation beneath him. Octave Mirbeau, friend and critic, had invited him to show his work at Georges Petit's gallery in October with Renoir and others. Perhaps this salon would be the one—the one to bring him true recognition, and not the negative kind. He wanted *her* to be there, to support him and witness his triumph. At this moment, that was nothing but a dream.

Auguste squeezed his eyes closed. The image of Camille's skin beneath his hands, her rosy nipple in his mouth, struck him immediately. He shook his head. He had to get a grip on himself, clear his head for the upcoming exhibition. Yet he could not. The vision shimmered in his mind once more: He kneeled before her naked form in adulation, idolizing her all-consuming beauty.

He shot up in his seat and fished cigarette papers out of his pocket. Quickly he drew a woman seated on a pedestal and a man on his knees, his head resting against her naked abdomen in surrender. It was he, surrendered at her feet, his *Eternal Idol.*

❦

Black storm clouds glared at one another, as if readying for a brawl. Wind swept over Camille and gathered under her skirts, making the lower half of her body appear bulbous. Auguste had really gone. She had behaved like a child, scolded him, and he'd left. She still could not believe it, and it had been weeks ago. She wrapped her arms about herself. The rain soaked her through, washed away her tempestuous behavior and anger. She must learn to hold her noxious tongue.

She sauntered down the gravel lane and through the fragrant bushes nestling against the stone cottage where she slept. The charming abode sat at the edge of a rocky cliff, not more than a meter from the sea. The Isle of Wight was her favorite of all the places she'd visited in England. Paul adored it as well and had gone fishing with Monsieur Lipscomb every day. Her brother found inspiration in the quiet mornings for writing and dreaming. The corners of her lips turned up in a faint smile. The men had yet to catch a fish the entire visit.

A wave arced over the slate waters and broke on the stone at the edge of the property. One violent tempest and the cottage floor would be engulfed. She relished the wild beauty of the sea, the push and pull of currents, and the whirling eddies of cold water that carved out divots in the sand. Water was the most powerful of all, breaking down all in its path, even if slowly; a true force. She lowered herself to the short drop-off to the sea, removed her boots, and dangled her legs over the surf. Auguste was an unavoidable force. Warring against her emotions grew tedious and tiring. Her limbs quivered when he was near; her heart leapt at the sound of his voice. But what of Rose Beuret? The subject had remained taboo. Perhaps it should remain that way for now. *Dieu*, she missed him.

A gust of wind sent a spray of saltwater on her face, a dose of cold reality on this vacation from her life. It was time to go home.

❦

Midnight sky consumed the last rays of weary light, and the single flickering lamp became inadequate in the cavernous room. Auguste had scrubbed and scoured three stones, kneaded a rope of clay, and cleaned all of his tools—menial tasks to occupy his hands. Now they itched to mold something, anything, but he couldn't focus, and he couldn't see a damn thing. He dropped his maquette and heaved a sigh. "We're finished here."

Giganti relaxed from his twisted pose and stretched. He ran a hand through his tumbled curls and dressed quickly.

Auguste was too old for Camille and he was her teacher. What was he thinking? He had looming deadlines, a show to prepare for—no time for such folly, and yet . . . He crossed the studio and stood beneath the skeleton of his *Gates of Hell*. A tormented male reached for a woman twisting away from him, lust and fear marking her features. He traced the figures with his fingertip.

"*Veux-tu fumer?*" Giganti placed a pinch of tobacco on a square of hemp paper and rolled it into a cylinder.

"No." Rodin shook his head. He didn't want to smoke; he didn't want to eat; he didn't want to do anything. He kicked a hunk of dried plaster.

"Everything all right?" Giganti asked, dragging on his cigarette.

Auguste grunted and bent to pick up a cloth that had slipped off a nearby figure. "Well enough."

"You don't seem yourself, if I may say so. Whatever it is, I hope it passes."

Auguste didn't know if it would pass. He'd never been so consumed, outside of work. He didn't even believe in love, yet he felt as if he were burning alive. He stared at Giganti. The model would be a better match for Camille. He was younger, less encumbered by his work. Hell, he didn't have a woman at home, waiting for him to return every night.

A tap on the door startled them, a fumble of the latch, and then it opened. Camille entered without a bonnet or overcoat, and her dress was speckled with raindrops.

Auguste's breath caught in his throat. He hadn't laid eyes on her since his visit to Peterborough and here she was, fresh, vibrant, and sprinkled with fall rain.

"Camille! Are you cold?" Giganti crossed the room and rubbed her arms. "I'm so glad to have you back!"

She pulled away from the model's touch and turned her eyes on Rodin. "I've come to see Auguste."

Chapter 21

꧁ꗥ꧂

Camille could not wait another minute to see Auguste. She had arrived home from the train station an hour before and raced to the studio. Her heart battered her rib cage.

And now, Auguste did not move a muscle. He seemed uncertain how to approach her. "Mademoiselle Claudel, you came to see me?"

Giganti raised an eyebrow and looked from one to the other. He ducked his head to hide his expression and slipped on his coat. "*Molto bene.* I will be on my way."

When Giganti had gone, Camille said, "I need to know more about Rose Beuret."

Auguste's face fell. "She is the mother of my son and a longtime friend."

"She lives with you."

"Yes."

"And you love her?" Camille asked, voice tremulous.

"In a way. But we have not been intimate for some time. Our relationship has changed into something different over the years."

Relief flooded her heart. "Monsieur Rodin," she whispered, voice husky, "fetch your charcoal." There would be no more running, only surrender. This force between them consumed her will until there was nothing left but him. Only him. She must show him how much he affected her.

Camille unpinned her damp hair and shook it free. Water droplets rained about her shoulders. She untied the sash at her waist and let it flutter to the ground, then began to unfasten her buttons, one by one.

Auguste's eyes grew round and he scrambled to his desk.

She laughed at his enthusiasm and kicked off her heels. He still wanted her. A burst of joy erupted in her heart. She climbed onto the pedestal and contorted her body into a pose, her creamy skin a moon in the black cavern of the studio rooms.

Auguste raced back, his face alight and eager to devour her offering. He reached out to touch her.

She laughed again. "Later, my love. Take what I have to give you first."

He stilled for a moment. "*Mon coeur*," he whispered.

Charcoal whisked over paper, shaping the small of her back, the peak of her breasts, and her soft abdomen. He finished one page and turned to the next. His cheeks grew ruddy in his excitement.

"Do I make a fitting model?" she asked.

His face turned serious. "There could be no other after you."

Auguste's hands moved swiftly, back and forth like a bow on violin strings, the soothing sound of hand on page, the soft scrape of charcoal. The thud of her heart. Camille closed her eyes and drifted. A menagerie of images flowed from one to another, made of smoke and blurred by a warm breeze. The rustle of fabric, a flowing skirt. Two lovers. The image danced on the edge of her consciousness. Soon, she would need her own charcoal.

A callused hand stroked her cheek. Her eyes fluttered open to thick, strong fingers stained red from terra-cotta clay with chunks of burnt orange under the fingernails.

She sat up, took his hand in hers, and kissed each fingertip, the pillow of her lips pressed gently against them. His delicious adoration, his strength, wrapped her in a cocoon, blanketing the last of her doubts.

"I tried to banish you from my heart but cannot." Camille threaded her hands in his hair. "You have taken hold of me, Auguste."

"And you have changed me. I am on my knees before you."

"*Je t'aime*," she whispered.

He pressed his lips to hers and took her in his arms.

❧

"Come!" Auguste said, as he led Camille through a series of rooms furnished with beautiful antiques, paneling with gold-painted detailing, and plush silk rugs from the Orient. Camille had even removed her shoes and stockings that morning to feel the rugs' softness between her toes.

"What is all the excitement?" She followed him through the front door and onto the drive. "You spirit me away from the city, but I have work to do," she teased. She was thrilled Auguste had asked her to vacation with him in a château in Touraine, regardless of the looming submission date for the coming Salon. The very thought of it brought anxiety that settled along the muscles near her spine.

"We'll only be here a few weeks," he said, his voice warm and ebullient.

The country agreed with Auguste. She noted his beaming face, the chuckle that came without cause. Sunshine poured over his frame, making his beige coat appear as if dipped in golden honey, and his copper beard, threaded with wisps of silver, shimmered in the light. A cloud of insects buzzed about his head and he waved a hand to dispel them. She caught his hand in hers and kissed his palm.

In a swift motion, he pulled her close, his mouth slanting over hers and taking her breath away. How Camille loved this man. She kissed him hard and then bit his lip. Startled, he pulled back. "What was that for?"

"Sometimes I want to eat you up." She cackled and nipped the end of his nose.

"Little wench!" He twirled her round and round, her skirts buoyed by the bubble of air beneath them. Camille squealed as her head dizzied and her view blurred.

The crunch of footsteps on gravel interrupted their gaiety. Auguste steadied her on her feet.

A footman who lived on the property emerged from the house. "*Bonjour*, mademoiselle, monsieur. Master Gerard instructed me to be at the ready for your ride. Would you like my assistance?" His voice was brittle, as if he might crumble and blow away in the autumn wind.

"Please," Auguste said.

Camille smirked at the footman's rigid demeanor, his perfectly pressed suit jacket. He could use some roughing up, or perhaps a tumble in the hay with a maid.

"Right this way." The footman showed them to an outbuilding, where he heaved open a sliding metal door.

Camille looked at Auguste with a questioning glance. "What is this ride we are taking?"

He smiled. "I've been told it's a marvel."

"So it is," the footman replied, pinching his lips. His eyes raked Camille's form, his disdain clear.

She gave the footman a pointed look. He clearly had better things to do, but he could at least be polite. Then it occurred to her—he didn't approve of her relationship with Auguste. He sat in judgment over her sharing a room with a much older man, especially as they were unmarried. She endeavored to hold her sharp tongue. No sense in ruining a perfect afternoon.

The footman yanked the coverlet from the mystery item and a cloud of dust swirled in the air. Camille coughed as the particles clogged her throat and tickled her nose. "What on earth is that thing?" It appeared to be a motorized bicycle.

Auguste squeezed one of the narrow wheels. "It's the newly invented vehicle you spoke of, powered by steam and straight from Prussia, though they call it the Benz Motorwagen."

Camille's eyes widened in surprise. "How did you manage this?"

"The owner is a friend of mine," Auguste said. "He has a connection with the inventor. Gerard is there now, in fact. I told him my lady had marveled over the invention and he insisted we take it for a ride."

She threw her arms around his neck and kissed him.

Auguste hoisted himself onto the small cushioned seat above two large rear wheels. Behind the seat, a series of cylinders and pulleys were fastened atop a wood box. Near the footrest, a long thin pole with a winding crank jutted upward from the floorboard.

Camille looked on in amazement.

"You turn this dial to steer." The footman gestured to each part. "And I will crank this wheel. The wheel clicks this dial to begin the process of heating the reservoir of water. As the water heats, it creates compression for the steam." Excitement crept into the footman's voice.

He had heard the instructions many times, that was certain, but still found fascination with the machine.

"How do you stop it?" Camille asked.

"With this lever." He indicated a rod with a black knob at the end.

"Shall we ride, Camille? There is enough space for two." He patted the seat beside him. "We'll ride to the big oak that marks the bend in the road." He pointed to a massive tree dressed in chocolate-colored leaves.

"Let's hope this thing doesn't explode." She gathered her skirt in one hand and allowed the footman to assist her into the seat. She watched him crank the wheel attached to a pulley. After several turns, the small engine awakened with a pop, hiss, and a shallow stream of steam. Auguste cheered and swung his beret around in the air. Camille laughed at his enthusiasm and they took off, bumping over the rutted dirt road.

The vehicle gained speed. "How fast does this thing go?" she asked.

"I haven't the slightest idea!" He shouted over the noise of the steam engine.

They bounced along under the autumn sky, until they reached the tree. Auguste pulled the break and the vehicle came to a stop. "*Incroyable!*" He turned in his seat and waved at the footman, who stood in the drive. The unhappy man returned a curt wave.

Camille slapped Auguste's knee. "It goes faster than I expected! Can you get it started again? It's my turn to drive."

"Are you certain that's wise?" he asked.

She shoved him playfully. "Don't play the misogynist with me. Of course I'm certain."

"Very well, my headstrong girl." He kissed her cheek and jumped to the ground, the thump of his feet against the dirt road sending a whoosh of dust into the air.

Camille scooted closer to the steering crank and brake rod. She grinned. Paul would just die for the chance to drive this thing. She couldn't wait to tell him she had.

Auguste turned the wheel and once again the *pish-pish* of steam and the clap of lids opening and closing surrounded them. "Off you go!" he shouted.

Camille screeched when the motorwagen lurched forward. As she gained speed, rolling countryside streaked by, a painter's palette of color in the blurred periphery of her vision. Cool wind blasted against her face and washed over her person; a cleansing air, dispelling the anxiety she had carried with her from Paris. If she held out her arms, perhaps she would fly.

After another hundred meters, Camille stopped the car and dismounted. She looked back toward the now-distant château. The footman had moved from his statuesque position at the end of the drive and was now a black ant on the front steps.

Auguste strolled up the lane, hands crossed behind his back, in the midst of fields of tilled wheat. A current of golden light eddied around him. He was the sun—her guide in the wilderness. Camille skipped down the lane toward him, her heart light.

Auguste laughed as she approached. "Amusing, isn't it? I can't imagine how much the damned thing cost Gerard, but perhaps one day there will be more of them. Imagine the roads full of motorwagens!"

"That sounds dangerous." She looped her arms around his neck.

His hands found her hips and rested there. "Anything new is dangerous. Dangerous to the sheltered world most live in." He grinned down at her. "I have something to ask you."

Camille's stomach somersaulted and she looked away, out toward the horizon. Perhaps he was leaving Rose to be with her, only her. She suddenly felt like the raven soaring above the wheat fields, its black wings beating against the cheery blue sky.

Auguste put a thumb under her chin. "I'd like to rent a private space, a studio where we can work together without interruption. *Our* studio."

She tumbled from her height. He did not want to leave Rose—she was nothing but a lovesick little girl, a student and a distraction to him.

Auguste read her expression and reached for her hand. "What is it?"

She gulped down her disappointment like a bite of overcooked fowl. "The rent of my own atelier is exorbitant and there is only Jessie and I left. I could not contribute to the expenses. I am going to decline the invitation."

The light in his eyes dimmed. "I would never expect you to share the expenses. I will afford the bills." He traced the line of her jaw with his fingertip.

Camille's disappointment turned to anger. She pulled free of him and dashed down the hill toward the château. He could find a way to drive the motorwagen back himself. Perhaps the merry footman would help.

"Where are you going?" he called after her.

"To work!" she shouted, without turning. How glad she was to have brought her sketchbook and clay. She would drown her girlish notions in work.

❧

After a month away and little contact with her parents, Camille dreaded their reaction, but she could not tell them the truth about her excursion. When the maid opened the apartment door, Camille smiled at Corinne, whose ivory nightcap was askew.

"Where have you been, mademoiselle?" the older woman demanded. "Your mother has worried herself into a tizzy! She's been in bed for days."

"And am I to believe that? Please, Corinne; I am not sentimental, nor am I stupid. Mother's theatrics are an attempt to control me as she does the rest of you, and we both know it." Camille pushed past her into the hall.

"Camille?" Papa's voice drifted from the salon. The sound of steady footsteps echoed over the wood floors until he stood before her, blocking her from the staircase, where she longed to flee. He knew her well.

"Where in God's name have you been this last month?" he said. "Your mother thought you had run off or lay dead in an alley somewhere."

"You mean she *hoped* I were dead."

Papa huffed and the curled ends of his mustache fluttered. "Don't be ridiculous."

"Please, Papa. If you'll excuse me, I am tired."

"No, I certainly will *not* excuse you." He slid on his overcoat. "We are going for a walk."

"Papa—"

"Now." He retrieved his walking cane from the corner and threw open the door.

The glow of the past weeks evaporated and Camille sank into a foul humor. She dropped her valise and followed him, reluctant to listen to his admonitions. She was twenty-two years of age, a grown woman with a career. She needn't tolerate childish reprimands.

"Humor an old man and let me escort you." He clasped her gloved hand and placed it on his forearm.

"Very well." She stared at the mauve glove on her father's arm. Its painted detailing curled around an oval cutout in the leather that bared her skin. Auguste had bought them for her. He had insisted when she had soiled her others irrevocably with turpentine. How would she tell Papa she had spent her time away with her teacher and lover? He would be furious.

They walked on in silence—not the scolding she'd had in mind and yet somehow worse, leaving her with her thoughts and guilt, a sentiment she did not experience often. Somehow Papa had a way of eliciting it in her. They turned a corner at the end of the street and walked in the direction of the Seine. Clouds swallowed the stars; the dark sky mingled with Camille's black humor and pressed down upon her.

The darkness would not envelop her. She would war against it.

When they reached the water's edge, a chilly gust brought the scent of muddy river waters rushing over their earthen fairway. She tasted their churning under stone bridges and curling around each bend.

"I adore that scent," she said. "Of clay along the riverbank." And this evening, it seemed particularly pungent. In fact, every odor did: the scent of her new leather gloves and the mélange of Papa's cologne with city smog and fall air.

"Are you going to tell me where you were the last few weeks? We were all worried. You sent one letter informing us that you were on holiday without location, dates of travel, or the name of your escort. What were we to think? It was cruel, never mind unacceptable."

Perhaps she should have written more often, yet what to say? She moved closer to the water's edge, where it lapped just over the pointed tips of her shoes. She lifted her skirts to clear the waterline. Any farther and she would walk straight into the opaque waters, wade up to her neck.

"I'm waiting." His eyebrows knitted together.

"Monsieur Rodin's atelier. I've been working late hours on *Shakuntala* and a couple of other designs. And then there are the pieces I must finish for Rodin. . . ." Papa's mustache twitched. "I lied about the vacation," she continued. "I did not want to worry you, though it seems that was unavoidable."

Papa's mouth curved down at the corners and he placed his hands on her shoulders. Camille's stomach tied into knots. He knew.

"Tell me you're not his mistress."

She didn't answer.

Papa shook her slightly. "Tell me!"

"Of course not, Papa." She turned her head from him. "And you may as well know, I am considering moving into my own apartment."

He sighed in defeat. "I thought you might eventually. I am against it— living on your own does not bode well for your reputation—but I will not stop you." They watched a barge chug upstream, parting the waters as it pushed ahead. "I am relieved you aren't sharing his bed. He is too old for you and will only use you. Men may carry on as such, but women cannot. Once branded his mistress, you will always be considered a whore."

Camille cringed at the insinuation. "Do you take me for an ignorant schoolgirl?"

"Don't take that tone with me. I am your father. I will always consider your welfare, whether you like what I have to say or not."

"Yes, Papa."

The ding of a ship's bell announced a tugboat's presence moments before it appeared on the rushing river. A clump of smoky clouds floated away and a sliver of moon carved a smile into the depressed night sky. Camille gazed at the stars, a fistful of glitter against black silk. The pinpoints of light pulsed brighter and brighter.

Camille snapped her head down, startled. Her senses seemed more acute tonight than usual. The smells, the stars . . . She must be imagining things.

Tea? Did Papa want tea? She turned to her father to reply. "Yes, I'd like a cup of tea."

Confusion marked Papa's features. "We did not speak of tea."

What was the matter with him? He had put the very idea in her head. Hadn't he? Frowning, she said, "You suggested it."

Confusion shifted to concern and the lines around his eyes deepened. "Very well," he said slowly. "There's a place at the end of the block." He led her up the riverbank and down the narrow expanse of street. "You are aware Monsieur Rodin has a wife?"

"She is his lover and hardly that, from what I hear." Venom dripped from her tongue. She despised the person who came between her and Auguste.

"Camille!" The light of a nearby lamp reflected off of Papa's spectacles. "Do not be a gossip—it will not help your relationship with your teacher. If he discovered that you say such things—"

"It isn't I who gossip, Papa. I am merely repeating what I have heard the entire atelier discuss."

"I hope you are not among them."

"I have neither the time nor the inclination to gossip."

"Very good."

As they continued their walk, Camille studied the pools of lamplight coating the worn stones. She'd never noticed how liquid light appeared, almost fluid and flowing from one spot to another. And the strange pulsing! She shook her head. She must be very fatigued after her trip.

They ducked into a brasserie. Once they had ordered, they sat in silence until two steaming mugs of tea and an apple tart arrived.

Camille's mood improved as a waft of cinnamon filled her nose. "If I am to be working for a long spell again, I will inform you in advance."

"Thank you. That is all I ask, *chérie*."

Camille added milk and sugar to her tea, a custom she had learned from Jessie. She had not seen her friend in weeks. She suddenly wanted to kiss Jessie for guarding her secret.

"Louise is to be married. Your mother is quite happy about the match." Papa sipped from his cup, then paused before adding, "She has asked me to find new suitors for you, as well."

"You cannot be serious." She put down her cup hastily, scraping the porcelain against its saucer. "You know how much my art means to me." She wanted to spit at the idea of being courted by some unworthy imbecile who would steal her away from her passion. Plus, to think of Auguste's despair at such a circumstance—her heart wrenched.

"Mother hopes a man will 'tame my wild ways.' What she does not understand is that I will always be myself—a woman in love with sculpture. Marrying someone she chooses for me will only end in disaster." She shoved her tea to the middle of the table. The cup wobbled in its saucer and toppled. Caramel-colored liquid spread across the table.

"Damn it, Camille!" Papa tossed a serviette over the mess and the liquid seeped into the flimsy fabric. "She wants you to be settled and loved like other women. That is all."

The edges of her vision clouded with red. She took a deep breath. It wouldn't do to lose her temper in public, especially with Papa. She could make him see her side.

Papa covered her hand with his own. "I would never ask you to marry if you weren't ready. Your work will make history one day. I do believe that. It is a matter of finding the right critics to support you. Any man who loves you would feel the same. But you must consider the financial strain your lessons and studio have placed upon us."

Camille exhaled a breath. So this was it; she had become a burden to her family, even to Papa.

"Monsieur Rodin pays me for my work in his atelier. I am one of his most skilled *praticiens*," she said. "I can pay my own rent, if you will still assist me with supplies."

He kissed her hand. "That would be a great help, not just to me, but in my argument with your mother." He smiled for the first time that evening. "I read the paper while you were gone."

She leaned back against the chair. "Did you see the news?"

"A bronze commission for *Giganti*. That piece has been so successful." He forked the last bite of tart into his mouth. "But the write-up I read called you 'an artist who mimics her teacher. One who lacks vision of her own.'"

Camille toyed with the tiny spoon in the sugar cube bowl. "I was furious. They treat me as if I don't have my own style. Rodin has fashioned his works around my ideas and I have done the same with his—as it is in any atelier. Yet he receives all of the credit. But I am working on several of my own that I am not going to share."

"You have a tremendous teacher, but I fear your career will be lost in his shadow."

"I have wrestled with this dilemma, but for now, he helps me secure showings in the Salon, even a private commission on occasion. I am to meet one of his critic friends."

She felt her father's eyes on her as he took in every twitch, her restless fingertips, her loosely pinned chignon. He nodded in his knowing way. "Be careful. That is all. *Fais attention.*"

⤕

Camille laced her fingers together and flipped her wrists so her palms faced outward, a good stretch after working for hours on stone. The marble had proved more stubborn than the last block, which she'd carved into a set of feet for *The Burghers of Calais.* She bent over and reached toward the ground, an impolite gesture in the presence of so many men. Luckily most rules of society were suspended within the walls of an artist's studio. With so many beautiful nude men and women moving about the premises, no one even looked up from their task.

Camille straightened once more and placed her hands on her hips. Auguste did not seem as preoccupied with the *Burghers* as before, not since the council had granted him the commission. His current obsession appeared to be the *Gates*, once more, and a commission of Victor Hugo, though rather than a mere bust for his personal collection, this Hugo would be a national monument placed in the Panthéon.

What must it be like to have so many opportunities? Camille kicked her heavy skirts, damp with sweat and water, and plopped down in a nearby chair. She sighed heavily.

"Why don't you apply, mademoiselle?" a fellow sculptor named Maurice asked. He scrubbed a piece of marble with a wire brush to prepare it for carving. "For a permit to wear trousers, I mean."

"And do all the paperwork with the Prefecture of Police? I would prefer to scratch out my eyes." She stifled a yawn. "Though perhaps I may steal a pair of my brother's pants."

Maurice laughed. "Now you're thinking." He rolled his sleeves over his forearms to his elbows.

Thinking? She'd had trouble focusing lately. After an argument with Paul, she had been too distracted. Her brother did not like her spending so much time away from home. He felt abandoned by her, his best friend. Though she assured him she loved him above all others, she knew she could not lie and promise him she would remain in the family home. She would move, if for no other reason than to solidify her independence.

To worsen matters, Giganti had promised to return to work after a midday repose last night, but had never shown. *Shakuntala* was at a standstill. She rubbed her forefinger and thumb together and focused her gaze on Maurice's hands while he worked. Giganti never went back on his word. Something seemed amiss.

"It should be ready now," the sculptor said to himself.

What if Giganti didn't show again today? Camille began to pace, still rubbing her fingers together. *Shakuntala* was her best work to date. Auguste and his critic friend had heaped praise upon it at first sight, even in its unfinished form. This could be *the one*—the one that made the art world stand up and take notice. She just had a feeling about it. Giganti wouldn't leave her stranded in the middle of a piece, would he? She grunted in frustration, then kicked a half-empty pail of dirty water. The bucket clattered against the floor, and lumps of half-dissolved clay splattered in every direction.

A man building an armature paused in his hammering. Another looked up from a plaster bust. One of the new female students, with ginger curls and heart-shaped lips, Elise Chevalier, glanced in Camille's direction. Their gazes met. The young woman was wealthy and sculpted as a hobby. She had joined the atelier just to say she worked with Master Rodin.

Camille's jealousy seethed. Why must Auguste take on admiring female students who did nothing but bat their eyelashes? There were plenty of real artists seeking his instruction. Though things had been wonderful, she had let him in at last and it terrified her. The thought of his eye wandering elsewhere left her cold.

She picked up a pail and tossed it under a worktable. A metallic tang flooded her mouth, the familiar taste that came when—

"What's gotten into you?" Maurice asked. "You're making an awful racket and huffing about today."

"What's it to you?" she snapped. Tension prickled along her aching shoulders and neck. Paul, Giganti, and now this silly woman—it was all too much. She needed fresh air.

"No need to be nasty," the sculptor said.

The skin on his face blended, then each hue stood apart in a multicolor palette: peach, pink, beige, the brown and silver of his hair, and a variation of every shade therein. Confusion muddled Camille's senses. She glanced from one artist to another. Each of their faces shifted from solid structures to nebulous shapes, painted with an array of colors. She shook her head to clear the odd sensation.

You are a thief. You copy Auguste's work. You are nothing and they know it.

The Voice, the evil one that mocked her—it had come once before, when Auguste had first kissed her. Her head swiveled this way and that in a panic to locate its source. But no one spoke to her. She blinked rapidly to rectify the blurred faces, the carnival of colors—to no avail.

Camille fetched her umbrella from the rack, ripped open the door with trembling hands, and rushed toward home.

❧

Rainwater speckled the windowpane, blurring the silhouette of a doe munching a mouthful of acorns. Auguste had avoided the atelier at the Rue de l'Université the past two weeks—too many people demanded his time and there was too much noise. He huddled instead in his refuge, a stable-turned-studio on the Rue Saint-Jacques. He could not deny the truth—he also hid away from wagging tongues. There would be a national monument commissioned for Victor Hugo, and Jules Dalou was in the running—against him. He must win, if for no other reason than to prove to Jules he was the better artist. His old friend's constant disparagement made him incensed each time he thought of it.

The doe perked its ears, suddenly alert to an intruder, and dashed into the cover of tangerine and gold leaves, the only line of trees in the small park facing his studio. Auguste's eyes blurred until he saw a vision of a man holding a woman close while a demon crouched, prepared to drag her through the gates of hell. He sketched furiously in the diminished light, adding to the dozens of drawings he had completed that morning. Camille's proclamations of love, her open affection and ravenous lovemaking had torn open a seam and a flood of creativity poured from his fingertips. *Dieu*, the woman filled his heart to bursting. He had never thought it possible.

A light knock came at the door before it swung open. Octave Mirbeau entered the stable. He removed his hat and glanced about at the many portraits of the *Burghers*, the torsos without arms, and the busts of several men he recognized. He took in the forgotten bales of hay in one corner. Many tools dangled from hooks along the walls.

"How in God's name do you work in here?" Mirbeau asked, his wooly dark eyebrows arching with disdain.

"It's quiet and I have plenty of lamps when I need them."

"*Ça pue comme merde,* Auguste." He wrinkled his nose in disgust.

Auguste cracked a smile. "At least it's horseshit. It could be worse." He stood and kissed Octave's cheek in friendly affection. "I've selected the pieces for the show next month. One of my assistants will help me install them at Georges Petit's in a couple of weeks."

"Fine, fine. But that's not why I've come." Mirbeau lifted his pinstriped trousers at the knee and stepped sideways to avoid a clump of dirty rags.

Rodin watched his friend with amusement. "I have an extra pair of boots, if you like."

"That won't be necessary. I will be brief. I wrote to Omer Dewavrin in Calais as you asked. He said he received your letter and intends to respond. I think he fears your reaction."

"Because I am so fearsome?" Rodin dropped his pencil and braced himself for bad news. He could not proceed on the final rendition of *The Burghers of Calais* until he had been paid. He simply did not have the funds to buy the supplies. "Omer is a friend. It's not as if I will berate him, for God's sake."

"Another bank collapsed in Calais. There's no more money for now."

"So that's it." Auguste crossed his arms over his broad chest. "I only requested two thousand francs more. Surely they can find that somewhere. It's not as if I am asking for a large sum."

"Where is the money to come from? Since the Union Générale crashed, banks have folded at an alarming rate. Surely you've noticed most of Paris is in a depression?" Mirbeau stroked his thick black mustache. "Another textile manufacturer went bankrupt last week. My brother-in-law is out of work and they aren't sure how they'll feed the children."

Rodin rubbed his eyes and forehead. "Of course I have noticed. But they pester me to finish the *Burghers* in time for the town's centennial and yet they do not supply the funds. How am I to purchase supplies? I've spent a fortune of my own money as it is."

"How close are you to finishing?"

"The second, larger maquette is complete, but I had hoped the life-size model would be ready by next spring." He let his hands thud against the tabletop. "Now that's impossible."

Mirbeau placed his hand on his shoulder. "You will finish in time. For now, you have other commissions to worry about." A look of consternation crossed his face. "You have heard Dalou is in the running for Hugo's monument as well? Several ministers asked him to apply."

He grunted. "One of my oldest friends competes against me. And he is consumed with jealousy. I fear what will transpire between us."

"Try not to take it to heart. Who wouldn't wish to preserve the image of one of the greatest men of our time?"

"Jules either avoids me or spits venom in my presence. This damnable business pits us against our own."

"He will come around," Octave said. "And if you do not get the commission, you have more than enough to do. How is the *Gates* coming along, and the monument of Vicuña?"

Rodin heaved a lumbering sigh. "Inspiration comes like a thunderclap, but the time . . . There's never enough time."

"Perhaps you need a little entertainment. Get away from the constant work." He smiled and pounded him on the back. "Come to my house this evening. All of our friends, the *Bons Cosaques*, will be there, Monet included."

Perhaps an evening with his writer and artist friends was what he needed. But he had not seen Camille in two days. "Do you mind if I bring someone?"

"Of course not. Mademoiselle Beuret?"

"Rose would never feel at home in our company. I will bring my student, Mademoiselle Claudel."

Octave gave Auguste a questioning look. "She's a talented artist. I have seen her pieces at various Salons. Exceptional for a woman."

"Exceptional for an artist," Rodin corrected him.

"She is very beautiful. Are the rumors true?"

Auguste looked toward the window through which he had seen the doe minutes before. A wind gusted against the pane and rattled the eaves of the old edifice. He looked back at his friend's face. "She is more than my lover. The woman owns me, Octave."

Mirbeau frowned. "Keep your wits about you. A woman like her could—"

"Devour me, body and soul? Yes, I know. It is too late."

Chapter 22

Camille sipped her single malt Scotch whiskey, something expensive, no doubt. Only Auguste's friends would offer liquors in abundance like table wine. And yet, she had almost turned down Auguste's invitation to attend Monsieur Mirbeau's soiree tonight. She still could not shake the vision of Elise Chevalier standing so near him, squeezing her crossed arms together to boost her décolletage. Auguste had smiled and seemed flattered by her sycophantic adoration.

She took a long drink from her glass. Elise had been the third female student in the past month to join his atelier. The place was now crawling with novices, and they were mostly women. Auguste didn't seem to know how to turn anyone away. She took another sip. Least of all Rose. She flipped open her fan and stirred a breeze around her face. She mustn't get caught up in that nonsense now; she needed to behave herself. Both Monsieur Mirbeau and Monsieur Geffroy, important critics and possible allies, circulated through the crowd. To lose her temper in front of the most famous art critics in Paris would be suicide.

She threaded through the guests and walked to the far wall to study the piece on the fireplace mantel. Auguste's *Crouching Woman* had been a gift to his friend. She continued her walk along the periphery of the room, surveying the collection of paintings purchased at Salons or given as gifts—one of Renoir's, two of Monet's. Monsieur Mirbeau had excellent taste. Perhaps he would purchase one of hers one day.

A hand tapped her lightly on the shoulder. "I see you enjoy Scotch, mademoiselle," Monsieur Mirbeau said. "It isn't a common choice for ladies, but I am told you are bold."

She swirled her aperitif in its glass. "Indeed."

The man had a full black mustache that swooped outward like a pair of wings, and thick eyebrows, but his eyes twinkled.

"I am so pleased you could join us this evening," he said.

"How could I resist seeing you again, monsieur?" They had met on one other occasion, at a Salon, and she had liked him instantly. "You possess quite the eye for fine art."

Monsieur Mirbeau warmed to her direct yet lighthearted demeanor. "I am not accustomed to compliments from such a beautiful woman."

Camille unleashed the full power of her smile.

He offered her his arm and took her on a turn through the room. "Congratulations on your showing in London. You're a rising star, mademoiselle. As much as a woman may rise in the art world."

She would have bristled at his words had she not caught sight of Auguste talking with one of the few women in attendance. A lady in lush pink satin, much older than she, spoke with such animation she appeared almost comical. As she waved her hands about, her diamonds sparkled in the candlelight.

Camille scowled. At least she had dressed for the occasion as well; she was certain she had never looked better. Her blue gown accentuated her eyes, and a flowered headpiece and silk gloves completed her costume, a gown Rodin had yet to see her in. She could not be dowdy in comparison to the high society she had been certain would attend, and she was correct. Now if only that woman would leave him alone.

Auguste met her eye that instant and excused himself. When he reached her side, he kissed her cheek in reassurance. "Madame Courbet asked if she might view your work. I invited her to the studio." He had read her thoughts. "Her husband is on the fine arts board so she might influence him to commission a piece."

"Wonderful," Camille said, her mood brightening once more. Suddenly she wanted time alone with the man she adored. Her doubts were for naught. "Monsieur Mirbeau, if you will excuse us? I have something I need to share in confidence with my tutor."

Mirbeau decanted a large Scotch from a crystal pitcher. "I will catch up with you both a bit later."

Camille led Auguste through the study and onto a narrow balcony overlooking the city. A brisk breeze rushed around them and they huddled together. They peered down at the cityscape, a black sea dotted with orbs of effervescent light, glittering on the cool waters in the fountain square, flickering in the smattering of streetlamps, and oozing from the buzzing electric lights that had cropped up in clusters throughout the city. How vivid the light appeared, a menagerie of gold and silver, pulsing with an aura all its own.

Camille cocked her head to the side, contemplating the pulsing light. The sensation came more frequently now, and she hadn't the slightest idea why. Goose pimples covered her arms. Should she have her vision examined?

"I have good news for you," Auguste said. "Mathias Morhardt has agreed to review several of your pieces. He believes in your talent."

She smiled, unable to hold back her joy. "Will I be able to meet him?"

He nodded. "He is a friend of mine, and he will give your work a proper critique. We must play the system in whatever way we can."

She paid him with an ardent kiss.

He crushed her against him. "I've been drinking in the sight of you all evening." He kissed her softly, then worked his way down her neck. Her breath came in short spasms as his strong hands played over the curves of her form.

"Come away with me," he said.

"Where?" she asked, breathless.

"Next week. To the Château de l'Islette in Touraine. We can work there, soak in our inspiration and the beauty of the countryside." He leaned his forehead against hers. "Be naked at midday and take our tea in a chemise if we choose."

"You always wax poetic, *mon amour.*" She kissed him softly, a gift for his beautiful words. "But what will I tell Papa?"

"That you're running away with the love of your life." He slipped his hand inside the front of her dress and cradled one of her breasts. He rubbed his thumb over her nipple.

"Auguste," she gasped. Her head fell back in pleasure while he stroked her softly. "Not here," she managed to say at last.

"We'll work, too." He kissed her again and straightened the front of her gown. "Bring what portraits we can."

"I will come," she said.

Auguste smiled and dipped his head toward her chest again. "*Dieu*, you are beautiful."

She pulled his face up to meet hers. "I will only go if you do something for me."

"Anything." His tone sobered.

"I want them to go."

"Who?" Another whisk of night air ruffled his beard and curling hair.

"All of them. The overeager students with no talent. The women who peer at you as if they share a secret with you. I can't stomach it."

He held her face in his hands. "You do not understand the extent of my affection. I don't eat or sleep at night if I don't see you." He caressed her thick bottom lip. "You hold my heart hostage. There are no other women but you."

His words always melted her defenses, but not this time. She needed his word that he would see only her. "I want you to agree," she said firmly. "It's bad enough you keep that . . . woman in your house."

He flinched at the reference to Rose. "You want me to turn away students?"

"They can find a new teacher. You're a busy man. And they don't need you. Not the way I do."

"Very well." He nodded.

Camille burrowed into his arms.

❧

A shadowy figure tiptoed into the salon, taking care not to slam into the footstool or step on the squeaky floorboard between salon and front hall. A pale hand reached out to stroke the costly silk tapestry on the far wall. Only one, other than Camille, would steal through the dark in the middle of night.

Camille remained still as death, not daring to alert the intruder to her position on the settee. In truth, she hadn't the energy to move anyway. The merriment of *Noël*, laughing guests, the clinking of fork against porcelain plate, the swirl of colored taffeta and silk gowns and

Mother's dull guests—it had all been too much. Her head still throbbed with stimulation hours later. To sit alone in a dark room seemed to be the only thing that helped.

A thump of bone against wood broke the silence.

"Ouch!" Paul said. He lit one of the lamps. "Oh! What are you doing here?"

Camille shifted her position to look at him. He sported his finest suit coat and tie, and a rosiness colored his cheeks. A heavy volume slipped from his grasp and hit the floor with a thunk. Shiny gold letters glinted in the lamplight: HOLY BIBLE.

"Where have you been at this hour?" Camille asked, eyeing him warily. "Reading your Bible?"

"I've just come from midnight mass."

She pushed herself into a sitting position. "What were you doing there?"

He sat on the edge of a chaise across from her. "Something has happened. I feel . . . changed. As if God spoke to me through the choir and organ. I felt my soul vibrating in my chest. The beautiful music." His voice lowered to a whisper. "He is real. It's all real. The angels, the spirits, God. I felt him as real as I feel your leg next to mine." He touched her knee for emphasis.

Camille stared at him in shock. After a moment, she threw back her head and laughed, deeply from her spine and belly, until tears sprang to her eyes. She wiped at them with the back of her hand.

Paul drew away from her and crossed his arms over his chest. "What are you laughing at? That I have found faith? I am saved. Pulled from the jaws of damnation and human suffering. I will worship him and be glad."

She snorted. "Your God will not save you from suffering. Quite the opposite. Believing he will save you will only cause you more suffering."

"You are wrong, sister. On this night, I can feel his truth within." He stood and began to pace, his long arms swinging at his sides. "I've been blind to it." He stopped. "Don't you see? This gives meaning to all of this." He waved his hands in the air.

"Tell your God to rescue me from this fickle business. A female artist is damned before she begins." She slumped against the cushion once more.

He sat beside her and embraced her. "You will finish *Shakuntala* and they will love you." He pulled loose from her heavy limbs and looked into her eyes. "I know you have worried over your last reviews. But they will see your talents. You must have faith."

"I will find a way," she said, her determination renewed.

"That's the spirit. Open your heart and God will lead you as he has led me." The glow of the lamp, or perhaps it was the burn of faith, reflected in Paul's eyes. She wished she could believe his earnestness, or better yet, believe in his God.

He continued, "There are others who will help you. You must know that."

She pushed out a weary sigh. "The only thing I *know* is that I must succeed on my own."

⤚❖⤙

Camille pressed the surface of *Shakuntala* with firm fingers to assess its level of moisture. Without properly moistened rags the clay would become too brittle to revive. She checked the clock on her desk. Exhausted, she put the teakettle on to boil and dropped into a chair. She pulled a cigarette from the tin on the table and lit its cylindrical end.

Giganti had left for a meal several hours earlier and promised to work again afterward—the third time of such instances from which he had never returned. She puffed on her cigarette and exhaled a filmy stream of smoke. She could no longer put *Shakuntala* aside. She was nearing a crucial point with the piece and she needed Giganti to be available daily. She would have to confront him, like it or not.

A rap on the door made her jump. She moved across the room and flung open the door to find a filthy young boy on the stoop. The boy lived on the streets; his shredded trousers and coat and soot-stained face betrayed him.

"You Ma'moiselle Claudel?"

"Who wants to know?" She peered down the street.

The usual crowd of artists in stained smocks, musicians toting weighty instruments, and students lugging loads of books stalked to their destinations. Several doors down—almost out of sight—a man leaned against a doorway. A large beard engulfed much of his face. Was it her Auguste? She squinted. Why would he be watching her from afar?

The boy flashed a square of paper in his hand. Camille grasped his arm and tried to pry the envelope from his fingers.

"What you doing, ma'moiselle?" He squirmed out of her clutches and backed away. "You won't have this unless you're Claudel."

She adjusted her disheveled frock and glanced at Auguste again. He had gone. "Who is it from?" she asked.

"Monsieur Giganti. He said Ma'moiselle Claudel would know him."

"I am Claudel; now, hand it over!"

He dropped the envelope at her feet and ran, his scraggly hair flapping in the breeze as he dashed away.

"Beat it!" she shouted after him.

He turned, running backward, and made a lewd gesture.

Camille mimicked him and the little imbecile laughed. After he'd gone from sight, she retreated indoors and tore open the letter.

Ma Chère Camille,

I do not have the courage to tell you this in person, but I am returning to Italy.

I am embarrassed by my conduct, but I cannot stay. A lover from my past has resurfaced—this time it is a serious affair and he needs my help.

I wish you luck. I have no doubt your work will enchant the art world as you have enchanted me, dear friend.

With Sincere Affection,

Giganti

Camille's mouth dropped open in shock. He was leaving her in the middle of *Shakuntala*? Her throat constricted in panic. She rushed to the window and looked down the street. Had Auguste put Giganti up to this? She'd seen him there, in the doorway. But why would he do such a thing? Surely he didn't wish to sabotage her work, did he?

She crumpled the letter and tossed it at the waste can. She fumbled with the cigarette tin and the remaining contents spilled on the floor. "*Merde!*" she shouted. She scrambled on her hands and knees and chose one poorly rolled cylinder. With a huff, she sat against the wall, lit the cigarette, and inhaled deeply.

Giganti had been a friend, even when Jessie had allowed her righteousness to come between them. The model had never thought her inferior for her choices. In fact, he had upheld her in the midst of her indecision and anxiety. A lump of sorrow formed in her throat. Camille burned through the cigarette and lit another. He was gone. He had abandoned her when she needed him, and now she wouldn't be able to finish. Her great work—her salvation from obscurity—would never see the light of day. She would have nothing to show for two years of work but a lost friendship.

She slumped against the leg of the table and wept.

Chapter 23

꩜

Auguste rapped on Camille's atelier door. Lights, though faint, still burned in the window, despite the late hour, so he knew she must be hard at work. She had been absent; for a week he had tried to reach her, but she seemed to know precisely when he was near. Or perhaps she had been ill and stayed home all of those days. If he weren't such a coward, he would have called on the Claudel household.

He removed his beret and wrung it in his hands. God, he had missed her. Was she angry with him?

Footsteps echoed from behind the door, and then paused on the other side of the oak barrier between them. Suddenly remorseful, Auguste berated himself for his stupidity, his desperation to see her. He should not have come so late. Perhaps she could only make out a male figure in the moonlight and did not wish to open her door. He looked over his shoulder and thought to steal home. She need never know it was he. He was a damned fool, a schoolboy sick with love. Camille might return his sentiment, but she did not scurry around after him like a child.

The click of brass key in lock sent his heart into his throat. As the door creaked open, a black cat with white paws darted past his legs. A gale of winter wind gushed down the street and rustled a pile of forgotten newspapers. Their pages flipped open and wrestled against a crackling wind laden with the promise of ice and snow. The cat pounced at the moving target—too great a temptation to ignore. But the pile of papers proved an unsatisfying toy as it lay trapped beneath her snow-white paws.

"Minou!" Camille darted after the cat without greeting Auguste.

The animal pawed at a crumpled ball of paper in the street. The ball bounced as if alive. Minou crouched, intent to pounce on the new plaything.

Camille paused to watch the cat's tail sway, her green eyes wide. Her paw shot out and swatted the paper. Minou pattered after it and batted the wad back and forth into the middle of the street.

Auguste couldn't help but smile.

Camille bent to rescue the cat just before it rolled into a puddle.

Rodin noted her hollowed cheeks and the purple-black wells beneath her eyes. *Dieu*, she looked starved and fatigued. He wanted to erase the dark smudges with his lips, cradle her in his arms, and bring her to bed. Something about her made him want to care for her.

"*Mon amour*," he said, sighing.

"Why are you here?" She walked briskly to the door and went inside. The cat twisted and squirmed out of her hands.

His heart sank at her clipped tone. She had not missed him at all. "Are you unwell?" he asked, following her inside.

A few candles flickered in the otherwise dark room, throwing shadows on the wall. Dozens of maquettes of *Shakuntala* and a piece he had not yet seen covered every table surface and sat in messy heaps on the floor. The odor of dead fish permeated the air.

Auguste held his tongue. He didn't want to say anything to upset her. Clearly she had been distressed already. Yet he had never seen the place in such a state of disgrace. And the darkness . . .

"Why does it smell like fish in here?" He looked under the tables and behind a chest to locate the source of the odor. Bits of a fish carcass lay scattered in the corner of the room near a bowl of murky water. "Is that for the cat?" He frowned. "What's happened, Camille? Where is Mademoiselle Lipscomb?"

Camille lit a cigarette. "She's been in London again, visiting her fiancé, but she returns tomorrow."

A flame consumed the last nub of wick in a solitary candle. A wisp of smoke snaked through the air and the odor of newly extinguished fire mingled with that of rotten fish.

"You'll need to tidy this place," he said. "She'll have no room to work as it is now." Minou wound between his legs and he squatted to pet the cat's silky fur.

"He's gone," she said, exhaling.

"Who is gone?" He watched as she paced in the small space, stopping to kick a maquette with a swift hit, launching it against the far wall. The dried clay whacked the plaster and burst in half.

"To Italy. Giganti left for Italy." She mashed the butt of her cigarette against a dried maquette and let it fall to the floor. "I'll never finish *Shakuntala*. Two years of work," she croaked, her voice heavy with emotion, "a complete waste of time. It was to be a definitive work for me."

"The bastard! I paid him for another month's work. We'll find another model to replace him." He laid his hands on her shoulders. Despite his regret for her, a guilty sense of relief rushed through him—Giganti no longer posed a threat to their relationship. "I am surprised he left, I must say. I thought he was in love with you."

A hollow laugh came from her lips. "Didn't you know he has a perversion toward men? With that face and body he had more lovers than I will ever have."

Auguste flushed in embarrassment. How had he not known? "I cannot believe I had never realized—"

"Why would you have known about his life outside of your studio?" She lit another cigarette.

He grunted. He did not expect the pinch of hurt at her words. He felt so close to his subjects, their movements, their emotions. He thought he knew his models better than they knew themselves, after so many hours observing them. It seemed he had been mistaken.

"What am I to do?" she asked, her expression forlorn. "No one looks precisely like him. It's impossible."

She put down her cigarette and with a fierce tug tried to open her desk drawer. The splintered edges slammed against the inside frame of the desk. She righted the drawer and yanked on the pull once more. Something cracked and the drawer propelled off its rickety track to the floor. Several pencils rolled under the desk and papers scattered near her feet. She fished the crumpled letter out of the pile and thrust it toward him.

Auguste took it from her cold fingertips, though his eyes never left her face. "What's this?"

"'I do not have the courage to tell you this in person, but I am returning to Italy.'" She recited Giganti's letter.

"I will take care of this," Auguste said. "You have a hundred portraits of him, and your sketches, the bust. We'll make do, I promise." He glanced at the rag-covered lump he knew to be *Shakuntala*. He would do everything in his power to help her. "We'll find another Italian with a similar build. You *will* finish. All will be well."

When her arms slid around his waist, he sighed in relief and laid his cheek atop her crown of curls. This precious, tormented woman. She needed him and he needed her.

After a heated kiss, he whispered in her ear, "I will take care of you, always. Even if you choose to give up sculpture—"

Camille went rigid in his arms. "You do not understand me at all. My humor has not been at its best, that is true. But am I not allowed to mourn the departure of both a friend and muse?" She stalked to her worktable once more, distancing herself from him.

He regarded the fire in her eyes, the determined set of her jaw. "Of course you are."

"You are just like them—those who wish I would accept my fate, a woman expected to find happiness in belonging to someone, in keeping a household and chasing children." Her voice went cold. "My dreams mean nothing to you. They mean nothing to anyone but me."

"That isn't true. Camille—"

She stubbed her cigarette out on the surface of the table, paying no heed to the sizzle of fire on lacquer. "It's true, whether you admit it or not. 'When will she outgrow this phase?' they all ask. 'When will a gentleman make an honest woman of her?' My mother and certainly your colleagues think so."

Rodin sighed. He could not argue with her. He had fought the prejudices of the *institut* on his own behalf many times, and on hers through his letters, though she did not know it. The result had always been the same: She was a woman, and certainly of lower status in their eyes. Suddenly, he was glad to be a man, a fact he had never given much thought to before loving *sa féroce amie*, his ferocious friend.

"Some think so, yes," he admitted slowly. "But I am not among them."

She crossed her arms. "You wish to take care of me, truly?"

"You must ask?" He reached for her.

She stepped out of his reach. "Bring them. Bring the critics to your studio. Let them meet me as your prized student with my works displayed. Show them I am a true artist. They will listen to you."

He nodded. "I would be happy to, but it must be on my terms. It is not just your reputation at stake."

"You are embarrassed by me?" she asked in a wounded tone.

"Of course not. But we are professionals and once tied together, we reflect one another in the public eye."

Camille's shoulders relaxed; her eyes became less guarded. "I am already tied to you as your pupil. But we must keep the truth of our relationship hidden or I will lose all credibility. They will see me as just another fool who wishes to follow in your footsteps. I would rather leave you than be branded a mimic of your work."

This was not the direction Rodin had intended to take the conversation. She did not need a reason to leave him outside of Rose. The thought of losing her made him want to curl inward and fade away. He cleared his throat to rid himself of the knot of emotion welling there.

"We needn't worry about their perception of our relationship," he said. "Your work will speak for itself."

The frown on her face melted into a smile. "I think so, too."

Chapter 24

❖

Camille massaged her fingers and wrists. She and Jessie had worked all morning without respite, without stopping for even a drop of coffee.

"You may break," Jessie said to a pair of models.

A mother and her young son stepped down from their perch, dressed, and sat to eat a hunk of bread and cheese. Camille's stomach grumbled as the aroma of a particularly pungent cheese filled the air. She picked over several apples in the basket on the table before selecting one.

"Monsieur Elborne should be here soon," Jessie said. "He'll take us for supper."

"What luck," Camille replied, her voice heavy with sarcasm.

Jessie's fiancé, William Elborne, had returned with her from England to see her studio and view the Paris Jessie had grown to love. Camille had disliked him on sight; his wide grin revealed a dreadful set of crooked yellow teeth and his innocent eyes gave him the look of an imbecile. He simply couldn't be as clever as Jessie, and he would steal her away, back to London for good. The first thing the cad would do is impregnate her to keep her tethered to his side. Her allowance for art supplies would diminish, and her love for sculpture would dissolve.

Camille's gut twisted in a knot at the thought.

"Will he allow you to work while he is visiting?" Camille asked. She couldn't help herself. Jessie would abandon her, their friendship, just as

Giganti had. She'd probably forget to write and never speak to her again, and it was all this man's fault.

"Really, Camille!" Jessie tossed the hardened heel of bread loaf into the wastebasket. "I know you do not care for him, but you needn't be rude. It's offensive."

The model pretended not to hear their squabble, and tousled her son's unruly curls.

Jessie poured tea for each of the adults and a cup of warmed chocolate for the boy. Little Julien's mother held the cup to his lips and he slurped it greedily, dribbling a sticky river of chocolate down his chin.

"He will destroy your dreams." Camille bit into her apple, its clean snapping sound a signal her opinion was final and the conversation closed—at least for her.

"And just what are my dreams? You seem to understand them better than I do," Jessie countered. "I must accept my responsibilities as a woman at some point, and I love him."

Would Camille marry Auguste if he asked? Perhaps, but she would not abandon her art, and he wouldn't ask her to. He would never propose anyway, she thought glumly.

"You must be a woman at some point!" Camille echoed Jessie's phrase. She hurled the apple core across the room. It smacked against the wall, leaving a glistening imprint before plopping into the wastebasket. "Am I less of a woman—are you—if we choose not to marry and have children?"

"Are we going to argue about this?" Jessie's eyes flashed. "You know I share the same views, but I have fallen in love and I want a family. That does not make me any less an artist than you." She looked longingly at the cherub on his mother's lap.

Camille thought of Paul at that age, his fattened cheeks and legs, how he had toddled around the house after his big sisters. She understood Jessie's desire for children. Her anger and annoyance evaporated and her vision blurred with tears. She'd had so few friends—certainly none who understood her. How lonely she would be when Jessie finally departed.

Jessie glanced at Camille and her face softened. "I'm not leaving so soon." She moved across the room and embraced her. "And I will miss you, too.

How had her friend read her so easily? She pulled away. Any warmth, any sympathy bestowed on her at all and the delicate band holding her emotion in check would snap.

A pounding came at the door, and Jessie's features shifted in an instant. She scurried to answer it.

"Darling!" she said from the doorway. "You've brought your camera?"

A male voice floated through the hall.

Camille listened to them prattle on in English until their voices dropped. She sorted through her tools, trying to ignore the sound of them exchanging kisses. Thankfully, the cherub clapped his hands and leapt off his mother's lap, happy to have a full belly. He was a welcome distraction.

Julien's mother stood and wrestled him out of his clothing. They would work another hour before supper.

"*Bonjour*, Mademoiselle Claudel," Elborne said, lugging a wooden box fixed with the long snout of a camera lens. In his right hand he toted a case, presumably for the stand. "Having a fine day, I hope?"

She shrugged. "I suppose."

Monsieur Elborne set the camera on the table. "Would you mind terribly if I took your photograph? With Mademoiselle Lipscomb, of course. I would like to capture the two of you working."

Work would soon end for Jessie—he may as well document it for her to remember.

"As you wish," Camille said.

Monsieur smiled, showing his buttery teeth, then moved like a cyclone in a frenzy of photograph paper and clanking camera parts. Jessie instructed the models to take their positions and began working once more.

Camille continued to work on *Shakuntala* while the buffoon fumbled with his camera. She didn't bother to look his way while he snapped several photographs.

"Have you seen the construction site?" the gentleman asked. "That fellow, Eiffel, had the ground cleared by the Champ de Mars. They've already begun construction."

"It's for the World Exposition," Camille said. "I can't imagine a metal monstrosity sullying the skyline. And we wonder why it's so dif-

ficult to land a commission! That so-called 'art' is the perfect example
of the ministers' hideous taste."

"I think a massive iron tower penetrating the sky is a symbol of
progress."

Camille snorted. "Penetration is precisely the problem."

The model tried to cover a giggle and Monsieur Elborne laughed
in spite of himself. Jessie shot her a warning look.

Camille did not care that she was inappropriate. Her tongue had a
mind of its own and she had given up trying to curb it.

"These ministers you mentioned, haven't they approved some of
your designs? I was under the impression you have had some luck."
Elborne adjusted the legs of his stand to a new position to photograph
Jessie on her own.

"I have had some luck with private commissions, yes, and a few
shown at Salon."

"That is more than Jessie," he said. "You must be pleased."

Anger ate at her patience. "Monsieur, I am not pleased to pit my
success against that of a dear friend, nor am I contented with showings
in which I was listed as a mere pupil. Even less so am I enthralled by
reviews that compare me to my teacher."

"You must understand it is a man's profession," he said. "Perhaps
you should channel your talents elsewhere."

Rage surged through Camille's limbs and set her temples to pounding. She threw down her chisel and it clinked against a pile of tools on
the tabletop. "And this is precisely why I am not supportive of your
union, Jessie." She whisked a cloth over her piece and tossed her smock
over the chair. "And you, sir, are not to return to this studio."

She bolted for the door.

❧

Auguste had come through as promised; he had found a suitable re-
placement for Giganti within days. To Camille's relief, she finished
Shakuntala in time for the Salon and now circulated among the other
artists and guests. Energy rolled off her skin—the compliments for
her work had come one after another all evening. With each additional nod of approval, she grew more excited, and by evening's end,

she wanted to dance. This was it! She had finally created something noteworthy, and the continual praise reflected it.

"You are beaming." Auguste leaned in closer. "And delectable in your gown. I am counting the minutes until we may leave."

Camille brushed her lips over his cheek. They grew bolder in displaying their affection for one another, despite her better judgment. Tonight, she did not care. She had worked too hard to come to this point, and now she couldn't contain her joy.

Mathias Morhardt crossed the room to join them, fresh wineglasses in hand. "*Shakuntala* is a success, Mademoiselle Claudel. You'll want this"—he put a glass in her hand—"because I have thrilling news for you. I've just been told your piece has won the Salon prize!"

Camille squealed and pecked the critic, and new friend, on his fleshy cheek.

Though taken aback, he smiled. "Congratulations. It is well deserved."

"*Félicitations!*" Auguste kissed her on both cheeks and held her face in his strong hands. "I could not be happier for you."

She had been given a prize at last! This was the beginning of many great things to come—she just knew it. Tears pricked behind her eyes. Acceptance as an artist meant more to her than she had ever realized. It meant everything, and now she had it all. Paul and Papa would be so proud. She could hardly wait to tell them. She gulped down half of her champagne and choked on the sting of bubbles in her nose and throat. Her heart was bursting with happiness!

"Oh, Auguste, I've done it." She wrapped her free arm around his neck.

Eyebrows raised, Mathias looked from one to the other, weighing the intimacy between them.

"I propose a toast," Auguste said, raising his glass. Mathias and Camille followed suit. "To achieving the dream, to my genius student, and most of all, to a bright future."

"To a woman blasting through their locked doors!" Camille added.

"*Santé!*" They all said in unison.

❧

A month later, an array of critics circulated through the Dépôt des Marbres. Auguste's assistants had spent a week organizing and cleaning the studio, moving Camille's pieces in progress and positioning them in an attractive arrangement. Even those she had carved for Auguste sat on display. Camille smiled. It had been facile convincing the critics to attend a private showing after her winning a prize at the Salon. All evening she had been pulling Auguste into his office or around dark corners and kissing him in thanks.

She laid a hand on her abdomen. They had feasted on creamed celery soup, spring lamb, and asparagus at a restaurant that afternoon to celebrate, and she was still full to the brim. It was the first large meal she had eaten since Giganti had left. He had taken her appetite with him when he left her in the lurch. But her luck had changed and with it, the success of her career. She had arrived.

"I am happy you are here," Camille said, clinking her glass against Paul's.

Though Paul claimed he wanted to be there for her, she'd had to convince him to abandon a prayer service that evening to attend. A shadow fell over her good humor. He had been attending daily confession, and mass almost as often. Even more disturbing was his incessant talk of saints. He no longer spoke of friends or his life outside the church. She had even witnessed him berating himself for his "sinful" behavior. She hoped the phase would pass—his obsession was beginning to worry her.

"I am so proud of you," Paul said. "I knew they would recognize your talent one day." He sipped from his aperitif glass and looked about the room, self-possessed and confident.

Camille had trained him well. Now her brother moved about the circle of writers, artists, and critics as if he were one of them, and he was. "Congratulations on your prize," she said, kissing him on the cheek. "I knew it, Paul. You've been destined to be a writer since you were a runt."

He laughed. "We'll see where the literary prize takes me. It could be a lark."

"Nonsense." She finished the last of her punch. "What are you reading these days?"

"A few works by Americans, if you can believe it. I've been meeting with American writers studying here in Paris, though they have gotten me into trouble a few times at the bar."

Camille wondered if the Americans were the reason Paul felt he must confess each day. She scooped another ladle of punch into her glass, the third of the evening. She shouldn't have more or she might say something inappropriate, but the alcohol prevented her vision from blurring and colors from searing her eyes.

"Take it easy," Paul said. "You'll be stumbling like a drunkard before long."

"You're the expert on that, aren't you? I can recall more than one occasion I cleaned up your vomit."

"Touché," he said, a smile curving his thin lips.

They walked toward a study of Auguste that she had just begun. The bust's figure was still barely recognizable.

"How did Monsieur Rodin manage to bring so many critics to a faux salon?" Paul asked.

"He promised to let them have a peek at his designs for a new piece; he's calling it *The Eternal Idol*," Camille said, eyeing a wrinkle in her bust's beard she needed to reshape. "As for the faux salon, I didn't like the idea at first, but if it exposes my work, I cannot complain."

"I saw your sketches on the table last night," Paul said.

She turned to him, truly interested to know his opinion. "What did you think?"

"They are all nude." He paused as if unsure whether or not he should continue. "They are perverse, I must admit. They make me uncomfortable just viewing them. I can't imagine what it must be like creating them."

Camille laughed. Her grown brother took offense to nude women? "You must be the only man in the world who feels that way."

"They're naked figures draped upon one another." He blushed from his suit collar to his hairline. "They're quite shocking. Sinful, even. I question Monsieur Rodin's motives in his teachings."

She could say many things about her own motives that would make her brother blush, but she could not bring herself to sully his innocence, even if his righteousness grated on her nerves.

At that exact moment, Auguste started in their direction with three gentlemen in tow.

"*Regarde*, Paul. You say the word and the Devil appears."

Paul flattened his lips in disapproval. "Look at his eager face. I bet the man is in love with you."

She smiled. "You can see it so easily."

He turned toward her, his gaze incredulous. "Are you his lover? Camille," he hissed under his breath, "he has a wife. You're committing adultery."

She lowered her voice. "Oh, for Christ's sake, Paul. Rose Beuret isn't—"

"Don't take the Lord's name in vain!"

She eyed him coldly. "Neither he nor I are married. And who knows? Perhaps we will be one day. You could support me instead of chastising me with your religion."

The muscles in Paul's jaw clenched. "He is despicable! Using you the way he is."

Auguste joined them, cutting their conversation short. "*Bonsoir*, Monsieur Claudel, mademoiselle. I would like to introduce you to Messieurs Leroi and Geffroy. And you know Mathias."

"Good evening, gentlemen," Camille said, pushing Paul's condemnation from her mind. Tonight was a happy event, another evening filled with praise and excitement, which she sorely deserved.

Mathias's cheeks were as ruddy as ever. He leaned over his large stomach to kiss Camille's hand. "It is lovely to see you again."

"Likewise." She smiled coyly at the gentlemen. Mathias had gushed about her works since their first meeting, at the Salon.

Mathias beamed at her. He seemed the quintessential round and jolly fellow.

"I was just saying to Rodin that I see pagan bliss and worship of the human form in his portraits of the *Gates*," he said. "In most of his works, really. Man prostrate to nature, or to woman. Yet yours convey an intimacy between figures. A yearning not of the flesh, but an internal beseeching to be loved and understood."

"That is what I hope they convey, monsieur. I'm pleased it's obvious."

"I am impressed as well, mademoiselle," Monsieur Leroi said.

His perfect cravat and wavy blond hair shone in the light. This man possessed an arrogance in his fine features, and a self-assuredness that suggested he had been granted all he desired in his life.

"I've never seen a woman with such promise," Leroi continued.

Camille smiled and he winked at her. Her smile froze on her face.

She did not know if Leroi was flirting with her or winking at her as if she were a child. In either case, she didn't like it. She was a serious artist and wanted to be seen as such.

"Likewise," Gustave Geffroy said, nodding stiffly. Giving praise to a woman seemed difficult for him. "I am looking forward to seeing your pieces in the next Salon."

"If they are accepted," she replied.

"They will be." Paul jumped to her defense.

"I agree." Auguste rubbed his beard. "I, on the other hand, may have an issue with my *Burghers*. The ministers still view me as an outlaw and are giving me trouble, but I won't give in."

Camille looked away to hide her withering look. Auguste yearned to be accepted, she knew, regardless of his brave words. She despised when he slipped into being *une victime de l'État*.

And you are his victim. He uses you for his own gain.

Camille pitched forward, startled by the Voice. Where had it come from?

"A persecuted master," Mathias said, oblivious to her stumbling.

"An artist who operates outside the lines of propriety," Paul said, his voice pregnant with disdain. "Perhaps that is why they will not accept your work."

Auguste raised a questioning eyebrow, then looked to Camille. "I beg your pardon, but I find the lines of propriety are not so clearly defined."

Geffroy pinched his lips together, his discomfort apparent. "If you will excuse me, I am just going to take one more look at your sketches, Auguste."

"I will join him," Leroi said. He smiled an oily smile at Camille that made her stomach flip with disgust.

Mathias looked from Paul to Auguste. "Mademoiselle, I would like to speak with you more later." Camille nodded and the gentleman followed the others.

Auguste turned to Paul once the critics had moved out of earshot. "And just what did you mean by your comment? It was rude and uncalled for in present company."

"You bed my sister, and sign your name to her pieces to further your own career, yet you have the audacity to keep a woman at home. It's shameful!"

Auguste's voice dropped to a menacing tone. "I am being lectured by a boy who knows nothing of my life? How old are you? Twenty?"

"Old enough to know a leeching bastard when I see one!"

Auguste gripped Paul's arm. "You'll not speak to me this way in front of my colleagues. If you have a problem, we'll discuss it elsewhere."

"Unhand me!" Paul jerked free of his grasp.

Camille's eyes darted around the room. The Voice had come back! The clack of heels on floor, the murmur of voices increased in volume. Laughter and chatter boomed in her head.

You are disgraceful. They are laughing at you.

She looked around the room again, frantic to locate the source of the laughter, the Voice. Who dared mock her on this night? Nothing but a blur of faces and orbs of color streaked by before her eyes. She blinked and looked to Auguste and Paul. They argued, but their conversation muddled and sloshed around in her mind. She envisioned their words as strings of pearls browning and disintegrating, before evaporating out of her ears like a stream of smoke. What in the devil was the matter with her? She cursed herself for drinking too much.

"Camille?" Auguste slid his hand under her arm. "What is the matter?"

"Get me out of here," she whispered. She could not let the critics see her in her confused state.

"Paul, fetch a cab. I'll escort her downstairs."

"Do not tell me what to do," Paul said.

Auguste stood a centimeter from his face. "Do it now," he growled. "Your sister needs us."

Camille watched in fascinated horror as the letters of Auguste's words flowed from his lips, hardened to black pebbles, and tumbled to the ground. She winced as they hit the wood floor and scattered beneath the furniture toward the fire.

She covered her ears and leaned against Auguste. "Make it stop!"

"What is it?" He dragged her from the room and out of doors to avoid a scene.

"The Voice! The noises." She clutched her head. "Your words," she said, her voice quivering, "turned to pebbles."

Bewilderment crossed his features. "You've had too much to drink. Let's get you home."

"No!" She thrashed against him in the street. "I can't see Mother like this."

Mother would berate her for being an embarrassment, lock her in her room, or, worse, call a doctor to assess her, but there was nothing wrong with her. It would pass. It always did.

A thousand thoughts streamed through her mind like landscape past a train window, dashing by too fast for her to make out details or their meaning.

Paul motioned to them from where he stood, a block down the street. Auguste pulled her tightly against him and walked her to the hackney.

"Get some rest tonight," he said. "You're overworked, excited by the critics." He kissed her on the forehead. "I'd say we're due a vacation. We'll discuss it tomorrow."

Too numb to respond, she mounted the step up into the hackney cab. Paul slipped his arm about her shoulders. He looked down at Auguste in his righteous way. "I will take it from here." Camille sank into her brother's embrace as the cab sped away.

Chapter 25

꧁꧂

Four weeks of bliss at the Château de l'Islette, in Touraine—working, making love, strolling through the fields and forest in leisurely bliss—and Auguste did not want to return to Paris. He stoked the bonfire and watched as glowing embers sprayed into the black sky and rained down in a shower of gold. The moon did not show its face and there was no stirring breeze; just the cool damp air of late spring that bathed the grass in dew and soaked into his bones. Camille sat wrapped in a blanket at the fire pit's edge, the flickering light dancing across her face. His Diana in the wilderness, by turns tender and fierce. He didn't know what to make of her spells. One day she seemed well, normal; the next a violence welled inside her and she lashed out. And then there were her suspicions that he followed her to steal her ideas, and the voice that she said spoke to her.

Auguste stirred the carpet of ash inside the ring of stones with his stick. Why would he use Camille? She inspired him, but he saw nothing untoward in that. Her beautiful and terrible mind intrigued him, but it seemed to torment her more and more. *Dieu*, but he loved her. If he could only take care of her in the ways he wished he could.

Camille rose to throw a log on the fire. The flames licked the rough layers of bark and singed the few dried leaves still attached. "I liked this trip best of all," she said. "Away from the noise of Paris. The screeching and clanking. All of the people. It crowds me and I can't think. I wish we could stay longer."

"I have to meet with Gustave Geffroy at the end of the week. I'm out of money for the time being anyway," he added quietly.

"Why do you have so many studios?" Camille asked. "How many are there? Five? You spend every franc you have on them." Her tone became peevish.

Wary at her change, Auguste proceeded cautiously. He did not feel up for a quarrel. "I need the space. The casts and life-size maquettes have taken over the studio. Where would we work, *mon amour*, if I did not stash my portraits somewhere?"

"There is more than enough room. I think you keep them because you like to boast about how successful you are. Such vanity. Those critics and your public care nothing for you. They gobble up the beauty we create like starved men. Starved to fill the void in their meaningless lives. And you, you scramble to do their bidding. Sometimes it is disgusting to watch."

"Why are you being so spiteful?" His voice raised an octave as his patience drained away. "I never budge from my vision, regardless of their reviews. I am not one of their academy. I am a beggar in their world of classicists, vying for respect. Striving to create what I know to be true and good and beautiful. Do not treat me as if you are better than I am. You would do well to follow my example and befriend the critics and ministers as well."

"I am but a lowly woman, remember? Who sculpts, according to those *cons*, exactly like you. My *Giganti*. 'The likes of Rodin's genius portrayed through Claudel's portraits. It would be best if she imagined her own,'" she spat. "Respect, indeed. Monsieur Leroi speaks kindly of my sketches while I am in the room and reserves his true feelings for the papers. Never mind his disgusting advances. I am not yet treated as your equal in intellect or being. How will I gain their respect, much less their friendship?" She drank from her cup. "Unless I spread my legs for them."

Auguste flinched at the unwelcome vision her words evoked. "You will never gain their respect if you are rude and treat them with disdain."

"As they do me?" Camille stood. "It is difficult to be courteous when they act as if I am beneath them!" She pulled the blanket over her shoulders and stormed toward the house.

"Stubborn woman! You sabotage yourself!" he shouted after her.

She broke into a run, stumbling over the folds in her dress. When she reached the door, she slammed it behind her.

So that was it, then. A perfect rendezvous spoiled by a tantrum. Auguste's shoulders sagged and he jammed his hands inside his coat, suddenly chilled. Paper rustled against his fingertips. He had yet to tell her about the letter Rose had forwarded from Paris that morning. The Claudels had invited him to visit their summer home in Villeneuve.

❧

For once Camille was grateful to be with her family, tucked away in their country home in Villeneuve, her favorite place in the world, far from the complication of Auguste and the art world's prying eyes. She brought a few supplies with her for the duration of the month, but she would need to dig up clay along the riverbank as she always had. Papa would ride with her after luncheons and later in the evenings; Paul would read to the family by candlelight. Best of all, Mother seemed deliriously happy when away from Paris and in her childhood home.

Camille tossed a pebble at one of the outlying boulders from her favorite spot in the rock garden of La Hottée du Diable. She watched the small stone ricochet from the crest of limestone into the trees just beyond. It would be Louise's last summer home before she married. She wondered what it would be like for Mother to lose her favorite child. She would probably latch on to Paul until he left. That would be soon enough.

She stretched and jumped down from her stony seat, sketchbook tucked under her arm. She felt almost like a child. Almost. The sun slipped toward the horizon, its fading rays highlighting Villeneuve's lonely landscape. Soon night's ink would seep into the sky, cloaking rocky knolls and barren fields in mystery. She traipsed through forest, over weathered paths and along the fallow fields. When she reached a junction in the path not far from the center of town, she stopped. A breeze stirred a mass of interlocking vines curling over a stone wall. The vine's leaves waltzed on a current of wind.

The rustle of fabric, intertwined limbs . . . a waltz! Camille dropped to the ground and flipped open her sketchbook. Her pencil flew over the page and two lovers emerged, embracing in the most intimate dance. The woman's head would rest on his shoulder and her dress would flow behind her lithe frame like ocean waves. Their love, their pain moved in solidarity with each step. One step forward, one back, or were they all sideways? She sketched rapidly, until she could no longer see, and skipped up the lane toward home. Giddy with inspiration, she entered the house humming under her breath.

Papa looked over the edge of his paper, the *Courrier de l'Aisne*, from his favorite chaise. "You are happy to be here."

Camille brushed her lips on his forehead. "Very."

He smiled. "Well, to add to your happiness, I have good news." He folded his paper in half. "Monsieur Rodin has accepted our invitation to join us tomorrow at midday. We'll dine in the garden and he will depart tomorrow evening to stay with a friend nearby."

Camille stilled. Her elation shifted to distress. She needed time away, yet their last meeting they had quarreled and she wanted to apologize.

"What is it, *ma chère?*" he asked.

"It's nothing." She whirled around and headed for the door again. It would be difficult to hide their affection from her parents. Under ordinary circumstances she failed at burying her emotions. How, then, would she manage her passion for this man?

"Where are you going?" Papa called after her. "It's dark!"

Camille did not answer, but hurried outdoors to let the night spill over her.

❧

The following morning, Camille peeled one eye open, then two at the sound of a rooster crowing in a neighbor's garden. The sun had not yet awakened from its slumber and the lingering darkness pressed against the windowpanes. She tossed in her bed. Auguste would arrive today. He had followed her once more. Would he seek her to the ends of the earth? Track her scent like a bloodhound to tap her well of inspiration and lap it up? Then there was Monsieur Leroi, the lout, who had called her work derivative. Mathias, on the other hand, praised her highly. Who was right? She wanted to ignore them all and disappear into her marble. She needed to work, to feel her hands thick with clay. She pushed back the covers and prepared for the day, careful not to wake Louise, who snored softly in the bed parallel to hers.

❧

Several hours later, Paul threw open the barn door. "Monsieur Rodin is here." He said the words as if they left a foul taste in his mouth.

Camille looked down at her smock smeared with dirt. Auguste had seen her far worse. Still, it would not do to look a mess at the table. She didn't need to row with Mother today.

"I'll just wash my face and pin my hair," she said. "Maybe throw on a fresh dress."

"Maybe?" Paul rolled his eyes. "Move quickly. We're serving aperitifs now."

She wiped her hands hastily and dashed from the barn to the house, careful to avoid being seen. Once indoors, she heard Auguste's voice in the salon. The melodious canter of his speech rushed over her and her body tingled with longing. Once changed and refreshed, she headed to the terrace. She touched the brooch at her breast. She could not wait to show him *The Waltz*.

The sound of chinking silverware and Mother's laughter filled the air. Mother loved to put on a good show for guests. A sudden lightness came over Camille as she rushed through the yard, her violet dress rustling about her feet. She'd even pinned a flower in her hair. Regardless of her reservation, of the Voice in her head, she loved Auguste with a tenacity that frightened her, and she would not run from him, or the blasted critics.

When she reached the edge of the table she stopped.

Louise, Paul, and her parents chatted with their guests—Auguste and a woman. The woman locked eyes with Camille and paused, the wineglass hovering near her lips. A glance of utter hate burdened her features.

Camille's mouth went dry and her throat constricted. It was *she*— the woman who held him captive. She stared back at Rose Beuret, unable to move. What, in the name of God, was she doing here? How dare Auguste bring her! Did he wish to humble her, to ridicule her in front of her own family? Her stomach roiled and she felt as if she might retch.

"*Ma chère*, Monsieur Rodin and his wife," Papa said, motioning to a chair at the table. "Monsieur's dedication to your progress is admirable. He has traveled from Paris to pledge his support."

Rose Beuret's pale skin blanched whiter still. She knew very well how dedicated Auguste was to Camille. The woman gulped from her wineglass to hide her trembling hands.

Auguste threw Camille a pleading look.

Her gaze shifted to Paul. He hid his frown behind his water glass.

"Join us." Papa motioned to the place at the table beside Louise, directly across from Auguste.

"For heaven's sakes, sit down," Louise said, tossing her hair. "We cannot begin without you."

After Camille sat between her brother and sister, she said, "Isn't monsieur's devotion admirable?" Her tone dripped with spite. "And how lovely to meet you, madame. You are the woman who keeps his house, correct?"

Mother's mouth fell open. "Do not speak to Madame Rodin that way!"

"I hope you will forgive me, *Madame Rodin*." Camille emphasized the false title. "I did not realize monsieur was married."

Rose opened her mouth to retort, when the maid and cook arrived, their arms loaded with platters.

"Would everyone care for cold potage?" Corinne set the tureen on the table. "I'll serve a vegetable next."

"Sounds delicious." Auguste tucked a napkin into his collar. He avoided Camille's withering stare.

Paul thumped Camille's leg under the table. She looked down at her soup. No one spoke. Spoons clanged and scraped against porcelain bowls. A happy bird belted a song from its nest in the bushes along the edge of the property.

"Paul," Papa said, breaking the uneasy silence, "tell Monsieur Rodin about your award."

"Yes, I hear you're a talented young man," Auguste said, thankful for the safe direction of the conversation. "Mademoiselle Claudel sings your praises."

Camille noticed the falsetto in Auguste's voice.

Paul wiped his mouth with his napkin. "Camille is my biggest supporter." He smiled at her. "I'm not sure where I would be without her encouragement."

"Likewise, brother." She blew him a kiss.

Rose sneered into her napkin. Camille smiled sweetly at her in response.

Thankfully, the remainder of the meal, Mother and Louise prattled on about the impending wedding. When the last piece of fruit had been finished, Papa waved his hand at the garden. "Would you care for a walk? Or perhaps Louise could play something for us?"

Louise sat taller, clearly pleased by the attention. "I would be honored to play for you, Monsieur and Madame Rodin."

Rose gave her a genuine smile. "That would be delightful, dear."

They all stood—all but Camille. She remained in her seat and watched everyone file inside. Her food had not been touched. Anger and disgust filled the cavity of her stomach instead. How could Auguste do this to her? She was nothing but a statue, an accessory in his life, someone to pass his time and to make him feel like a man. A tide of pain rolled through her and flooded her throat. How much she had suffered at his hand. She couldn't bear it. Auguste had no intention of leaving Rose and clearly did not take his relationship with Camille in earnest.

Hot tears pooled in her eyes. She stumbled through the yard, fleeing the party, and her pain. She lost her footing on lumpy lawn in her haste to get away and tumbled to the ground. The flower tucked in her hair fluttered to her lap and her beautiful violet gown was smeared with dirt.

She must leave him. The wretched voice had been right. Auguste used her, but the thought of never seeing him . . . A forlorn sob racked her body.

"Are you hurt?" Auguste strode toward her.

Camille scrambled to her feet and strode away from him. "Leave me, please. Just go."

"My darling, wait." He chased her across the lawn and into the field abutting the Claudel property. Her knees wobbled and she stumbled once more. His strong hand caught her and pulled her into his embrace. "I had no choice. Rose's name was on the invitation. She opened it and replied before I had even seen the letter. I tried to tell you in Islette, but we argued and you left. In a panic, I penned a letter and sent it right away to warn you."

Camille's eyes grew wide. "I never received it." And there was only one person who might read her mail and keep it from her: Mother. She knew about them—she must. Tears fell freely, staining her cheeks. Every dream she had of spending their lives together collapsed, every happy memory turned to a dagger, stabbing her insides. The pain. She wanted to crawl into a dark room and disappear.

Auguste fished his handkerchief from his pocket and wiped her tears with a tender hand. "*Amour,*" he whispered, "there is only you. I love you. Since the moment I met you there was no one else."

"If that were true, she would not be here, humiliating me in front of my family." She sobbed. "Did you see the look she gave me?"

Auguste pulled her into his arms. "She is the mother of my son, a longtime friend. I cannot just throw her into the street. Please understand that. Her presence in my house does not diminish what I feel for you. You have my heart. My soul." He pressed her hand to his heart. "It will always belong to you."

Though Camille wanted to slug him, she could not find the strength. Instead she laid her head against his chest and the tears flowed, soaking his linen suit jacket.

"Shhh." He stroked her hair. "I am here for you, always. Rose will never stand in the way of our love."

She did not understand him. If she meant so much to him, despite his friendship with Rose, he would want to be with only her. His words rang hollow. Auguste served only himself, while she and Rose were made to suffer.

She wrenched free of his grasp. "I don't want to be anywhere with you."

"Camille—"

"Just go!" She shoved him. "Leave me alone!"

"You are upset. You need time to refresh yourself. Enjoy the country, the clean air, the birds. When you are revived, come to me. I will be waiting for you."

"Your poetry will not sway me. This—whatever this is between us—is finished."

Fear filled his eyes and his mouth tugged down at the corners.

"Camille?" Mother stalked toward them. "You look a fright! Monsieur, I trust all is well? Your wife asks after you," she said, tone clipped.

"*Bien sûr*. Madame, thank you for your hospitality." He looked at Camille one last time, sorrow deepening the lines on his face. "Thank you, Mademoiselle Claudel. I hope you enjoy the rest of your visit in Villeneuve."

Camille watched him amble toward the house. Once he was out of sight, Mother dropped any semblance of polite speech. "You little whore!" She slapped Camille's cheek with force. "You're fornicating with him!"

Camille staggered backward. Her hand flew to the stinging flesh where palm had connected with skin. Her right eye felt as if it would catapult from its socket. She had never been hit so hard, or at all.

"Mother," she breathed.

"I saw him embracing you!" she hissed. "He has a wife! And now she's here, dining prettily at the house of her husband's mistress! How can you live with yourself?"

A grim smile crossed Camille's face. "They aren't married, Mother. You might say we are both his whores."

Mother's face registered confusion, then shock. "Then you truly are a fool. If he will not choose you when he isn't encumbered with marriage, when would he?"

Her words stung far more than the slap. Camille turned to the open field once more and ran, skirts flapping about her ankles.

"Come back here this instant!" Mother called. "You need to send the guests off."

Camille's chest felt as if her heart had been cut from her body. She flew over the vast carpet of summer grass, under an indifferent blue sky. Mother had hit her! Reflexively her hand flew to her still-warm cheek. But she was right. If Auguste did not choose her now . . . Another sob caught in her throat. She willed her legs to go faster.

The sound of her breathing filled her ears as she ran. The rhythm of her legs and the pounding of her heart lulled her racing thoughts until she calmed. Above her, a raven soared on a current of air.

Camille knew what she must do.

Part Three

1887–1898

La Vague
The Wave

Chapter 26

❦

The sun relinquished its fiery hold on the city and the first cool breeze of evening tiptoed through the open studio windows at 113 Rue d'Italie. Camille dipped a sponge into a basin of clear water, wrung it out, and patted her face and neck. She had worked steadily all day on *The Waltz* and it was nearly complete. Her shoulders and back ached, but soon, Monsieur Debussy would come for her. Her composer friend insisted the music at Robert Godet's salon was sublime inspiration for any artist. She had not been out for weeks and had agreed at the last minute to accompany him.

She wondered how Auguste would feel if he saw her with Debussy. A vision of his pained expression made her stomach clench. She did not regret severing their union, despite the aching hollow in her chest and the yearning for his touch. A watery mist obscured her vision and the room swam. She dashed a hand across her eyes. She could not cry now. She slipped behind the crude partition in the rear of her studio to change into a fresh dress. At least she had gained a new atelier, though its location had proven difficult. Auguste had done anything he could to keep her near him, even renting a space for her just a few doors down from his own, despite their parting. It would not last, but she would use it while she could. After Mother had slapped her, she had moved from the family home into her own apartment, and the new studio, for good. Damn the rumors and her reputation—or what was left of it.

Camille ran a brush through her hair and pinned loose curls in place. She still shared the atelier on Rue Notre Dame des Champs with Jessie, but in mere weeks her friend would depart for England and the atelier would close. As would a chapter in both of their lives.

The hollow in her chest throbbed again when she thought of Jessie leaving. First Giganti, then Auguste, and now Jessie. Paul was all she had left. When she emerged from behind the partition, a shadow caught her eye—the silhouette of a woman—in the window. Someone peered in from the street.

A tremor ran the length of Camille's body. Who in the devil was that? She rushed first to the window, then to the street, spooking her intruder.

"You there!" she shouted. "Why are you spying on me? I could have you arrested!"

The retreating woman glanced over her shoulder. Though she had dashed away too fast for Camille to make out her features, she would swear it was Rose Beuret.

కోడిలో

Footsteps echoed in the staircase outside Auguste's bedroom door.

"It's Octave. Let me in." Mirbeau's voice came from the corridor.

Rodin pushed up in bed. He had been unable to face the mountain of work awaiting him at the studio without *her* in it—he could not even bring himself to say her name. Rose berated him, then pleaded with him every day to forget *sa féroce amie*. Yet he could not banish the image of her wilting in sorrow in his arms. He had betrayed her, their love. He was a coward.

"I am not receiving visitors." Rodin left the house only to post letters, then returned to the dimly lit room and relinquished himself to the blessed escape of sleep.

"Open the door this minute or I will break it down," Octave said firmly.

Rodin heaved a sigh, hoisted himself from bed, and padded to the door. "I am in my chemise."

"No matter," Octave said, stepping into the room. He placed his hands on Rodin's shoulders. "This must end. Come away to my summer home in Normandy. We'll spend a month there, take in the sea and the salty air. It will do you some good."

"I don't know. I have so much to do—"

"Which you aren't doing even now. You suffer from heartbreak and anxiety. It will pass with time. A little perspective from afar will help."

Auguste had written to Octave about *her*. There weren't many he could tell, but both Octave and Mathias had proven to be good friends—unlike Jules, from whom he had still not heard despite the approaching Salon.

"Well?" Octave prodded, stroking his signature mustache. "What do you say?"

Auguste stared into his friend's face and saw the concern brimming in his eyes. "When do we leave?"

⋅⋙⋘⋅

Camille strolled with Jessie through the vast Jardin du Luxembourg in search of a shady spot beneath a tree. They had spent hours in the studio and needed a change of scenery. The late summer haze had crawled from the streets and through their open windows. The odor of urine and rotten garbage mingled with the scent of clay and their own sweat. Camille wanted to rip off her gown and lie in her undergarments, float down the river Seine.

Jessie grunted as she swung a basket at her side, heavy with food and wine. She had offered to provide the picnic this time because of her guilt. She had used the last of Camille's clay for the third time that month without asking, and she still owed her share of rent on the atelier—not to mention a small fortune for an assortment of supplies. Why Jessie had not asked her parents for money, Camille didn't understand. The Lipscombs lived on a huge estate and had all the money they needed. Was Camille supposed to feel sympathy for her? Her friend's life had been easy—her parents adored her and now she had a fiancé.

Camille pushed aside her negative thoughts; she didn't want to ruin one of the few remaining days she had with her friend. Jessie had forgiven her easily after she'd treated Monsieur Elborne with such disdain, and she owed her friend a bit of generosity in return.

A couple walking their poodle neared them on the gravel path. The dog leapt toward Jessie's picnic basket to sniff it. After a moment of investigating, he pawed at her skirt.

Jessie laughed. "I'm sorry, little dog, but this isn't for you."

"César, *ça suffit!*" The dog's owner yanked on the leash. He did not appear amused.

"That's a big name for a little pup," Jessie said.

"His character is grand, believe me," the woman said, mopping her forehead with a pale green handkerchief that matched the bodice of her gown.

César barked and then his tongue fell from his mouth, showing his dog smile. Camille fixated on the outline of the dog's body as it distorted and blended with the gravel path until there were not two objects but one: a ball of gray fur with black pupils against vivid whites. She squeezed her eyes closed and opened them again. She glanced from one face to the next. César's owners' cheekbones and ears, the planes of their faces distorted. She clutched her head.

The gentleman tugged at the leash. "Come, César."

"Camille?" Jessie's concerned voice cut through the fog in her head. "We need to get you out of the heat."

"I just need to sit down," Camille said, as an arm slipped around her shoulders. She allowed herself to be led to a bench under the shelter of a shade tree.

"Have a drink of water." Jessie fished a glass bottle from the basket, uncorked it, and poured water into a tin cup.

Camille gulped it down greedily, then stretched out on the bench and closed her eyes. "The Voice has come back and my vision . . . sometimes I cannot see. I don't know what to do." She threw her arm over her eyes. "And the poodle? I couldn't distinguish where he ended and the gravel path began. He was a gray blur with bright devil eyes."

"What voice do you mean?" Jessie asked, her tone cautious. "You are hearing voices?"

Camille groaned. "Some days. It isn't frequent, but the other things . . . What's wrong with me?"

Jessie sat down beside her. "You have been working so hard lately and you are under a lot of pressure. Then there is Rodin," she added quietly. "Do you miss him? He wrote to me again and asked after you."

As if a dam had burst, a hot flood rushed down Camille's cheeks. "And what did you tell him? That I am a nightmare of distress, debts, and demon voices?"

"Perhaps you should consider a holiday. Get away from Paris for a while."

"And who is to pay for my vacation?" She looked up through a hank of frizzy hair. "I can hardly pay rent. I sold another plaster, but that isn't enough. Papa has given me so much money already. I can't ask him for more."

Jessie watched a pair riding bicycles. The chime of their bells rang merrily in the sunshine. "I owe you money," she said. "I am sorry; truly I am. My father's fortune is at risk and they have stopped sending my allowance. Tutoring has been the only way I've been able to manage."

"Hasn't your father just earned his fortune?" Camille snapped. She didn't believe the mansion and lavish vacations of which she had partaken only last summer had vanished. "You take my things. You tell your students you're as good a sculptor as Auguste. We both know that isn't true. You're a liar," she said with vengeance. "How can I believe you anymore, Jessie?"

The bicycle bells chimed. Their vibrating fused into the sharpened point of a saber to stab her brain. Camille groaned. "And you share my secrets with *him*." She looked about, frantic. "You're not my friend. You use me. You use Auguste."

The bells again. Her head rang and a metallic tang flooded her mouth.

"What are you talking about?" Jessie demanded. Her face registered her alarm. "You are unwell, Camille. You aren't yourself—"

Camille's head swiveled from left to right as she scanned the pedestrians in the park around them. "What are you scheming now? Auguste writes to you. Are you planning something with him?"

Shock registered on Jessie's face.

"Get out of my sight!" Camille screamed. "Get your things from my studio and leave. I don't need someone who betrays me."

Jessie stood and gathered her basket of things. "You have lost your mind! It is true I have failed at doing the right thing at times, but I have always been your friend." She turned to go, but stopped suddenly to add, "I am as talented a sculptor as you, and likely as Auguste. It is not a lie to tell my students thus."

Camille laughed, a hollow, unnatural sound. "Even if that were true—which it is not—your sculpting career is finished the moment you set foot on that ferry back to England, and you know it."

Jessie's shoulders drooped. "If you continue to treat people as you do, you will be alone—alone with no one to care for you, and all of the success in the world will mean nothing. Good-bye, Camille. I wish you well."

"Keep telling yourself you are as skilled as Auguste!" she shouted at Jessie's retreating back. "You are a liar and a fake, desperate to be something you aren't." Camille was suddenly confused, her own words echoing in her ears and ringing somewhere deep within her core. A liar and a fake, *she* would never be as skilled as Auguste.

When Jessie had disappeared from sight, a pang of remorse stole Camille's breath away. She gripped her sides to hold in the pain. Her friend was gone, and would likely never speak to her again. Why had she treated her that way, regardless of her shortcomings? Had she become like Mother? She curled in on herself, around her leaden despair.

⚜

Though Auguste had spent the fall seeing Camille's face in every block of marble, her supple form posed upon a platform smiling for only him, his spirits revived. A letter had come, awarding him the commission to create Hugo for the Panthéon. He had rejoiced at the news, and found solace in poring over his sketches once more. He closed the ledger and returned it to his desk drawer. He did not need more work with his *Burghers* yet to be finished, and then there were the *Gates* and several private pieces, but working on Hugo gave him a reason to get out of bed in the morning.

Truman Bartlett, artist and critic, poked his head into Auguste's office.

"Come in." Rodin slid a silver-plated letter opener under the flap of an envelope sent from the Société des Artistes Français. He looked up as Truman entered.

"Are you ready to dine?" Truman removed his hat.

"*Oui*, in one moment." Rodin skimmed the letter. "I cannot believe it." His eyes bulged and he reread it for good measure. "I've been awarded the Légion d'Honneur. The bastards have finally accepted I'm here to stay." He sat back in his chair. As the news soaked in, a giddiness he had not felt in months warmed his blood. He slammed his fist on the tabletop. "I've done it, Truman! I've really done it. If only my father and sister were alive to see it."

Truman extended his hand. "Congratulations are in order. And a toast."

Auguste stood and shook his hand vigorously. "Thank you, my friend." A hearty laugh escaped his lips and he ran his hands over his hair. Rodin stood motionless for several moments while he basked in his newfound happiness. "I can't believe it. This day has finally arrived."

A cloud darkened his sudden good humor. There had been scandals that involved artists paying for the award and, consequently, much gossip circulating. It belittled the honor and insulted those still hoping to attain it. But Auguste had not paid for it and damn those who thought he had. He had never cared for what others thought of him anyway. Why would he begin now?

He slipped into his overcoat. "What do you think of the scandal?"

"No one will believe you paid to win, if that's what you mean," Truman said. "You're one of the most talented and well-known sculptors in Paris these days, probably in all of Europe. It shouldn't have taken them so long to award the ribbon to you in the first place." He shrugged. "But you can always refuse to accept it if you're truly concerned with the rumors. Degas, Courbet, Daumier all denied the ribbon, though I think it foolish. It proves nothing, but making them look like stubborn old men."

Auguste puffed out a breath. "Yes, I know. Antibourgeois, anti–Napoleonic Empire sentiment and all that. Never mind the many talentless hacks who have toed the line for the *école* all these years. But frankly, I have bills to pay so I'm happy to accept a commission from anyone, bourgeois or not. Rent for my ateliers, all of the supplies." He rubbed his eyes. "Do you think they will snub me?"

"Who? Your friends?"

"The critics, my friends. Geffroy, Mirbeau, Monet. Dalou, especially. They scoff at it like it's a label of mediocrity."

Truman grasped his shoulder. "It is an honor. Be proud and stand behind it. Very few men can boast they have won such a prestigious award."

Auguste's friend had toiled as an artist and as a critic. He knew well the prestige associated with a national award. Still, the scandal worried him. Would his friends disapprove?

"Take time to think about it," Truman said. "For now, let's eat!"

Auguste nodded, though perhaps he would skip right to the drink.

❧

A month later, Auguste looked over the adorned heads of the crowd. His cravat strangled him, or perhaps his unease came from all those eyes upon him. He touched his precious Légion d'Honneur, pinned at his lapel, and now wove through the crowd to his place at the table. A ball of anxiety, he had not eaten all day, but now the aroma of meat wafting from the belly of the building sent his stomach to grumbling. If only Camille had accompanied him. God, he wanted to share this moment with her, to fill her full of fine food and parade her across the dance floor in an elegant peacock blue gown, the shade of her lovely eyes. How she would laugh at the bureaucrats stuffed in their tailored suits and the women plucked, preened, and pasted with false smiles. They would exchange secret smiles, knowing looks. But he had not heard from her in many months.

Auguste sat and tucked his serviette into his collar. A beautiful woman to his right turned a flirtatious smile on him. "*Félicitations*, Monsieur Rodin." She fluttered her painted eyes and tipped her head at a coquettish angle.

He had seen her at another event. Madame Barder, queen bee in her circle of wealthy lady friends and their self-made husbands. Her gold and pink taffeta gown set off the rosy blush accenting her cheekbones and strong jawline. A long, creamy neck and cascade of blond hair threaded with silver gave her a regal look. If he were to create her portrait, her complexion would demand to be carved in the most delicate alabaster.

"*Merci*—Madame Barder, is it?" he asked.

"*C'est moi*," she replied. "I would love to see your work, Monsieur. Perhaps a visit to the Dépôt des Marbres is in order. To be one of your subjects would be"—she smiled—"titillating." She leaned forward so he might peer down the front of her dress.

Despite her beauty and apparent willingness, a tumble in bed with a stranger couldn't be further from Auguste's mind. Suddenly uncomfortable, he glanced at her husband across the table. The woman possessed bravado, though not the kind he admired. He was thankful for the rumble of laughter and voices that drowned out her words. He must be cautious, lest Monsieur Barder think him a rogue. Rodin had just been accepted into this circle and didn't want to be pushed out once more—especially over a woman he did not want.

"One of my assistants would be happy to escort you through my studio," he replied.

The maître d'hôtel, dressed in black-and-white livery, rushed from the kitchen leading a flurry of his staff. They carried soup tureens filled to the brim with creamed winter vegetable soup and baskets of fresh bread—the first course of the evening. Auguste could smell it from his place at the table.

Madame Barder changed her tactic. "Aren't you buzzing with happiness? To be recognized as an artist of national merit is such an honor." She smiled and a twinkle lit her gray eyes. "An honor well deserved."

"Thank you, and yes, I am very honored." He hoped the award meant his legacy would be ensured. An indescribable sentiment bloomed in his chest at the thought. Pride? Elation?

Gratitude.

His works would not be forgotten or degraded—perhaps he would even make history. He felt his imprint on the art world had meant something, but that did not mean his contemporaries felt the same way. His reviews over the years had proven that.

"Has the controversy affected you?" She touched the back of his hand lightly. "I know you would never purchase your award. You are too upstanding for such a thing."

Auguste nodded and drank from his water glass.

"I'm assuming you have seen Octave Mirbeau's response to your acceptance in the journal?" she continued.

He stared at her in surprise. The woman had not only propositioned him in front of her husband, but she was a gossip. Yet he knew he must tread carefully.

"I've read the article *Le Chemin de la Croix*, yes," he said. "Monsieur Mirbeau wishes me well, though he is unhappy I accepted the award." Auguste had to admit the article had stung, but he knew Octave had his best interests at heart. Truly, his friend lashed out at the institution and not at him.

"I'm certain he wishes you well. Mirbeau may as well have called you a genius in that article, but he did not hesitate to express his thoughts, *publicly*. That must have been quite offensive."

Auguste chewed a mouthful of bread. He had known madame for mere minutes and she expected him to pour out his heart. He wished he could change his seat at the table.

She raised her preened eyebrows expectantly.

He attempted to keep his irritation in check. "I assure you I am quite happy with the honor and that all is well."

"Take heart, monsieur. Scandals bring recognition and that can only mean good things for your art."

"I am not one for scandal, madame. It insults my integrity."

"Oh, come now. A secret or dash of impropriety adds a sense of mystery to an artist. Not that you need a single thing, monsieur. You're positively alluring as you are. Artists are so intriguing." Madame Barder dabbed at her mouth with a serviette, erasing the faded rouge from her lips. "Why don't I come to your studio next week? I might find a portrait or two to buy, or at the very least recommend to friends."

Rodin saw through her ruse. She wished to buy him, to keep him at her heel as she did her friends. He could see it in her glittery brooch and diamond earrings, in the expensive adornments her lady friends wore, and worst of all in her flirtatious manner. He would not sell himself to her—he did not need money that desperately.

But Camille did.

The staff returned to cart away their empty bowls and replace them with plates of whitefish dressed with crème fraîche and a chiffonade of herbs.

"This smells divine, but I must save my appetite for the duck course. A woman should look after her figure." She sipped from her wineglass instead. "So what do you say?"

"I know the perfect piece for you," Auguste replied. "It possesses *la tendresse de l'amour*, forgiveness, adoration, and is crafted by an expert hand, but it is not one of mine. It's called *Shakuntala*, by a Mademoiselle Camille Claudel. It's brilliant. I assure you, you will not be disappointed."

"The prizewinner at Salon last year?"

"That's the one."

"I would like to see it again."

"Morhardt, Mirbeau, and Geffroy sing her praises. Her work has become quite popular." A bit of a stretch, but he must help Camille in any way he could. If he struggled against the blasted *école* and the expectations of a fickle society a thousand times, she struggled ten thousand. His chest tightened at the thought of his ferocious one.

Yet she wasn't his at all.

"Monsieur?" Madame Barder covered his hand with hers. "Are you all right?"

Auguste removed his hand from the table and placed it in his lap. "I am well, thank you."

God, he missed Camille. The reprieve of happiness dissipated as melancholy clutched him once more.

❧

A hand broke loose and fell to the floor with a crash. Camille walked to where the appendage lay, kicked at the severed fingers, and crunched the terra-cotta palm beneath her boot. She hated this piece anyway. It had done nothing but give her trouble. She had wrestled with all of her works since her split with Auguste. She could think of nothing but him. Had he moved on? Forgotten their love and fawned over another young student? Those stupid women who flocked to him didn't understand him. They did not know his heart. Rage surged through her veins. With a violent shove, she pushed the broken statue over. She stomped on the piece, a tide of anguish, fear, and the sting of rejection pouring from her. The release of her hopes and disappointments trickled down her spine and into the soles of her boots. She smashed until only a rusty powder and shards of dried clay remained.

Out of breath, she flopped down in a chair. She needed to get hold of her emotions. Auguste would move on and so would she, eventually. She glanced at a statuette of a young girl in a sheath. It nestled beside her bust of a slave. Both pieces had evoked such excitement in Auguste, she had reveled in his praise for days. How proud she had been! Now they sat, alive, with no one to see them.

Still agitated, she rustled through a stack of envelopes on the table. One was a bill from her landlord; the other showed an address from

Aisne, the *département* in northern France where she was born. Curious, since she knew no one in Aisne. She snatched a chisel from her worktable and slit the envelope open.

Étienne Moreau-Nélaton, minister in Aisne, thought her works inspired and had written to the town council on her behalf. He believed he could secure a commission for her—a noble piece to represent the republic to be set in bronze for the town center.

Camille leapt to her feet, excitement pulsing through her. It would be her first public commission! She did not need Auguste's help! *Shakuntala* really had bolstered her career. Her monument would stand in the town square for posterity!

She wanted to tell someone. She looked around at the myriad of tables, pails of clay, and tools scattered throughout her work space. No sounds of a fellow artist shaping her work emanated in the silent space—no laughter, no cursing over an unruly block of marble. Even Minou emitted not a sound, sleeping in a shaft of pale sunlight. The furball had not even roused when she destroyed the piece.

Suddenly the space grew to a yawning hole, echoing her solitude.

Jessie had left for England and probably hated her for her behavior when they last met. Giganti had abandoned her and now she had lost Auguste. Better not to love anyone at all, lest they leave her—and they always left her.

Camille picked up a pointed shard of dried clay and crushed it in her hands. Blood seeped from a fresh cut in her palm. But she did not need them. She needed her art, only her art.

Chapter 27

꧁꧂

The coach sat in congested traffic as they approached the Exposition Universelle. Their guiding beacon beamed electric red, white, and blue lights across the evening sky.

"Eiffel's tower," Claude Debussy mused. "Three hundred meters of iron. I think it's hideous."

"You and half of Paris." Camille leaned forward and pushed the coach door open. "We should have taken the train. Let's go. We can walk the remainder of the way."

Claude scrambled out behind her and they strolled along the boulevard to the Champ de Mars. Camille had spent a lot of time with Monsieur Debussy in the past few months. He was a good friend—and could be more if she allowed it. If only. Thoughts of Auguste tormented her. *Dieu*, she craved him. Yet each time she would surrender to her heart and set out to throw herself at his feet, the Voice would return to deride her.

She looped her arm through Monsieur Debussy's as a gust of autumn wind sent a whirling funnel of dead leaves into the air around them. They walked past buildings constructed in styles native to the countries they represented—Bolivia, Russia, Japan, and many others. Debussy smiled and his thin mustache twitched at the corners.

"You can't wait for the performance," Camille said, stretching her own frozen face into a smile. The unseasonal chill bit at her earlobes and fingertips.

"Of course, but I am looking forward to the sculpture exhibit as well," he said, almost as an apology.

"You don't have to pretend to enjoy it. I am perfectly happy on my own. You can sit at the bar or visit another exhibit while I'm there."

"Of course not," Monsieur Debussy said. "You know I love art as well. But I'd like to go there first." He pointed to a massive pavilion. "It's the largest vaulted building ever built."

When they entered the pavilion, Camille gazed at the hinged iron archways supporting the ceiling. "Incredible!" she said.

They stopped to admire the indigo ceramic tiles and paintings of Byzantine life of *le dôme central.* The edifice was an astonishing work of iron and glass. Tourists milled about in their native Oriental silks, African robes, and South American headdresses. Many languages swirled around them; foreigners had traveled far to witness the latest world's fair, in the grand city of Paris.

"I wouldn't have guessed so many would come from so far away."

"Remarkable, isn't it?" Monsieur Debussy led her to the massive Galerie des Machines, a hall packed with hundreds of steel and iron machines hitched with rubber and wood contraptions, fueled by steam or powered by electricity.

Despite the impressive display, after an hour of touring Camille grew anxious to see the Palais des Beaux-Arts. She knew Auguste would show at least one piece there, and suddenly she needed to see it. *Now.*

"I'm ready to move on." She tugged Debussy's arm. "There are some pieces I really need to see."

He raised an eyebrow at the urgency in her voice. "Very well. Let's go."

Without a second thought, Camille pulled him through the crowd to the exit. Somehow, seeing Auguste's work would soothe her spirits. An image of him laboring over a swath of clothing or the bulge of fleshy lips flitted through her mind. A need filled her chest until it squeezed her lungs and she could hardly breathe.

Once outdoors, she moved faster, dodging pedestrians as she went.

"Mademoiselle, slow down." Debussy raced after her. "Is something wrong?"

"I need to see him now."

"Who? I thought we were going to see the art."

Camille stopped in her tracks. Monsieur Debussy smacked into her, sending his hat tumbling to the pavement. "*Dieu*, what is that?" she asked.

Within a large fenced area, several families of South Americans roamed about in their tribal dress, their silken black hair free-flowing over bronzed shoulders. Strings of shells ringed their necks and wrists and vivid white teeth stood out against copper skin. One woman scratched her bared, sagging breast. Another rolled a stone cylinder against a rock to crush what looked to be corn kernels. A ring of males sat around a fire and passed a pipe between them. The smoke did little to cover the scent of livestock and human waste.

Debussy fetched his top hat and placed it on his head. "It's a human zoo. Have you not read about it? There are more of them here. Africans, peoples from the Orient. Apparently they are one of the more popular exhibits at the Exposition."

Camille stared at the natives in shock. Who would devise such a thing? "How horrifying," she said at last. "Can you imagine being gaped at all day? I'm sure they are heckled."

Amusement played across his features. "I presume they have been paid handsomely."

Laughter came from somewhere ahead of them on the path. Camille turned from the odd display to find the source of such a jovial sound. A broad-shouldered man with a burnt orange beard walked with a cluster of male companions.

Her pulse quickened. Was it *he*? The shoulders, the beard, his gait. She resumed her rapid pace toward him. It had to be her dear Auguste. No one resembled him. The cool air stung her nose and cheeks; the clack of her heels on pavement thundered in her ears.

"Mademoiselle, wait!" Debussy trailed her.

Her breath came in uneven spasms. "Rodin! Monsieur Rodin!" Too engrossed in his companion's story, *he* did not turn, despite her calling after him. She broke into a run, ignoring those who stared, until she reached the gentleman's side. "Auguste," she breathed, placing her hand on his shoulder.

The gentleman turned. "What's that ye say, miss? Are ye looking for someone?" His thick Irish accent did not match *his* voice—the voice of her precious one, her tormentor.

A crush of disappointment took her breath away. The gentleman's orange beard and barrel chest, his cane with brass knob had fooled her. Her unbidden hope deflated.

"Do ye need an escort, lass?" the Irishman asked. He glanced at his friends with a knowing look. "We was headin' to see the wild west show."

"Oh, rats. I didn't bring my chaps," she said. The gentleman frowned. He did not understand her French. He tipped his hat and went on his way.

"Is something the matter?" Debussy said, catching up to her.

She blinked rapidly to contain her tears. "I thought I saw someone I knew."

He searched her face. "Is everything all right? Should we leave?"

A need throbbed inside her. To see Auguste—despite the Voice, the critics, her brother—was the only cure. She turned to the entrance of the Palais des Beaux-Arts. She shook her head. "Let's go."

Debussy grasped her hand and placed it on his forearm. They entered the building, carefully constructed in iron with thousands of glass panes similar to those in the Galerie des Machines, set to illuminate the hundreds of paintings, sculptures, and lithography works inside.

Camille inhaled a breath to steady her nerves. She would go to Auguste tonight. She must. But what would she say? Did he still love her? Perhaps he had moved on to another fresh-faced young artist to fill his inspirational well. No, she could not do it—go to him to find he had moved on, or worse, to see him still in Rose's clutches.

As Debussy led her through the halls, Camille noted a few well-made sculptures, but most displayed inferior execution and inspiration compared with those she had seen in Rodin's atelier. And then she saw them—her *Young Girl with a Sheaf*, but it was called *Galatée*, and her *Slave* bust was now *Tête de Rieur*. She froze.

Auguste had stolen her ideas and created his own exact replicas.

She skipped from one piece to the next, heart thudding against her ribs, searching out her works labeled with his name. How could he, without telling her?

"Mademoiselle?" Debussy said. "Is everything all right?"

Camille combed the entire section, but found no others that were hers. She inhaled a deep breath. They had, in truth, worked on the pieces together. She reminded herself of the many works he had inspired, and their give-and-take in the atelier. They learned from one another. Right? Yet she deserved to have her pieces shown in this space, with *her* name on them. And she would, one day soon, she reminded herself.

"Let's move along," she said, suddenly ready to be somewhere else. Seeing Auguste's works had not calmed her yearning for him, or her nerves, as she had hoped.

Debussy nodded and led her to an *allée* of paintings.

Camille stopped to study a tableau titled *Maternity*. A woman traveled through a barren landscape of brush holding a baby, with a young son at her side. Where was the woman going? The tableau, flushed in grays and blues, emphasized the woman's hopeless state of poverty, or at the very least her loneliness. Camille could feel the crackling grass against her legs and the sandy path underfoot, the desolation of the landscape as raw as the woman's in the painting. She would never have a child. The thought at once relieved and depressed her. She would be an awful mother. To re-create her family's home would be the worst thing she could do to another human being. And to be as poor and alone as this woman.

"What do you think of this?" Debussy stood before *A Rajah of Jodhpur*, a scene of the Indian king atop his elephant cavalry. "The saturation of light and color is brilliant."

"It's the desert. Of course there's light," Camille said, ever sarcastic. "It's nice, though it's not inspired. It lacks emotion." She moved to the next painting.

The sensation of being watched sent a chill down her spine. Her heart pumped faster. That sentiment had come more often of late, and it made her already poor sleeping habits worse. God, she did not understand what was happening to her. And whom could she tell who wouldn't call her . . . the word she refused to say? She rubbed her thumb and forefinger together. But it was there, the burning of two eyes into her back. She turned to locate the source of her discomfort.

Auguste, face contorted in pain, stood opposite her in the aisle.

Chapter 28

A couple linked arm in arm pushed past Auguste while he stood motionless in the walkway. The air had left his lungs. How had Camille managed to come the same day at the exact same time? The exposition had been open for months. The cauterized wound in his heart ripped open and emotion poured from the gaping hole. Her skin, the wicked blue of her eyes. *Dieu*, his love for her was like a sickness.

Camille walked toward him, cautiously. A man he vaguely recognized trailed behind her. Her escort? His heart seized in his chest. He couldn't bear to know that she had moved on. He would rather drown in his misery than learn she did not love him. He turned on his heel to flee.

"Auguste." Camille's voice rang out across the space like bells in a fog. "How are you?"

He turned to face her. "I am surviving. God, Camille. To see you again." He looked away, afraid he had revealed too much. But why hold back now? He had already lost her. He met her gaze once more. "Each day without you has been hell. I am a lowly man writhing outside your gates, longing to enter, to hold you again. I—"

Camille closed the distance and wrapped herself around him. The indomitable force that bound them tightened its hold.

Auguste did not understand it, but the draw to her, the strength of their affection filled him once again with awe and foreboding. He would never be free.

"*Pour toujours, mon amour.*" He held her against him, oblivious to the crowds swarming around them. "Always."

Breathless, she rested her forehead against his chin. "You have cursed me."

"And you have crucified me." He cupped her face in his hands.

She laid her head against his chest. "I have been in a wretched state without you, no matter how hard I fight it."

"Mademoiselle Claudel?" Her escort cleared his throat. "Would you care to introduce me?"

Rodin took in the man's scraggly mustache, his thin black hair and angular head. He had an interesting profile; his face reflected a deep melancholy that had settled into his bone structure.

Camille turned, surprised she had forgotten the gentleman. "Monsieur Debussy! Yes, of course. May I present Auguste Rodin, the sculptor."

Recognition flickered in Debussy's eyes. "Ah, yes. Monsieur, you create beautiful works. I am honored to make your acquaintance."

"Likewise." Rodin shook his hand. "You are a composer."

"Indeed." Debussy looked at Camille.

"If you will excuse us a moment, Monsieur Rodin." Camille pulled Debussy to the side.

Auguste strained to decipher their fierce whispers, but could not. Monsieur Debussy kissed her hand. Surely the man did not think to woo Camille after witnessing their reunion? Auguste clenched his jaw.

"It's a pleasure to meet you, monsieur, but I must be off," Debussy said. "There's a musical performance I am anxious to see. Something from the Orient."

Relief surged through Auguste. "I hope you enjoy the show," he said with a polite nod.

Camille kissed the man's cheeks and threw herself in Auguste's arms once more.

"I have a reservation at the Restaurant Russe in Eiffel's tower." He placed tender kisses on the tip of her nose and her eyelids. Each contact with her skin sent a river of warmth through him. "Come with me."

Hesitation perched on her features; she warred within, still.

Auguste held her eyes. "Come for the succulent beef and a spectacular view of the city. I cannot share it with anyone but you, *amour.*"

The last of her doubts evaporated from her face. "Take me with you. Take all of me."

❧

Smoke filled the back room at the Café Américain. The Société Nationale des Beaux-Arts had convened officially for the first time two hours before and now a few remaining members enjoyed dinner and a round of drinks. The conversation had, thankfully, steered clear of the topic of Auguste's Légion d'Honneur. Since Camille had come back to him, he had been content, though overworked, and had no desire to stir up controversy at his acceptance of the award.

Auguste slipped his hand under the table and squeezed Camille's knee. She puckered her lips slightly in a mock kiss. They had been open about their affection since their reunion.

"Lovebirds," Jules Dalou said, blotting his mustache with his napkin. "You two are like children."

Jules had deigned to show his face despite their broken friendship, but he refused to make eye contact with Auguste. Since the appointment of the Hugo monument, he had not answered a single one of Auguste's letters. Auguste didn't know why he insisted on trying to maintain the friendship—it only brought him heartache.

"You just wish I would kiss you instead, Monsieur Dalou," Camille said in a biting tone, though she puckered her rouge lips once more. A chorus of laughter met her comment.

Jules held up his hands. "I'll admit it. I am jealous of Auguste."

Camille laughed, though her eyes seemed to hold an emotion Rodin could not decipher, as if she had a secret with Dalou. Auguste tensed, but forced a good-natured chuckle. "You have plenty to be happy about, my friend."

Jules's smile faded into a scowl. "I suppose I do, though I should have been selected to design the monument to Victor Hugo."

The murmuring around the table stopped.

Jules had said it at last. He thought himself above Auguste, clearly, and any other artist who had submitted designs. Auguste squirmed inside. If he weren't in the company of so many of his colleagues he would give Jules the tongue-lashing he deserved. After many barbed comments over the years, Jules's constant avoidance and badmouthing, Auguste had had enough. His former friend had destroyed anything good they had shared as young men.

"The best man wins," Camille said bluntly. "Monsieur Rodin will do a fine job with Hugo, and I, for one, am not sorry he was selected."

Though Auguste wanted to kiss her for coming to his defense, he shot her a warning look. He could fight his own battles.

"He may do a fine job, but it is difficult to respect an artist who will accept a medal from a corrupt government," Jules replied. "It's unfortunate you did not have the conviction to stand up to the *école*, Auguste. Sadly, you lick their boots, instead. Now it is difficult to take you seriously."

Anger blistered over Auguste's skin. "I do nothing of the kind!"

"Christ, Jules, what has gotten into you?" Mathias's usual good humor dissolved as he jumped to his friend's aid.

"Why won't you stand up to them?" Jules pressed him.

"I won't apologize to you, or to anyone, that I accepted the award. I have worked like a madman for many years and defended myself in the journals when I felt it necessary." Auguste felt his face flame. "I have earned the recognition. My battle is won by creating beautiful sculpture, not through spite for the administration."

"You're a darling of the press is all," Dalou said, balling his hands into fists. "And I don't find it so well deserved."

Mathias's eyes flashed. "That's enough!" He arose, his portly middle bumping the table. "You will not talk to your colleague—nay, your friend—like that."

"I may be a darling of the press," Auguste said, "but it does not belittle my hard work." He stood and slammed his chair into the empty table behind them. "Apparently our friendship has meant nothing to you. I'm finished with your abuse. Steer clear of me or you will regret it, Dalou!"

Jules crossed his arms and glared in response. Camille pulled on her pelisse and retrieved her handbag.

"Gentlemen." The barkeep rushed to their table. "Is there a problem here?"

"I was just leaving." Auguste put his hand under Camille's elbow. "Good night." They stormed to the exit.

❧

The gardens at Château de l'Islette flourished in the summer sun; rows of pruned hedges lined the paths, a trellis sagged under the weight of bursting rose vines, and the skirts of willow trees billowed over patches of verdant lawn. Camille adored spending time in such an idyllic setting. Today she would go for a walk and do some sketching in the shaded nook beside the pond. She glanced at her young model fidgeting in her chair. The walk would need to happen sooner than she had expected. Madeleine Boyer, the little girl before her, would not last much longer. The château's owner had allowed Camille to sketch her five-year-old granddaughter for a bust—*La Petite Châtelaine*, she would call it. The old woman was honored to have young Madeleine preserved in time. Camille felt honored herself, to make the sweet, vivacious girl immortal.

Madeleine picked at a long blond hair that tickled her nose. Camille wished she could portray the smattering of freckles across her nose, her long lashes and caramel-colored eyes. She trimmed a thin cord of clay from her maquette, highlighting a rope of hair that braided and buckled over itself as if blown by a brisk wind. She brushed the debris away with a delicate hand.

A vision of Louise came to mind, her four-year-old giggle erupting from somewhere behind a bush. Camille had chased her little sister until she managed to escape and hide. But Louise had not remained hidden long; her infectious laugh gave her away, and the hem of her blue-and-white dress showed through her leafy cover.

"I see you!" Camille launched at her little sister, wrestled her to the ground, and tickled her.

Louise's giggles became waves of laughter and then happy tears. "Stop!" she called through her laughter. "Stop!" After several minutes, Camille helped Louise to her feet and freed a snared leaf from her curly mop. She loved to play with her when their mother allowed.

"Let's play again," Camille said. "This time, I'll hide and you find me."

Rodin entered the room, wiping his hands with a towel. "Shall we break? I'd like to go for a stroll around the pond and through the wood."

Camille started at his voice. The memory had been so vivid she felt as if she were there, chasing Louise, the brisk wind of Villeneuve whipping across her face and through her hair. She shook her head to dispel the fog. She had loved children then and still did.

"What do you say?" Rodin asked. "Care to walk with me, *amour*?"

"We are finished for today," Camille said to Madeleine, smiling.

La petite slipped the top of her dress over her shoulders and Camille helped her button it closed. She had not requested the girl be naked— it would be indecent to ask such a thing from a child not raised to be an artist's model.

Camille touched the end of Madeleine's nose. "I will see you again tomorrow. Please thank your *mémé* for the tart. It was delicious."

Madeleine jumped down from her perch in a flash, happy to be released. "*Oui*, madame." She smiled, displaying a dimple in her right cheek, and skipped from the room.

Camille was no madame. In fact, she couldn't be further from being Rodin's wife. *C'est un collage*—living together out of wedlock—was what they were doing, and not even full-time at that. Fury and self-disgust brewed in the pit of her stomach each time she was reminded of the truth of her situation . . . and of Rose.

"I have a surprise for you." Auguste tossed the soiled rag among a scattering of supplies.

"What is it?" she asked, swallowing her less-than-pleasant emotions.

He took her in his arms. "Your little Madeleine shall be in marble."

She gasped. "How did you manage that? Who wants it?"

"I purchased the stone myself. Think what a mark it will make at the Salon—a woman's work in marble."

Camille squeezed him with all her might. And this was precisely why she could not stay angry at him for long—his generosity, his obvious desire to help her succeed.

He laughed. "I see you are pleased."

"*Merci, mon amour.*" With a happy heart, she pressed her lips to his.

❖

Rodin did not wish to attend another dinner where he must be engaging. He had neither the wits about him nor the appetite—his stomach felt raw, chewed alive by the stress of so much work to complete. The *Gates*, the *Burghers*, *Hugo*—not to mention several of his personal projects—needed finishing. But to ensure his legacy and to pay his mounting bills, he could not turn the work away. As he grew older and his days numbered, he feared he would not leave enough of his works behind. Now he vied for a national commission of Honoré de Balzac, but another sculptor had been the favored contender—at least that is what a friend behind the scenes had told him.

"*Bonsoir*, gentlemen," Auguste said, sitting at a table of critics and friends. He turned to the man on his right—the reason he had agreed to attend the dinner in the first place—the newly appointed president of the Société des Gens de Lettres.

Émile Zola smiled, softening his staid countenance. "Monsieur Rodin, it is a pleasure to see you again."

The writer had visited Auguste's atelier nearly two years ago, but he had seen him only a handful of times since, and from a distance. "Thank you for the invitation," he replied. "I am truly honored. Tell me, are you working on another book? I have purchased my own copy of *L'Argent*."

Zola frowned and pushed his oval spectacles up his nose. "That novel has not garnered the praise I had hoped."

Auguste spooned steaming cabbage soup into his mouth. "Don't let it bother you. Many allow their religious prejudices to speak for them, rather than their sentiments about your style. I understand your frustration, but your novels are poignant and will be remembered as such for posterity."

"Jews and Christians have been at war for centuries," Zola said. "And yet, writing about their struggle in modern times is as controversial as ever." He soaked a hunk of bread in his soup until it grew heavy with savory liquid. "I have some business to discuss with you."

Bracing himself, Auguste set down his spoon. He already knew what Émile would say. To attain the commission of not one but two national heroes would be a coup. It did not surprise him that he had not been selected, yet he couldn't help but feel the letdown. "Balzac has been granted to Monsieur Vasselot," he said, voice matter-of-fact.

"The opposite, in fact," Zola said, smiling. "I have selected the sculptor myself and elicited the committee's approval."

"Oh?" Auguste's stomach churned with wine and cabbage broth.

"You are the artist to capture Balzac's naturalism, his greatness."

"I don't know what to say." Auguste shook Zola's hand vigorously. "Thank you." Victor Hugo and now Honoré de Balzac! A wide smile crossed his face.

"I have no doubt you will create a marvel of a piece," Zola said.

"I will do my best."

Zola ate another bite. "We can discuss stipends and delivery dates next week after I meet with the committee."

A shower of anxiety dampened Auguste's excitement. Another due date. He forced a smile and downed another bite of soup.

⋞⊱

Auguste riffled through his bills and shoved the latest into a leather binder before hiding them in his desk. One day he would no longer be able to help Camille financially, and he did not look forward to that day. The only remedy would be to help her find work—and he would do his best to ensure it happened.

"Auguste!" Rose called from the salon downstairs.

He sighed. He had not seen her much in the past months, or even the past two years, with his constant travel with Camille, but he still did his best to keep her satisfied—and out of his hair.

"Auguste!"

Muttering under his breath, he headed downstairs to the salon.

Rose sat in a chaise mending a pair of her stockings. "There you are. Since you've been back from Touraine, you've either dashed out the front door or been locked in your office."

Auguste sat on the sofa opposite her and chose a newspaper from the stack in the wicker basket. "I've had bills and such to tend to."

Silence followed, broken only by the occasional rumple of newspaper pages. After some time, Auguste looked up. Rose watched him intently. A bonnet covered her graying hair and she wore her favorite faded apron.

"What is it?" he asked.

"I want you to stop seeing her."

"Stop seeing who?"

"After all this time you are going to treat me as if I am blind?" Her voice rose an octave. "The artist. You made *The Eternal Idol* for her, didn't you?"

Auguste rubbed his tired eyes. The piece in which a woman leaned backward on her knees, her eyes closed in pleasure as a male figure kneeled at her altar—his love, his inspiration, his very being. He was that male figure. Yes, he had made the piece for Camille.

"We wouldn't live like paupers if you stopped supporting your whore. You parade all over the country buying her things," she said. "You think I don't read the receipts?" When he didn't reply, she crossed her arms. "She doesn't even make you happy. You've brooded and skulked ever since you met her."

"Perhaps you should find a lover of your own." Fatigue throbbed in his bones. "Someone who makes you feel alive. Clearly that person is not me and it hasn't been me for many years."

Rose stood and her mending tumbled from her lap to the floor. "You would toss me out? Cast me aside like a worn pair of shoes?" Her face turned a frightening shade of purple.

Auguste grabbed her hand and pulled her toward him. "Calm yourself. Your heart—"

She yanked her hand free of his grasp. "You make me sick!" She clutched her chest.

"Sit down!" He guided her to the settee.

Before she reached the cushion, she crumpled and fell to the floor, gasping for breath.

Chapter 29

"Rose!" Auguste bent over her limp body. "Take a deep breath." He loosened the buttons of her collar and the front of her dress, then cradled her head in his lap.

"My chest . . ." she squeaked through blue lips.

"Jeanne!" he shouted. "Come at once! Jeanne!"

The maid's footsteps clamored in the corridor.

"Send for Doctor Moreau! She's had a *crise cardiaque*. Go now!"

Jeanne gasped. "Right away. Oh, mademoiselle." She threw a shawl about her shoulders. "I will return as soon as I can."

Rose gulped in several breaths and attempted to sit up.

"Do not try to get up," Auguste said.

After several minutes more, the color seeped into her lips and her breathing regulated. "The pain," she groaned, clutching her chest.

Auguste pulled a blanket from the nearby armrest and wrapped her in it gingerly. "You frightened me." He kissed her on the forehead.

"I am sorry," she whispered, her voice hoarse.

"I regret how much I have hurt you." He ran a thumb across her cheek. "You do not deserve it. I have failed you." He gathered her hand in his. "But I can control my feelings no more easily than you can control yours."

She closed her eyes. "I know, Auguste. I know. I just wish things were different."

"So do I," he whispered.

⤬

The crumpled letter sailed across the room and bounced off the rim of the wastebasket to join other discarded missives on the floor. Camille poured a glass of wine and imbibed it in two gulps. The crimson liquid dribbled from the glass and streamed down her chin. She poured another. She should not have placed her hope in Monsieur Moreau-Nélaton. The town council of Aisne had rejected her republican monument—they did not see it fitting for a woman to create a portrait of national pride. They feared the town would be offended by her piece.

"Idiots!" she shouted. She guzzled another glass, despite the early morning hour. It had been her second piece of bad news in a week. A critic had called her latest showings tasteless and outside the realm of a woman's scope. Sensuality burst from her work and every ninny in the Ministry of Fine Arts shifted in their seats to see it come from the hands of a woman. It was the Third Republic, for Christ's sake. A revolution of machines and progress! How could they yet be so prudish and prehistoric in their thinking?

And now Camille had to restrain her disillusionment and face Mother and Paul. She wished with all her might she had said no to Paul's plea to visit. She hadn't set foot in the family apartment the length of her stay in Touraine, nearly two years. She would not go back to living under Mother's roof, regardless of her hateful reproaches.

Camille dressed in overcoat, gloves, and hat and set out for the family home. She would lift a few foodstuffs from the Claudel pantry to add to her own meager supplies. And she might ask Paul for money—she needed plenty of it, always. The sum she'd attained through her most recent commission had dwindled with the cost of plaster for *The Waltz* and other supplies. She climbed the stairs to the front door and knocked. She felt a stranger on her family's doorstep, her residence for more than ten years. She brushed a lock of hair out of her eyes with impatience.

When the door opened, Corinne's mouth fell open. "Mademoiselle Claudel . . ."

Camille rolled her eyes and pushed past her, removed her winter wear, and walked into the salon.

The maid placed a tray on the table, stocked with a cup of warmed chocolate, milk, and sugar. "Thank you." Camille prepared her cup and drank deeply, grateful for its rich sustenance and warmth.

Mother descended the stairs and entered the salon, carrying her sewing. "You've come home, I see." Her eyes reflected a faraway look, as if she were lost in a daydream. A smile played on her lips— something Camille had not seen in so long, she couldn't remember the last time she had seen her teeth.

"I am here only for a visit." Camille cradled her cup in her hands. "I won't live under your roof again, Mother. Not to worry."

Mother narrowed her eyes at her. "I didn't say you needed to leave."

"I used the power of my intellect and surmised it."

She ignored Camille and held up the tiny pair of trousers for closer inspection.

"Is someone having a baby?" Camille asked.

Mother's pleasant demeanor faded and a hardened shell replaced it. "It's for your brother, of course."

Her sunken cheeks and skin possessed a pallor Camille had not noticed at first. What in hell was wrong with her? Stunned, she said nothing. Her brother? As in her dead infant brother, or was Mother pregnant? Camille glanced at her abdomen. "You aren't with child? At your age—"

Mother exhaled with an angry huff. "Of course not!"

The front door closed with a bang. "*Bonjour? C'est moi*," Paul called from the entrance. He walked into the salon and kissed Mother's cheek.

"I have missed you." Camille stood to embrace him.

"Likewise, sister. You have been gone too long. I didn't know how I would get along without you at first." He sat on the edge of the flowered chaise, brushed invisible wrinkles from his trousers, and prepared his own cup of chocolate. "I want to hear about your sojourn and what you have been working on—"

"Spare us the details of your time with that man," Mother spat. She smoothed the *petit pantalons* and plucked a wooden spool wrapped with navy thread from the basket beside her chair.

Paul gave Mother a silencing look. "As I was saying, I want to hear all about your works, but first, I have a favor to ask of you and if I don't out with it now, I will lose my nerve."

"Go on, then," Camille said, setting her cup in its saucer.

"I am applying to the diplomatic corps."

"Paul!" Mother exclaimed.

"You are not!" Camille gasped. "You wish to live abroad? Our little Paul?"

"I'm twenty-five and a grown man."

"Of course you are." Camille winked at him. "And I am an old maid at twenty-nine." He laughed. "So what is this favor?" she asked.

Paul brushed his immaculate trousers once more. "I would have a much greater chance of gaining the position if someone of influence could put in a good word for me. Someone, perhaps . . ."

"Like Monsieur Rodin?" Camille finished his sentence.

He nodded. "Yes, someone like Monsieur Rodin. I know we do not have the best relationship."

"You mean you detest him," she corrected.

"I am not his biggest supporter, no. But you know why—"

"I know. And yes, of course I will ask him to help you. He is not very fond of your righteous outpourings either, but you are my brother."

"So you will ask him?"

"Of course."

"Thank you!" He clasped her hand in his and kissed it. "I owe you so much."

She laughed. "You may repay me by lending me some money."

"Whatever you need." He radiated contentment. "Yet, I still have more news."

"More than being a foreign diplomat?" Camille's mouth formed an *O* of mock surprise. "Do not keep us in suspense."

He laughed and said, "*La Ville* is to be published!"

"Oh, Paul, you are incredible!" Camille leapt from her place on the settee and kissed his cheek. "You have always been talented, but this! A playwright and a diplomat. I could not be prouder, baby brother."

Mother patted his knee. "You honor this family, unlike your sister."

"Yes, your sister is quite the harlot," Camille retorted, "but I've heard she has a way with a chisel and hammer. Even still they have decided against a commission for the republican monument in Aisne, despite her skills. Those bastard old men."

"Watch your tongue in my house," Mother said.

The foul mood reared its head again and Camille could not corral her words. "Will I corrupt the baby's innocence?"

Mother's eyes grew round. "You make a mockery of me in my own house? Get out! Get out, you hateful child!"

Camille slammed her cup on a side table, rattling the china. "Have it your way. I wasn't feeling up for a visit anyway. Paul, congratulations. We'll talk more about this later."

"Camille, wait," Paul said. "We haven't seen you in so long. Must we quarrel?"

"I am not welcome here, and frankly, I don't wish to be." She turned to go.

"The day you became Monsieur Rodin's whore, you lost your welcome here." Mother's voice became flat, cold as marble on a winter's day. "You are no longer my daughter. I don't want to see your face again. Not until you can live with integrity."

Camille gaped at Mother's hateful words. "You would disown me?"

Mother looked down to thread her needle.

Camille had not expected the pain that slammed into her, after so many years, after a lifetime of being rejected by her own mother. Yet its full force bore down upon her and she staggered. She would never be enough. Never. Somehow she had hoped that would change.

She threw on her overcoat. In an instant, she ripped open the door and was met by a blast of frigid air.

Paul clamored after her. "Camille!" He flew into the street and crossed his arms against the cold. "You must forgive her. She doesn't know what she does. Pray for her; pray for acceptance."

Camille's unwelcome tears crystallized on her face in the icy wind. "Spare me your religious outpourings, Paul. How am I to forgive a woman who despises me? She has disowned me. Her own daughter! As if I don't struggle enough. She regrets my existence, and you know that to be true."

His face drooped and his shoulders fell in resignation. "But I wanted to spend more time with you. You have abandoned me in all of your success."

She squeezed him with all her might. "I am not so very successful, brother. And I will never abandon you. There are not many I love in this world, yet you are among them."

"I worry about you," he whispered. "You cast off any sense of morals. You live in sin."

Camille fastened the last of the buttons on her coat. "To pour your soul into something you love, to make it beautiful, is the highest form of spirituality there is. You understand that better than most, Paul. To share it with the world is to inspire the godliness you are so fond of. You should know this, yet you condemn me for it. Your writing means everything to you."

"Not everything," he said softly.

"I'm going home." She pulled her hat down for good measure and raced down the street against the black cold.

❧

A drumming sound beat inside Camille's head, or was it in the wall? She rolled over on her belly and covered her head with a pillow. She wished everything would fade away. All she wanted was sleep.

The drumming grew louder.

"Open the door, Camille!" Auguste's muffled voice pounded between her ears, behind her eyes, in her chest.

Auguste was the cause. This was his fault. He had sucked her into his world, taken her into his care, his little mistress, and paraded her around so he could feel like a man.

To take credit for your work. He doesn't love you. He uses you.

"Shut up!" she screamed. The Voice had plagued her since that horrible day when the rejection had come—the day Mother had turned her back on her for good. She groaned at the pain. And what of the voices? She had gone mad! Insane like the men who shuffled through the city streets, mumbling to themselves in the seedy parts of town, or those wretched souls who were locked away in a tower. She sobbed, soaking her sheets with bitter tears.

She would be one of them, locked away from the world.

The drumming came again. "I am coming in!" Auguste called.

She sat up and pushed her gnarled locks off her face. "Don't come in! I don't want you here."

The turn of key in lock, the creak of door hinges, and his footsteps boomed in the ceiling, against the walls. Camille covered her ears and fell back against her pillows. "Please," she whimpered. "Leave me alone."

The booming ceased next to her bed and a shadow fell over her. "Darling, you have not been to work all week," Auguste said. "Are you ill?"

She ran a hand over her rumpled chemise and pulled the bedcovers to her chin. "I don't want to work today. I'm too tired."

He frowned and sat beside her. "You have been in bed for more than a week."

She threw her arm across her eyes. "They don't want me."

He stroked her hair. "Who doesn't want you?"

He will seduce you, have his way with you, and leave you with nothing. Just like the others. Push him away! Bite him!

She thrashed in the covers. "Make it stop!"

"I am here." Auguste scooped her up and held her close, rubbing her back.

"The Voice." Camille quivered in his arms. "It taunts me and tells me to do terrible things."

"Let my voice be louder." He kissed her forehead, her cheeks, her eyelids. "*Je t'aime.*"

His voice will stamp out your own. He sets you on fire and watches you burn in agony.

"*Je t'aime,*" he said again, cradling her gently in his arms.

She burrowed closer to him. The soothing scent of his skin wrapped around her like a blanket.

"I am here," he whispered, stroking her hair. "I will help you. We must find a way to treat this . . . thing that has seized you. We'll find a doctor."

"No!" she said. "They will lock me up with the crazies."

Auguste stared at her as if unsure how to respond. Finally he said, "Very well, but I don't want you to spend so much time alone."

"But they don't want me," she said with labored breath.

"Who, *mon amour*?"

"The town council, the ministers—or Mother. There's to be no republican statue, no commissions. Mother has banished me from the house. The old cow. She was sewing baby clothes for my dead brother!" She peered at him through swollen eyes. "She has lost it, Auguste. And I'm"—a sob rose up in her throat—"I am like her."

He cradled her face in his hands. "*Écoute-moi.* You are a true artist. Do not let those . . . those rudimentary—"

"Blowhards!"

His eyebrows shot up in a question.

"Paul has befriended several American writers."

He smiled and gathered her hands to his lips. Her humor had returned. "Do not allow those blowhards to rattle your confidence. You have never allowed them to in the past. Don't begin now. We will show them your wonderful pieces and one day, they will feel foolish." He kissed her forehead. "As for your mother, she is a simple woman who is both jealous and frightened of your talents. Your brilliance instigates fear. I have suffered from it myself for many years."

"I despise how my sex defines me in their eyes." The words left a bitter residue on her tongue. "It does not make me less of a sculptor."

"Quite the opposite." He squeezed her hands. "You are one of a kind, my darling, and one day they will champion your work. But you must be strong."

Camille melted in his embrace once more. She would fight the men controlling her fate the only way she knew how—by creating more, by pushing harder, by leaving them breathless with emotion when they examined her sculptures. They could not force her to create something banal, a betrayal of her luminous inspiration. She would not ignore her need to portray beauty.

"I will heat some water for a bath," Auguste said. "Take some time to soak and relax, and then we'll meet Mathias for dinner. He has an idea for a commission for you. The bust you made of my large head is exquisite." He smiled.

"You love only yourself." She punched him playfully in the arm.

Auguste's laughter bellowed, sending a warm rush, the first in a week, through her body. She gathered her hair and twirled the ends together into one long, twisted mass and slipped out of bed.

She would try again.

Chapter 30

⎯⎯⎯⎯⎯⎯⎯

Auguste turned to a clean page in his ledger and sorted his bills into piles. He had been in a foul mood all week—ever since he'd received word the ministers did not care for his design of Hugo, slated to be placed in the Panthéon. If he did not have their blessing, the commission would go to someone else. He glanced at the clock on his studio wall. Any minute, he would have his answer. He *must* control his emotions. Losing his temper would not help his cause.

Monsieur Blanchet knocked at the office door.

"*Entrez.*"

The gentleman entered, removed his hat, and turned it round and round in his hands. "Monsieur Rodin." He nodded.

Auguste's mood darkened further. The man had bad news.

"I will come right to the point," Blanchet said. "We have decided against your piece for the Panthéon."

Auguste tossed his quill pen on the desk. "I give you an innovative design, something powerful, but you wish for trite and overwrought. Something Victor Hugo would be appalled by if he were still alive."

Monsieur Blanchet grimaced and looked at the floor. He was a timid gentleman and clearly felt uncomfortable delivering such news.

"*Merde!*" Auguste shouted. To hell with tempering his emotions.

Monsieur Blanchet's shoulders sagged like those of a scolded schoolboy. "But wait, Monsieur Rodin. It is not a complete loss. I made a proposal to the committee on your behalf and they have accepted it—if you agree, that is."

"Go on," Rodin said through gritted teeth.

"We'd like to keep your version of Hugo and place it in a garden in Paris, and commission another. One that matches the proportions needed for a building as grand as the Panthéon."

Auguste went silent. He did not have time for a second monument, and yet, this was not only a generous offer; he was certain it was the only offer he would receive. If he did not comply, they would ask Jules Dalou. And he'd rather lose an arm than let that happen.

"I expect to be well paid," Auguste said at last. He pointed to the door of his atelier. "And you may see yourself out."

Blanchet paled. "Monsieur Rodin, I—"

"I accept." Auguste grabbed a nearby maquette and squashed the form between his strong hands. "Now, as you can see I am extremely busy. I have another masterpiece to throw together."

Blanchet's jaw set in a grim line. "Good day, monsieur. I look forward to your next concept."

Once the man had left, Auguste threw the wad of clay with all his might, knocking a study of Camille to the ground. The piece cracked open on impact.

༺❦༻

The swish of buffing cloth over marble soothed Camille's nerves. She dipped her cloth once more in the polish made of pulverized lamb bone, and rubbed the bust of *La Petite Châtelaine* with a loving hand. In truth, the piece needed no more polishing—its diaphanous surface already gleamed. But Camille needed to keep her hands busy. Monsieur Dayot, fine arts minister, would arrive any moment to assess both the plaster and stoneware versions of *The Waltz*. The overwhelming positive response at the Salon last month had captured his interest—proof that what she needed to succeed was to be seen.

She wiped her brow with her arm. The sour odor of nervous sweat permeated her dress sleeves. It was unfortunate she must meet the minister before she'd had a bath. She looked down at her trembling hands. She must gather her wits. She grabbed the carafe of wine on her worktable and filled a glass to the brim before gulping it down. Her future lay in Monsieur Dayot's hands. If he liked the piece, he would recommend it to the fine arts director for purchase in marble or bronze. She needed the money—and the recognition—desperately.

A tapping at the door interrupted her thoughts.

"*J'arrive!*" She removed her stained smock and opened the atelier door.

Monsieur Dayot was a smartly dressed, handsome man with high cheekbones and silky auburn hair. A cigarette dangled from his full bottom lip. "Mademoiselle Claudel?" The cigarette tumbled to the ground. He covered it with his foot and twisted several times with force. After inspecting it, he stamped on the stub again to verify the fiery glow had been snuffed out.

Camille raised an eyebrow at his vehemence. "I'm certain we have no chance of fire."

Monsieur Dayot laughed and his cheeks flamed in embarrassment. "My cousin's house caught fire from a cigarette and they lost everything they owned. One must be vigilant."

"And vigilant you were, monsieur," Camille said, not bothering to hide her amusement. She motioned him inside. "You are here to see *The Waltz*? Right this way."

He followed her indoors, pausing to take in her work space: the secondhand worktables stacked with abandoned maquettes, a few chairs crusted with dried plaster, and a myriad of pedestals and wire armatures.

"I will show you *The Waltz*, of course, but would you care to see anything else?" Camille did not wait for his response, but moved around the room removing sheets and towels from her works.

Monsieur moved from one bust to another. "You created this without assistance?" He touched the cool marble bust of *La Petite Châtelaine*. "Your tutor is Monsieur Rodin, yes?"

"No one assisted me. Well, except for the fairies and elves that sneak into my studio at night."

"The elves?" He laughed, a smart, short laugh reserved for noblemen and those who are impressed by their own power.

"Why, of course." She smiled to soften her sarcasm. "Let us be honest, monsieur. No woman could do such work without help. We both know that to be a fact."

Monsieur Dayot gazed at her as if deciding whether or not she was serious or speaking in jest.

She smiled and led him to a stand near the window. "Here is *The Waltz*."

Two dancers whisked over a dance floor in a passionate stance, their faces emblazoned with the rapture of music, of love and uncertainty of their future.

His eyes widened. "I am speechless."

She smiled. "I hope that is a positive reaction."

"The movement is magnificent. They appear alive." He bent closer to examine each surface. "But the sensuality . . . it's erotic." His face flamed at the word.

Camille had never seen a man blush so often.

"And they are nude," he continued.

"Why, yes they are," she said, her tone light. "There is nothing more beautiful than the human form, wouldn't you agree?"

He moved around the piece slowly, a frown ever present on his features.

He doesn't like it. Save yourself the humiliation. Smash it with a broom handle!

The Voice. Camille froze. Why did it have to come now? She glanced around the room, suddenly frantic.

Monsieur bent over the piece, absorbed.

She moved swiftly to the wine carafe, poured, and took several large swallows. She would drown the hateful words.

"Their organs are rather close." Monsieur Dayot straightened. "This piece would scandalize the director. Perhaps if you clothed the pair—"

"Clothed?" Her voice cracked. "Their nudity adds to the pair's sensuality, their longing. To cover their forms would hide all that is striking about this piece. Such prudery is antithetical to my vision."

He stiffened. "I cannot recommend this in good faith as it is. The sensuality overwhelms the piece. The director would not agree to something so erotic made by a woman's hands. I'm sorry. You clearly have talent, but the image is too profane."

Desperation clawed at her hope. "If I rework the piece, will you reconsider?"

"I don't know—"

"Please, monsieur. You said yourself I am talented. Give me a chance to prove it."

He turned back to the piece and stared at it for a long moment. "Very well."

A rush of air left her lungs. "Thank you. I will send word when it has been adjusted and is complete."

Monsieur Dayot stalked to the door and placed his hat on his head. "I look forward to hearing from you."

Camille closed the door behind him. Monsieur Dayot was handsome and self-assured. He must have had lovers. How could he see this piece as profane?

Because you are a harlot. You sell yourself and he can see that plainly.

"No!" She squeezed her eyes closed against the wretched voice that belittled her at every turn. "Leave me alone!"

She poured herself another glass of wine.

⋙⋘

Camille lifted the edge of her gown and stepped over a puddle in the street. The odor of urine burned her nostrils and she increased her pace. A romp through Montmartre meant an assault of odors: Fresh baked bread alternated with human waste; savory pork crackling mingled with cheap perfume wafting from brothel doorways. By day, artists littered the streets; by night, the whores, thieves, and those seeking entertainment of the most sinful kind emerged. A city within a city, boasting a colorful gluttony of pleasure. Camille squeezed Auguste's arm. She had looked forward to going to the infamous *Le Chat Noir* since she'd arrived in Paris more than a decade ago. Her former male classmates had raved about the club. Polite society considered it an abhorrence, which made it all the better, she thought.

"They want me to start over." Auguste matched her stride.

He had been chattering about his commission, though Camille found it hard to focus on his words. Too many sights and sounds swirled around her.

"I can't believe they did not like Hugo," she said. "What faults could they possibly see in it?"

A metallic tang tingled in the back of her throat. She wet the pad of her tongue against the roof of her mouth in an effort to dissolve the taste—the warning that the Voice was hovering on the edge of her mind.

Not tonight, she pleaded. She wanted to enjoy herself.

"They did not like the shape of the base or Hugo's state of undress," Auguste said. "But I covered his manhood, for Christ's sake."

"When will you cease to care about their opinions? You are established. You have many admirers and regular work." She pushed away the envy that curled her toes when she compared his success to her struggle.

"I can't just ignore their request. It's Victor Hugo." Auguste tucked his hand under her elbow and maneuvered her around a gaggle of rowdy bourgeois, decked in top hats and their best suits. They waited for Moulin de la Galette to open, though they had clearly been drinking for hours.

"*Soûlards*," he muttered.

"Precisely," Camille said, ignoring the pack of drunks. "It's Victor Hugo—the very reason you should cling to your vision. The man would balk at a trite representation of himself. And the public would shrug at another hero in bronze, volume tucked under his arm, or worse, a sword in his hand to slay injustice." She rolled her eyes at the thought.

When they reached 12 Rue Victor Massé, they joined the steady line of patrons streaming inside *Le Chat Noir*. The converted house rocked on its foundation to the beat of a party tune on the piano, and the hum of laughter and voices. Light blazed in every window. Camille glanced up at a sign swinging from its balustrade: A black cat sat on its hind end, its feline grin an invitation to join the mischief.

A smile played on her lips. "I wonder which part I will like best."

"Rodolphe Salis is hilarious," Auguste said. "You will appreciate his humor."

"The host?"

"And owner, yes." He held the door open for her.

A piano and platform sat opposite the entrance, flanked by dozens of tables. Paintings and gilded mirrors covered the walls, and statuettes of cats poised to leap from their sconces decorated every corner of the room. Patrons in glittering evening gowns or silk laughed, sipped their alcohol-laden beverages, and cheered for the chansonnier, who concluded the final note of a bawdy tune.

Camille peered through the cloud of cigarette smoke in search of an empty table.

"On the second floor there's a shadow theater. Mostly artists and writers loiter there." Auguste motioned to the staircase.

The mention of writers brought Paul to mind, and her promise. "I need to ask you something."

"Here?" He frowned.

"Now, or I will forget after a few drinks. It's about my brother."

Auguste grunted. "Your brother who despises me."

"He wants what is best for me," she shouted over her shoulder as they wound through the room. With each step, she peeled her shoes from the sticky floor. By the staircase, she paused. "He has applied to be a foreign diplomat, but he needs a reference from someone well connected. That someone could be you—if you are willing, that is."

"I can't imagine it will do him much good, but I'll send a recommendation. For you, not for him."

She smiled, relieved to have that task out of the way. Despite the men's mutual dislike of one another, they both loved her, and that still meant something.

"Shall we go upstairs?" Auguste asked.

"Let's." Camille lifted two glasses of brown liquid from a server's tray and started up the stairs.

"You had better pay for that, lady," the man said through a thick black mustache.

Camille eyed his sweat-stained shirt and damp hair, then sipped from one of the glasses without bothering to retrieve her coins. Surely he would offer a lady a drink?

Embarrassment crossed Auguste's face. He retrieved a franc from his pocket and laid it on the man's tray. The man did not thank him for the generous gratuity, but continued to snake through the crowd, balancing the nearly full tray over the heads of seated patrons.

"You do love to tease them, don't you?" Auguste said.

Camille placed a wet kiss on his cheek, leaving an imprint of her rouged lips on his skin. He wiped his face with a handkerchief and glanced around the room.

She noticed his unease. "I can't mark you as mine?" Though her tone was light, her mood shifted. Earlier, Auguste had wanted to show everyone their love; now he appeared . . . embarrassed. Or perhaps he was hiding something. Another lady friend? A heaviness lodged in her gut.

"Isn't it obvious I belong to you?" he asked.

He claimed to be hers, yet he still slept in another woman's house. Camille chewed the inside of her cheek to hold back her words.

"This way, darling." He led her up the staircase.

They slid into the few remaining empty seats.

"Monsieur Rodin!" a gentleman said. He had a pointed beard that looked like a goat's and melancholy eyes. Camille knew that face—she'd seen the famous gentleman once before at a salon, though they had not met. Émile Zola, journalist and author, president of the Société des Gens de Lettres.

"Monsieur Zola!" Auguste shook the writer's hand briskly. "Do you frequent *Le Chat Noir*?"

"I wouldn't say I frequent the place, no. I visit occasionally."

Auguste motioned to Camille. "May I present Mademoiselle Claudel? She is a student—"

"Yes, I know who she is," Zola said, tipping his head in her direction. "Pleased to make your acquaintance, mademoiselle."

She frowned, confused by his statement. Had Zola seen her at the salon that evening when too much absinthe had been poured? He couldn't have. They had been in the same room only once the entire night and were never introduced.

"Do we know each other, monsieur?" she asked.

"We have not met, no." Zola's eyes gleamed with an unknown emotion. Condescension? Perhaps he had heard rumors of her liaison with Auguste and regarded her as a young plaything—not the respected artist she should be known as. The metallic tang on her tongue grew stronger, but she managed a tight smile.

"How is the monument coming along, Auguste?" Zola stroked the tip of his beard. "My anticipation to see your *Balzac* grows every day." He adjusted his spectacles, though they did not need adjusting. "I have assured the *société* of your talent—and that the piece will be finished on time." A not-so-subtle hint that Auguste produce, or the *société* would decide against purchasing his *Balzac*.

A retort dangled from the tip of Camille's tongue. She took another drink from her glass to wash it down. It would not help Auguste's cause.

"A masterpiece takes time." Auguste's eyes turned grim. "Something with nouveau lines, a fresh perspective."

"Can I get you anything to drink, Monsieur Rodin?" A woman in an ill-fitting corset leaned over their table. Her breasts appeared as if they might spring free at any moment, layers of shiny beads sat atop them, and netted gloves squeezed the flesh on her arms.

Camille eyed the woman coldly. How did she know Auguste?

The blare of music from the first floor thumped in her ears. The tap of the woman's finger on her tray beat against her skull.

Tap, tap, tap.

Auguste smiled. "*Bonsoir.* I'd like a brandy." He put his hand beneath Camille's elbow. He nodded to the two glasses on the table before her. "Are you happy with that concoction or would you like a proper drink?"

Tap, tap, tap.

She gulped the remainder of her drink down and sucked in a steadying breath.

"I guess she'll have another," the woman said, showing a toothless smile.

Had Auguste slept with this woman? Or perhaps tucked change in her bosom for a kiss? She clutched the arms of her chair. He meant to drive her out, once he had drained her of inspiration, or stolen all her ideas. The image of her *Young Girl with a Sheaf* flashed in her mind. Her throat clogged with emotion.

Tap, tap, tap.

She despised it—this mind of hers played tricks on her. The noise, her senses, the Voice.

"What is it?" Auguste peered into her face. "Do we need to leave?"

Her eyes darted from the woman's overt leer to Zola's proud countenance, and back to Auguste's worried expression. She yanked on the faux-ruby cameo encircling her neck. She couldn't breathe.

He will suffocate you. Auguste will smother you with false affection and leave you for his band of pirates to poison you, finish you off.

Camille stood quickly, knocking the table. Her second drink, still untouched, wobbled uncertainly for an instant, then tipped. Its contents splashed the gown of the woman serving them.

"What is the matter with you?" She turned her furious glare on Camille.

"Perhaps now you'll find a dress that fits," Camille snapped.

The woman drew herself up to her full height, compressing her bosom further. The pressure on the stays was too much. A lace snapped and her naked breast bounced into plain view.

"Oh!" She frantically stuffed the large mound into her corset. "I apologize, messieurs." Monsieur Zola stared in horror.

Blaring music, the laughter, the stabbing light. Nausea swam in Camille's stomach. Auguste's concerned face hovered near hers. "Get me out of here," she said. "My head."

He gave a quick conciliatory explanation to Zola.

Laughter, singing, and the roar of voices hovered in the space around her and pressed upon her. She tugged at her cameo once more and stumbled toward the staircase.

"Camille, wait!" Auguste followed her.

A black weight crushed her. She leaned against the stairwell wall, panting.

"What is the matter?" He reached for her and slipped his arm about her. "Are you unwell?"

"It won't stop. The Voice, the noise." She melted against him in defeat. "I can't make it stop." Tears slipped down her cheeks.

He is the reason. He makes the Voice come.

She squeezed her eyes closed. Was it his fault? She didn't know what was real anymore.

"Shhh." He stroked the soft skin of her neck. "I am here, *amour.*"

Camille tucked herself in his embrace and let him lead her home.

Chapter 31

⚜

"Don't cry." Paul rubbed Camille's back. "It will happen, but you must believe. 'The darkest hour of the night is just before the turning of the morning,' as the psalm says. You're nearly there, sister. I have been praying for you."

Camille leaned against her brother on the park bench. She had spent six months reworking *The Waltz* and Monsieur Dayot had approved the new piece with delight. He had even secured six thousand francs for an advance—until the director of fine arts voided the commission on the grounds of it being inappropriate.

A torrent of tears streamed down her cheeks and dripped from her chin. "It's hopeless. I give up."

Paul held her at arm's length. "So that's it? You are finished, then? You won't sculpt any longer?"

Not sculpt? The thought made her insides turn to sand. Who would she be without her art? She had nothing. She was no one. Even to Auguste she was an addendum, just someone to soothe his loneliness and make him feel a man.

This is his fault! He turned them against you. He fears your ability and will not stop until he destroys you.

"What is it?" Paul asked. "Your eyes—are you ill?"

"It's the Voice. It haunts me. It makes me do things. . . ."

"You must stop chastising yourself." He embraced her. "You've always been too hard on yourself. If you spent some time in prayer, you would feel better."

Paul did not understand; neither did Auguste. She tried to explain, but each time she spoke of the Voice, they looked at her as if she had three heads. Perhaps hers was broken.

Camille wiped her eyes with her sleeve. "I am nothing without my art."

"That isn't true!" He shook her slightly. "You're a beloved sister, a daughter. It's true you have a gift, but use it another way. Teach others and create for the love of your art rather than to make a name for yourself. As you used to," he added softly.

"Teach others? As in students?" She recoiled in revulsion. "Why on earth would I do that? I have no interest in wasting my time on amateurs." And she did not like people all that much. They looked down on her—or betrayed her.

"There is more to you . . . and to life. You are well loved."

"By whom, exactly?" she said. "You and Papa?"

"And that adulterer who shall remain nameless."

The one who will destroy you.

Camille shook her head.

"What is it?" Paul asked.

"You would be fulfilled without your quill pen and paper because tutoring and a family's love is enough?"

He looked down.

"Just as I thought. You would no sooner give up your passion than I would."

"I would become a disciple of God." He sniffed. "If he wished for me to give up my writing, I would."

"Do not make me vomit, Paul. I'm serious."

"So am I."

Camille stood and paced across the lawn, leaving him alone on the park bench. He could be so infuriating with his self-righteous, godly existence. It made her want to strike him. The worst part was she knew he lied to her face. He would no sooner give up his writing than she would her art.

"Wait!" He raced after her, keeping pace with her rapid strides. "Listen to me. I understand. I would do the same in your position."

She stopped and met his eyes with a stony glare. "But you aren't, are you? In my position."

"I will help you." He squeezed her hands in his. "Once I have made a name for myself."

"With two published works, you are well on your way." She threw her head back and gazed up at the sky, willing herself to control her emotions. She detested the jealousy she felt for her own brother. The shame of it made her hate herself.

"I have . . . something to tell you," Paul said slowly. "You won't like it, but it's the reason I wanted us to meet today."

"I am happy for your success, regardless of my situation," Camille said. "You know that."

He nudged an anthill with the tip of his shoe. A frenzy of miniature insects marched out of their home to locate the source of the disturbance.

"Well?" she said.

"I've been appointed First Vice-Consul of France. I depart in two weeks for America." A shy smile spread across his face.

Camille stood in stunned silence. She could see the happiness oozing from behind her brother's guarded countenance. He harnessed his joy for her sake. America? Her darling Paul was not just a playwright, but a diplomat. He would leave her and join the ranks of her former friends—Giganti, Jessie, and even Mother. One by one they had abandoned her. And now he would.

"Well?" he asked. "Are you happy for me?"

She regarded his shiny blond hair, slicked to his head with pomade, his expensive coat and foulard. He looked the part of a diplomat.

"Of course I am!" She ruffled his hair as she had when they were children and squeezed him hard. "But how can I part with you? You will be so far away." A clot of despair clogged her throat.

"I will write to you. And I will write to those blasted ministers and to the papers. They'll regret they have turned away the sister of a diplomat."

"And the sister of a famous playwright." She kissed his cheek. "I am so proud of you."

Paul beamed at her acceptance.

Camille forced a smile for his sake. "We should celebrate."

They would celebrate his going away, and her oblivion.

⤖

The crackling of old plaster coming loose echoed in the vast ceilings of the château Folie le Prestre, Auguste's crumbling estate with overgrown gardens and nymph statuettes. Camille adored working in the abode. Though located in the middle of the restless city, it felt like a vacation home, far from all of his assistants and his swarm of admirers. They had multiplied in number in the past year and their presence had become almost unbearable.

Camille caressed Auguste's face and the silvery hair curling all over his stout chest. He sighed in contentment.

A glint of light winked in the window. Curious, Camille propped herself up on one elbow. There was nothing metallic in the garden. She waited for several minutes more, but the light did not flash again.

Someone has been following you. It's Rodin's band! They have come to drag you away.

She reached for the wineglass she had abandoned just before they made love. She finished the remainder in her glass, then his.

Auguste ran his hand over her shoulders and back. "You should eat something. You haven't touched a thing all day."

Camille glanced at the third version of *La Petite Châteleine*, now in plaster. She had created a dozen maquettes of children in the past months. Their innocence and vibrant eyes made for beautiful expression, and filled a new ache inside her.

"You have only one son," she said. "You have never considered more children?"

Auguste pulled on his shirt and helped her into her chemise. "They're expensive and drain you of energy. They disappoint you." A look Camille could not decipher shadowed his face.

"You had one with Rose." Her jealousy left a vile taste in her mouth. "That old hag you live with."

"You do not want children of your own, do you?" he asked, giving her a wary look.

She ambled to the worktable near the front window. "I've never yearned for children the way my sister always has. My art has consumed me all my life." She leaned against the sill and stared through the warped glass at the unruly bushes. "A child would only hamper my work and my dreams."

Auguste came up behind her and wrapped his arms around her middle. "And imagine this world without the beauty Camille Claudel has created." He shuddered dramatically.

She smiled weakly. "I would be a terrible mother at any rate."

She heard the movement in the room before she saw it. The clack of heels on wood floor, the rustling of petticoats.

"Get away from him!" A shrill voice sliced the air.

Camille and Auguste spun around to see a woman. Shock painted Auguste's features. "For God's sake, Rose! What are you doing here?"

It was *she*! The woman between them, the woman who kept Auguste from her. *Rodin's lover.*

Rose Beuret pointed a pistol directly at Camille. "You filthy prostitute!" she screeched, waving the gun. "He is twice your age!"

"Put the gun down, Rose." Auguste took a step toward her. "Jesus, do you want to go to jail?"

"He uses you." Rose stepped closer. "And he will discard you like he has the rest."

"He loves me because I'm nothing like you," Camille said in a steely tone. "I understand his passion. I *am* his passion. And you— you're nothing but a mother to him!"

Auguste lunged at Rose. The pop of the fired gun sent Camille to her knees. She scrambled behind a worktable for cover.

"He's mine! Do you hear me? Mine!" Rose sobbed.

Camille hunkered lower to the floor, heaving in gasps of air. The woman had lost her mind. But now, at long last, Auguste must choose. Relief mingled with fear in the pit of her stomach.

Another shot was fired. A bullet ricocheted off something metallic, then a bust exploded, sending chunks of hardened clay in every direction. Auguste grabbed Rose's arm. She flailed about and her elbow smashed him hard in the nose. He stumbled backward, blood oozing down his face.

A male figure barged through the front door. "Put down your gun!" a familiar voice called out. Sergeant Alphonse Bertillion stepped into the room, a pistol in hand.

Camille gaped at her former suitor. What was he doing here? She shivered at the uncanny coincidence. Here, in the dilapidated studio of her lover, her former suitor had found her once more, and saved her from *un crime passionnel*. Fate mocked her. She should have married Bertillion when she had the chance.

"Madame," Sergeant Bertillion said, "put down your gun or I'll shoot."

Rose's shoulders slumped and she let the gun fall to the floor. "How did you know to follow me?"

"When I saw you exit the omnibus, you gripped something in your bag," Bertillion said. "Call it intuition, but I have learned to follow a hunch."

Rose burst into tears. "I am sorry. I—I did not know what I was doing—"

"Nothing happened," Bertillion said. "That is what matters."

Camille stood and brushed debris from her chemise. No sense in hiding from him; the sergeant would see her sooner or later.

Bertillion's eyes widened when he spotted the object of Rose's scorn.

"Monsieur Bertillion, we meet again." Camille grinned.

Auguste looked from one to the other, his face set in a mask.

"Mademoiselle Claudel? How is this . . . possible?" The policeman's eyes never left her face.

Auguste crossed the room and wrapped Camille in a blanket to cover her state of undress. "Are you hurt?" He brushed the hair from her face with a soft hand.

She withered at his touch. "Your lover needs you."

"Camille—"

She turned her head to the side. "Just go."

Auguste's hand dropped to his side in defeat. "Very well, but I will return for you."

Bertillion cleared his throat. "Will you see this woman home or shall I?"

"I will," Auguste said. "She is my responsibility." Rose stuck out her chin, triumphant to be stealing him away.

In an instant, Auguste finished dressing and the trio departed.

Camille collapsed to the floor in defeat, self-disgust, and despair. Auguste had chosen Rose again. Camille was nothing but a second choice. Her hand flew to her stomach. She had not even found the right moment to tell him—the washing syringe had not worked this time. She had missed her monthly courses.

Chapter 32

꧁꧂

Camille studied her reflection in the framed looking glass on her atelier wall. She appeared the same on the outside: undulating chestnut tresses bulging from their combs, bright eyes, and a weak chin that receded before it should. But she wasn't the same. She pulled the fabric of her dress flush against her abdomen and placed a hand on her flat stomach. How far would it extend? She could not see herself round and waddling through her studio, lugging blocks of marble with a heavy load around her middle. What would she do with the child?

Fear wrapped around her throat. What would become of her career?

She needed air. She lifted her wool overcoat from the plaster bust where she'd left it. Rodin's sloping forehead and grizzled brow stared back at her. Those all-seeing eyes, even in plaster, watched her every move.

"Stop watching me," she snarled.

Camille dashed through the door. A blast of icy air whipped against her face and the bubble of warmth over her frame dissipated. Would Auguste leave her to toil on her own? He had yet to leave the crazy old hag, even after Rose had attempted to shoot her! Despair hit her like an ocean wave, filled the hollow of her chest, her lungs, until she felt as if she would drown. She perched in the doorway of a condemned building and sucked in steadying breaths.

Then it dawned on her—the alternative way Auguste might view her pregnancy. He might be overjoyed. Not for the sake of the child, but to make her dependent on him, a woman at home with a child to raise. She would pose no threat to his own fame and she could never truly leave him. He had impregnated her on purpose!

Fury replaced her despair, and propelled her forward once more. Auguste would love her for a time and then abandon her for his art, chase the next beautiful woman who excited him. Though he wouldn't have to chase them—they already swarmed his studios to be near the Great Rodin.

Camille stalked past two little girls holding hands and giggling as they skipped in front of their parents. Such a happy family, she thought, as envy radiated through her limbs.

The slick soles of her boots slid on a patch of ice and she pitched forward.

"Steady there." A man on the street caught her.

She righted herself and glanced briefly at the man. A painter, he toted a tableau under one arm and his supplies in the other. Even as an unknown artist he had a greater chance of success than she did, she thought bitterly. She pulled her coat tighter and continued.

A wayward bicyclist weaved between the pedestrians over the uneven cobblestones. At the last moment he dodged a young boy carrying newspapers. "Watch it!" the paperboy shouted. He pushed his cap out of his eyes and promptly slammed into Camille.

Her hand flew to her stomach. Had he knocked it loose?

"Watch it yourself, you ass!" She huffed and moved around the boy.

The roads widened and became more crowded as she pushed down the street. The faces of the pedestrians melted and their bodies became misshapen blobs of color moving in a stream on either side of her, all a blur but their eyes. Their pupils stood out against their glowing white eyeballs as if they were demons. There it was again—that shift of shape as if the human form was not rigid at all, but pliable clay. Camille ducked into a large doorway, slid to the ground, and covered her eyes. She rocked back and forth. Rocking like Papa in his favorite garden swing, like Paul on the rope dangling from a limb of the giant oak in Villeneuve.

Rocking, rocking, rocking.

Minutes became threads, then wisps of smoke. Camille reached out to catch them, but the image wavered and slipped through her fingers. A sharp metallic rattling came from across the street, so loud she could feel it in her teeth. She covered her ears. The rattling grew louder, cutting through the noise on the street, through the web of confusion and sensations. It split open her sadness. God, how it devoured her head, her heart, her will.

Rattle, rattle, rattle.

Camille peeked warily through one eye to find its source. A woman's misshapen form in a tattered dress and shawl sat huddled against a nook where a tavern wall met a café. Her daughter rattled a tin cup of coins.

"Spare some change, madame?" the little girl said to an elegant woman passing. The woman's gait did not slow and she continued on her way. The little girl's dirt-smeared face fell and her mother squeezed her hand.

Camille stared on in bleak dismay. She would end up this way— abandoned in the street with her baby. Mother already wanted nothing to do with her, and Papa would be disgusted at her shame.

Dispose of it. You can't even take care of it yourself. Your baby would only hate you as you do your mother.

A hot current of sorrow piped up her throat and the tears began. How had she let this happen?

Rattle, rattle, rattle.

You ungrateful wretch. Do something! If you don't, Rodin's band will hunt for you and kill you both. Go now! Dispose of it, or they will kill you!

Camille shot to her feet in terror. Colors bled into each other and the demon pedestrians continued to stream by her. As they approached, she screeched and turned back in the direction of her apartment. Where was Rodin's band of men? Home—she must hide where it was quiet and safe. Through a blur of tears and agony, she raced away.

⌘

Camille shifted uncomfortably in her bed. Minou repositioned herself in the warm spot in the sheets and curled into a ball next to her. The cat was the only one who was there for her. The procedure had been horrid—far worse than she expected. The catholic pills the doctor had given her, the grinding cramps in her abdomen, and the sharp instrument. Bile bubbled in her throat at the memory. She turned on her side as vomit streamed from her lips and puddled on the floor. She'd done it—she'd rid herself of the threat to her career, saved herself from death.

What threat? Rodin is the threat! Not the child. It is his fault.

She whimpered in pain and exhaustion. The Voice tormented her even now. Where was the relief? It had lied to her! She had saved herself from nothing, from no one. And she loved Auguste—how very much she loved him, in spite of all. Yet where was he? She slipped from bed to clean the mess. He wasn't there for her. Though she had told him to stay away before, he had never listened, but tracked her like an animal—until now, when she most needed him. Now he avoided her completely.

It's Rose he wants.

Sweat broke out across her forehead. God, he did want Rose. The desolate truth of her solitude soaked into the hollow inside her and she slid to the floor. A lump of forgotten red clay sat underneath her chair. She dipped it in Minou's water bowl. A few minutes of reworking the clay between her hands and it regained its moist texture. She put it to her nostrils and inhaled, desperate for the smell of earth, for the memory of Villeneuve's windswept lands and the wild beauty that had matched her own at one time. What she wouldn't give to be cradled in the Devil's rock garden under the moonlight, far from the disillusionment of Paris, from her tattered dreams and the child she would never have. Far from the man who loved her and destroyed her.

Camille dipped the clay into the water again, until the clump became a slick paste. She smeared the red mass on her cheeks and forehead, along her arms. Anything to bring her closer to home, to the time when all was innocence and hope and she did not hate herself. To the time when she knew who she was.

Chapter 33

～☙～

Auguste sat at his worktable, poring over a sketch of *Balzac*. He had found a proper model at last with similar build, heavy brow, and the same fleshy lips as the great writer. In fact, the model could be his brother. Now to capture the spirit of the intelligent, legendary man—in one month's time. Auguste wiped his hand on his smock. It was a ludicrous idea. He would not finish the maquette alone for months and months. Zola would be furious—furious like Camille.

Somehow he managed to enrage all those who were important in his life at one time or another. He had let Camille down, again. He frowned. He had tried to take care of her; he paid her rent, helped her gain commissions—he loved her with every bit of his strength. He had even sent three different doctors to her door to assess her, but she had refused them all. He didn't know what else to do, outside of contacting her family. He reshaped the head of the maquette to make it more square. The result made the forehead too elongated. Frustrated, he squished the head between his fingers until it was flattened and un-recognizable. He couldn't contact the Claudels—not after the scene in Villeneuve. Never mind the fury he would face from *sa féroce amie*.

He smashed the remainder of the figure and rolled the lump into a ball. Last night Rose had asked him why he didn't leave her. She had pointed out that he loved Camille, so why bother with her? What *had* kept him at Rose's side for so long? He couldn't say, but it must be love. The thought of Rose no longer being a part of his life after so many years terrified him, made him feel weary and old, cast-off. She was family and to cut her out would be like severing a limb.

Marcel popped his head into the office. "Someone's here to see you, Monsieur Rodin."

"Who is it?" he asked.

"The mayor and his wife."

"I don't have time for this," he grumbled. Then he remembered the robust, naked male posing in the central room of the atelier. He scooted quickly from behind his desk and darted into the work space as if his pants were on fire. "Get down!" He motioned to the model. "Quickly, now!"

"Why?" the model asked.

Auguste pulled the naked man down from his pedestal and shoved him behind a block of marble. "Madame Maire must not see you. You'll scar her eyes."

Laughter erupted in the studio. The smile that spread over Auguste's lips felt strangely foreign, but welcome. The model covered the exposed area between his legs.

Monsieur le Maire and his wife strolled through the atelier, pausing to admire a smattering of busts and half-finished statues.

"Good day, Monsieur Rodin," the Mayor said when he had joined Auguste by the marble station. The abundance of pomade in his hair made him look like a greased weasel.

"Monsieur le Maire." Auguste shook his hand. "Madame."

"I see you are hard at work."

Auguste said, "An artist's work is never done."

They chatted politely for a few moments until Madame Maire grew restless and began to look around. Auguste glanced at the marble block where his model hid. He needed to move them to the next station so the naked man could escape unseen.

"I've heard we have monuments to Balzac and Baudelaire to look forward to as well," the mayor said.

The model peeked out from behind his cover.

"Quite right," Rodin said absently. He kept his eyes glued on the mayor's wife. The marble room sat opposite the model's hiding place, but if he could stand in front of it . . . "Would you care to see the marble room?"

The woman's face perked up at the suggestion. Auguste inched toward the hiding place to intercept Madame Maire—too late.

"Oh!" she gasped. "I never!"

The model bowed. "Madame Maire, it is a pleasure to meet you."

A dainty hand shielded her eyes. "Why on earth are you hiding in the nude?"

"To shield you from my naked ass, madame."

More laughter rippled through the atelier. Monsieur le Maire chuckled at the impropriety.

"I beg your pardon, madame," Auguste said. "I would be honored to show you the variety of stones we use."

Crimson stained her cheeks. "Yes, please."

Auguste smothered a sigh. The last thing he needed was to waste time playing host. *Balzac* awaited. But one could not turn away an important guest, especially an important one who might lobby to secure him funding.

⤋

Though Auguste thought it impossible, the crowd grew after luncheon at the Salon. Seven thousand works, he had been told, graced the vast space of la Galerie des Machines, the very same that had housed the Exposition Universelle almost ten years earlier. *Monument to Balzac*, in all its revolutionary glory, stood positioned in the center of the hall, just down from *The Kiss*.

Auguste found the juxtaposition of the two works ironic: the one, a monument to his enduring love for Camille; the other, a representation of the changing art world—the pivot to his aesthetic.

"It is a chef d'oeuvre." Gustave Geffroy motioned to *Balzac*. "A monument to modern sculpture."

"Thank you," Auguste said. "Seven years of my life and my final state commission. This one nearly killed me."

Gustave eyed his friend with curiosity. "And *The Gates of Hell*? It will remain unfinished?"

"I'm not dead yet."

Geffroy laughed, then drank from his brandy glass. He wiped his mustache with a handkerchief after each drink. Auguste had never heard the serious man so much as chuckle. He considered Geffroy's amusement a victory.

"Rodin!" Octave Mirbeau spotted them through the crowd and made his way to their side. "Congratulations. It's an absolute marvel." He clapped him on the back.

"So *Balzac* isn't a slab of beef?" Auguste asked. "A snowman beginning to melt? Or my personal favorite, it's Balzac in a straitjacket being led to an asylum."

Octave chuckled, his wing-shaped mustache looking more comical than ever. He stopped abruptly when he noticed Rodin's expression. "Those criticisms are from the *bons bourgeois*. They know nothing of art. Surely you aren't listening to them?"

"And Zola?" Auguste challenged him. "He hasn't answered my letters."

"He has been busy, I suspect." Octave sounded amused.

"*J'accuse!*" The three men said in unison.

Zola's newspaper article accused the government of anti-Semitism for condemning a Jewish man without proof, creating national outrage.

"It's about time someone stood up for the poor bastard. Dreyfus is innocent," Geffroy said.

"Don't say that too loudly or you'll find yourself in a brawl," Octave replied. "There are plenty who would like to see him hanged."

Auguste shuffled his feet. He knew better than to state his views about the exiled soldier. To be vocal about such a volatile topic could undermine his connections. The country had been divided on the integration of Jews since the Middle Ages. He would not dip his toe in that pool. It could be career suicide.

Octave's dark eyes widened. Geffroy and Rodin followed his gaze to a clot of artists and spectators gathering around *Balzac*. As the group grew larger, the din boomed from the rafters of the glass building. Several gentlemen shouted at each other and waved their arms about as if preparing to fight.

"What are we waiting for?" Octave said, a gleam in his eye. He always liked a good story. "Let's see what all the commotion is about."

Gustave and Octave made their way to the monument, but Auguste remained rooted to the floor. Within moments, both gentlemen had joined a shouting match of their own.

Rodin eyed the crowd with apprehension. He neither knew nor cared why they argued, and to hear more mean-spirited comments about *Balzac* along with bearing Zola's snub was too much to carry today. Weariness throbbed in his bones. He was an old man of fifty-eight, dressed in a black redingote, attending what felt like his funeral. The *Monument to Balzac* was complete; he was proud of the piece. He had nothing more to say on the topic. All he wished for was peace, a block of marble, and a quiet room. He sauntered silently, alone, toward the exit.

⚜

A golden tide of sunshine flowed through the windows and cascaded onto the floor. Camille cursed the blasted rays. Her head throbbed and the early summer heat did not help. Soon she'd have to leave the studio for food and wine after many days indoors. Weeks? She squinted at the blinding light. At least she'd managed a letter to Paul, who was far away in China. She had told him about the wretched clinic, about her confusion and remorse, though she didn't know why. Paul had not comforted her in her time of need, but condemned her. He had called her a sinner, told her she had blackened her soul and would be damned unless she repented.

"'Truly children are a gift from the Lord; the fruit of the womb is a reward,'" Paul had quoted the Bible. "'Thou shalt not kill'" and "'Unrepentant murderers cannot enter the kingdom of heaven.'"

But Camille would never be fit for heaven. She had never been pure of heart or deed, a dutiful child—or adult, for that matter. She had merely followed her heart and her passion. Surely Paul's God could understand that? And hell? What could be worse than the torment she now suffered? She boiled in her own hate—hatred of the ministers; of those who professed their friendship and love, yet abandoned her.

A new image had come to her in the night. A young woman on her knees, her hands in the air, imploring a man to stay with her, but a dark angel spirited him away, the angel of age. *The Age of Maturity*. She had scrambled on all fours to the desk and scratched the name and a rough outline of her vision on the back of an envelope.

She cackled at the irony—a new idea recorded on the envelope carrying her latest rejection. She had her art in spite of them! She would make more beautiful things for the world, whether they wanted them or not. And one day, someone would look on her collection and be grateful, inspired. She still believed that. They could not defeat her.

She launched herself to her feet. "Screw them all!" She stumbled over a chair leg and fell face forward. Her abdomen smashed against the floor. She cried out and clutched her middle.

A pointless gesture.

"Thank God there is no baby," she said bitterly, to no one. The feeling she had done the right thing had yet to flood her senses. What would fill the gaping cavity in her chest? Instead, her disquietude was the final stroke in a barrage of loss.

"When?" she screamed. When would it be gone? The guilt, the horror of that day. The grief for all she had lost.

Paul had lectured her. "You serve your art, but it consumes you as greed would. And that is all this is, Camille. Your lust for success has no merit. Repent and find your strength. The voices you hear are a rebuke from the Devil."

How she had wanted to scream when she had read his words. He parroted phrases that condemned a beloved sister in need of his help. The Voice was not a punishment, but a symptom of her regret. So much regret.

A thudding came at the door.

"Go away!" she said in an uneven timbre.

"Camille, it's Auguste. Let me in."

The Devil has come! He wants to cage you, drag you with him to hell.

She cradled her head in her hands. "I don't believe in the Devil."

But you do. You made a pact with him, don't you remember? He is here for you.

More pounding. "Open this door or I'll break it down!" he shouted. Auguste wouldn't try to poison her in daylight, would he? "Camille!" If she did not open the door, the neighbors would give her trouble. "I need to see you," he said.

She moved to the door and swung it wide. Auguste pushed inside and kissed her cheek in greeting, the way he would a friend. Camille's arms dangled lifelessly at her side. What would she say to him?

He walked from one worktable to the next, studying a series of busts she had begun—all of young girls. "These are magnificent." He fingered a groove of brow bone.

"Don't touch them!" Her voice came out garbled, rusty from disuse. She moved frantically from one to the next, covering them with rags. She could not let him steal these from her as well.

"What could I possibly do to your portraits?"

"You rob me of my inspiration and call it your own."

Auguste looked at her with a dull expression, as if all of his emotion had been drained from his body these past months of their separation. Until the sketch of *The Age of Maturity* caught his eye. He picked up the envelope to get a closer look. "Is this a farce of our lives together?" With his finger, he traced the drawing of a young woman on her knees. "You don't intend to make this? I would be ridiculed."

"You think this piece is about us and that vile woman, don't you?" She scoffed at him. "You're as self-centered as I always suspected you were. This woman represents youth; the man is the present and is being spirited away by the angel of age to the grave."

He put down the sketch. "You have shut me out, Camille. I have made our love foremost, always, but you reject me."

"Foremost? Like the afternoon you brought Rose to Villeneuve to humiliate me? Those many nights when you were finished with me and you returned to her? And then there is the matter of Rose trying to kill me, yet you comforted *her*. You escorted her home and you left me alone. With child."

Silence echoed in the immeasurable space between them.

"You are pregnant?" Emotions warred on his face. He glanced down at her abdomen. "When? When are you—"

"There is no child."

"You have terminated it? God, Camille." He clenched his fists. "You didn't even speak to me about it. A child with you . . ." He rushed toward her. "*Mon amour*, if I had known."

She stepped out of his reach. "And what would we have done then? You would continue to spend all of your hours in the studio while I chased the babe?" A high-pitched laugh escaped her lips. "That's how you would have wanted it, isn't it? To keep me out of the way."

His face twisted in pain. "How can you say that? I have loved you since the moment I met you. I will never love anyone the way I do you."

"Yet you would not leave Rose to be with me, make an honest woman of me."

He stood stock-still. The silence grew as her stare burned through him. In a soft voice, he said, "Why didn't you come to me first? We could have talked about our options at the very least."

"The Voice told me what I should do."

"The voices are back?" He stroked the soft spot on his beard in agitation.

"It never left."

He reached out to her. "Let me help you. I can find someone—"

"You have helped enough." She motioned to the door. "Now, get out. I don't want to see you ever again."

Desperation crossed his face. "Camille, don't do this!" He yanked her arm and crushed her against him.

"Let go of me!" A desperate panic rose inside her. He would crush her and do away with her! She pushed against his chest. "Leave me!"

He tightened his hold. "No."

"You're a coward!" she screeched as panic strangled her.

He held her fast against him. After several minutes of struggle, she relaxed. "Let me help you," he whispered in her ear.

"You have helped enough. I never want to see you again. I mean it, Auguste. The sight of you, your scent, your art make me sick."

He released her.

"Just go." She wrapped her arms around herself, the fire of her anger suddenly extinguished. A chill cooled her blood and penetrated her bones until her teeth began to rattle.

Tears shone in his eyes.

"I have made the great man cry." She mocked him.

"More than you will ever know." He fumbled for the handkerchief in his pocket before moving to the door. He paused to look at her a last time. "Good-bye, Camille."

"Don't you mean good riddance? You are free of me."

"I will never be free of you," he said, voice soft.

With that, he disappeared through the door.

❧

Auguste sat across from Cazin, Monet, and several other members of the Société Nationale des Beaux-Arts. They discussed matters of the next salon and various topics, but Rodin had barely heard a word. He stared into the bottom of his beer glass. He could have had a child with Camille, but now it was finished. *They* were finished. For good. Each time the sorrow drained away, it welled inside him once more until it oozed from his pores. He ran his fingertip around the edge of his glass. Yet despite the pain, his relief was still stronger. An illness had seized her beautiful and terrible mind and she could not prevent it, nor control it. She could not raise a child. She could scarcely support herself, but still, she turned away the money he had sent. An exhaustion consumed him, one so profound, some days he could not leave his bed.

The pitch of the conversation around him changed.

Claude opened a clipping of newspaper. "Auguste, have you seen this?" Monet smoothed the rumpled paper clipping, smudging the black ink. "Your *Balzac* is 'the polemic of the moment. Before long it will be necessary to be for or against Rodin, as it is necessary to be for or against Esterhazy'."

Monet scrutinized his face—for what, Auguste didn't know. He had no opinion on the matter, at least not one he would share, and he knew for certain Claude was decidedly pro-Dreyfus.

"The journalists align your supporters with Dreyfus and the nay-sayers as traitors of the republic." Monet drained his beer and speared a slice of cured ham with his fork.

"How they came to that conclusion baffles me," Cazin said, then sipped from his brandy glass. "Zola is a Dreyfusard, yet he is the one who has denied *Balzac*—"

The stirrings of anger arose inside Rodin. "I've read them all. All of the spiteful reviews and hate directed at me. I am an artist, not a political tool. The bastards will ruin me." His pulse thundered in his ears. "Now Descaves claims I am organizing a Jewish cavalry to overthrow the government. What complete nonsense is that? I'm an old man, for Christ's sake."

"Why don't you take a stand?" Monet's eyes challenged him.

Auguste clenched his fists. "And be caught up in the scandal? I want to be as far from that *merde* as possible."

Monet's characteristic passion rose to the surface. "It's an important national issue, Auguste. Why not speak out?"

"The Gens de Lettres have rejected the commission." Auguste stood. "Zola has turned his back on me." He waved his arm about in frustration. "I slave for them and they belittle me in their papers. Leave me with empty pockets. I have no interest in speaking out. It seems it has been done for me." He ran a hand over his hair and put his beret firmly in place. "I've had enough." He tossed a few coins on the table.

"Where the hell are you going?" Monet asked, his face scrunched.

"Away." Auguste departed in a rush.

Speeding cabs, the prattle of omnibus over cobblestone, and the rush of people to and fro—all of it—bore down on him. When he reached his home, he slammed the door behind him.

"What's happened?" Rose rushed to him from the salon.

"We're leaving. Away from the city racket and these idiotic journalists. I need space from it all."

Rose touched her lips in an attempt to hide her smile. "Whatever you wish, *chéri*."

He uncurled his fists and took her in his arms. "Thank you."

"For what?" she whispered.

"For always loving me. For standing beside me. I don't deserve you, but I am grateful."

She kissed him lightly. "You are my home."

"We'll go to Meudon after my meeting with Mathias at the end of the week."

"Very well," she said.

Auguste released her and clomped up the stairs to his office. He lit his lamp and a stray candle atop his desk. After riffling through a stack of articles and reviews, he formed them into a neat pile. One by one, he held the articles over the hungry flame and watched their edges singe and disappear.

❧

Auguste wrapped his fingers around the heft of brick he'd found at the Dépôt des Marbres that morning. Someone had shattered one of the front windows of the atelier. It could have been a coincidence, but he wasn't a betting man. Someone had sent him a warning. He glanced at a maquette of *Balzac*, one of his first studies. With a quick thrust, he launched the brick at the dried clay, knocking it over in one hit. He reached for the brick and pounded the statue, breaking its limbs, crushing the duck lips and large nose on the face of the man he had so wished to replicate. An angry laugh strangled his throat. He beat the statue again and again, until only rubble remained. Satisfied, he dropped the brick and brushed his hands against each other to dust off the debris.

At that moment, Mathias rapped on the office door, in the rear of the atelier.

"Come in." Auguste said, breathless. He would make this meeting fast—he could not wait to leave.

Mathias closed the door behind him. He raised an eyebrow at the dust covering Rodin's suit before continuing. "I have good news. We've collected more than half of the sum we need to purchase *Balzac* from Zola and the Gens de Lettres. We'll find a placement for him in Paris yet.

Auguste shook his head. "I don't intend to sell the piece. Please return the funds."

"You cannot be serious!" Mathias's eyes bulged like a bulldog's in his round face. "Hundreds have donated to see *Balzac* erected in public."

"I will not be associated with a public outcry. It would pit me against the other side. No," Auguste said firmly. "My works represent a truth about humanity and I have no agenda other than illustrating the beauty of those truths."

"But if you withdraw it, your enemies will win."

"And who are my enemies?" He paced in the confined space. "The Gens de Lettres? The bourgeois? Or is it those who believe Dreyfus is an enemy of the Republic? I don't know who they are! At any rate, I have written a rebuttal to the nonsense about my Jewish plot. It will run on the cover of *L'Aurore*. After that, I am finished with *Balzac*, once and for all. It will remain in my studio."

"But they will crucify you," Mathias said.

"They already have!" Auguste raised his voice. And he was done with it all.

Mathias watched him in silence. "And those who champion your cause?"

"Can do so without me. I appreciate their patronage and friendship, but I am not a political martyr. I am an artist."

"You flee confrontation." Mathias's chubby cheeks puffed indignantly. "But that is your choice."

His friend's words stung. Auguste detested making impossible choices. Camille and Rose. Camille's final letter had praised *Balzac*, and had given him greater happiness than all of the critics combined. She had found it perfect in its simplicity. She knew his heart, understood his longing, his vision. Yet he had not known his own—and he had left Camille for Rose again and again. Now it was done, just as he was.

"Auguste?" Mathias leaned toward him, his round middle bumping the desk.

"I won't hold that comment against you because we're friends," he said. "You may sympathize with me, but you are not an artist. You can't truly understand what it is to bear your soul for others to ridicule. I will not lay myself before the vultures so they can pick my bones clean."

All he wanted was the buzzards to leave him in peace. And her. God he still wished for *her*. But Camille was no more attainable than the minister's approval—or pleasing anyone beyond himself.

Mathias sighed and opened the door to go.

"Wait." Auguste stood. "Camille . . . She's in desperate need of money. I've sent a student her way for tutoring, but she refused her. Can we find a way to secure a commission for her? Even a bronzing?"

"I will do all I can."

He shook Mathias's hand and gripped his arm with the other. "You are a good friend."

Chapter 34
March 1913

⌘

Drip, drip, drip.

A trickle, unbearable in tenor, beat against the empty sound. A leak in the ceiling, perhaps? Or a rivulet of poison Auguste had dispensed to rid his world of her. Shredded paper curled from the vast plains of wall and disintegrated in the puddle-soaked floor in the apartment at the Quai de Bourbon. The smell of rotting garbage hung in the air, thick as a coastal fog.

Camille kicked aside a pile of rubble and swung the mallet again. It connected with a terra-cotta bust, cracking it in two. She cared nothing for the pieces she had smashed.

Drip, drip, drip.

"Again!" she shouted, her voice hoarse. She pulverized the bust and its orange dust rained to the floor. The shattered sculpture would join the other worthless pieces, an array of busted heads and nymphs, shattered bodies, and children's faces.

Drip, drip, drip.

Camille panted; her breath billowed from her lips in little clouds. She hadn't enough wood to heat the place more than a few days at a time. She looked around her atelier at a broken armchair, the dozens of empty wine bottles. But those did not pose a threat to her livelihood. No, it was the maquettes, all emblems of her precious ideas—

she must smash them all before Rodin stole them away. He was a thief and a liar, a man absorbed only in his own fame, and he would stop at nothing to ruin her. She had seen his band of spies, waiting in the dark corners of the street to nab her and poison her. She shivered at the thought, suddenly glad she had barred her door with plywood. Yet the dripping—would it poison her? Her eyes darted from one leak in the ceiling to the next. She gripped her mallet in her hands once more.

The Dawn, the portrait of a young girl's face full of promise, caught her attention. The girl's inquisitive eyes implored her to cease the destruction. Camille dropped her mallet and ran her hands over the smooth planes of the face and hair. The piece was too beautiful to destroy.

"You must outlast me," she whispered to the little girl. "Show them your beauty when I am gone."

In a sudden burst of energy, Camille jumped to her feet and raced around the room, sweeping dirt off of all her remaining pieces. "All of you. You will remain when I am dust. You must show them! Show them the power of your beauty."

It was true, and her heart was glad. Part of her would remain behind in this world, always. She could not be defeated!

When Camille had cleaned the last sculpture, Minou—a new cat named after the first and just as beloved—stole out from behind her cover and butted her head against Camille's leg. She scooped the cat up and snuggled her in the crook of her neck.

"Are you hungry again? Maybe I can take you to Villeneuve to catch a bird or a mole. You'd like that, wouldn't you, girl?" Her cats were the only ones who understood Camille, who had stayed with her through it all. The cat's throat whirred in its comforting way. She licked Camille's hand.

Though I walk through the valley of the shadow of death, I fear no evil, for you are with me; your rod and your staff, they comfort me.

Camille did not fight the Voice any longer. It came and went as it pleased, in time to torture her, and disappeared again. But she could not suppress it.

Drip, drip, drip.

Her eyes fell upon a tear-stained letter on the desk. A wave of grief hit her with force. Papa was dead and in the cold ground. Mother had

not informed her of his funeral, nor had Paul or Louise, and the cere-
mony had gone on without her. That was the day her destruction had
commenced.

A memory came, vivid as the day it had happened. Louise, Paul,
and she had taken bread from the kitchen to feed the neighbor's
chickens.

Paul slipped his hand into Camille's, and Louise skipped after
them. The brittle wind of Villeneuve pushed against their faces, yet
they did not care. They ripped their hunks of bread into pieces and
scattered it on the ground. The hens' bobbing heads made them laugh
as they raced toward the food. Their clucking and cooing was so satis-
fying.

Young Camille tossed a ball of clay in the air and caught it, then
launched it high again. The final time she caught the ball, she stopped
to inhale its earthy scent.

"Why do you love the dirt so much?" Louise asked her.

Camille smiled. "I can shape it into something pretty and let it dry
so it will last forever."

"The flowers don't last forever," Paul said in his little boy voice.
"They die."

Papa joined them in the garden. "Are you going to make me something, Camille?" He gestured to the clay in her hand.

"Yes," she said. "A bird family. So they can peck at each other."

"Like we do." Papa laughed and kissed her on the head. "You are
very good at making things, *chérie*."

A pang coursed through Camille's body. She would never forget
the sound of Papa's laughter. She leaned her weary head against the
wall in defeat. She couldn't do it. Not this, not anymore. She needed
help from someone—anyone willing to care for her, to show her the
way out of this oblivion. But she had no one at all.

An odd and distant thud resounded in the cluttered room. Someone was at the door?

"Camille!" Paul's voice cut into her consciousness. "Open the door!
It's me, Paul."

"Paul!" He was here! "Paul!" she screamed. Camille picked up her
mallet once more and beat at the wood hammered tightly across the
door. Her brother was here. He was really here! He had come for her.

He had promised to be by her side, always, and he was here! At long last. He would rescue her from Rodin and his band.

Another whack with the mallet and the wood cracked and split. She yanked at the splintered wood and unlocked the door.

Paul burst inside. "God in heaven, Camille. What was all that noise?" His eyes grew round at the sight of the wreckage, and of her. "My dear sister, you are emaciated." He stroked her bony cheek.

Camille could not understand how she had come this far—how her life had sunk into despair. If only she hadn't been so stubborn, so foolish.

"It will be all right," Paul said. "I am here to take care of you. I'm going to take you away."

She looked at him, confused.

"Come." He wrapped her in his coat and led her by the hand to the doorway.

"Where are we going?" She pulled out of his grasp. "I can't go out there. Rodin's band will kidnap me."

Paul watched her closely. Finally, he said, "Monsieur Rodin has been shipped out to America. He won't bother you now. You're safe." He squeezed her shoulders. "I'm going to bring you to a hospital, to make sure you are properly fed."

"No. His spies are everywhere. I won't go." Camille ran to the window and peered out, searching out the wicked men who watched her. But she did not see Rodin's followers or the Devil himself. Perhaps she was safe with Paul at her side. Still, she must talk quickly and nail the door closed before Rodin returned.

"You'll only go to the hospital for a little while." Paul cajoled her with a soft tone. "Until you've regained your strength and made your penance."

"Made my penance?" she asked, whirling around to face him.

He pressed his lips together. "You have sinned against God, Camille, and now he punishes you."

"What are you talking about? Really, brother, sometimes I wonder if you have lost your mind." Her harsh laughter split the air.

The *douceur* left his voice and his blue eyes turned cold. "The abortion, of course. You have taken a life and now God has taken yours. You have lost your faculties. Some recovery time, some prayer, and you may yet be forgiven."

"God punishes me for being a woman!" Camille snarled.

A team of horses pulling an enclosed wagon rounded the corner and pulled into the drive. Camille made out the words: *L'Hôpital de Ville-Évrard*.

Paul pulled on her hand. "It is time."

"No! I'm not going with you! He will find me," she hissed. "He will steal my work."

"Please, Camille, I'm trying to help you." He gripped her arms. "Have I ever let you down?"

She stared at him with incredulity. "Yes! The day you left for America, then China. The day you buried my father and didn't tell me!" Her shrill voice echoed in the ceiling.

"I have her," Paul shouted to the men who had descended from the enclosed wagon. They filled the doorway with their dark coats and sullen faces. Rodin's band—it was they! They had come for her!

"No!" She stomped on Paul's foot.

He cursed and pulled her against him. "This is what is best for you. You will thank me one day. I will write to you, I promise."

Camille sank her teeth into the tender flesh between Paul's thumb and forefinger and fled to the opposite side of the room. She ducked behind a partially dismantled armature fashioned in the likeness of a man. Minou jumped into her arms once more.

"She's there," Paul said, motioning to her feeble hiding place.

Paul was in on it! He worked with Rodin to lock her away. The pain of that realization ripped through her and filled her legs with lead. She sagged against the wood base of the armature. She could not escape him—Rodin would travel to the ends of the earth to find her. And with Paul in on it . . . with his God, she could not hide.

A man with gray whiskers lunged at Camille from one side of the armature base. She shrieked and fled to the other side—into the arms of the other man. "Let me go!" she screamed.

"Calm yourself," Paul said. "We are here to help you."

As the men pushed Camille toward the door, Minou squirmed in her arms. A feral scream split the air. "Not through the door!" she screamed. "He's there! He's waiting for me in the alley."

Both men held her fast on either side.

"Through the window," she panted. "Please! You must sneak me out. Rodin will not see me if we are clever."

The Dark Men looked at each other and then to Paul. Her brother nodded and rushed to the window to unlatch it and swing the panes open. "I'll help catch her on the other side." He ran around the building to the front window.

"Hurry!" Her eyes darted to the door. "He will be here soon."

The Dark Men lowered her over the edge of the windowsill and into Paul's waiting arms. He clutched her tightly around the middle until the others joined him.

Camille looked up at the rooftops of the neighboring building. A flock of ravens peered down at her. *Les corbeaux*—the keepers of secrets—smiled their vicious smiles. What did they know? Did they know when Rodin would come? Were the Dark Men here to help, or to take her straight to him? She glanced from one face to the other, her panic arising once more.

"Come with us, mademoiselle." One of the men held out his hand.

They couldn't make her go, could they? She glanced at the open window of her studio and an oppressive cloud suffocated her.

"All will be well, sister," Paul said. "You will find safety there, away from *him*. God will take care of you."

She nodded numbly. She didn't know what she needed, but she could no longer face the days in the studio, alone.

"Will you take care of her?" Camille asked, still clutching Minou to her chest. "While I am gone?"

A tear slid down Paul's face. He wiped it quickly and held out his hands. "Of course."

"I will rest and be well. I'll come back for you soon." She kissed the soft fur on Minou's head. "And Paul? Will you take care of them, too? My sculptures?"

More tears fell from his eyes. "Nothing would make me happier." He brushed a matted lock of hair off her forehead and kissed her cheeks.

Camille handed Minou to her brother, and glanced at her studio one last time. She did not regret her suffering or the perception it had brought; it had taught her everything—it was a gift, even, allowing her to know, to *absorb* the emotions of others in all their intimacy, so she might depict their joys or exquisite pain. The beauty—that which she left behind—would transcend the tragedy of her life. This truth tingled in the depths of her soul and somewhere within she was proud.

Camille gathered her courage and blew Paul a last kiss.

The Dark Men half-carried, half-dragged her to the wagon. She looked over her shoulder at her brother and cat, and the single bird with jet feathers that alighted in the courtyard.

This bird knew her, her dark companion since the very beginning.

"It is done," she whispered.

Epilogue

꧁꧂

"I visited our friend two days ago." Mathias frowned, an unusual expression on his jovial face.

Auguste felt a familiar pang. It had been years since he had laid eyes on Camille, yet a day did not pass without a reminder of her, even if in some small way. "Was she at home?" he asked. "I arranged another commission for her, but that was months ago now. I never heard a thing about it."

"Her studio looked abandoned," Mathias said quietly. He paused, as if weighing his words carefully. "I peeked in the windows and the place appeared as if it had been ransacked by thieves. Something didn't feel quite right so I inquired with mademoiselle's family."

Auguste's chest tightened. "Go on."

"She has been committed. To the asylum at Ville-Évrard by her brother Paul and her mother."

He sat very still as a tide of pain, then pity rolled through him. After a long moment he stood. "I have to go."

"But our dinner should arrive any minute," Mathias said, placing his hand on his distended abdomen.

"I'll pay you for mine later."

Mathias sighed. "You still care for her."

"I do not exist a single moment without loving her." Auguste's words came out strangled. He stuffed his hands into the sleeves of his coat and left the restaurant. He knew Camille had been ill. Still, he could not wrap his mind around its truth. She was gone—locked in a facility where no one loved her, and that crazed brother of hers condemned her as if he knew better than God.

Cane in hand, he climbed into a hackney and rode across town to the Quai de Bourbon. Camille's apartment on the bottom floor sat dark and lifeless. Spring rain fell steadily, wetting his hair and coat. He sucked in a breath of damp air, gathered his courage, and peered inside. Heaps of garbage and puddles of water, wine bottles, and smashed maquettes filled the apartment. He could imagine her there, bent over a piece, oblivious to the rest of the world. She would look up from time to time, say something funny and irreverent, then kiss him with force before ignoring him completely again. A lump lodged in his throat.

Auguste remained there, clutching her windowsill, until nightfall.

When the sky blackened, the ravens in the courtyard dispersed, and his coat was soaked through, Auguste turned to go. Later, he arrived home in Meudon and changed into his chemise. Rose had fallen asleep hours earlier. He lit a lamp and climbed the stairs to his office. His brave, *féroce amie* had gnashed her teeth at convention. She had been an outlaw as he had, creating only for herself. And when he had fallen into the trap of pleasing others, she had set him on track once more.

The golden glow of lamplight bathed his paper. He dipped a steel-tip pen into its inkwell and paused. Was she truly mad, or too impassioned to contain her emotions? He did not know. Didn't they all possess some degree of madness? He, for his work—and for her. They all toiled in their humanity, and for what? Love did not conquer all; it only made life more bearable for a short time before it consumed its victims. They had both striven to capture love's essence in marble and clay, to shape it and perfect it.

To leave a mark of beauty on the soul of humanity.

Black ink seeped into the paper as Auguste wrote a letter:

Ma Chère Camille,

> *Where do I begin? My heart is crowded with words unspoken and regret. I have failed you. I could not leave Rose—I did not have the strength. She is my family, a confidant, and yes, a woman I have*

loved. I do not desert those in my heart, as I have not deserted you.
I will take care of you, forever, in any way I can. I always have.

I wrote to Paul to discuss your collection of works. Upon my
death, my art will be bequeathed to the French state and will reside
at the Hôtel Biron, a property I hope to make my museum. It is
spacious and beautiful—a place befitting for us. I say us, because,
you see, I have requested that rooms be reserved for your work as
well, for all to admire. You will be known as I have known you,
loved as I have loved you, your Eternal Idol. We will reside, side by
side, and never be parted. I will fulfill that promise to you in death,
as you deserved all along.

This is my confession and my plea for your forgiveness.
I will never stop loving you.

Yours,

Auguste

When he finished, he hobbled across the room and tossed the letter
on the fire. He watched as the flames devoured it. Paul would help him
gather what had not been destroyed. Her brother would do this for
her—he must. And the eternal struggle of the artist, of one great love,
would never be forgotten. His eyes blurred with age and unshed tears.

Auguste sat at his desk once more and opened his sketchbook.

AUTHOR'S NOTE

Camille Claudel's career reached its apex in the first years after her final split with Auguste Rodin. Her hard work, as well as Rodin's tutelage, had begun to pay off, and she exhibited her work somewhat regularly in Paris. In an effort to delineate her vision from her lover-teacher's, Camille ventured in a new direction, experimenting with materials and ideas yet unexplored by either of the pair. If Rodin produced grand-scale works in the nude, she created smaller pieces of intimate scenes, figures clothed; if he worked with soft marble, she utilized the hardest jade and onyx, demonstrating her immeasurable talent for crafting with difficult materials.

During this time, Camille's interest in Japan blossomed, along with a fascination with Art Nouveau—a style emphasizing curved lines and natural scenes. Her most notable works of this period include *The Age of Maturity*, *The Wave*, and *The Gossips*, among others.

Though she battled progressive mental illness, Camille continued to work and exhibit until 1905. As promised, her brother, Paul, donated her pieces to the Musée Rodin, but not without repeated prompts from Rodin himself and his critic friend Mathias Morhardt. Today, the largest collection of her works resides in the museum at the Hôtel Biron in Paris.

Much can be debated about the life of Camille Claudel. Did her style derive from Rodin's experience and artistic lens? Certainly, as her style also evolved from her own inspirations and those of her first art tutor, Alfred Boucher. But Camille influenced Rodin a great deal as well, as shown in his "beautiful period," between 1883 and 1898, the dates coinciding with their relationship. In this book, I demonstrate this co-influence.

Another question arises about the date of Camille's final break from Rodin. While some sources cite 1893 as their separation, others favor 1898, the date of Camille's last letter to Rodin, in which she praises his *Monument à Balzac*, the controversial piece entwined with the Dreyfus affair. Since relationship lines blur and the lovers had such a tumultuous affair, I portrayed their final days together in the later year.

In addition, some histories assert Camille's mental diagnosis to be dementia; others, schizophrenia. The rash behaviors and violent outbursts that intensified for Camille around age eighteen and progressed through adulthood, as well as the crippling isolation and paranoia later in her life, are characteristic of schizophrenia, as are the variable waves of its symptoms. Whether or not Camille heard voices is up for discussion, but it is one of the most common symptoms of the illness. I chose to use these voices to highlight the inner workings of her mind and the ways in which she battled not only the male-dominated art world, but herself.

Fictionalized elements in the story include policeman Alphonse Bertillion's courtship of Camille, though he was, in fact, the earliest known criminologist. While there is a historical account of Rose Beuret shooting at Camille, the policeman on the scene was not Bertillion. Other fictional elements involve Camille's tutors Monsieur Colin and Alfred Boucher, who both visited her originally in the town of Nogent-sur-Seine, rather than at the Claudels' summer home in Villeneuve. I also invented Jules Dalou's flirtation with Camille, of which there is no record; and his attending Victor Hugo's birthday celebration in 1883, though he attended a fete in 1885. Finally, Camille's works *Young Girl with a Sheaf* and *Head of a Slave* were claimed by Rodin and labeled *Galatée* and *Tête de Rieur* three years after Camille had designed her own, as illustrated in the novel, but neither piece was exhibited at the 1889 Exposition Universelle.

Though all letters and reviews have been fabricated, they are based upon authentic letters and journal reviews. The only exception is one in which Rodin quotes reviewer Jules Claretie from *Le Temps*, May 5, 1898, regarding his *Monument à Balzac*, which is, indeed, authentic.

For more information about Camille Claudel's life and times, visit my website at www.HeatherWebb.net.

ACKNOWLEDGMENTS

There aren't enough words in the English language to express my gratitude to Michelle Brower, the kind of agent writers dream of. And to the entire team at Plume, especially my lovely editor Denise Roy and my publicist, Mary Pomponio—I thank you from the bottom of my heart. Also, there's no replacing a great copy editor, so thank you, Kym Surridge.

While I am lost in the rabbit hole of research, certain questions arise that demand the input of experts. For *Rodin's Lover*, I owe special thanks to Chris Troup, Kerry Schafer, and Andrea Catalano—authorities and friends.

I'd like to thank early readers and dear friends Susan Spann, Julianne Douglas, Kris Waldherr, Chris Troup, and L. J. Cohen for all of their input and cheerleading. I'm not sure where I would be without you.

To my rockin' critique group, the SFWG, for their continued support and love: Amanda Orr, Janet B. Taylor, Marci Jefferson, Candie Campbell, DeAnn Smith, and Arabella Stokes. Writing in a bubble without friends just isn't as much fun.

I owe much gratitude to my former student-turned-artist, and a brilliant one at that, Joshua DeLillo, for beautiful renditions of Camille's pieces: *L'Aurore*, *La Valse*, and *La Vague*. I hope to view your works in a museum one day, Joshua.

Lastly, my beloved family and friends—you inspire me with your love, courage, and wisdom daily. You make this life, and this passion of mine, an incredible experience.

Also by Heather Webb

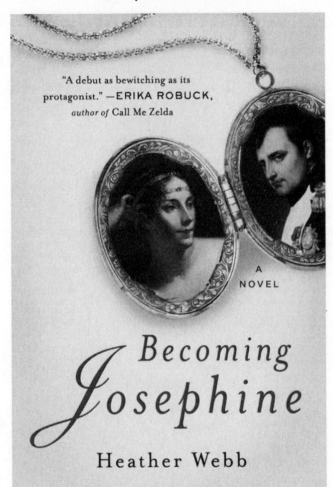

"A debut as bewitching as its protagonist." —ERIKA ROBUCK, *author of* Call Me Zelda

A
NOVEL

Becoming
Josephine

Heather Webb

978-0-14-218065-5

Available wherever books are sold

PLUME